Jan Coffey
Fourth Victim

MIRA®

ISBN 0-7783-2057-X

FOURTH VICTIM

Copyright © 2004 by Nikoo K. and James A. McGoldrick.

www.MIRABooks.com

Printed in U.S.A.

To Linda, Shannon, Arhonti, Karen, Dr. Hafti and all the other wonderful people at the Hunter Radiation Therapy Center at Yale–New Haven Hospital. Thank you for your excellent care, for your compassion…and also for being such great fans of our books.

We dedicate this book to the women and men who are going through breast cancer treatment right now…and to the millions of survivors.

There is great hope. Keep on living.

Prologue

The bright desert moon clearly illuminated miles of scrub pine and yucca on either side of the highway. Flares and a trooper funneled the late-night traffic on Interstate 10 into one lane, and three ambulances, three state police cars, a tow truck and the local sheriff's black-and-white blocked off the rest of the westbound lanes, putting on a light show that could probably be seen as far as Albuquerque.

A few passenger cars and a number of trucks crawled past as the drivers gaped at the wreckage of the station wagon that was lying with its wheels in the air beside a knocked-out section of guardrail. A hundred feet up the road, an eighteen-wheeler was sitting on the shoulder of the highway. The shaken driver sat on the cab's running board, making statements to a trooper. News of the accident was already on the local station, advising travelers to take alternate routes.

The acrid smoke from the flares burned everyone's eyes as they worked. Pebbles of glass covered the road, crunching beneath rescue workers' shoes as they tried to extricate the passengers from the station wagon.

There was already one fatality that they knew of. A toddler, thrown out of the car when the station wagon flipped over repeatedly before coming to a stop. No car seat. No seat belts. The middle-aged woman who was driving had been unconscious when they took her out in an ambulance to Deming only moments earlier. The three other passengers in the back seat were all minors. A baby tucked between two young teenagers.

It was a few more minutes before the rescue workers successfully removed the seat that had trapped the children in the car. The state trooper who'd arrived first on the scene stood back as two EMTs gently removed the wailing infant and the teenage boy from the wreck. They put the boy carefully on a stretcher and strapped the baby into a special carrier. A few cuts and bruises. Neither seemed seriously hurt, only upset. The same trooper had pulled out the driver.

He crouched down and flashed his light into the vehicle. The last passenger was a young girl, maybe ten or eleven.

"Everything will be okay now," he said calmly. "They'll be back to take you out in a minute."

With the car upside down, she was twisted on her side. But her green eyes were open. They glistened in the light. No cries, though, no moans, no complaints. No response at all to the blood streaming from the ugly gash in her forehead, soaking the short curly brown hair and running down her pale face.

The trooper felt the tap on his shoulder as another EMT came for the girl. As he stood up, a cool breeze swept in off the desert, mingling the smell of pine with the scent of gasoline from the overturned vehicle.

"Head injury, concussion. She's not responding," the first man called out, crawling inside the vehicle. Two others bringing a stretcher arrived at the car.

The trooper touched the letters BDM stenciled beneath a gold crescent moon on the mangled driver's door, and went around the car. Flashing his light inside, he searched the glove compartment for any documents they might have missed. They had already found the car's registration, but there was no purse or ID on the driver.

"Be careful now," he said. Two of the EMTs were slowly handing the girl out. The officer hustled around to help the other worker bring the stretcher closer. The green eyes were still open, and as the workers placed her on it, the girl focused on him and said something under her breath.

He leaned closer. Her face was deathly white. She whispered it again.

"...me!"

"What did you say, hon?" he asked softly, crouching down on one knee as they strapped her in.

"Take me away. Please...take me..."

He placed his hand on her icy fingers. "They're taking you to a hospital. You'll be as good as new in no time."

She abruptly began to shake and started straining against the straps. "Don't leave...me...here. Don't..."

"You'll be okay. Everything will be okay." He tried to hold on to her, but the EMTs rushed her toward the ambulance.

He stared as the back doors closed. A moment later, the sirens began to wail, and the ambulance pulled away.

The station wagon had come from the compound of a religious group led by Reverend Michael Butler. The Butler Divinity Mission—made up mostly of women and children and a few retired folks—lived and worked on a two-hundred-acre ranch little more than a half hour south of here. Interrupting his thoughts, the barracks captain from Deming called to him from his cruiser.

"Dispatch says there's no answer out at Reverend Butler's place," the captain said. "I want you to ride out there and let them know about the accident. See if you can get the reverend or one of his deacons to come into the hospital in Deming. We're going to need someone to ID the deceased boy, too. Take Mac with you."

Ten years older, with nine years seniority, Mac was a veteran compared to the number of recent academy graduates working out of the newly built state police barracks in Deming. Southwestern New Mexico was growing, and the force was growing with it.

They drove in silence for a while before Mac started in. "So, I hear you're just back from your honeymoon."

"Yeah. Today was the first day back on the job."

"Where did you two lovebirds go?"

"Back East. That's where Anne's family is."

"Big family?"

"She's got enough aunts and uncles and cousins to pack a football stadium." He smiled. "And I'm only talking about the ones that I met during the ten days we were there."

"You wanna talk about big families? In my first year on the force, it seemed like every goddamn car I pulled over was some cousin of mine, or a neighbor to a cousin, or a girlfriend to the cousin of a neighbor to a cousin."

Mac had a story for everything, and he continued to ramble on as they took the exit off the highway.

The young trooper had already heard a lot of the officer's stories, but he enjoyed hearing those about family. Everything he could put together from his own past wouldn't fill a five-minute coffee break. A father who ran off when he was too young to remember. A mother who was always working to make ends meet. No brothers or sisters, no aunts or uncles or cousins. Certainly no family reunions. His mother never talked about her folks, and he'd never asked. Then one day she'd fallen asleep at the wheel coming home from a second shift job. She was dead by the time they got her to the hospital. It was too late to ask anything, then.

He'd been a loner until he'd fallen for Anne. She'd made him complete in more ways than he could say. After seeing what he'd been missing all his life, having a big family was something that he was looking forward to immensely over the next sixty or seventy years of marriage.

"Your Anne must get a mite homesick with none of her folks around."

"I don't know. I keep her pretty busy."

"Wash that damn newlywed grin off your face, or I'll put in to have it surgically removed," Mac threatened. "B'sides, you just wait a few years. All that will change. Believe you me."

"I don't think so."

"Well, I was talking about when your sweet ass is at work, lover boy. What's she do with herself?"

"Anne is keeping her job," he replied.

Mac answered a call from the dispatcher and told her their destination before continuing with their conversation. "Shoot, and here I've been telling everyone how you robbed the cradle. That gal looks like she's still in school."

"She graduated this past May. Had a job waiting for her."

"That a fact? Where?"

At a colorfully painted, oversize mailbox, the trooper turned off the state highway onto a dirt road.

"Department of Child and Family Services."

"Both of you dipping into the New Mexico public trough. Way to go, fella."

"Hey, she works hard."

"I know," Mac said seriously. He shook his head. "Family Services is tough. Juvenile delinquents, welfare cases, drunken fathers, abuse. You'll work with them plenty. I don't envy her none."

"Actually, Anne got lucky. She works in this new program they're trying out with a bunch of teenagers in test groups across the state. It's kind of a..." He slowed the cruiser and turned his spotlight on the brush to the right of the road. He thought he saw something or someone come out of the dark and then disappear again into the sparse brush.

"What was that?" Mac asked.

"You saw it, too?"

Mac looked at the open stretch of land to his right, where the figure had disappeared. There were no other cars on the road. No lights other than the cruiser's as far as they could see. No houses. Nothing.

"I'll tell you the truth. This area has spooked me since I was a kid. All them stories about ghosts haunting these hills. Indians and Spaniards and God knows what else."

"Come on, Mac. That's a bunch of crap." The young officer turned off the spotlight and put his foot on the gas. "Those are just stories to give little kids nightmares."

"And I s'pose you don't believe in no ghosts."

"I don't think anyone sane over the age of five does."

"That right?" Mac huffed. "Well, a few do. Anyway, that's how this guy Butler was able to pick up that ranch and all this land for a song."

"Well, however he got it, having somebody use it for a good cause is better than having it sit empty and rot."

"That's what I keep hearing." Mac turned to him. "You know him?"

"Not personally."

"Been out here before?"

"No, but some of Anne's kids are staying at the Mission, so she's been visiting them pretty regular. She can't say enough nice things about the place and the reverend. She calls him Father Mike."

"Watch out there, fella. That's how it starts."

"What starts?"

"The chick magnet." Mac grinned devilishly. "Word is, that Divinity Mission is packed with women. Young women. Pretty women."

"And kids," the younger man responded defensively. "Kids whose fathers have shit for brains. These women come out here because they have no place else to go. They're running for their lives, some of them."

"I know how that goes," Mac admitted. "Did I tell you about this loser that my sister Adele is dating?"

Mac launched into an involved tale about how his younger sister was blind to some guy's faults and her plans of moving in with the creep. The young trooper quickly lost interest in the story, though, when he drove over the crest of the hill above the Mission compound. The silvery landscape glowed beneath the full moon. In the valley below, a handful of buildings hunched together, giving the appearance of a toy village. There was a parking lot with a dozen cars on the south side of an adobe building with a cross on top. An old windmill, the tallest structure in the landscape, stood two fingertips away. With the exception of a few lights in the distance, the Mission lay in total darkness. A new range fence encircled the cluster of buildings, but the gate was wide open.

"It must be past curfew," Mac commented, turning in his seat as they drove past a hand-painted wooden sign, welcoming them to the Divinity Mission, Rev. Michael Butler, Pastor. "You said your wife comes out here a lot?"

"Yeah. Almost every day. In fact, I think she was stopping by this afternoon."

"This is the worst part of the job," Mac said quietly as they drove slowly down the hill to the compound. "Bringing people bad news at all hours of the night."

"No dogs," the young trooper muttered as he pulled in next to the first building. "Anne said they kept a bunch of dogs out here for the kids."

Another hand-painted sign encouraged the visitors to sign in at the Mission office.

They sat silently for a few seconds. No one was out and about. No lights had come on in any of the buildings. Even the radio in the cruiser was totally silent for the first time since they'd set out.

"What do you say we just do the job and get the hell out of here," Mac said in an attempt at sounding cheerful.

They both got out and approached the office. Mac knocked as the young trooper looked behind them at the dark buildings. It was dead quiet. They waited for a few seconds, and this time Mac called out, identifying himself and knocking again. Still nothing.

There were no locks on the door, so he pushed it open. The door swung noisily on rusty hinges. The light switch was right beside the door, and Mac flipped it on. A single bulb came to life overhead. In the office, there were two cluttered desks and a four-drawer file cabinet near a window.

"Nice to have a nine-to-five job," Mac commented good-naturedly.

"I think that's the only phone in the place." He picked it up. There was a dial tone. "Well, it's working, anyway."

Mac nodded and the two went out of the office. They walked along a gravel path, looking at the dark buildings. There was no sign of life. They exchanged a look.

"Your guess is as good as mine," the young trooper said. "Where should we start?"

There were three single-story buildings that looked like dormitories on either side of the walkway. At the end of the path was a larger adobe building that looked to be the chapel.

"You take that door, and I'll take this one. We knock until we get hold of a live one. Go ahead. I'll watch your back."

Not far off, the distinctive yip of a coyote cut sharply through the night and made the hair stand up on the trooper's neck. He looked over his shoulder and found his partner already poised to knock on the first door. There was no answer at either building.

"You sure these folks ain't on spring break or something?" Mac called across to him as they walked toward the next building.

"If I hadn't seen those signs, I wouldn't be sure we're even in the right place. This is starting to look like a set from one of those Hollywood westerns."

"Yeah, a ghost town," Mac chipped in.

"All we need is a saloon with a skeleton for a bartender." He knocked on the next door and at hearing no answer, he pressed his face against the window. Total darkness was the only thing that greeted him inside.

"How about a lame dog?"

"I don't remember that in any movies." He looked over his shoulder at his partner.

Mac was approaching something tentatively. By the corner of the building, a black dog was growling fiercely at the trooper. Before Mac could reach it, the animal turned and limped away into the dark, dragging a leg behind him.

He hurried over as Mac backed away. The two men peered into the darkness around them, their hands on their pistols.

"I don't like this, kid. Go and call for backup."

The tone had changed. Before he could move a step, he saw the older officer focus and move toward another dark shape in the shadow of the church building.

Mac turned to him. "Tell them we're going to need ambulances."

The trooper made it to the cruiser in seconds. While

radioing in the information, he saw Mac moving to the door of the chapel. Drawing his weapon, Mac pulled open the door.

He stood still for a moment, and then staggered backward.

Throwing the handset on the seat of the cruiser, the trooper drew his own weapon and rushed toward the building. He hadn't heard a shot.

"Are you hurt?"

Even in the darkness of the night, he could tell Mac's face had turned chalk white. The older man leaned against the building, and a strange growl escaped his throat. "Don't go in there."

The young trooper focused the flashlight on his partner. No stab wound. No blood. He turned the light on the door.

"No. You don't…want to see it."

He was crying. Mac was crying. Unable to stop himself, the officer took a step toward the open door. Immediately, his gaze was drawn to the candles sputtering beside a pulpit at the far end of the building, although they shed very little light. Smoke from burning incense was rising from a small table beside the door. The smell was sickeningly sweet.

The beam of his light flashed into the church. Bodies. Right inside the door. Three bodies wearing red robes. A woman with two children in her arms. They were lying on the floor. Her legs stretched out along the threshold. Their eyes were open.

He stared at the boy. The little face was contorted from pain and fear no child should ever feel.

The trooper inched forward. There were more. White candles had been lit and blown out. They lay next to the bodies. He felt the blood drain from his head as he stared at the scores of lifeless bodies. The body of a man in a white robe lay on the altar behind the pulpit.

The smell of death hit him, paralyzing him. He heard himself saying that it wasn't real. It couldn't be real.

He didn't know that his vision had blurred until the images in front of him came sharply into focus. He flashed his light on the faces. All those innocent faces. So many of them children.

He stepped unsteadily into the church. He could barely breathe. Shining his light at the foot of the pulpit, he saw a baptismal font. Paper cups lay next to it on a small table and filled a wastebasket beside that.

As he moved closer to the pulpit, it felt as if the air was moving around him. Thoughts of spirits trapped inside the closed doors stopped him in his tracks. He could feel them around him, swirling in the amber-colored air like wisps of smoke. A light touch on his shoulder caused him to turn, his flashlight cutting through the near darkness. Nothing. The caress of a small hand on his wrist. He looked down. Nothing.

Suddenly, he couldn't breathe. Pressure on his chest, like some huge gloved hand, was squeezing the air out of him. He pulled at the collar of his shirt as he gasped.

How could this all be real? Denial again took hold
of him. This was a lie. It had to be. They were staging
this. They couldn't all be dead. Then he felt the bile
rising into his throat. He had to get out of this place.
He turned toward where the door was, but he couldn't
see it. The flashlight rotated wildly in every direction.
Along the walls, the floor was covered with bodies in
red robes. There were more of them around the pulpit.

A hand took hold of his elbow. He could not turn
to look. He had to get out. He could feel each finger
pressing into the flesh through his shirt. The hand was
pulling at him, forcing him back toward the pulpit,
back toward the baptismal font. Panic washed through
him, and he tried to yank his arm free. The fingers
felt like steel pincers, cutting into his flesh.

Still, he could not turn. Images of the dead were
rising up in front of him, dancing like macabre spec-
ters in some horrible dream. The walls were beginning to pulse in and out as if they were made of
rubber. There was no air anywhere.

He had to get out. He had to get to the door. But
his legs felt as if sacks of sand had been bound to
each ankle. He inched along, seeming to make no
progress. The pincers biting into his arm were ready
to cut through the bone. The pain was so intense that
he was afraid he would lose consciousness. Finally,
he whirled and looked at his captor.

Nothing.

He turned and tried to move again toward the door.
His boot touched a hand and he stopped, shining his
light on the dead woman.

Anne.

One

The hundred or so cheering onlookers were sweating profusely on the aluminum grandstand seats that stretched along the faded white tile of the indoor pool. Parents, grandparents and family friends took turns calling out encouragement as cameras flashed and video cameras tried to capture each stroke of the dozen and a half three- and four-year-olds splashing noisily across the width of the pool. Graduation day at the duckling-level swimming class had brought all the families out.

The health club on the state road between Errol and Colebrook was a popular place every spring, drawing not just people from northern New Hampshire, but families from Vermont, Maine and even the province of Quebec for the swimming lessons. The managers knew how to take advantage of having the only indoor pool in the area, and made sure that the families who brought their children in for lessons knew about the special rates available for the racquet courts, Nautilus rooms and a range of other programs geared more toward adults.

Kelly Stone was only interested in one thing, though, and that was her daughter. For the past two and half months, three times a week, she had been driving Jade here for one purpose—socializing. The little girl was a competent swimmer already, thanks to being raised on a lake by a nervous mother. Kelly had made sure her daughter learned to swim at the same time that she was taking her first steps. The lessons were unimportant. Mingling with other kids, making friends, knowing how to act and talk and play like a child—that was their reason for coming. Although she was little more than three and a half years old, Jade wasn't too strong on being a kid. Never had been. But what could one expect when the little girl was constantly surrounded by adults?

Kelly owned and lived in a renovated inn tucked cozily away in the New Hampshire woods. The clientele was, for the most part, young couples, antique dealers and an occasional pair or trio of upscale hunters. Certainly, the small group of people who worked at Tranquillity Inn didn't have any experience dealing with children, so Jade wasn't really treated like one. Their closest neighbors were the clusters of cabins on the far side of the lake. Empty for most of the year, they were occupied only during the months of July and August by one youth camp or another. The closest village was Independence, five miles away. The closest child Jade's age? Kelly looked at the young swimmers lined up at the side of the pool. This was where she'd hoped to find them.

Her plan should have worked. A budding friend-

ship. A giggle here and there. But nothing. Even
Kelly's direct attempt at initiating something—an invitation for a few of the girls and boys to come to the
inn for a little luncheon—had failed. The parents had
been polite but reserved. Their children treated Jade
with the same awkwardness that she treated them.

Standing at thirty-two inches tall and weighing just
under forty pounds, she was smaller than any of them,
but she talked and acted like Miss Manners.

The little hand rising out of the water and waving
in Kelly's direction brought the whole pool area into
sharp focus for the young mother. She waved back
proudly at Jade, who was holding on to the edge of
the pool and preparing for the final task of swimming
to the other end. Kelly turned on the video camera as
the three-year-old tucked a tendril of wet hair behind
her ear and twisted the belt holding the white plastic
floater around her thin middle. Jade easily undid the
clasp and tossed the floater up onto the tile. She'd
hated the nuisance from day one but had agreed to
wear it so she wouldn't be pushed into the older age
group. This was the last day, and Jade had told Kelly
on their drive in that next year she would just as soon
take the class with the teenagers. At least they thought
she was cute.

"Look at that little one!"

"What a good swimmer she is!"

"She's amazing."

Kelly swelled with pride as the whispers of praise
rippled through the parents and grandparents. She bit
her lip to fight her emotions and brought the camera

to her eye and started taping. Jade reached the end of the pool in the same time that it took the other little ones to cover half the distance.

There were a few in the audience who actually cheered for Jade, as if it were a race. Kelly knew that Greg would have been cheering the loudest if he were still alive. He would have been not only a proud father, but a loud one, too. He would have been telling everyone on the stands which one of those children was his and how young but accomplished she was, and a hundred other things. He'd been ready for fatherhood from the first moment she'd given him the news. Kelly would never forget how he'd announced at dinner to everyone on the Caribbean cruise ship that he and his wife were pregnant.

Unfortunately, he hadn't lived long enough even to see his daughter born. The video camera continued to tape, but Kelly's vision blurred.

A moment later, she realized the parents were moving off the aluminum seats. A group was forming a circle in the area where the instructors were handing out certificates to the children. She shut off the camera and put it in the bag, before rummaging around in her purse for a tissue to wipe her eyes.

"I want a Band-Aid, too."

Kelly looked up in surprise to find her daughter standing before her. The oversize towel she'd wrapped around her was dragging on the wet tile floor. A certificate, spotted with wet fingerprints, was being held out to her. Kelly quickly came off the grandstand and took the child—paper still in her hand—in a tight embrace.

"I am so proud of you. You were incredible."

The three-year-old shrugged. "I want a Band-Aid."

Kelly put the certificate in the bag with the camera and sat down on the first aluminum bench, pulling her daughter onto her lap. A Band-Aid was their cure for everything, and not just cuts and bruises. On the first day of swimming classes, Jade had put four Band-Aids on her stomach to take care of the nervousness.

"What's wrong, baby?"

"I'm not a baby." A little pout formed on her lips. There was a slight tremble in her chin.

"No, you're not." Kelly wrapped the towel tighter around the child's shoulders and gave her a growling bear hug. "You're a big girl. A talented one. And a very strong one. In fact, you're one tough cookie."

"I'm hungry."

"Me, too." Glad for the distraction, Kelly put Jade down and held her hand as they headed for the changing room. The circle of families around the swimmers had not broken up yet. Parents were thanking the instructors. She didn't miss the wounded glance her daughter directed at the circle as they passed it. Even at her age, Jade clearly understood the difference in her life from the lives of the other swimmers. Kelly knew she felt a little jealous that she didn't have a big family to adore her and admire her every accomplishment, no matter how small. Today was just another day designed to make her realize how tiny her fan club really was.

"Let's do something fun for lunch," Kelly suggested as she ushered Jade inside the shower room.

"Let's get cookies and soda."

"Cookies and soda?" She tickled her daughter, helping her with rinsing off. "How about a pound of sugar?"

"How about a billion M&M's on an ice-cream cone?" Jade gave a belly laugh and went on to ask for all her favorite candies and cookies and every other outrageous thing that her young mind could think of.

Kelly was relieved to see her daughter's mood improve, and she hurried to get the child out of the locker room before the rest of the children and their parents came in. Jade cooperated every step of the way. It was like her to be so attuned to her mother's moods.

They made a compromise by stopping at the new ice-cream shop near Errol and ordering a Belgian waffle with ice cream and all kinds of toppings. An hour later, as they turned onto the gravel road leading to Tranquillity Inn, Kelly looked in the rearview mirror and smiled at her sleeping child.

She was planning to send Jade to a preschool south of Independence two days a week starting this fall, even though she knew it would mean many tears and moods and emergency calls for Band-Aids. There would be Father's Days, Grandparents' Days, school plays, sporting events, parent-teacher conferences.

She and Jade would have to go through them all on their own. Kelly yanked the wheel to go around a large pothole in the road. She'd have to start buying Band-Aids in economy-size packages.

Enough for both of them.

Ian Campbell looked from the small tray of business cards to the plate of chocolate chip cookies on the corner of the reception desk, then at the face of the old lady studying the page of the reservation book. Thinning cotton-white hair, cut very short and styled. Pink-rimmed glasses matched the color of the woman's jogging suit. He didn't miss the cane leaning against the wall near her chair.

"I'm sorry, Mr. Campbell. But we have no reservation in your name."

He checked the nameplate on the desk again. "Miss Maitland, isn't it?"

"Mrs. Maitland. But please call me Janice," she said, flustered. "Perhaps your secretary, or whoever made the reservation, gave you the wrong—"

"I called myself. And I spoke to a young man named Dan. Dan Davies. Do you have an employee by that name?"

"Well, yes…"

"Would you be kind enough, Janice, to check through your reservations again?"

A deep blush crept into the wrinkled cheeks. Ian leaned back in the chair across from her as she started running a thin finger down the scribbled list of names on the open page of the reservation log. Yellow sticky notes jutted out every which way from a book that looked more like a ledger than any kind of calendar.

A door to the left of the reservation desk was open, and Ian could see into a small, cluttered office. Right next to it, a long hallway led to an exterior door that was also open, letting fresh air in through a screen door. The voices and dramatic music of a soap opera drifted down from the end of the hall, mixing with the chopping sound of a knife going to town on a cutting board. He leaned over and helped himself to one of the cookies as he glanced through the open double doors to his left into a large, bright, enclosed porch with half a dozen tables. A door led out onto a deck overlooking the lake.

Footsteps behind him made Ian turn in his chair. He smiled politely at a round-faced young woman carrying an armful of tablecloths and napkins through the lobby. With a brisk nod of her head, she went around the reception desk and down the hall.

"Great cookies. Mind if I have another?"

"Absolutely. Please help yourself." Janice pushed the plate toward him as she turned a page of the reservation book.

Ian took another cookie and shifted in his seat. The large, open parlor and sitting room extended behind him. The walls were white, giving the room an airy feeling that was tempered only somewhat by a large stone fireplace that dominated one wall. Over the mantel, a moose head stared brightly into space, its huge span of antlers stretching for four feet on either side. An ancient Winchester hunting rifle had been mounted beneath the moose, with crossed snowshoes and a variety of Native American artifacts completing the decor on that wall. There was a collection of painted and decorated gourds on the mantel that looked southwestern. The windows in the room were open, with large screens that were undoubtedly hung every spring letting in the fresh New Hampshire air and keeping out the blackflies. Ian had heard the blackflies were vicious during the summer months. Comfortable sofas and chairs sat in inviting clusters around the parlor.

A wide stairway graced another wall, turning at a landing a few steps up and passing above the wide front entrance. Ian had stopped and looked at the wraparound porch before he'd entered the vestibule leading to the lobby. The line of rockers stretching around the side of the house had been artfully arranged to entice visitors to sit and enjoy the view of the lake.

Janice's fingers paused on a line after flipping two more pages. The darkening of her cheeks and the deepening of the furrow in her forehead told Ian that she didn't care for what she'd found.

Ian tried to recall what he'd read about Tranquillity Inn in a write-up in a tour guidebook of New England inns. The northern New Hampshire inn was owned and managed by Kelly Stone. Overlooking Lake Tranquillity, the book said the inn was sure to live up to its name, offering pleasantly simple accommodations, a country experience and excellent food. Though the inn lacked the modern conveniences—or inconveniences—of televisions, Internet connections and phones in its five guest rooms, the hotel guests were welcome to use the office phone or fax in case of emergencies. When he'd called a couple of weeks ago to make the reservation, the young man on the phone had even given him the choice of any of the rooms, making Ian think that he might be the only guest this early in the season. When he'd driven into the inn parking lot, he'd seen only two cars with New Hampshire plates. He'd assumed they belonged to the people working here. Ian took one more quick look at the empty parlor before turning his attention back to the woman behind the desk. Janice was now rummaging through a folder.

"Any luck?"

"Yes, I did find your reservation, Mr. Campbell." She was avoiding eye contact. "Unfortunately, a grave error was made by the person who took down your information."

"Dan Davies."

"Yes…you see, he's our summer help. And the day you called…I believe might have been his first day on the job. It appears he had the reservation book open to the wrong page. We weren't expecting you until the last Friday in June."

"I specified the dates I was interested in staying here," Ian responded, putting a sharp edge in his tone.

"I'm sure you did, sir. I'm positive the mistake was Dan's and not yours. In fact, I've found another reservation for that same day…taken by Dan…and I'm afraid that couple may be arriving today, as well."

She slid a color flyer toward him. "If you'll give me a minute, I'll make a call to this place for you. The Peacock Inn is owned by a good friend of ours. I'm sure we can place you there. It's a lovely inn and less than a half hour's ride from here. You'll find their accommodations outstanding. In fact, we'll be happy to—"

"I am not moving to another inn, Mrs. Maitland."

"I was going to say that your stay there will be at our expense, because of the inconvenience," she said, totally flustered. "You'll absolutely love—"

"It seems we're having a hard time understanding each other. I made a reservation, and I agreed to have you charge the first night of my stay to my credit card in advance. That confirms my reservation," Ian said in a low voice. "I'm here, and I don't care if you have to go and stay at Peacock Inn yourself. I expect to have a room here, in this inn, on this lake. Do I make myself clear?"

Janice's face looked as if she'd gotten a third-degree burn. Ian noticed the woman's hand trembling as she shuffled paperwork aimlessly. "I...I should get my husband...perhaps he can better explain the problem we're facing. There are only four guest rooms available for this coming week. We...we have a reservation for every one of them."

"Have the other guests arrived?"

"No, but we're expecting them anytime now."

"I believe the applicable term, then, is first come, first served. I'm here, Janice. You can make some other arrangement for one of the other guests."

Whatever composure the old woman had left disappeared. She started to say something a couple of times, but her voice was too unsteady to speak. This complication was obviously beyond her. The sound of tires crunching on the gravel outside indicated another arrival. In a huff, Janice snatched up the flyer she'd pushed toward him and stuffed it back in her manila folder.

A woman carrying a sleeping child over her shoulder came in through the screen door at the end of the hall. All Ian could see of her was curly brown hair pulled into a ponytail and a quick glimpse of her profile. Glancing over her shoulder, Janice saw the woman and child. The young mother didn't pause or say anything and disappeared at the first turn, where he guessed a back stairwell might lead to the rooms upstairs.

"If you'll wait here, Mr. Campbell, I'll get someone else to…to try to explain our predicament to you better…and make other arrangements."

Ian thought about Janice's threat to get her husband. He had an image of an eighty-year-old holding a shotgun to his head before escorting him to his car.

"I'll only speak to Ms. Stone."

"Pardon me?"

"Ms. Stone. She is the owner and manager of the inn, isn't she?"

"How do you know Ms. Stone?"

"I know her from her card. This one, right here," he said with a hint of sarcasm, taking one of the business cards from the desk and pushing it toward the woman.

"Ms. Stone has just arrived. It might take a few minutes before she'll be available to speak to you."

"That's fine. I'll look around while I wait." Ian rose to his feet. Pausing, he gestured toward the cookies. "May I?"

"Of course. That's what they're here for."

To the older woman's obvious dismay, he took the entire plate and walked to the porch dining area. Behind him, Ian heard Janice push the chair back and go into the office, complaining loudly to someone. He guessed she was calling upstairs to Ms. Stone.

He paused in the doorway to the porch. With obvious attention to detail, someone had tastefully placed a miniature hurricane lamp and a small vase of flowers in the center of each table. He pushed through the door to the deck overlooking the lake.

Turning around, he gazed up at the inn. He could see there were three floors. Several additions had been made to the original house. Pale yellow clapboard and black shutters were the color scheme for the building. Turning his attention back to the deck and the grounds around it, he saw a small garage or carriage house, separate from the main building. With window boxes overflowing with flowers and a couple of deck chairs on the front lawn, the place was obviously being used as a residence by someone.

Beyond the carriage house, there were two small, somewhat dilapidated cottages by the edge of the water. Ian wondered if either of them might be available.

Straight down from the inn, a small sand beach extended to a large boathouse with a removable dock. A swimming float was anchored not far from the dock. A young man, perhaps a college kid, was working on a sign near a half-dozen small boats and canoes sitting in the grass nearby. Ian wondered if that was Dan Davies.

With the plate of cookies still in one hand, Ian started down the steps, hoping to make an ally out of the kid and get him to show him the rest of the grounds.

Descending the stairs from the deck, Ian's attention was drawn to the bottom step. Three medium-size boxes were stacked on top of each other, ready to be brought in. They all had the same markings. The top one was open. He looked in. There were dozens of white candles stacked neatly inside.

"I guess there's a first time for everything," Kelly said good-naturedly as she scanned the large ledger book Janice had pushed in front of her face. They were sitting in the little office behind the reception area. She had no sooner tucked Jade in her bed than the intercom had buzzed her from downstairs. She could hear from Janice's tone that there was a problem. "Think how much better this is than last summer. You remember how we were struggling to fill the rooms? This is a good problem, Janice."

"You clearly don't realize the enormity of the situation." Without getting up from her chair, the old woman reached out with her cane and pushed the office door closed. "I'm telling you that we're not going to have an easy time sending him anywhere. The man is as stubborn as a mule. He would not listen to reason. Also, he eats like a horse. He took the entire plate of cookies I keep on the reservation desk."

"A fresh supply is coming. When I came down, I saw Wilson taking two more sheets of cookies out of the oven." Kelly took out a clean piece of paper and wrote down the numbers of the rooms before looking down at the registration book again. She couldn't blame Dan for making a mistake. The system was all Janice's, and no one else seemed to be able to understand it. On this particular page, the scribbling was barely legible, and with all the added notations and scratch-outs and sticky notes, it was a miracle that Janice herself could make any sense of it. The only decipherable notes came a couple of pages later…the ones Dan had written in.

She looked at them closely. It was only two reservations. Perhaps they could do something with them. The first was for a single guest, Ian Campbell— a San Diego address was listed and no preferences as far as the room or private bathroom or anything else. The other was for a couple, made under the name of Victor Desposito. From Philadelphia. Their request specified a private bath, preferably with a claw-foot tub. A queen- or king-size bed, no feather quilts or pillows. Nonsmoking room. Lake view. She shook her head as she read through the half-dozen other requirements that included a list of food allergies and ended with "no use of blue-dyed sheets."

"I think dealing with Mr. Campbell should be a piece of cake compared to what we've got coming with the Desposito couple."

"Maybe the boy smartened up and registered that couple for the right date," Janice said, still exasperated. "I swear, Kelly, we don't need that smart aleck. He makes one mistake after another."

"You know why he's here. Besides, Bill is getting too old to do all the heavy work."

"We've always gotten along fine before. That's all I'm saying."

"Right." Kelly looked down at the notes again. "Let's see…Desposito."

Dan had taken the reservations back to back. And he'd written today's date on the top corner of the block.

"No, my guess is they're coming this afternoon." She flipped the page back to Janice's notes and pushed the book toward the older woman. "Don't worry. We can work it out. There is always room five."

"Aquarius is only half-painted. It's a mess, Kelly."

"A minor detail. We can clean it up and, so long as we apologize profusely and put the right person in there, it'll be a go. There's also the extra room on the third floor."

"We haven't rented that out since you and Jade moved in up there. That's your floor. And you always said you wouldn't have any privacy if we put someone in there."

"Well, at a hundred and twenty dollars a night,

plus whatever the person spends on drinks, it's worth it to me right now.''

''Kelly, that room is way too small. The eaves are so low. There is barely any furniture in there. It has no bathroom.''

''There's a bed and a dresser. We can spruce it up in no time. And the quest can use the bathroom on the second floor.'' Kelly watched Janice struggling to make the adjustments in her head.

In her efforts to get over Greg's accident—which had come so soon after her father's death and just before her mother passed away—Kelly had tried to spend as much time as she could with her daughter. In doing that, however, she had let Janice and her husband, Bill, take on the lion's share of work in running the inn. More and more, however, she realized that they were not up to handling even small complications like this.

''Okay, Janice, let's not worry about what's wrong with those two rooms. Tell me who else we have arriving today.''

Janice grudgingly pulled the book onto her lap. Kelly wasn't about to be critical, but she was glad that Mr. Campbell had not let them move him to a different inn at their expense. That would have been a ridiculously unnecessary expenditure. Janice and Bill might have been involved with running Tranquillity Inn forever, but during this past year or so Kelly had come to realize there was a direct connection between the lack of concern the couple had about the business and the inn's income.

Kelly was trying to make a success of it, but the business was difficult. She'd stayed open during the mud season for the first time ever this spring, but it was a rare occasion to have even fifty-percent occupancy during the weekends for those two months. And though trails around the seven-acre lake were perfect, she realized that they hadn't been doing enough to bring in the cross-country skiing types in the winter. The bottom line was that the bills were mounting, and this overbooking was a gift. Kelly knew she had to squeeze the guests into the rooms they had, even if it meant inconveniencing herself and Jade with a guest on the top floor.

Janice adjusted the pink glasses on her nose and looked at her notes. "Incidentally, I never charged the first night's stay against Mr. Campbell's credit card, since I didn't even know he was coming. So technically…"

"Give it up, Janice. I'll warn him about not stealing your plate of cookies again," she said brightly, and then decided to take the lead. "How many parties of guests are arriving tonight?"

"Four. That's not counting the Deposit…or Depo…whatever this other couple's name is."

"Desposito," Kelly corrected. "Who do you have staying in number one?"

"The Sagittarius Room. That would be…" She checked the book. "Burke. Ken Burke. You remember him, and his girlfriend. She goes by the name Ash and models in all those racy lingerie catalogs. They were here over the Columbus Day weekend last fall.

He called to make the reservation and insisted on the same room.''

There was no way anyone would forget Ash. Tall, brunette and very beautiful, she was hard to miss. Kelly also remembered Ken Burke. The photographer. There was something oddly familiar about him, though she couldn't place it. She wondered if they'd run into each other in New York during her days of working for the newspaper, or at one of the events other photographers showed up to cover.

Sagittarius. Kelly wrote down the names on her tab of paper. Casually, she picked up a three-by-five index card she always kept on a corner of her desk. It was a cross-listing of the numbers of the rooms with the zodiac signs Janice always insisted on using in referring to the rooms. Just another case of the old habits never dying for the aging couple. The Maitlands had been associated with Tranquillity Inn for at least twenty years. When Frank and Rose Wilton, Kelly's parents, bought it nine years ago, the couple had simply stayed on to help after the sale.

The decision had been a good one for everyone at the time. And even now, despite their occasional disagreements, Kelly treasured Janice and Bill and everything they'd done for her. They were very special people. She gave a nod of encouragement to her old friend to continue.

''I have a pair of newlyweds by the name of Marisa and Dave Meadows staying in the Pisces Room. This is their first time with us.''

"That's room two—the smaller bedroom with double bed."

"And the claw-foot tub." Janice moved her fingers down the list. "I have the Sterns and their two sons returning, as well. They'll be in the Libra Room."

Kelly's check of the index card told her that the Libra was the suite on the second floor with the good-size bedroom and a small living room with sleep sofa and a private bath and balcony. "I don't think I remember the Sterns."

"A very nice family. They used to come and stay with us every year when your parents were still alive and their sons were young. Those two boys must be strapping teenagers now."

Kelly was certain that Mr. Campbell must be getting impatient. "And room four?"

"Taurus. The antique dealer who comes in twice a year. Shawn Hobart."

"He has to use the bathroom down the hall. Twin bed."

"Yes."

"He is kind of short. Isn't he?" Kelly tapped the pen against the table.

"Don't even think of moving him. He's a creature of habit and a steady customer. And he's very particular about that room. I think he likes the price. That's why he always comes back here. It's far more important to keep someone like him happy than these one time guests. Also, you have one week reservations for all these guests, and the way I read it, both of these new people are only staying for the weekend. I really think we should just find them another inn.''

There was no point in arguing with Janice. The older woman had decided where the customers she'd booked were staying. Ian Campbell and the Despositos could obviously go bunk in with Dan in the crappy little cottage by the lake.

''I'd like you to get Rita to spruce up both of those rooms—room five…uh, Aquarius, and the one on the third floor. Maybe she could get Bill to help her hang some of the pictures back up in Aquarius. And leave the windows open,'' Kelly suggested. She waited until Janice nodded. ''I'll talk to Mr. Campbell and explain that the only thing we can do for him would be the room on the third floor. I hope he's not too tall.''

''Six feet…maybe six-three. I really don't think he'll be comfortable.''

''Well, that's the best we'll be able to do for him. And please let me know when Mr. and Mrs. Desposito arrive. We can discount their room big-time and offer them a complimentary lunch or something.'' She rose to her feet. ''Oh, and please don't forget to tell Wilson in the kitchen about the extra guests, too.''

''He won't be happy,'' Janice grumbled.

''Wilson is *never* happy, so this shouldn't make any difference.'' She opened the office door. Kelly didn't know exactly when everyone at the inn had become so cranky. There was too much gloom and doom hanging over the place. Maybe Tranquillity Inn and most of the people who worked here had been around too long.

Well, summer was almost here. Kelly pasted a smile on her lips and stepped out of the office, just as Rita was coming back from the kitchen.

"Oh, good timing! We've had a mix-up and there are going to be a couple of extra guests. Janice will tell you what needs to be done."

"You've got to be kidding," Rita complained, huffing off before Kelly had a chance to offer any help.

Kelly didn't let the sourness further ruin her mood. She went out through the porch onto the deck, where she'd been told Mr. Campbell had headed. Taking care of a new guest would actually be quite pleasant right now.

Two

Ian walked down the slight embankment across an area of unshorn grass toward the lake. The ground was soft beneath his feet, the grass wet and slick. As he neared the water's edge, he looked out into the distance, surprised by the curtain of white fog that had descended over the view.

He glanced up. The sky was still clear above the inn, the sun shining high in the sky.

"Storm coming?" he asked as he drew near the boathouse.

The college-age kid didn't look up right away. He was wearing a navy T-shirt with the arms cut off and a well-worn pair of jeans. He had two hoops in each ear and a Celtic knot tattooed on one muscled bicep. His hair appeared short, though Ian couldn't be sure with the baseball hat worn backward. The young man glanced up, scrutinizing him briefly.

"Nope," he said finally. "It gets this way every afternoon."

"You must be Dan." Ian shifted the plate to his left hand and extended his right toward him.

The young man nodded and accepted the handshake without getting up. "And you are?"

"Ian Campbell. You were the one who took my reservation a couple weeks ago."

He stood up and stretched his back. They were about the same height. "It's a miracle. I did something right."

"Actually, right now they're scrambling to find me a room that they supposedly don't have. The old lady behind the desk told me she wasn't expecting me for another two weeks."

Dan cursed under his breath and shook his head. "You'd have to be a frigging Einstein to figure out that reservation system of hers. I was damn lucky that Kelly moved me away from it after the first day behind that desk." He motioned with his head toward the plate in Ian's hand. "So, was that a peace offering for not finding you a room?"

"No, they'll find me a room," Ian said, stretching the plate toward Dan. "I took these hostage to make sure they do." He took it immediately back, though, when the younger man helped himself to three of the cookies.

"So what brings you to Siberia?" Dan asked, stuffing the cookies into his mouth and bending over the sign he was attaching to a post.

"You must get an occasional tourist up here," Ian answered wryly. "You a native?"

"Half a dozen moose and a guy who carves animals with a chain saw are about the only natives I know. Traveling with the wife and kids?"

Ian sat on the hull of an overturned sailboat. "Yeah, I have them locked in the trunk of my car."

"It must be damn crowded in there." Dan motioned with his head toward Ian's rental car, visible in the parking area next to the inn.

"They don't complain much." He bit on another cookie. "Janice told me you're pretty new at the job. So, do you live in town?"

"Nope. Right there." Dan pointed at one of the two ramshackle cottages beyond the boathouse. "But I'm not giving up my room, if that's what you're getting at. I know I took the reservation, but I forget how long you said you're staying."

Ian looked out at the lake. The fog was spreading across the water toward the inn. "The place is much more attractive than I thought it'd be. I might just stay a couple of weeks."

"Don't you have a job?"

"I've got good vacation benefits."

"There's not much going on around here. Unless you like country music and ice cream…or watching a guy with a chain saw carve animals."

"Maybe I'll take up fishing." Ian heard the squeak of a window opening behind him. He glanced over his shoulder. The same woman he'd seen pass through the lobby pushed open a couple of windows on the third floor. "Do the rest of the people who work at the inn live here, too?"

"You mean here on the inn property?"

"Yeah."

Dan gave him a long appraising look. "You ask an awful lot of questions for a guest. What are you doing, casing the joint for Al Qaeda?"

"With someone like Janice in there to ferret out our sleeper cell? Not a chance." Ian gave a fake shudder. "She already warned me about her husband, too. Sounds pretty tough."

"Bill's not so bad. Just a quiet old guy. Likes his music. And not the kind of music you'd expect. We got talking about different groups one day, and he told me he once met one of the Beatles. Janice arrived then, though, and he shut right up. Still haven't been able to find out which one."

"Fascinating."

"Yeah, isn't it? Life here in Siberia is just a thrill a minute." Dan picked up a hammer and pounded a couple of times on the sign. "Have to get back to work. The boss just came out on the deck. I think she's looking for you."

"Thanks." Ian pushed to his feet and fixed his gaze on the slender young woman standing on the top step of the deck. A white, short-sleeved, collared shirt was tucked into a pair of khakis. Flat sandals. Curly brown hair pulled back into a ponytail. He started toward her, and her features came into focus. No makeup. Only large green eyes dominating a pale face…and a thin scar on her forehead.

Kelly didn't know why, but her stomach twisted as the stranger neared. She did, however, suddenly understand Janice's hesitation in wanting to find him a room.

Broad shoulders, narrow waist enclosed in a black polo shirt and khakis. Tall and imposing, he moved with the smooth power of an athlete. She couldn't imagine him being the kind of man who spent too much time behind a desk...nor could she imagine him fitting comfortably into the tiny bed in the third-floor room she'd intended to rent to him.

As he drew closer, she noticed a touch of gray staining his temples. His wavy dark hair curled over the collar of his shirt. He was overdue for a haircut. She looked up into his face and saw a look of hardness there. A broken nose above thinly drawn lips and a square jaw. The dark eyes were challenging, and Kelly felt the intensity of the gaze from the second he'd turned and noticed her.

Kelly fought her inclination to go back inside and face him with the safety of a reception desk between them. She pushed away from the railing and straightened up. "Mr. Campbell?"

"And I suspect you must be Ms. Stone?"

She was relieved when he stopped at the bottom step. They were eye level. "Everyone calls me Kelly."

He extended a hand and took hers in his firm grasp. "Strange, the young man down there referred to you as the boss."

She felt like a diver who'd run short on air, and she didn't enjoy the feeling. She took back her hand. "First of all, I have to apologize for the confusion. Janice and I spoke about it, however, and we're readying a room for you on the third floor. I'm afraid that the accommodations might not be of the same caliber as the rest of the rooms here at Tranquillity Inn, but—''

''You're putting me in the broom closet.''

''Not exactly.'' She smiled. ''The room we're putting you in was rented out to guests before my daughter and I moved into the inn. It's small, but I think you'll find it very comfortable.''

''How long ago was that?''

''Do you mean, since we rented this room?''

''Yeah. How long have you been at the inn?''

''Well, it's been a couple of years, I guess,'' she responded vaguely.

He motioned with his head toward the carriage house. ''I would have thought that's where you lived. A nice little place.''

''My parents used to live there. But it was easier for my daughter, Jade, and me to take over the third floor of the main house and move Janice and Bill in there. Those two are getting too old to climb that many steps every day.''

''You're a very considerate employer.''

The softer tone surprised her, and Kelly found herself blushing. She scrambled to explain. ''The Maitlands are the very heart of the inn. Plus, they're like family to me.''

He leaned on the railing and took one of the last two cookies that were left on the plate. ''What happened to your parents?''

He must have seen her watching his actions as he extended the plate toward her. Kelly shook her head.

''They're both deceased.'' She rubbed her hands

together, suddenly uncomfortable with the coziness of standing there and chatting with him. "Rita should have your room ready in about an hour, Mr. Campbell. In the meantime, you're welcome to sit here or inside, or walk around, or whatever. There is also a new plate of cookies on the reception desk that you are welcome to, as well. And we'll be putting some liquid refreshments out in the parlor, as soon as I go inside and get to work."

"So I should make myself at home."

"Absolutely." She took a half step back as he started up the steps.

"And is someone going to give me a tour of the place? Or should I just poke my head into everything."

She wiped her sweaty palms on the seat of her pants and glanced hopefully at Dan.

"He's pretty busy," the guest stated.

"Well, someone will definitely show you around. We'll just need a little time to get organized. So if you'll forgive me…" Kelly turned and practically ran toward the door to the porch dining room. She just couldn't understand the nervousness this man created in her.

She must be crazy, putting him up next to her own apartment.

Lauren Wells stared out at the green blur of trees as the bus sped along the state highway. It seemed as if she'd been on a bus forever, and the air-conditioning on this one hadn't been working right since she boarded it in Concord.

Well, she thought, they had to be getting close to the village of Independence.

She opened her travel bag and took out the schedule and the "Inns, Hostels, and B&B's of New Hampshire" map she'd gotten at the bus terminal. An index card was paper-clipped to the map. She adjusted her glasses and peered at the schedule. The numbers on the paper were just too darn small, but the bus driver had told her they should get there about ten past two. Trying not to jostle the young man dozing in the seat next to her, she pushed her bag to the floor and carefully opened the map. It didn't give her much detail about the area, but the inn seemed to be reasonably close to Independence. She tried to figure out the distance from the village to the numbered spot she'd circled.

"Going to Independence?" the young man asked, startling her. He was smiling and looking down at the map.

"Why...er, yes I am."

"Me, too," he said cheerfully. "Me and my four friends back there are all going to Independence Village. Or near there, at least."

"That's nice," she replied, glancing over her shoulder at the people behind them. They looked like a pleasant group, talking quietly amongst themselves. She casually refolded the map. "Coming home from college?"

"Not exactly, ma'am." He was a nice-looking

young man, clean-shaven with short blond hair and bright blue eyes. "You're right about the college part, but we're all up here for jobs at a summer camp for kids."

Lauren looked away. "Are there many camps around here?"

"Four or five of them," the young man laughed. "We work at a…a camp that teaches kayaking and outdoor sports to disabled kids. This is the second year for all of us working there."

"Oh," she said, feeling relieved.

"I'm Caleb Smith."

"Nice to meet you, Caleb. I'm Lauren Wells." She adjusted her glasses.

"So, Lauren, you home from college for the summer?"

She glanced at him and realized he was teasing her. They both laughed. Lauren knew she looked every bit her seventy-seven years. She was still in reasonably good health, except for her failing eyesight, but the years had definitely left their mark on her wrinkled skin and snow-white hair.

Lauren looked down at the map in her hand. The index card clipped to it was facing up, and the oversize printing on it was easily readable: *Kelly Stone. Tranquillity Inn. Independence, New Hampshire.*

Putting the papers back in her bag, she sat and looked out the window again.

"Are you staying at that inn? The one on the card?"

She looked over at him. He was just being friendly. "Yes, I am."

"Is someone picking you up?"

Lauren considered telling a lie, but he seemed like such an earnest young man. Plus, he was getting off the bus at the same stop. "Actually, I was hoping to get a cab at the bus stop."

"I doubt they have one. There isn't much of anything in Independence. Maybe you could call out to the inn for a ride. Some of these places have courtesy vans."

"That's a good idea," she said. "I'll call when I get there."

"Which is right now," he replied, gesturing out the window.

The bus was pulling into a combination general store and gas station. A little A-frame breakfast-and-lunch place sporting a sign that read, Alpine Chalet Family Restaurant was right next door, and an old-fashioned telephone booth stood between the two parking lots.

The five college kids and Lauren were the only ones getting off here, and she let them pile out in front of her. The driver opened the outside trunk for them, and they hauled out backpacks and bags. She waited until they started across the parking lot toward the store, where there was a blue transport van parked by the door. As she went down the steps, she slung her bag over her shoulder and watched her travel companion talking to the driver through the window. The others were piling their things into the van.

The bus pulled out of the lot, and Lauren walked toward the telephone booth. The fresh air felt good after the stuffy confines of the bus, and she breathed in the smell of pine. Just as she reached the phone, the van pulled up behind her, and the front window opened.

"Hi again," Caleb said. "Listen, we're going in the same direction that you are. We can drop you at the Tranquillity Inn."

"Well, I…" Lauren thought about it for a moment. "I'd hate to take you out of your way at all."

"It's no problem, ma'am. We'll be happy to give you a lift."

Lauren looked at the phone and then back at the van. Finally, she decided. "Well, Caleb, that's very nice of you. I think I'll take you up on that offer."

"Great!" He hopped out and opened the sliding door to the van.

She could see the other four had seated themselves in the back two bench seats, leaving room for her on the seat behind the driver. As she settled herself in, the door slid shut with a bang, and the young man hopped back into the front seat.

"All set," he said brightly, pressing the door lock.

Too late, she saw the small silver crescent moon hanging from the mirror, for the van was already pulling out onto the state road.

Three

There were trails into the woods. Trails around the lake. Trails to take you to other trails and to rutted fire roads and to more trails. A rough carving on a wooden sign next to the parking lot showed the layout of the hiking trails and the lake. The map showed the borders of the inn property around half the lake, and the trails seemed to end abruptly where a camp on the far side was situated. Ian's interest, for now, anyway, was focused on the inn and the people in it.

Walking back toward the main building again, he saw a round-faced young woman who must be Rita looking out a second-floor window at him. She appeared to be on the run and obviously wore several hats in the operation. After moving his car to a better spot in the parking lot, Ian also noted a heavyset biker-type with a shaved head dropping a garbage bag into a Dumpster. The man was wearing a white T-shirt and apron. Ornate tattoos covered every inch of his arms. He only grunted in answer to Ian's greeting before disappearing back inside what had to be the kitchen.

Ian entered the inn and settled down at a table by the windows on the porch. From that vantage point he could see both the reception desk and the lake. The sun was warm and comfortable. Ian got up once, when the cook appeared with a bin filled with bottles of water and soft drinks. The baldheaded bruiser didn't even look at Ian, though, and retreated immediately.

An older man that Ian guessed might be Bill, Janice's husband, appeared by one of the lakefront cottages a few minutes later, backing an old pickup right to the door. Looking out the porch window, Ian watched him use a key on a padlock and disappear inside the building for a few minutes. When he came out, he was carrying another box the same size as the ones Ian had seen on the steps near the door.

More candles.

After padlocking the door again, the old man put the box in the back of the pickup and looked up at the inn. Spotting the boxes by the deck, he climbed into the truck and drove across the soft grass up to the deck. Ian watched him as he lifted the three boxes into the pickup. He was still pretty fit for an older man, Ian thought as the pickup pulled around to the front of the inn.

It wasn't long before Dan came trudging up from the cottage. He had changed into khaki shorts and a white polo shirt. On the breast, Ian noted the logo of the place. The words *Tranquillity Inn* were surrounded by a simple, stylized rendering of a lake, a mountain and a small crescent moon above that. Dan entered directly into the lobby and gave Ian a quick nod as he went by the door to the porch on his way toward the kitchen. The young man didn't get far, though, as Ian heard Janice calling him.

Ian stood up and looked out the window again. The fog was still blocking any view of the far side of the lake. He was considering taking a walk, when he felt a tug on one pant leg. He looked down into a small face with huge green eyes, still puffy from a nap. Long curly hair that had escaped the clip holding the rest in a ponytail stuck out in every direction.

"Can you read?"

Half a dozen books that collectively weighed probably as much as the girl herself were stuffed under one arm. She was a tiny thing.

"Can *you?*" he asked.

"No, silly. I'm only three and a half."

"You're old enough to work here. You must be old enough to read."

"I don't work here." She scrunched up her nose and looked up at him with new interest. "Ohhh…you must be the Cookie Monster."

Amused, Ian crouched down on one knee until they were eye level and lowered his voice. "Who told you?"

"My mom," she whispered, taking Ian's chin and turning it toward the reception desk. Kelly was greeting two men who were just arriving. "She told Wilson in the kitchen to make more cookies because we have the Cookie Monster staying with us."

"Hmm…so she's on to me," Ian whispered. "But I thought the Cookie Monster was blue."

She considered that for a moment. "Maybe you keep your fur suit in your bags."

The books were getting too heavy for her, and as she adjusted them, one slipped out, hitting the floor. Ian picked it up. "And you'd like me to read to you, is that it?"

"We can start with that one," she said firmly. She pointed to the door. "I like the rocking chairs on the deck when it's warm and sunny out."

For a second Ian tried to put himself in the young mother's position, mulling over how he'd feel about a daughter of his going outside with a total stranger. He wouldn't like it.

"How about those chairs in the parlor there by the fireplace. I have to stay close to the cookies, you know."

She shrugged and took his arm, helping him up. He'd never been a parent and wasn't used to being around kids, but this one definitely ranked high on the adorable scale.

Ian was watching Kelly as the moment of panic hit her. Her eyes scanned the area, looking for her daughter, and then relief showed in her face as the two of them walked into the sitting area. She looked at Ian, at the books, at Jade, and then back up at Ian.

He motioned toward the leather sofa where Jade was putting down the books. "I'm about to be tested on my reading ability."

"That's really not necessary, Mr. Campbell. Her baby-sitter is supposed to arrive any minute."

"No problem. We might get through one of the books."

"Are you sure?" she asked, looking uncertain.

He nodded. "This way I can keep track of you and Janice and make sure you don't give my room away to somebody else."

One of the guests she'd been speaking to, a very short man with expressive hands, approached Kelly after a brief conference with his friend. There was no question in Ian's mind that the two were gay, and this one—with his styled hair and muscular body—looked like a miniature cover model.

"Come on, Cookie Monster." There was a tug on Ian's hand, and he turned his full attention to the bossy thing at his side.

"I've got a name, you know," he said, letting her lead him to the sofa. "It's Ian."

She climbed up and patted the seat next to her. As he sat down, she extended her hand toward him. "Nice to meet you, Ian. I'm Jade."

Her tiny fingers disappeared inside his hand. She was dead serious, and he somehow succeeded in keeping a straight face. Then it was right down to business. She opened the first book, a counting book.

"You can't rush through the pages, like *some* people, because I like to look at the pictures, too."

"Okay." He glanced at the first few pages. There were no more than a dozen words on each page. This would give him ample opportunity to keep an eye on things.

Janice had seated herself at the reception desk and,

after a quick look in his direction, was focusing on some guests who were just arriving. The woman was definitely an old hand at this, playing the part of hostess to perfection. She greeted the couple—a guy and a beautiful woman who looked familiar—with the enthusiasm and familiarity of a woman welcoming family home. From the conversation, Ian realized he'd seen the woman on a number of magazine covers.

Naturally, Kelly was introduced to the newcomers, as well, who were apparently returning guests. But it was obvious that her department was to deal with problems—such as where to put the gay couple and Ian himself. She was standing by the porch with the two men. A pull on Ian's sleeve brought him back to a page showing eight little eggs. Embellishing on the text, he gave Jade his version of the best way to have them for breakfast. Somehow, watermelon, peanut butter and sweet-pickle ice cream made it into the description.

She giggled. "You're funny," she said, immediately flipping the pages back to the beginning. "We'll start again. And this time, tell it *your* way."

It was difficult to understand, but the little girl's approval had an effect on him. He looked down at the top of her head and the tangle of light brown curls. This tiny human, so open and honest, actually liked him. It was as simple as that.

"Mmmmmm…one pig…a side of bacon."

"On a burger?" she asked.

Ian nodded. "With mustard and ketchup."

"And marshmallows."

"On a cheeseburger?" Ian made a face.

Jade nodded exuberantly. "And blue M&M's for a topping."

"Are we still talking about the pig?"

"No, the cows." She smiled, turning the page to where pictures of two cows filled the space.

"Back to the burger."

Ian felt Jade become tense beside him.

"What's the matter?"

"She's here," Jade whispered, cuddling closer against him.

"Who's here?" he asked, looking around the parlor. A family who had checked in earlier were back downstairs. The younger son, cookies in hand, was already raiding the refreshment table. The couple Kelly had been speaking to earlier was leading Dan out to the car to get their luggage. Ian saw the object of Jade's obvious unhappiness. A teenage girl with a red backpack slung over one shoulder had just come into the inn by way of the hallway behind the reception desk. "Her?"

Jade nodded. "That's Cassy."

"Your baby-sitter?"

"I'm not a baby. I don't need her." Jade half hid under his arm, glaring fiercely across the lobby.

The child's discomfort sat wrong with Ian. He looked more closely at the teenager. On the surface she was just another Britney Spears look-alike. Maybe sixteen years old. Spiky golden hair and the requisite band of skin showing between the shirt and low-slung jeans. Pierced naval. She had a bright and expressive face, and she spoke up intelligently as she approached Kelly.

"What don't you like about her?"

He got a shrug for an answer.

"What do you two do when she comes over?" Ian asked, hoping for Jade to elaborate.

Again, he got a shrug.

"Is she mean to you?" he asked seriously.

The child's head shook from side to side, making the ringlets dance. The little fingers clutched at his sleeve when Cassy looked in their direction as she continued to talk to Kelly.

"Why don't you tell your mom that you don't like her?" he whispered back as the baby-sitter approached, suddenly feeling uncomfortable at the way Jade was clutching at him.

"I want to read more," Jade said, burying her face against his arm. "I want to stay here."

There was no way the girl could have missed hearing the complaint. Without thinking, Ian put his arm around Jade's shoulder, drawing her more protectively to his side.

"I hear somebody had a short nap today. Hi, I'm Cassy Harper," she said brightly to Ian.

"Hi. I'm Ian Campbell."

Swinging her pack down, Cassy crouched before them, patting Jade's knee and trying to draw her out. "Your mom told me to ask you about your swimming class today. She is so proud of you." She reached for the child and peeled her away from Ian and into her own arms.

Ian didn't like the way Jade went limp and agreeable the moment Cassy touched her. All the fight had suddenly drained out of her. The books lay forgotten on the sofa. The teenager, holding the little girl by the hand, stood up.

Ian immediately rose himself. "Is school still in session?"

"Yeah, for a couple more weeks," Cassy said, lifting her onto her hip and shouldering her pack. She started toward the door.

Ian followed them. "Do you come here every day?"

"No, only when things are busy. Usually Fridays and Sundays. You know, check-in and checkout."

Ian touched Jade's hand. It was ice cold. "So what's the routine?"

"We go for a long walk. I'll bring her back by dinnertime. It doesn't matter how crowded or busy this place gets, Kelly insists on having dinner with this little munchkin. I think she's looking for you," Cassy motioned with her head toward the owner of the inn. "And we've gotta go."

The teenager went out with the little girl, and Ian stood watching them. Jade didn't look back, instead putting her head listlessly on the sitter's shoulder. She was a different kid than the one who'd been sitting next to him a minute earlier.

Kelly came up behind him. "I think we finally have your room ready, Mr. Campbell. And if you like, I've got time to give you a little tour."

"You have a very cute daughter." He turned to her.

"Thank you."

"How long have you had this sitter?" he asked in a no-nonsense tone.

"Cassy has been watching Jade for me from the time I relocated to New Hampshire. She's the only baby-sitter my daughter has ever had. Is something wrong?" Kelly asked, a note of apprehension in her tone.

"No, I suppose not." He frowned. "Maybe things are different in New Hampshire, but did you ever do a reference check? A police background check? Drug or alcohol testing?"

Kelly looked at him steadily for a moment, then began to bite her lip, obviously trying to hide her amusement.

"This isn't San Diego, Mr. Campbell. We live on the very edge of the boondocks. The total population of Independence and Errol and the surrounding area is just under five hundred on a good day...and that's counting the dogs and cats and tourists. The deer outnumber the people around here, and everybody knows everybody else. We have two men who constitute the police, and they're actually state wildlife conservation officers. Even if I needed them, there isn't a real police department within thirty miles."

"So does that mean you didn't?" he asked, still serious.

"No, I didn't. But I know Cassy's mother."

Ian nodded and said nothing more.

"Thanks for your concern, Mr. Campbell, but I work pretty hard to raise my daughter in a safe environment, and we all look out for each other up here. Now, how about if I show you around."

Leading him along the main floor, the inn's owner ran through a rehearsed speech about the place, its history, its amenities.

"Though we serve three meals a day, we're very flexible for people who wish to take a lunch for a hike in the wilds or on a sightseeing drive. And if you're a connoisseur of wine, we have one of the finest collections of—"

"What is there to see around here?"

"Around Independence?" She scrunched up her nose the same way Ian had seen Jade do. "Miles of forests and hundreds of lakes. Within an hour's drive, there are mountains, too. If you're interested in driving to White Mountains, we can pull out some maps and—"

"No, you have exactly what I'm looking for."

Kelly Stone had very expressive eyes, and Ian saw the question form and go unasked, before she whirled and pushed through the door leading from the porch dining area onto the deck. There was no sign of Bill or his pickup. Two boys were tossing a Frisbee on the small sand beach. The younger boy missed a catch as he paused to watch them for a minute.

"I saw you talking to Dan before, so he probably explained to you about the lake and the boats and the safety rules we insist all of our guests follow."

"Actually, we never talked about any of that," he

said. The fog still shrouded the far side of the lake. "Does it get foggy like this all the time?"

She followed the direction of his gaze. "Janice always tells me that it's bad for business to admit it, but I'm not too good at keeping any secrets. Yes, half of Lake Tranquillity is covered in fog nine out of ten days." She tucked her hands into the pockets of her pants and leaned against the railing. "I was told there's a logical explanation for it, though. Most of the lakes in this area are spring fed…some are cold springs, some warm. The spring that feeds this one is warm. If you go in swimming, you'll notice the difference. They tell me that's the reason for the fog, too."

Ian liked real things. Whether they were obstacles, walls or people, he like them solid and tangible. He'd never cared for fog. "What's on the other side of the lake."

"A summer camp."

"What kind?"

"The owner leases it to different groups every few years, so it changes. I have no reason to go over there, but I was told that last year there was a camp for inner-city teens for most of the summer."

Ian had other questions about the camp, but Kelly turned her back on the lake and led the way inside. On the porch, she pointed out a buffet table that was well stocked with snacks around the clock. Ian's mind, though, was still outside. He didn't pick up on her comments about the kitchen only serving cookies up to eleven at night until it was too late to make a comeback.

"Would you like me to ask Dan to bring your luggage up while I show you upstairs?"

"No, I'll get it myself later."

"By the way, we only have you down for the weekend," she commented as they trekked up the stairs. "Do we have that right?"

"Would it be a problem if I decided to stay longer?" Ian asked, sure now that he would be staying.

"No problem at all. Of course, you haven't seen your room yet. You might change your mind." She shot him an impish smile before stopping at the second floor to show him the full bath he was supposed to share with several other guests.

At the top of the stairs, the floor was old, highly polished hardwood, and there was a small alcove set up like a sitting room. In front of a window overlooking the lake, a comfortable upholstered chair, a ladder-back chair, a child's rocker, a small table containing a number of books and a reading lamp had been artfully arranged. Fresh flowers sat in a vase on the table. Ian stopped and peered out, checking the view. Dan was down at the dock, getting the two boys outfitted with a canoe. The fog in the distance was impenetrable.

"The house is old, and the locks aren't too trustworthy. So we have a little sign here that we ask our patrons to use when using the bathroom." She showed him the hand-painted slate sign hanging from a hook next to the bathroom door.

Ian glanced at the slate. Aside from the word Occupied, it was decorated with astrological markings of moons and stars and signs of the zodiac. "Who's the artist?"

Kelly touched the sign. "I really don't know. It seems like the slates have been here forever, from when my parents first bought the inn. Every room has a unique plaque of its own."

Ian looked down the hallway and saw the plaques hanging beside each door.

"Each room is named after an astrological sign. I'm no good at any of that, myself. I suppose I shouldn't tell you this, but when I'm in the office, I have to use a little cheat sheet to remind myself which room number is Sagittarius and which one is Aquarius. I just can't keep them straight." She motioned him down the hall. "I have to apologize, but you'll have to take the back stairs up from this floor. There's only one set of stairs that go from here to your room."

At the far end of the hall, a variety of delicious smells wafted up a narrow stairwell from the kitchen. This was obviously the way Kelly had brought Jade up earlier. She opened a door behind them, revealing stairs going up to the third floor that were steeper and even tighter.

"At one time, this section was only an attic," she explained, leading the way. "I'm told some fifteen years ago, the last owner added the dormers and the bathroom and made it into an apartment.''

They reached the top, where one of the dormers opened up the small sitting area at the landing. Like the rest of the house, the space was cozily decorated with a braided rug, rocking chair and small bookcase. To their left, a door was open, and Ian peeked inside at what he could only describe as a doll's room. The eaves ran down steeply from the peak of the house and the narrow area from the door to the window was the only place with enough headroom to walk. The walls were a pale pink. An antique twin bed with a white metal frame swallowed up most of the available space. The bedcovering was a checkered quilt of white and pink. The rug matched the color of the quilt. A white end table held a lamp with a pink lampshade. On top of a white dresser, near the foot of the bed, sat a row of teddy bears. Ian noted that even they were wearing pink shirts and coveralls.

''Is this Jade's room?''

''Jade hates pink.'' She cleared her voice, but it didn't help. The words came out as a croak. ''This is yours.''

He looked inside again, trying to imagine how he could possibly fit inside the place, never mind sleep in it. Pink.

''If you're not claustrophobic, you'll find the bed very comfortable. And your room will come with your breakfast included. Did I mention that Tranquillity Inn is famous for its outstanding meals?''

After a moment, Ian turned around and Kelly took

a couple of steps back to give him room. He touched the chair at the top of the stairs and watched it rock back and forth a few times. He wondered if he could sleep in it. On the other side of the stairs, there was another door that Kelly was blocking.

She followed the direction of his gaze. "This leads to the apartment where Jade and I live. We're both really quiet types. There'll be no early-morning noise."

He tugged on an earlobe.

She stepped away from the door. "We'd be delighted if you decided to stay with us, but of course I would understand if you preferred to have us find you another inn with better accommodations."

He noticed the slate plaque hanging by the door of her apartment. He looked back at the plate by his own door. His was Cancer. Hers was the Moon.

Unlike Kelly, Ian actually knew quite a bit about the zodiac and astrology, and he had no problem remembering the signs and their properties. The Moon's symbol was a crescent. The visible part symbolized the conscious mind; the dark side, the unconscious. The Moon was a feminine sign, and appropriately connected with water. Perhaps even more appropriately, he thought wryly, the Moon ruled in Cancer, a nighttime house.

He turned to her. "I'll take the room."

Four

"Yo, Blade. You in here?"

Dan entered the kitchen, but the cook was nowhere to be seen. No matter, he thought. He knew what he had to do.

He looked up at the television positioned on a shelf and shook his head. Wilson Blade was an addict when it came to soap operas. Dan was pretty sure that the guy didn't fit any demographic group that normally watched soaps, but that didn't make any difference. The cook, who on the surface was probably one of the scariest people Dan had ever seen, knew every character, every plotline and every history of at least a half-dozen shows. He'd heard him talking to Rita about them. This was a new one on Dan, though. It was a French-language soap out of Quebec.

Dan reached up and switched the channel to the Montpelier station, which was the closest thing to a local station they got up here. The early news show was already half done, but he knew the weather would soon be coming on, so he left it there and got to work.

The kitchen was, as usual, immaculate. A couple of sauces were simmering on the huge old stove, and it smelled as if a roast was in the oven. Wilson—who had told Dan when he first started to call him Blade, no matter what the others called him—was a surprisingly clean worker. He was also a damn good cook. When Dan, on his first day, had jokingly asked him if he'd learned to cook in prison, though, Blade had nearly taken his head off. Wilson Blade was obviously not a person to be trifled with.

Digging through the bins in the walk-in fridge, Dan found the bag of sweet potatoes he was supposed to peel and cut up. He hefted it to the sink, dragged a stool up and picked a sharp knife out of the drawer. He'd just finished his second sweet potato when the weather guy began to tell the anchorwoman about a festival in India that was coming to a climax.

"...celebrating an astrological event in which Jupiter is halfway through its journey around the sun. The round trip takes a little more than twenty-two years, and in four days the planet enters Aquarius on the zodiac, as the sun enters Aries. Now—pay close attention, Monica—when the sun, which represents rational intellect, encounters this specific relationship to Jupiter, which happens to be the spiritual master, it guides the moon, which represents the human mind, thus resulting in immortality of the self."

"Wow," the anchorwoman joked. "I'd better get my house cleaned."

"Seriously," the weatherman continued. "Here in northern New England over the next few days, we'll get to enjoy the largest moon we'll see this year, but that always means some weird stuff is bound to happen."

"Will the loonies be out in force, Jay?"

"Well, you were still in grade school when it happened, but the last time these planets aligned in just this fashion, a cult in New Mexico committed mass suicide, leaving only—"

The television clicked off and Dan looked up, startled, slicing his hand in the process. "Shit!"

Blood began dripping into the sink, and he grabbed a towel to stop the flow. Turning, he saw Wilson Blade glaring at him, the cord of the TV in his hand.

"What's your problem?" Dan asked, focusing his attention on his hand.

"This is my fucking TV."

"Yeah, so?" He frowned at the chef. "You weren't around, so I—"

"It's mine. Don't you ever touch it again. Ever." Blade stepped toward him threateningly. "You got it?"

"Whatever. Don't blow a gasket."

Plugging the cord back in, Blade switched the channel back to the Canadian soap. Stalking to the far side of the kitchen, he said nothing more and started to set up his pasta machine.

"I'm getting a bandage for my hand from the office," Dan said, moving to the door.

Blade snorted, and Dan went out, patting the deep cut and looking at it. The sound of the soap followed him down the hall.

"Weirdo," he muttered under his breath. "Who'd have guessed the guy even spoke French."

* * *

Jade was too heavy to be carried the whole way, and Cassy put her down right after they left the inn. As soon as they were on the trail through the woods, of course, the little girl's energy kicked into gear. The teenager chased after her through the forest up a long hill, all the while shouting warnings not to veer off the trail into the woods, not to stumble over the rocks, to watch out for poison ivy, and a dozen other things. As soon as the sitter caught up to Jade and got a firm grip on her, however, the energy disappeared, and the girl started to dawdle, dragging like an anchor along the trail.

"Mommy loves these." Jade bent over to pick another flower from a patch of grape hyacinth. They'd been seeing these all along the wooded path.

"Come on. You already have a bunch in each hand."

"One more," Jade pleaded. "These are the prettiest ones."

Cassy glanced at her wristwatch. She should have let the little monster race the entire way. They were definitely going to be late now.

"Come *on!*" The sitter urged, letting her frustration show when Jade took two more steps and spotted another patch of flowers. She changed her tack. "If we walk this slow, we're sure to get eaten by bears."

"My mom says that bears won't hurt you if they don't have babies to protect."

"Please, Jade," the sitter begged. "It's important that we keep going."

"Why?" The little girl dropped one bouquet and

ran off the path to a lilac that was still in bloom. "These are *so* beautiful and they smell *so* good. We've *got* to get some for my mommy. Help me?"

The teenager stared at her charge, one hand on a hip. "If I do, will you walk faster and stay with me?"

"I promise."

Following the little girl to the shrub, she reached up to break off a cluster of the fragrant flowers, when she heard the sound of an engine in the distance.

"He's here," she said, turning toward the sound.

Her bargain forgotten, Cassy reached down and hoisted the child on her hip, then ran along the path.

"Mommy's flowers," Jade croaked in a soft voice while clutching tightly to the remaining bouquet in her fingers.

Cassy paid no attention to the child's complaint. She hardly felt Jade's weight, and the pebble that had gotten inside her shoe was forgotten. She broke over the crest of a hill with a smile beaming on her young face. A moment later they came to a place where a deserted logging road crossed the path.

The old Jeep coming down the narrow lane had no top or doors, and the driver gave her an enthusiastic wave as she stepped back onto the trail. He roared up and skidded to a stop.

"Caleb!" Cassy called out to him. "When did you get back?"

"Early this afternoon."

"You got a haircut." She admired the short blond hair.

"Yeah." He ran a hand through his hair and the

blue eyes focused on the child in Cassy's arm. "How's she doing?"

Jade was clutching tightly to the sitter's shirt. Cassy noticed the crushed flowers that the child still held in the other fist. Her head was tucked against the teenager's shoulder, and she refused to look up at the young man in the Jeep. Cassy walked around the back and climbed onto the passenger seat, jostling the little girl as she settled her on her lap. "This is a new thing with her. She acts shy around people."

"But we're old friends." Caleb reached over to touch the child's hand, but Jade withdrew it sharply, breaking some of the flowers from the stems. The child's green eyes stared at her loss.

"I want to go home," she whispered to Cassy and started to cry softly.

The young man gave a worried glance to Cassy. The teenager pulled Jade closer into an embrace. "She'll be all better when we get there."

"I hope so," Caleb said. "Father Ty is very anxious to see her. He wants to introduce her to the new people."

Ian moved the little lever on the tarnished brass plate of the antique doorknob. He could feel the lock click but when he reached around the bedroom door to test it, the outside knob turned without the least bit of resistance. He pushed the lever the other way. He was sure the mechanism inside was doing something. He tried it again. The knob turned. Trying the lever again, he fiddled with the knob and the spring-loaded bolt protruding from the edge of the door. He gave up. He'd need a screwdriver to get into the works of the lock, and he probably wouldn't be able to fix it, anyway.

He should have known not to take Kelly's warning about the locks too lightly.

He closed the door and pushed a straight-back chair—the only furniture in the room not painted pink or white—against the door, jamming the back up under the knob. He put his suitcase on the bed.

Dinner would start at six. Cocktails and hors d'oeuvres in the lobby at five. That was his chance to get introduced to the other guests, perhaps ask one or two questions. He opened the suitcase and took out his pistol and a cartridge. Loading the weapon, he checked it, unloaded it, and laid the gun on the quilt beside the cartridge. Ian pulled out a manila envelope stuffed with papers and dropped it next to the gun, as well. All the clothes from the suitcase fit into the first two drawers of the dresser. He put a smaller bag containing his bathroom stuff on the top. Pausing, he took his cell phone out of his pocket and looked at the display. No service in this area.

As he pulled on a clean shirt, Ian's eye caught sight of a small photograph that had fallen onto the bottom of the suitcase. He picked it up and looked into the smiling face of the young woman.

"Soon," he whispered, tucking the picture into his shaving pouch. The pistol and the envelope went back into the suitcase. He spun the dials on the combination lock and tested it before sliding the case under the bed.

Ian looked at his watch. It was already five-thirty. Time to get the ball rolling.

The tantalizing aroma of various foods drifted out of the kitchen and down the hall. None of the guests had come downstairs yet to taste Wilson's delectable appetizers. Bill had established himself behind a portable rolling bar near the fireplace and was polishing glasses while he waited. Janice was sitting at the reception desk and speaking to someone on the phone, her reservation book open in front of her. The afternoon breeze was mild and comfortable, and all the windows were still open.

Kelly looked anxiously toward the door to the porch. No sign of Jade and Cassy yet. She checked her watch. They were not technically late, she told herself. She stepped into the porch dining area. Rita was just finishing setting the last of the dinner tables.

"You've been on the go all day. I'll help you with serving the tables tonight," Kelly offered, trying to give the young woman some relief.

"Whatever," Rita said in her usual rough, no-nonsense manner. She picked up the blackboard they updated every night with the dinner entrées.

"Let me do that." Kelly took the board from Rita's hand. "Why don't you go have your dinner. Sit and veg for a few minutes before the insanity starts."

The only reaction out of the woman was a shrug before going out in the direction of the kitchen.

Though she was only in her early thirties, Rita was another old-timer at the inn. She'd been working there since she was eighteen, right out of high school.

From about the first week Kelly was here, she realized that dealing with Rita was no bowl of cherries. The woman's moodiness, her lack of communication skills and her confrontational attitude when she disagreed with anything were a little tough to take at times. But trying to look past those things, Kelly had soon seen that the woman was a workhorse. With no husband or kids, or even a boyfriend that anyone knew of, putting demands on her time, Rita was very dedicated, spending every minute at the inn when they needed her. There were days like today when Kelly knew that she could not have hired three people to do what Rita accomplished in one afternoon. And that was if she could *find* three people in the Independence area willing to drive back and forth to the inn every day. Help was difficult to find around here.

Over the course of two years, the two women had learned how to deal with each other. Or at least, Kelly had. She just told Rita what had to be done, then she got out of the way fast.

Kelly's eyes followed the trail along the shoreline, hoping for a glimpse of Jade and Cassy. No one. The nerves in her stomach cinched up tightly. It was all Ian Campbell's fault. She wouldn't be even thinking about this if it weren't for him planting all those ideas in her head.

She took the chalk and the board and headed for

the kitchen. She'd offered to do the job for Rita, but she didn't know the exact menu for dinner.

The couple from Philadelphia had appeared. They were standing by the bar cart and chatting with Bill. The three smiled at Kelly as she walked through the parlor. Ian Campbell was coming down the stairs, as well. His gaze met Kelly's, and then he glanced at the sofa and at Jade's books, stacked on an end table. A pang of worry went through her again as she realized she wasn't alone in wondering about her daughter's whereabouts.

They'll be along, she told herself.

As she went by the desk, Kelly whispered to Janice, "Be nice to *all* of them."

The old woman smiled. She already had her hostess face on.

On her way to the kitchen, Kelly slipped into the office and buzzed the intercom for her apartment upstairs. There was a slim chance that Cassy had brought Jade in without Kelly seeing them, and they'd just gone straight upstairs. There was no answer.

In the kitchen, Kelly found Rita and Dan sitting at the counter. Dan was having his dinner and Rita was fazing out, staring at the TV. She was glad they were there. If there was one person who really bothered Kelly, it was the inn's cook, who was standing by the stove. There were a dozen times she'd considered letting Wilson Blade go, but he was a tremendous asset to the inn. He was easily one of the best chefs in the area, and his dishes brought in a good number of extra dinner guests once the summer season really got roll-

ing. Why, she'd seen him twice turn down offers from
the Balsams to go and cook for them. Besides, he
never really gave her a concrete reason to fire him.
Like so many other things around here, Wilson Blade
was something she could not easily change. Still, he
bothered her.

"I need to copy the dinner menu," she said, laying
the blackboard on a counter near the door. Finish and
leave, she told herself.

Wilson's hand paused in stirring a sauce, and his
gaze warmed as he turned and looked at her. Kelly
felt the hair stand up on her neck, and she glanced
away. This wasn't the first time—not even the hundredth time—that he made her feel uncomfortable
like this.

He was always watching her. He hovered over her,
and it gave her the creeps. The weird thing was that
he wasn't looking at her like some construction
worker ogling a woman on the street. He didn't stare
at her breasts or her butt. It was difficult to define…it
was something in his eyes. He acted like a guard dog.
She didn't need one—hadn't asked for one—and
never encouraged his behavior in any way. From the
moment she'd met him, Wilson stared at her as if she
were some treasured cut of beef.

The whole thing was too strange. There were many
nights when she thought he had gone home, and she
would gaze out her apartment window and see him
standing outside, smoking beneath the trees. Sometimes he would look up at her windows. On a few
occasions when she'd taken Jade to a local fair or a

sale, she'd run into him. He seemed to be everywhere she went. If the activities in the area were not so limited, she might have considered him a stalker, but she couldn't quite bring herself to that point.

Still, Kelly never allowed Jade to go into the kitchen alone, and she never put herself in a position where she was alone with him. He'd never made an inappropriate advance or said or done anything overtly out of line, or that would have been the end of his employment. But even so, her skin still crawled.

"Blade, didn't you write the stuff on that piece of paper for Rita to copy onto the board?" Dan said, coming to her rescue and pointing to a single handwritten sheet sitting on the counter above the warming drawers for the bread.

"It's already been changed," Wilson growled, going over and crumpling the paper before tossing it into the trash bin.

Kelly wouldn't have been as uncomfortable about Wilson's behavior if he were consistent. If he were one bit pleasant to others—if there were even a trace of civility in his conduct with his fellow workers or with *anyone* else—she would have felt somewhat better about his oddly protective behavior. Added to that, Wilson Blade's past was a bit of a mystery. No one knew a thing about him. Neither Janice nor Bill would admit to hiring him in the first place, though he was already here when Kelly's parents bought the place. The Maitlands were also both quick to name a hundred reasons why Kelly should keep him any time they sensed she was becoming aggravated with him.

The funny thing was that she'd tried exactly what Mr. Campbell had suggested with Cassy. The park conservation officer she'd talked to about running a background check had looked at her as if she had two heads when she'd mentioned it. It was not something he was regularly asked to do, but he took the information she gave him and made a call to the police station in Colebrook and to the state police barracks in Twin Mountain. Wilson Blade was an ex-biker who'd had many brushes with the law in his younger years. No prison, but lots of minor arrests for alcohol and drugs before finding Jesus and getting sober. He had been a model citizen ever since, as far as the State of New Hampshire was concerned. It didn't appear that she had anything to worry about, the cops had told her.

Well, maybe not from where they were standing, she thought.

"What should I put on the board?" Kelly asked again, trying not to show her uneasiness as Wilson continued to scrutinize her silently.

He wiped his hand on a towel next to the stove and told her what the three entrées were.

She started writing down the dinner choices. "And what's the soup?"

"Cream of broccoli."

She made a mistake in spelling *broccoli* and his hand was right there, wiping the word for her.

Goose bumps rose on her arms, and she edged away from him.

"You look cold," he said. "You should go up and put a sweater on."

"I can look after myself, Wilson," she replied testily. "Any appetizers?"

"It ain't a good idea putting that stranger on the third floor. He's too close to you and Jade."

She was about to remind him that it wasn't his job to worry about where the guests were placed, when she heard the screen door open and close. She immediately moved away from him to the hallway, relieved to see Cassy carrying Jade in.

"She fell sleep," the teenager whispered as soon as she saw her. "I'll take her upstairs."

Kelly looked at her child's face, her dirty hands and muddy shoes.

"No, I'll take her."

She peeled her daughter away from Cassy's shoulder and took her in her arms.

"Was she feeling okay?" she asked, touching Jade's forehead. She wasn't feverish.

"Yeah. She's been running around like a maniac since we left. She got exhausted and wanted to be carried about twenty minutes ago." Cassy pulled out a leaf that had gotten tangled in Jade's hair. "I hadn't realized we'd gone so far. It was a hike carrying her back."

"Jade is getting too big for that."

The teenager shrugged. "She's a trouper, for the most part."

Kelly motioned toward the kitchen. "Why don't you get something to eat, and I'll get Bill or Dan to drive you home."

"That's okay. My mom is coming to get me." She caressed Jade's hair one more time. "So, do you need me tomorrow, or should I come back Sunday?"

"Sunday. But I'll call you if I need you sooner," she told the teenager as Dan came to the kitchen door and offered to finish writing the menu on the board for her.

Kelly used the back stairs to take Jade to their apartment. She was working her child harder than she should. The swimming classes were a lot, and then letting Cassy take her for a long walk on top of it was too much. And Jade hadn't had any kind of nutritious lunch to speak of. And now, the three-year-old was asleep and would miss dinner, too.

Kelly knew guilt's whisper well, and she could hear it now. Anytime Jade was sick—or fell and got a bruise—whenever her daughter had cried, no matter the reason, the voice was in her ear. She tried, but she just didn't know if she was being a good mother or not. She'd never had anyone to use as a model—at least, not when she'd been Jade's age.

At the top of the stairs, she spotted the little table that had been moved next to the door of her apartment. Jade's books from downstairs were stacked neatly on top of it. Next to them, two chocolate chip cookies sat on a napkin.

Kelly smiled as she pushed open the door. She didn't know anything about Ian Campbell. Despite the type of business she was in, she was always wary of strangers. She and Jade were slow to trust. Slower to accept. But there was something different about Mr. Campbell.

Five

Victor Desposito was flamboyant. At least, he was as flamboyant as a man can get at five foot five. His companion, Brian, more heavily built and six inches taller, was far more reserved.

Saying a simple hello to Victor had been enough of an encouragement to launch him into a complete history of himself and his friend. Within just a few minutes, Ian learned that both men were from Philadelphia. Victor was in the antique business. Brian was an artist, who worked side jobs as a carpenter. The absolute best hands in Philadelphia, if Victor was to be believed. Ian decided to take his word for it. Brian also worked part-time in the antique store that Victor managed for a dealer named Ellie Littlefield. The two of them were up here for some "fabulously" important auction that Ellie couldn't come up for herself.

This was more than Ian needed to know about the two men. He glanced around the lobby, hoping to learn as much about some of the other guests. But with their drinks in hand, Vic and Brian were right on his shoulder as he introduced himself to Marisa and Dave Meadows, a young couple here on their honeymoon.

Pleasant and somewhat shy, the two had a whole-some look. Ian noted the wary look on the part of the husband toward the gay couple. Before Ian could say anything beyond the initial introductions, though, Victor was talking.

"My Lord, look at the bone structure on this girl," he expostulated, moving next to Marisa. She had one or two inches on him, at least. "Are you two Amish?"

The wife and husband were both at loss for a minute before Dave answered. "No!"

"Why would you think...?" Marisa started to ask.

Victor waved a hand, speaking directly to her. "Your skin, honey. Gorgeous. No blemishes, no squint lines, and no smudges that say you're using any four-step system to keep your skin looking retro. Now, that one..." He motioned with his drink toward the very tall woman being escorted into the dining room by a shorter man, carrying a photography bag over his shoulder. "That's Ash. She's a model. And he's her personal Ken doll...I mean, photographer."

Ian couldn't help but smile, not only at Victor but also at the young couple as they looked and listened in wide-eyed wonder to everything he was saying.

"She's been using this amino acid antioxidant ex-foliator for two weeks now. She even told me the brand." He shook his head and nudged Marisa con-spiratorially. "Babe, even if I could afford it, I would never do that to my skin."

He brought his hand up and motioned for Marisa

to touch the back of it. She complied, to the obvious horror of her husband.

"Silky soft, isn't it? Strictly low-fat moisture lotion, street brand. I buy the stuff for about twenty dollars a tube."

"Well, looks like everybody is sitting down for dinner," Dave said, taking his wife by the arm. "And look, they've set a table for *two* for us by the window."

"Lucky you," Victor said as they moved off. He scanned the passing people for his next victim.

Ian turned to Brian and nodded toward the model and her boyfriend, who were just being seated in the porch dining area. "She's got 'buzz off' stamped all over her. So how did Victor here get a chance to talk to the ice princess?"

"Girl talk," Victor responded. "We ran into each other in the hallway upstairs. She liked my belt."

He jutted his hip out so Ian could see the silver Native American decorative work and the turquoise gemstones. Ian tried to look appropriately admiring.

"I told her how much I liked the ads she was doing," the shorter man continued. "But I told her she absolutely had to cut back on the dark lip liner. The natural fullness of her lips with that foxy-red color Bliss has out this season would complement her brunette complexion much, much better."

"Of course," Ian said, shaking his head. "Why didn't I think of that approach."

"It's a gift."

"And she didn't scratch your eyes out?"

"Christ, no!" Victor smiled at them. "They both live in Manhattan. She just finished a big shoot in Florida. She and Ken doll are taking a couple of weeks off before the next job. Anything else you wanted me find out for you, honey?"

"No. Thanks, though." Ian drank some of his beer and studied Victor with new interest. Short but well built. Obviously strong and very agile. He was good-looking with a carefully polished edge. Urbane and very astute.

"Oh my gawd!" Victor said, gesturing toward the porch. Ken had taken a Nikon camera out of his shoulder bag. The huge flash attachment had a piece of paper covering the bulb area with a rubber band, but the whole room lit up as he snapped a half-dozen shots of Ash—who looked incredibly bored—in rapid succession. Moving around the room, he managed to get everyone in the dining area in one shot or another.

"Some people just can't leave their work at home," Brian said with a shake of his head.

The family of four passed before them on their way to the dining room. Ian already knew their last name was Stern, and the boys were Craig and Ryan, fourteen and twelve years old. He had not yet met Mr. Stern, but his wife, Rachel Stern, had much the same coloring and build as Kelly. The eyes, though, set the two women apart. Kelly's eyes were more beautiful than anything Ian had seen in years.

"Speaking of work, did I mention my boss, Ellie Littlefield?" Vic asked, moving between Ian and Brian and nodding to the parents as they went by.

"You mentioned her name," Ian answered.

"Did I tell you she's married to a hunk?"

"No." Glancing into the dining room, Ian watched a brief and casual exchange between Mrs. Stern and the model. Their chairs were back to back, but there was something about the way the two women spoke, or acted, that gave Ian the impression that they might know each other.

"His name is Nate Murtaugh," Victor announced. "Do you know him?"

"Who?"

"Nate Murtaugh, Ellie's husband."

"No, should I?" Ian asked.

"He was an FBI agent."

Ian shot a curious look at Victor before shaking his head.

Brian broke in, speaking for the second time since Ian met the two. "Never mind him. Vic is into that 'degrees of separation' thing. He thinks everybody is related or knows each other or knows someone who knows someone else."

"I know for a fact that it's true," Victor said. "My mother was at the Vatican last year and had an audience with the pope. Think about it. What head of state hasn't he met? None. And what big pop star hasn't met a head of state? I'm only that many degrees of separation from Madonna. And that's only going through my mother. Think of Ellie and Nate and the people they know…"

"He has a point," Ian said to Brian, but the other man rolled his eyes.

Everyone else was seated in the dining room. Ian's gaze went from a couple of empty tables to a guest sitting alone at the far end of the room, his back turned.

"Nice talking to you guys," he said, walking away.

Ian had seen the man arrive. In his fifties, traveling alone, he hadn't stopped to order a drink in the parlor before going into the dining room. He didn't really fit in with the other guests.

"Mind if I join you?" he asked, reaching for the back of one of the chairs across the table from him.

The man looked meaningfully at the two empty tables on either side of him, before looking up at Ian. "I guess...not."

"Fabulous—I just love double dates," Victor said with enthusiasm, taking the chair to Ian's right and motioning to Brian to sit across from him.

The older man appeared at a loss for words for a few seconds at the intrusion, but Victor took care of that very quickly.

"I'm Victor Desposito. This is my friend, Brian Moore. And this is Ian Campbell. No relation to us."

"Shawn Hobart," the man said gruffly, making a production of spreading the napkin on his lap, and picking up his glass of water.

"Your first time at the inn?" Vic asked before the glass reached the man's lips.

"No, I'm a regular guest here."

"Fantastic." Vic stirred his mixed drink. "And what do you do, Shawn?"

"I'm in antiques."

"Get out of here!" Vic said excitedly. "You have a store?"

Ian sat back and watched the older man clear his throat.

"Yeah, I do."

"We must be here for the same auction," Brian commented to Ian, moving the plates, silverware and glasses around in front of him to make room for his bottle of beer. "That estate sale Vic was talking about earlier."

"When is it?" Ian asked.

"Tomorrow morning," Vic answered. "The preview is bright and early at seven sharp. The first item goes up at nine."

From across the table, Ian watched Shawn beginning to sweat. The older man took another long drink of water before looking anxiously over his shoulder at where Rita was explaining the dinner menu to the Sterns.

"If you're a regular here, you must be an old pro at finding your way around these back roads. We're from Philly. How about if Brian and I follow you tomorrow morning to the sale."

"I'm not going," the man said abruptly.

Vic's look of surprise was anything but restrained. "I know dealers who're coming all the way from Richmond and D.C. for this thing. The advertisement for it has been running in every trade paper from Maine to Virginia. And we're…what, an hour away from it, and you aren't going?"

"No, I'm not."

Victor stared at him for a moment. "Oh, I get it. You have your connections. You got a private viewing of the stuff before," he said, looking satisfied with the explanation. Shawn didn't say anything to contradict him. "How about giving us directions to the place, then. It's supposed to be right over the border in Vermont."

All eyes at the table turned on Shawn Hobart. The older man stared at the empty water glass before him. For a change, Vic fell quiet.

"Ask at the front desk. They'll help you out," he said finally. His mouth clamped shut, his downward gaze discouraging any more questions.

Victor and Brian exchanged a look, and an awkward silence descended on the table. Ian watched Kelly hurry into the dining room. She'd changed into black dress pants and a white button-down shirt with her sleeves rolled up. Her hair was gathered on top of her head. A few loose tendrils were dancing around her face. The change in hairstyle made her green eyes large and arresting. On a whole she looked slick and smart. She and Rita exchanged a few words near the blackboard menu. Ian realized Rita was wearing black and white, too, but the two women looked entirely different.

"So, Ian…" Vic finally drawled, obviously unable to stay quiet for too long.

Ian got a sympathetic glance from across the table. He drank from his beer. "Yes, Victor."

"Brian and I never had a chance to ask. What

brings *you* all the way from San Diego to Tranquillity Inn, here in deepest, darkest New Hampshire?''

"Vacation," he said casually. "A little R & R."

"Why here? Why not someplace with more…" Vic turned his palm up and searched for the right word. "More pizzazz? You know, you're pretty hot-looking…in a tough, Marlboro-man kind of way. Why not go to the beach or one of the club resorts with those girls in bikinis and guys in G-strings parading around? You know, somewhere where you can accomplish two things at once."

"I thought R & R were two things. Rest and recreation."

"Vic prefers S & R," Brian put in with a chuckle, finishing the last of his beer. "You know—sex and recreation."

"Nice talk," Vic said in a hushed voice, looking around the room. "There are young families around, you know." He turned a hundred-watt smile back on Ian. "So, why not some S & R?"

"Too much trouble. A place like this is exactly what the doctor ordered."

Vic picked up on the word right away. "You really mean doctor, don't you, hon? This is no vacation."

"I'm on medical leave."

Victor leaned back in his chair and gave Ian a once-over of whatever he could see. "Must be a head doctor, then, cuz you look pretty good to me."

"It's for stress. I was letting my job get to me," he said, watching Kelly come across the room.

"What do you do?" Brian asked.

Ian returned Kelly's smile as she reached their table. "I'm a cop."

It shouldn't have mattered at all what Ian Campbell did for a living, but Kelly found herself distracted from the moment she heard him say the words. He was a police officer of some kind. And he wasn't so much telling the three men at his table what he did for a living; he was telling her.

The same knot Kelly had felt form in her stomach when she first met him was back. There was something familiar about him that she couldn't explain. He talked tough and his actions gave her no inkling about what he thought of her or why he was really here. Still, her hackles weren't raised. She didn't feel like running. If anything, she was curious to learn more about him.

"There isn't much more to do here, if you want to go up," Rita said to her after the tables were all cleared and the dining room nearly prepped for the morning. There was still plenty to do in the kitchen, though.

"It's been a pretty long day for you. Are you sure?" Kelly asked the other woman. She appreciated the offer, all the same.

"I'm sure. I didn't bring a car today. Wilson is dropping me home. He's not even close to being ready to leave."

Kelly would have sworn that in the two years since she'd been here, she hadn't seen Rita and Wilson say more than a dozen words to each other. Still, it was a common thing for them to share a ride in from the village.

Kelly gently squeezed the other woman's arm. "You were great today. I appreciate it."

Rita nodded and turned away.

In the parlor, Kelly was happy to see a few of the guests were sitting around talking. The lights had been dimmed, and everything had been tidied up and tucked away. But Bill was always good about seeing to that. He especially took his job as the "portable bartender," as he called it, very seriously.

Janice, coming out of the office, answered a phone call just as Kelly approached.

"No, I'm sorry… No, we have no one by that name staying with us," she said in response to the caller. After a few seconds of someone speaking at the other end, Janice spoke again. "No, I'm very sorry. You have the wrong number."

"Who were they looking for?" Kelly asked as the older woman hung up.

Janice looked up at her. "They had us mixed up with someplace down around North Conway." She motioned to the intercom Kelly left on whenever Jade was napping upstairs alone. "I haven't heard a peep from her. She must have been exhausted."

"Tell me about it. But she had no lunch or dinner. I feel horrible."

"She'll manage. Kids are tough," Janice said gently. "How was dinner?"

"Good. Everyone seemed very happy with their meal." From this angle, Kelly could see Ian Campbell, sitting in one of the leather chairs by the fireplace. He was listening to something the shorter of the two men from Philadelphia was saying. The fourth person at their table, Mr. Hobart, had retired as soon as Kelly had taken away the dessert dishes.

"I know it's only three more people, but the dining room seemed so much livelier having extra guests tonight. Maybe if I get Dan to finish painting room five—"

"Aquarius."

"Right, Aquarius. If that gets painted as soon as the Desposito party leaves, we could start renting it out next week. Also, I wouldn't mind at all having someone staying in the room on the third floor. So long as we warn them about the size and the color."

"You're getting ahead of yourself," Janice said with a smile, closing the books and putting them in the drawer of the desk. "Let's get through the weekend first, then we can talk about it."

There was no point in arguing with Janice about such things. Actually, there was no point in arguing with her about anything that constituted change. From experience, Kelly knew that she just had to start the ball rolling herself and then tell the older woman later. Heck, all she really had to do was put Dan on the reception desk for one afternoon, and she'd have more extra bookings than they could handle.

Kelly glanced one more time around the sitting area. It looked as if Ian was getting ready to leave.

"I need to go up and check on Jade. I'll come back down later and lock up."

"No need," Janice told her. "Dan's disappeared somewhere, but I know he'll be back. Bill went to our place to watch one of his baseball games on TV, but he'll be back, too. Between the two of them, they'll take care of things. Why don't you get a good night's sleep."

Kelly didn't commit one way or the other whether she was retiring for the night, but said good-night to Janice and went up.

The sound of the television could be heard from the kitchen, but Kelly didn't poke her head in. Thanking Wilson and congratulating him on another spectacular meal would wait until tomorrow morning, when there was at least one other person in the kitchen. On the second floor, all was quiet. Kelly saw the light on under the door of the suite of rooms where the Sterns were staying, but there was no sound of voices coming out. It was about nine o'clock, and she wondered if they'd gone out or somehow wrestled their two sons into bed early.

She made a quick check of the bathroom that was being shared on the floor and made sure there were enough towels and other supplies for the guests. Going back down the hallway, she continued up to her own floor. It took a few seconds at the top to get used to seeing both doors—the one to the guest room and the door into her apartment—closed. She'd been spoiled, having the whole floor to herself, and although she really never used that room, she enjoyed the cross breeze she usually got in the warmer months with everything open.

The only renovation Kelly had done to the house since moving back had been in the apartment where she and Jade now lived. Before, the place had consisted of three smaller rooms, very much like the one Ian was staying in. The Maitlands used them as a bedroom, living room and a sewing room or study.

Kelly immediately had all the walls knocked out and the ceiling, as well, opening the space beneath the roof. A couple of skylights were added to let in more light. Now, with the exception of a kitchenette and a small bathroom with a shower, the entire apartment was open.

She liked the fact that the living and sleeping areas she shared with Jade were all one space. The arrangement allowed her to watch over and be with her daughter, no matter what they were doing. It was just the two of them, and Kelly hated being separate from her. They were the only family either of them had left.

The air in the apartment was cool. She looked at Jade first. She was cuddled up with her old yellow blanket, sound asleep. Kelly sat down on the edge of the bed and touched the silky dark ringlets. She caressed her daughter's forehead and cheeks. The little upturned nose creased a couple of times, and the child snuggled deeper under the blanket.

No real lunch, no dinner, no bath, no cuddling in bed and no reading of any stories before she fell sleep. The guilt slithered back in. Kelly's gaze wandered to the end table that separated the two twin beds. Greg's face smiled up at her; his expression was reassuring.

He trusted her. He'd always been confident in Kelly's abilities. He'd always made her feel that she was doing the right thing.

"You would have been really proud of her today," Kelly murmured. "Your daughter was a champion, inside and out."

Kelly touched the edge of the picture frame. God, she missed him. It had been so long. It felt as if she and Jade had been alone forever.

Dozens of framed photographs of all shapes and sizes could be seen on every bookcase, table and wall. A couple of oversize black-and-white photos of Jade walking in the woods had been fastened to the sloping ceiling. Kelly got up from the bed and walked to the end wall, where she'd arranged and hung so many pictures.

Greg. Her parents. Greg and Kelly at their wedding. Her mother, Rose, so proudly holding Jade at the hospital when she was only a day old. Greg and Kelly during the cruise, taking their own picture. She looked at the dozens of pictures she'd put up for her and Jade. Even when everyone was alive, their family circle was so small. She wanted Jade to know them, though. Kelly wanted her daughter to know every loving face.

A cool breeze coming in made Kelly shiver slightly. She shut one of the windows and was about to close a second one, when she saw Ian Campbell walk down the steps from the deck.

Six

Ian stood in the shadow of a tall maple in the grassy area and looked out at the lake. The night was damp and cool, and he pulled on the black cotton sweater he'd brought out with him. Through the mists swirling overhead, the moon looked like a cold, white disk hanging in the sky, more like a stage prop than something real. His shoes were wet from the dew, and the smell of the earth filled him with thoughts of his past.

The distant yip of a coyote startled him. It was a familiar sound to Ian, but he didn't expect to hear it here. He thought for a moment that he might have imagined it, but an answering yip cut through the darkness from somewhere across the lake. He gazed out in that direction. The forests were black and unbroken, a vast area where a person could walk for days and never see another human being. It was a place where one could die and never be found.

At the far side of the lake, the fog was not as thick as it had been during the afternoon. Lights were on in the camp, and he could see them flickering as the mists broke and then closed up again, tantalizing him. The sky above the camp was brighter where the light dispersed in the fog, giving the place a white shifting glow, like some cheerless, unfixed halo. The coyote's call cut through the night again. It was closer than before, though it might have been a third animal.

He turned and looked up at the house as the door from the porch opened, and the newlywed couple, Marisa and Dave Meadows, slipped out. The lamps by the doors were still on, and he could see them clearly. They stopped at the railing for a minute, talking quietly. Standing in the dark shadows cast by the tall tree, Ian knew they couldn't see him, in spite of the moonlight. They appeared to be disagreeing about something. Finally, Dave won out, and with a quick look back into the dim-lit parlor area, the two came quietly down the steps and moved across the grass toward the lake.

Ian edged back a little farther as they went by him. They were not holding hands or showing any of the affection you'd expect from two honeymooners. As they passed, Dave pulled a penlight on a key ring from his pocket and flicked it on. The grass ahead of them glistened under the beam of light. He handed it to her. When they reached the lake, she took down two paddles from the rack as he turned over one of the canoes and dragged it toward the water's edge. The hollow sound of the canoe sliding across the grass was muffled. A moment later, she took her place in the bow and switched off the penlight as her husband pushed them off the shore.

Frowning, Ian watched the canoe glide noiselessly away, disappearing immediately into the gloom. They appeared to be paddling toward the camp.

He stood there for a few minutes, listening to the sounds of the night. A pair of owls had begun to call back and forth, each hoot raising the hackles on Ian's neck. A mosquito landed on his cheek, and he brushed it off. Guessing that the couple was not returning right away, he left the shadows and strolled down to the edge of the lake. He considered taking a canoe himself, but decided it would be a bad idea to be caught out there. He turned and looked at the inn and the outbuildings.

From what he could see of the small parking lot on the far side of the inn, a number of the guests' cars were gone. The battered rental truck belonging to Victor and Brian was visible. They had been the last ones remaining in the parlor when Ian had left.

The carriage house where Janice and Bill lived was lit up, though there were no signs of activity. The two cottages by the water were dark. With a casual look back at the inn, Ian wandered past the one where Dan lived. Reaching the second cottage, he looked in a window but could see nothing. Moving around to the door, he pulled gently at the padlock.

"Can I help you with something, Mr. Campbell?"

Ian recognized Kelly's voice. His hand dropped from the padlock. Turning around, Ian saw her standing ten feet away from him. She was wearing a white sweater over the shirt she had on before. The sweater was unbuttoned. In the moonlight, she appeared almost ethereal.

"Ian. Please call me Ian," he said before motioning over his shoulder at the cottage. "I was wondering if you kept any kayaks in there."

"No kayaks. Canoes are all we've got. And a couple of Sunfish that nobody takes out. There's never enough wind to sail them, it seems." She looked over the lake. "Was it my imagination or did someone take out one of the canoes?"

"The newlyweds," Ian replied, walking over and standing next to her. "You could at least have given them a private room and bath."

She sent him a sidelong glance and didn't answer. Ian saw the smile, though, pulling at the corners of her lips. A moment later, she glanced back over her shoulder at the inn.

"Will you stay for a minute?" To entice her, he pulled a couple of Adirondack chairs to where they were standing.

Her look this time was at the third floor of the house.

"You know, I don't think the Meadows couple took any life jackets. You should stay here for a few minutes, at least, in case they capsize the boat and need help."

"Dan told me they took out a boat this afternoon, too. I believe he probably explained all the safety mumbo jumbo to them."

"Stay, anyway."

She rubbed her arms, as if she was warding off the cold, and after a moment's hesitation sat down on the edge of one of the chairs. "Only for a couple of minutes."

Ian sat down, too. She looked over the water at the lights coming from the camp. Her eyes glistened in the moonlight. Her cheeks were high and sculpted, her mouth wide and her lips full. With some makeup, he supposed even Victor would consider her a very beautiful woman. But she didn't do anything to enhance or bring any attention to her features. She did nothing to hide her flaws, either. He stared at the thin scar on her forehead, visible even in this light.

She turned and looked at him over one shoulder.

"You have a beautiful place here. Each season must be so different," he said before she had a chance to ask any questions.

Kelly looked around, obviously trying to see the place through the eyes of a visitor. "I think the inn is the prettiest on a crisp fall day when the sky is a deep blue and the leaves on the trees are a hundred different shades of red and yellow. The water on the lake reflects the colors like a mirror. I have to say autumn is the nicest time to be here."

"You must book up solid during those weeks."

"We do. In fact, that's usually the only time of year that all our rooms are full." She leaned back and relaxed a little. "The way we filled up this weekend is very uncommon. Of course, I really have Dan to thank for that."

"He says he's new this summer," Ian commented. "Not like the rest of the people working here."

"That's right…thank goodness." She laughed and then lowered her voice. "I shouldn't have said that. That was a horrible thing to say."

"No, it wasn't." He smiled. "You inherited the whole bunch of them, didn't you?"

She shrugged. "It's tough finding enough people around here to work. The few year-round residents that we have commute to the big resorts, which pay better. I was lucky to have any kind of crew at all."

"Dan gave me the idea that he's not from around here."

"No. He's from Tarrytown, New York. He goes to school in Boston. He'll be a junior next year, I think."

"How did you lure him all the way up here?" Ian asked.

"I didn't have to do a thing. His mother called me. Sally and I worked together at a newspaper in New York a few years ago. We've more or less stayed in touch since I left." Kelly brought up her legs and gathered her knees to her chest, getting more comfortable. "Sally wanted Dan out of Boston for the summer. His grades weren't as good as she would've liked. He was hanging around with the wrong crowd, I guess."

"So she asked you to do her a favor."

"She was doing *me* a favor. And I told her so. Despite his grumbling, I think even Dan is happy with the arrangement. He's making decent money, and there's nothing around here to spend it on. He's putting it all away."

"How has the old guard taken to the new kid in town?"

"You have a funny way of putting things." She smiled. "They took him in. A couple of mistakes here and there. A few complaints. But all and all, I'm happy to have him here.''

They both turned to look as a pair of headlights and the accompanying crunch of gravel announced the arrival of a car. A van pulling an open trailer appeared in the lot, its lights shining down toward the lake before the driver swung around and parked out of their line of vision by the front door of the inn. Two doors opened and slammed shut.

''More unexpected guests?'' Ian asked lightly.

''I hope not.'' She stared up at the inn.

Just then, the door from the parlor opened and two young men came out, descending the stairs and coming across the grass toward the cottages.

''I think I know what this is about. Funny, though, I thought…'' She let her words trail off, and got up from the chair. ''Hi. Are you looking for me?''

The two came directly to them, and Ian stood up behind Kelly.

''Hello,'' the first said. ''Ms. Stone. They told us you were outside somewhere.''

He was tall and clean-cut, a good-looking kid, from what Ian could see. College age. He shook hands with her and shot a quick glance at Ian. The other had the same size and look, but said nothing. He was looking at the cottages.

''I thought you guys would be over from the camp during the day to clean this stuff out.''

''We were setting up. So if it's okay—''

Ian broke in and touched her arm. ''If you'll excuse

me, I've got to get my briefcase out of my car before
I turn in. Good night, Kelly.''

Ian was certain he noticed a touch of regret in the
look she sent him, but she nodded and went back to
talking to the two men.

He walked up to the parking lot. As he rounded
the corner, he could see they were moving toward one
of the cottages.

They'd come in a transport van, and Ian hurriedly
jotted down the registration number and noticed the
small stencil on the driver's-side door. *BDMMDB.*
Pulling a small light from his khakis, he flashed it in
the windows. He gaze fixed for a moment on the crescent medallion hanging from the rearview mirror. He
continued to look around the inside. They'd removed
the bench seats from the back of the van. As he
flicked the light around the empty space, Ian's eye
was caught by a small, folded slip of white paper that
had been pushed under the track of the driver's seat.
There was nothing else in the van.

As quietly as he could, he opened the passenger
door and climbed in. Reaching around the driver's
seat, he plucked the paper from under the seat and
pocketed it. He also took a quick look at the registration slip in the glove compartment. The van was registered to a Joshua Sharpe. The address was a P.O.
box in Independence, New Hampshire.

Climbing out, Ian carefully pushed the door closed
and crossed the lot to his car. Unlocking the trunk,
he slammed it shut and walked back to the inn.

No one was in the lobby, and Ian climbed the stairs

to his room on the third floor. Closing the door, he looked out the window before switching on the light. Kelly and the two young men were walking back toward the inn. When they disappeared from sight beneath him, Ian turned on the light and sat on the bed. Unfolding the paper from the van, he saw it was a credit card receipt for a bus trip.

The name on the slip was Lauren Wells.

It took them a while to move all the boxes from the cottage, loading them carefully into the van and the trailer, and it was almost eleven when Kelly watched the van finally pull away from the inn. There was still no sign of Dan.

She took a quick look inside a cottage that was now completely empty. Ten months a year, it was rented out as a locked storage shack for the camp across the way. It was an arrangement made years ago prior to Kelly's move to New Hampshire. Just one more thing that Kelly had inherited. Still, she wondered if there was any chance she could do some renovations to the cottage and have it ready to rent out during the summer. The roof looked solid, but the walls lacked drywall, and the floor gave a little as she walked across it. The only plumbing was a laundry sink with no running water, and the electricity consisted of a single bare bulb hanging from a wire Thomas Edison probably discarded. The cottage had possibilities, but it would be too much work and too expensive for this year, she decided.

The cottage Dan stayed in was used for storing

some things, too—tents and boxes of old sporting equipment. It wasn't in any better shape than this one. Even if she could find a spot for Dan, there was not much chance of using that cottage either, she decided.

She was wound too tight to go up to bed and try to sleep, but she walked up to the inn, anyway. Janice was gone by the time Kelly went inside. All the lights were out except the one lamp on the reception desk that they left on every night. The kitchen was dark, as well, and Wilson's car was gone.

Kelly checked the monitor/intercom. All was quiet in her apartment. She turned on the lights in her office and dug out the accounting books and the bills that she had finally wrested from the grasp of the Maitlands. She opened her laptop and switched it on.

It had been a struggle taking control. Moving to Tranquillity Inn, Kelly had hoped to lose herself in the work and in raising her daughter. Bill and Janice were not ready to give up the running of the inn, though. She knew that the Maitlands half expected her to take the same hands-off approach as her parents had adopted, leaving them to manage things.

Little by little, though, she was trying to assume control of the inn. Taking over the books had been the start of it. Using the computer and spreadsheets to balance their income and expenses had made it a guarantee that the job was solely Kelly's. Neither Bill nor Janice were interested in learning anything about that.

While the computer booted up, Kelly picked up the day's mail from the in-basket and thumbed through it. She hadn't had a chance to go through the pile today. As always, there were just the essentials. Janice was usually working at the front desk when the letter carrier came in for his daily chat and cup of coffee. While they sat and talked, Janice always sorted the junk mail and duplicate catalogs out of the stack they received every day.

Several envelopes slipped off her lap and fell to the floor when Kelly reached over to open the spreadsheet file on the laptop. She leaned under the desk to retrieve them...and stopped.

She could smell distinctly the acrid odor of burnt paper. Tossing the mail on the desk, Kelly pushed back her chair and pulled the small metal wastebasket out from under the desk. Guests sometimes used the office phone, since there was no cell phone reception in the area. And despite the sign and the gentle reminders, people occasionally ignored the No Smoking poster and lit a match when they were in the office. This smell was not from cigarette smoke, though.

Kelly saw the charred papers in the partially filled basket. She stirred up the contents to make sure there was no possibility of fire left in them. Part of an envelope grabbed her attention. The sender's address had been mostly burned away, but she picked it up and peered at the section that was left. Her name was handwritten in blue ink. Below was the name of the inn, but the rest of the address was torn away.

Kelly sat back, staring at the piece of the envelope and wracking her brain. She was sure she hadn't seen the letter before, and it bothered her. It could have been a personal letter from someone she knew. Why would Janice—or anyone else—destroy the letter before Kelly saw it? The idea was very disturbing. There was nothing left inside this part of the envelope. She checked the trash bin, looking closer at the charred pieces of paper. The corner of one piece of paper caught her eye. The same ink color—the same handwriting. She could see part of the date, but only the year was left.

She shook her head. Digging through the wastebasket, she found another small section, and then another. She laid them out on the desk as if she were doing a puzzle. The letter had obviously been torn first and then the pieces burned…that much she could tell. Also, the shaky handwriting looked as if it belonged to an older person, or someone who had trouble controlling his or her hand. She was about to dump the entire trash can on the desk and go through it more closely, when the sensation of being watched stopped her. Kelly lifted her head.

The boy was standing a couple of steps beyond the door, staring into the office at her. She breathed a sigh of relief.

"Hi!" she called out in a friendly tone. Kelly could only imagine how crazy she must have looked to a child watching what she'd been doing.

He didn't answer. As if in a trance, he just continued to stare.

Kelly put the wastebasket back under the desk. Casually, she gathered the few pieces of paper she'd salvaged and covered them with the day's mail, pushing them to one corner of the desk.

"Can I help you with something?" she asked in a gentle voice, getting up.

The boy didn't move, didn't say anything...only stared.

Kelly remembered the child's name was Ryan. He was twelve. The younger son of Rob and Rachel Stern. Different possibilities came to her mind. Maybe he was sleepwalking. She dismissed that. The boy was wearing his normal clothes and sneakers. Did that make a difference? Kelly told herself she didn't know enough about such things. Maybe sleepwalkers dressed in their sleep, too. She had no idea. She came around her desk and stepped out of the office.

"Ryan, right?" she asked softly.

He gave the smallest of the nods. Well, he was awake.

"Looking for something to eat, Ryan? I can get stuff out of the kitchen if you're hungry."

The boy gave a slight shake of his head, declining the offer. Kelly was relieved that they were at least communicating. Still, the way he continued to look at her was unsettling. He had a sort of smile on his face, but his gaze was so focused on her. So...impressed looking. Like she was Nomar Garciaparra and Derek Jeter and Jim Carrey put together. This close, he looked practically starstruck.

"Did your mom or dad send you down for something?" she asked, deciding she could play Twenty Questions.

He shook his head again, the admiring little smile on his lips still there.

"There are some young-adult books in the bookcase next to the fireplace, if you're looking for something to read. There are at least half a dozen decent board games in the cabinet below them, too, if you want to take any of them upstairs to play with your brother."

He shook his head and continued to stand there, watching her.

Kelly should have felt uncomfortable. The situation was awkward, to say the least. But the innocent fascination in the child—as if he was looking at something or someone special for the first time—confused her more than anything else. He had to have seen her this afternoon when they'd arrived and then again during dinner.

"Ryan! I was wondering where you disappeared to." Mrs. Stern came down the last steps and hurried across the lobby.

"I found him just standing here," Kelly said with a smile at the young boy. "I was trying to interest him in something to eat, or maybe taking a book or a board game upstairs."

"That is so kind of you. We got back from town not long ago, and the boys rushed upstairs ahead of us. I assumed both of them were in their room, but this one always likes to wander." The woman put both hands on her son's shoulders and turned him toward the steps.

Kelly wondered which town the Sterns had gotten

back from this late at night. The village of Independence rolled up the sidewalks at five-thirty in the afternoon.

"Do you have everything you need, Mrs. Stern?" she asked instead. "Are your rooms comfortable?"

"Just perfect." Rachel Stern nudged her son toward the steps. "We'll see you in the morning."

She watched the mother and son go up the stairs. The child's gaze was once again on Kelly as they made the turn at the landing halfway up. The same peculiar look was back on his face.

"I could always use something more to eat."

Kelly practically jumped out of her skin. She turned around, holding a hand to her racing heart. In the dark hallway, Ian Campbell was leaning a shoulder against the wall. He must have taken the back stairs down from his room.

"Don't scare me like that. I almost had a heart attack."

"Sorry. Didn't mean to." He straightened up from the wall. "Are you some former teen idol or something?"

"Not since the last time I checked."

"There isn't something you've been hiding from the rest of us, is there?"

"I guess you saw the look on his face, too." Kelly said, shaking her head, glad that it hadn't been her imagination. "I think Ryan's older brother must be playing mind games with him. He must have confused the poor kid, mixing me up with Ash, our resident supermodel." She turned on the light in the hall.

"He won't look my way twice tomorrow morning, once he knows the truth."

"I don't know about that," he said, giving her a slow once-over. "If you ask me, you're much better to look at…any time of the day."

Kelly felt herself become flustered for a moment, but was able to find her voice. "There's no need to fake any compliments around here. I'll feed you, anyway."

"In that case, can I ask another favor, too?" he asked with a smile that made him look so much younger and very handsome. "Can I use your phone?"

"Of course," she managed to get out. It was a good thing that he hadn't turned on the charm when they were figuring out the room situation. He would have ended up with the best room in the house, the other guests be damned. "You can use the phone in the office. It's more private."

"Thanks," he said. "I'll only be a minute."

She didn't want to eavesdrop on his call, so she hurried into the kitchen and turned on the lights. The place was sparkling clean. All the pots and pans had been put away, the dishes stacked neatly in the cabinets. The floor had been washed. This was Wilson's ritual every night before he left. Because of it, Kelly felt funny even walking into the place after the cook went home, figuring he probably checked for scuff marks and fingerprints when he arrived in the morning.

Fighting off her misgivings, she opened the fridge

door and stared in. She had no clue what Ian was hungry for. She also had no idea why she felt so skittish.

This wasn't the way things generally went at Tranquillity Inn. Guests came and went. While they were here, they ate. They went for hikes and swims, and they took the boats out on the lake. They ate some more, and they went to bed. The next morning, everything started all over again.

Usually, the only conversation between Kelly and the guests was polite small talk. A little chitchat about the weather or the lake or the mountains. A little give-and-take of compliments. But nothing really personal. None of this meeting by the lake or for late-night snacks. Kelly closed the fridge door and walked over to a corkboard where Wilson's note was pinned, listing jobs for Rita and Dan. She scanned the sheet, looking for a hint about tomorrow's dinner menu.

"Thanks for the use of the phone," he said, startling her again.

She turned away from the note. "I didn't know what you were in the mood for. There are all kinds of cold cuts in the fridge, but I think you might have wiped us out in the chocolate chip cookie department. And there's—"

"This'll do." He took an apple off the fruit bowl and tossed it in the air. "Actually, it's the company that I was looking for, more than the food."

Kelly leaned her back against the sink and eyed him curiously. "So, another night owl. Maybe I should have asked the Stern boy to stay downstairs.

The two of you could have played one of those board games.''

He sat down on one of the high stools by the island in the kitchen. "Let me say it right this time. *Your* company is what I was hoping for.'' He took a bite of the apple.

His words threw her for a loop. It had been way too long since anyone had made a move on her. And the humorous thing was that she was so out of practice that she wasn't even sure if he was.

"Why?'' Kelly finally asked.

"Because I'm curious.'' He put the apple down. "When I made the reservation and came up here, I expected people like Janice and her husband to be running a place like this. I could have even expected Rita...or your oddly anal-retentive biker chef...and certainly a college kid like Dan working up here for the summer. But what I can't figure is you and Jade. A photographer for the *Times?* What are you doing all the way up here?''

Kelly blushed immediately. Her office, she told herself. That was how he knew about her former career. As a going-away present, some of her co-workers had framed and inscribed an award-winning photo she'd taken. Vanity had Kelly hang it in the small office. It was just a little reminder that for a short time, at least, she had seen the world.

"I didn't want to raise my child in the city,'' she said simply, tucking her hands between her butt and the sink.

"What's wrong with the suburbs?''

"Nothing, but my parents were here."

"I got the impression from you that your parents are deceased."

"They are…now. But when I started planning the move, my mother was still alive." Kelly straightened from the sink. She felt suddenly cold. "That was a rough year. Three people I loved very much all died on me that same year."

"Jade's father?" he asked quietly.

"He was the second," she said hoarsely.

"If you don't mind me asking, how did he die?"

"A car accident." She looked up at him. "You know, I'm not really that great when it comes to being good company. There's not much that's interesting about my past."

"I'll bet there's a lot that's interesting about you," he said, getting up from the stool. "This place is too sterile. It's like an operating room."

"Which explains why I feel like I'm being dissected," she said, rubbing her sweaty palms on her pants.

"I didn't mean to make you feel that way."

"That's okay. Anyway, it's getting late."

"Do you have a few minutes to go for a walk, or just to sit out on the deck? I promise to behave and not ask so many questions."

Strangely, Kelly wanted to, but she glanced up at the clock hanging on the wall. "It's midnight. I have to be up early."

"Do you walk around and lock up?"

"I usually walk around and double-check on

things," Kelly admitted. "Turn off the lights, turn the keys in the locks...if they have them. But all in all, we don't worry too much about security around here. No fancy alarm systems. We're so far into the woods that any kind of crime would probably be an inside job."

"And has there ever been an inside job?"

"I was joking." She scrunched up her nose. "This must be a professional hazard of your job. A cop is always a cop...even on vacation?"

"You eavesdropped on our dinner conversation."

"I think you made sure you said it when there was no way I could *not* overhear," she challenged him, taking an apple off the fruit bowl as she started for the door.

"I guess I did." Tossing his half-eaten apple into a trash barrel, he followed her.

"Why?" she asked, turning off the lights in the kitchen.

"Single male in his midforties, traveling alone. I wanted to give you some reason not to be nervous about me."

Kelly closed the back door. "You thought I'd trust a cop?"

"I figured I'd have to take my chances." He reached around her and turned the dead bolt on the door. "You didn't hear everything, though. There was a little detail about me being out on medical leave because of stress."

"Pressured to write more parking tickets?" she teased, starting back toward the parlor.

"Nah. They frowned on me handcuffing so many wisecracking women."

"In that case," Kelly said lightly, "I hope they confiscated your equipment before sending you this way." As they reached her office, she paused and switched off the light inside.

"I managed to smuggle out a few vital pieces."

She pulled the door closed and turned around, only to run into Ian's chest. She immediately took a step back, flustered by how close they were in the narrow hallway outside her office.

"I still have to check the front door...and the door from the deck...and..." Her smart mouth had started this, but now her mind was mush. She tingled in unmentionable places. Her body's reaction was too embarrassing.

"After you," he said, edging back but not giving her too much room to maneuver.

As she slipped past him, her body brushed against his, pushing her senses into overdrive. The lights in the porch dining room were off, but Kelly noticed some of the cushions had been left on the chairs on the deck.

"This is more than you bargained for. I might have to put you to work." She walked to the door leading outside.

"I'm here to serve," he said easily, right behind her. "Do with me as you please."

Kelly waited until she was on the deck and had picked up the first cushion from one of the chairs. "Are you flirting with me, Mr. Campbell?"

''Would that be a bad thing?''

''I don't know.'' She picked up the next cushion and the next, not looking at him. ''I can tell you right now, I don't date. I don't have affairs. I don't get especially friendly with the guests at the inn, ei-ther…for reasons…well, like this.'' Her arms were full. She straightened up and he was right there again, in front of her.

''I guess I am hitting on you,'' Ian said. Reaching over the cushions in her arms, he kissed her lips.

She was too shocked to move, or say anything, or even kiss him back. At that moment, all she could think of was how good it was to feel this way. To be kissed. To be wanted. The cushions slid out of her arms and fell onto the deck. She tore her mouth free and backed up, looking at him in shock. Then she quickly bent down to pick up the cushions. Ian bent down at the same time, and they bumped heads.

They both looked up, both of them rubbing their foreheads.

''I used to be a little more dignified than this,'' Kelly said, unable to stop the laughter from bubbling out.

''I'm a little out of practice myself,'' he said with a chuckle, picking up the cushions she'd dropped and tucking them under one arm.

She looked down at his left hand, trying to remem-ber if he'd been wearing a ring. Hoping that he wasn't. Feeling guilty that she hadn't thought to ask first. His hand was hidden under the mounds of cushions.

"No wife," he said, reading her look. "No children. No live-in girlfriends...or boyfriends," he added with a smile. "I thought I should mention that after the dinner conversation I had with Vic and Brian tonight."

"Victor is quite a character." Kelly lifted the lid of the bench storage bin she used for the cushions. Ian stacked them all inside. "He's never short on words, is he?"

Ian's attention shifted to the lake. A moment later Kelly realized what had distracted him as she heard the bump of a paddle against the side of a canoe.

"I think our newlyweds are back," he said just as the boat left the line of the trees and became visible in the moonlight.

"I should have done a count of the cars and the boats. I could have totally forgotten about them. I can't imagine they would have liked to be stuck out on the deck for the night."

"There are worse things than making out under a moon like that," he said quietly. "But those two don't strike me as being all that romantic."

Kelly agreed, but she kept her comment to herself. Standing next to Ian, she watched Dave and Marisa Meadows step out of the canoe and pull the boat out of the water. The oars went where they belonged. The efficiency with which they worked together was practical...and not at all romantic. There was no joking, no laughing or hugging. Watching them walk up toward the house, Kelly noticed that they were not holding hands. But then, the couple might have seen them on the deck.

"Nice night, isn't it?" Ian asked casually as the two drew closer.

The woman jumped, and a quick whisper passed between the couple.

The husband answered. "Yeah, it's a great night."

"How was the water?" Ian pressed, casually slipping an arm around Kelly's waist.

She didn't understand what he thought he was doing, but she didn't step away.

"The water?" Marisa answered as they came up the steps onto the porch.

"Yeah, we were thinking about going for a swim."

She would have given him a sharp jab with her elbow if it weren't for the peculiar look that passed between the Meadowses. Kelly couldn't really describe it. It was almost a look of disapproval, like they were making a judgment. What business was it of theirs? she found herself thinking. She leaned more closely into Ian, and his arm tightened around her.

"It's definitely too cold for that," Dave Meadows commented, ushering his wife toward the door. "By the way, what time do you start serving breakfast?"

"Seven," Kelly replied crisply. "Good night."

The couple disappeared inside, and Kelly wished she had an ounce of Jade's stubbornness. Ian would've gotten a kiss that would really give the Meadowses something to be judgmental about. Unfortunately, she was an utter coward.

She reluctantly pulled away and sent him an apologetic look. "I'm ready to pack it in for the night."

"I'd be happy to accept a rain check," he said pleasantly, opening the door for her.

Kelly went inside ahead of him. "And what is it exactly that I'd be giving you a rain check for?"

She never gave him a chance to answer though. As soon as she was inside, she heard Jade's voice on the intercom. She was scared and calling for her.

"You go," Ian said gently. "I'll lock this and check the front door."

Kelly rushed toward the steps, anxious to reach her daughter. To be honest, she was also a little thankful to Jade for getting her out of whatever it was she was getting herself into with Ian Campbell.

Seven

At midnight, all of the lights in the compound were extinguished except for a single bulb that illuminated an open area at the center of the camp that spread up from the edge of the lake. Beneath the old-fashioned light, a raised covered platform, called the Pavilion, had been built of rough timber and planks. In the center stood a single chair and a small table. Wires ran from some audio equipment at the side of the platform under the planks to large speakers mounted on the two front corner beams. All the electronic equipment had been carefully covered with plastic sheeting. A pit for bonfires had been dug in front of the platform, and smoking embers smoldered in dying colors of red and orange. Split-log benches, arranged as in an amphitheater, spread out in concentric crescent rows from the pit and the Pavilion.

Around the Pavilion, long log cabins for attendees extended in pairs like rays from the sun. They started to the right, not thirty yards from the lake, just beyond empty racks built to store dozens of canoes, and continued in a large arc two-thirds of the way around the center. There, a cluster of other log buildings had been built, including a very large dining and recreation hall, several administrators' and counselors' cabins, and a nurse's office. Latrines and showers were interspersed among the array of campers' cabins.

With the exception of an occasional crackle or spark from the dying fire, the camp was deadly quiet. The place was orderly and clean, even though over a hundred new arrivals had been coming in all day. Families, small groups and individuals had been transported from the commuter parking lot out by the state highway, where they had all left their vehicles. The only sign of habitation, aside from the glowing embers in the pit, was a large white banner that had been strung from the roof of the Pavilion, behind the chair and table. On it, in red letters, *"BDM~MDB"* were arranged like a mirror image. Those in the camp knew what the letters stood for. *Butler Divinity Mission~Ministry of the Divine Blood.* Beneath the letters, three red drops were depicted falling into a cup from one tip of a golden crescent moon.

The beams of two flashlights cut through the darkness by the long cabins. Two young men wearing heavy belts and holsters containing pistols were making their security rounds. Shining the lights into every dark corner, they worked their way up and down between the cabins, checking the showers as they went. With a gesture at his partner, one of them led the way into the woods beyond the cabins toward the path that defined the perimeter of the camp. In half an hour, they would be back doing the same round, again and again, until the time came.

* * *

Exhaustion had set in hours earlier, and Lauren Wells found herself fading in and out of consciousness. She was somewhat surprised that they hadn't already killed her. Perhaps they figured she'd just die on her own and save them the trouble. One thing she was sure of, no one would ever see or hear of her again.

She'd known what was coming the moment she saw the crescent moon in the van. There was no escaping them. She'd tipped over her bag on the floor at her feet, hoping to find something to use as a weapon, but she had nothing. As she replaced the items, she'd pushed a receipt under a seat, but that wouldn't help her much. She might as well have put a message in a bottle. One of the ruffians had moved next to her soon after that, and they'd overpowered her as the driver pulled the van off the road. If she'd been fifteen years younger, she thought, she would have given them a much better fight.

After taking her glasses, they taped her hands and feet and mouth with thick duct tape and covered her with a sleeping bag on the floor. Then they'd driven for quite some time. She knew the moment they left the main road. The jarring left her bruised and sore, and by the time they carried her from the van into a cabin, she could barely hold her head upright.

The cabin was pitch black and the bunk they'd laid her on smelled musty and old. She had no idea what time it was. She was dreadfully thirsty, her head ached, and her bladder was about to burst.

When a door creaked open in another room, she

wasn't sure if she was awake or dreaming. Trying to focus on the sound, Lauren was nearly blinded by the light that flooded the room when several people entered.

She struggled but was unable to sit up in the bunk. There was no feeling left in her bound arms and feet. She tried to breathe through her nose and made a muffled noise as she looked in panic at the group.

"This is no way to greet an honored guest," the man standing in the center of them said gently. "Remove the tape that binds her."

The voice was one she'd heard before. Through the blur of her vision, she tried to focus on him. The tapes was cut off her wrists and feet. The one pulling away from her mouth left her gasping for air.

"Welcome back, Lauren." The voice was tranquil. Strong fingers touched her forehead, moved to rest on her head. The warmth seeping through the man's hand gave her a familiar jolt.

Lauren looked up and tried to focus on the face that had separated itself from the others. The light of the room made him look pale. His hair was thinning on top. The eyes were puffy and had dark bags under them. But the blue stare was the same.

"Ty?" she asked uneasily. "Brother Ty?"

"It's Father Ty now, Lauren," he said softly. "And yes, you've come back to us again."

"Us?" she whispered, blinking at the man, trying to distinguish between sleep and reality.

This was the only name she knew the man by. He was one of Michael Butler's ministers, one of the top

lieutenants in the organization, when she went to the
Butler Divinity Mission twenty-two years ago. He'd
been the one to meet her at the office in Albuquerque
when she first arrived in New Mexico. He'd personally taken her out to the compound in the desert.

Lauren Wells had gone to take her daughter and
grandson back home with her to Indiana. Debbie had
gone there with the idea that Reverend Butler's mission was a safe place for runaways and abused wives
and children, for people who had no one to protect
them and take care of them. Everyone thought so.
Sixteen years old and six months pregnant, Lauren's
daughter had run away from home and her abusive
father. It had taken Lauren a divorce from Debbie's
father and almost two years of constant searching before she'd found her daughter and grandson at the
Butler Mission. Once there, though, she'd soon realized that leaving was not an option.

"Yes, you're back with us. With your brothers and
sisters."

"There was no *us* left after Reverend Butler was
done," Lauren said bitterly, the memory of her last
hour at the mission still vivid in her mind.

She had stolen a set of keys to one of the cars.
Everyone knew something horrible was going to happen that night. They'd been rehearsing it for days. But
Debbie wouldn't leave with her, so Lauren had taken
her grandson instead. The toddler had come to her
with open arms. Then, when another young mother
realized what Lauren was doing, she had pushed her
baby daughter into Lauren's arms. That was Sydney,

less than a year old. William, was fourteen at the time and wiry as a starving rat. The State of New Mexico had put him there only three weeks earlier, and he didn't like the looks of things. The talk going around was that this was the end of the line, and he wasn't buying it. He was in the station wagon and waiting before Lauren got there. The last one had been Kelly, with her large green eyes. She looked as delicate as an angel. She'd stood there beside the car and in the tiniest voice had whispered to her.

Please take me. Don't leave me.

Lauren glared accusingly at the self-styled Father Ty, who had obviously taken on the mantle of his predecessor. "The only *us* left after that massacre were the innocent children who escaped twenty-two years ago. But someone killed Sydney. And then they killed William. Those were no accidents...I know that. It was *you*. You and your people!"

He sat next to her on the cot. His smile was false and cold. "You're tired. Hysterical. You've forgotten that our mission is not about taking lives but directing them to a higher level—to an eternal one."

He wasn't denying her accusation. She inched away from him on the cot. "You're sounding as crazy as Reverend Butler did before he died."

"Lauren, you've never been able to live past the guilt you bear for robbing your grandson of the gift of eternal peace. You stole him away from his chance at timeless bliss. It's very sad that he had to die at your hand in that car accident." His fingers came to rest on her shoulder, but she pushed his hand away.

"Debbie, however, has moved on. And now she's waiting for you and for the rest of us to join her."

"You're talking nonsense."

"I'm promising you the chance to make peace with your daughter. She's ready to forgive and forget. This is the moment of our Khumba Luxor. This is the time that God has aligned Saturn and the sun and the moon. The government is bent to destroy us, but this is the opening of the path for us, the true believers. This is our moment to follow those who went before. That's why you're here."

"I'm here because your people tricked me and abducted me at the bus stop. I came to New Hampshire to warn Kelly that Sydney and William are dead, and I'm too old to believe in coincidences." She cringed and moved off the cot when he tried to touch her. Her legs barely held her and she stumbled, her shoulder striking a wall.

"Sydney and William were both given a chance," he replied. "They were once the children of the Mission, like the rest of us here, like all those who are arriving here this weekend. They could have joined us. But they turned their backs on us. They joined forces with our enemies. They threatened to expose us, so they had to face the consequences."

"You're a hypocrite. If you believed in all of this nonsense, then you should have killed yourself with the rest of them. But no, you ran away." She pointed a finger at him. "You're a coward…and a thief. No one ever found even half of the funds the Mission had been collecting. Don't you think everyone knows that you took that money?''

He came abruptly to his feet. The chilling smile was still painted on his face. ''Lauren, Debbie is not the only one who forgives you. We forgive, too. All of us.'' He made a sweeping motion at the handful of people standing behind him.

Lauren did not look at them. She didn't trust Tyler Somers enough to take her eyes off him for a moment.

''You're a hero to all of us. You're the reason we've been blessed with a second chance at immortality. You're the cause of us coming back to the surface from under ground. We will finally be able to join the ones who went ahead of us with our prophet Michael.''

''You can't lay your guilt on me. You will not murder more people and say it was because of me,'' Lauren said sharply. ''I had nothing to do with you people back then. And I'll have nothing to do with you now.''

''But you have everything to do with us,'' Ty argued. ''Like a prophet carrying the Ark of the Covenant…like the Baptizer, pointing the way to Him…like Serapis Bey, holding open the door to Paradise…you have accomplished the divine task God gave you.''

''That's a lie!''

''It is *truth*, sister,'' the cult leader said forcefully. ''You delivered up to us our new messiah. After twenty-two years, the universe is once again aligned.

The path is open. And you alone have given us the Chosen One to lead us to our destiny.''

Lauren was trembling violently, trying to comprehend what the man was saying. After all these years, she still could not forgive herself for not doing more—for not acting sooner. All the children that had been in that camp! All those young people…dead! She edged away and shook her head.

''No! You're wrong. I simply took away a child. She's not part of this.''

''What a child she was,'' he said solemnly. ''What a woman she has become.''

''She will not go along with any of your madness.''

''Come with us, Lauren!'' Ty walked toward her. ''You're old and at the end of your days. Come and rest in the arms of your daughter. Come and find the bliss of immortality.''

''No!'' She had to warn Kelly. She had to get to her before these people did.

Shoving away his outstretched hands, Lauren turned and tried to run through the people by the door.

''As you wish,'' she heard him say.

Out of the corner of her eye she saw the arm of one of the ministers flash upward as she shoved at those blocking her way. She never felt any pain when the blow struck her skull, but was surprised when the world exploded in a brilliant flash of reds and yellows…before everything around her went black.

Eight

The first rays of dawn had barely lightened the eastern sky when Ian heard the creak of the hardwood floor right outside his bedroom door. He was awake immediately, his mind clear.

He'd left the window open, and a cool breeze made a low whistle as it found its way under his closed door. His gaze fixed on the door handle as he slid his hand under the pillow. His fingers slipped with practiced familiarity around the handle of his pistol.

Last night, he hadn't bothered to try the lock again. He hadn't tried to jam the wooden chair up against the door, either. The chair was too light and impractical, even for sitting in.

There was another creak. Time seemed to stand still for Ian. His senses were keenly alert. The smell of lilac and pine traveled on the breeze.

A dozen thoughts went through his mind, but the look exchanged between Dave and Marisa Meadows was the one that stuck. The floorboard outside squeaked again, and he moved his pistol from beneath the pillow, sliding it under the blanket so that it was pointed at the door. The door handle turned, and he undid the safety catch.

The door began to open. Ian's finger tensed on the trigger. He held his breath as the breeze came through stronger, causing the curtains in the room to flap gently.

The door swung open and a small face appeared around the edge.

The relief came like a bucket of cold water. He let out the breath he'd been holding. His entire body relaxed, and he flipped on the safety as he pushed the gun back under the pillow.

"Cookie Monster?" Jade whispered from the doorway.

This was the nicest name anyone had called him in many years. But he had no shirt on and was sleeping in his boxers. If he didn't say anything, maybe she'd think he was asleep and go back to Kelly. That would be the best thing for all of them.

"Ian!" she whispered in a more insistent tone.

"Yes, Jade," he responded, giving up and lifting his head from the pillow.

"Are you asleep?" she whispered in her quieter voice again.

He looked at the small clock next to the bed. "Why would I be sleeping at five twenty-five on a Saturday morning?"

"You're awake," she decided for him, immediately pushing open the door and coming in.

He noticed the pile of books tucked under her arm, and he almost panicked when, without being asked, she started climbing onto the bed.

"Wait...wait. I'm getting up." He looked around the bed for his pants.

"But I want to cuddle and read in bed," she said in a very cute little whine.

"No, that wouldn't be..." He found and grabbed a pair of shorts he'd put out, and dragged them under the sheet. Hurriedly, he pulled them on. "We'll read in the chair in the hallway."

"But I'm cold," she argued, rubbing one bare foot on the other.

"We'll grab a blanket." Jumping out of bed, he straightened the sheets and quilt over the pillow. There was no way he was going to move his pistol while a little girl with eagle eyes was watching.

"You have really hairy legs," Jade noted in a grave tone, pointing them out to him.

"Thanks." He grabbed a T-shirt from the top drawer and pulled it on.

"You can use my mom's razor to shave your legs, if you want," she offered, walking around the room and watching everything he did with obvious fascination. "But you should probably ask first. I can't touch those things now. But she said when I get older, I can. Of course, first I have to get lots of hair on my legs, like you."

Ian wondered if all three-and-a-half-year-olds were this talkative at five in the morning.

"In the hall," he ordered, turning her around and starting her gently toward the door when she became curious about his shaving bag and the other belongings he'd left on the dresser.

"I'm cold," she whispered again before leaving the room.

Stopping, he closed his window and then pulled the door to his bedroom shut behind them. A window was partially open in the sitting area at the top of the stairs. He closed that one, too.

"Better?"

She shook her head from side to side and dropped her books on the table. Ian watched her run through the open door across the hall. Enough morning light was coming in from the skylights and the windows that he had a good view of the entire apartment. The open space, the white walls, the oversize pictures decorating those walls. At the far end, he spotted a pair of twin beds. He guessed the body with the sheet twisted around it had to be Kelly. Jade grabbed something that looked like a small blanket from the other bed and tiptoed back.

"She's really sleepy because I was up a lot last night," Jade explained to him in a very mature tone when she was back in the hall.

"Some people consider now nighttime, too."

"I didn't wake her up. I woke *you* up this time," she said in a logical tone. She pointed to the rocking chair. "Sit."

"Yes, ma'am." He sat down.

"I'm not a *ma'am*, silly." She started climbing on the chair, too.

"What're you doing?" he asked, expecting her to sit down in the chair next to his.

"Getting comfortable." She climbed on his lap,

nestled against his chest, and tried to spread the blanket on herself. "Help me."

Like an obedient servant, he tucked the well-worn yellow blanket around her.

"Book, please." She stretched a regal hand toward the table.

Ian took the top one. "Will this one do?"

"Perfect," she said with a comfortable sigh, leaning into him and waiting for him to start.

She was perfect, Ian thought. This activity was perfect. The moments he and Kelly had spent alone together last night—even their awkward kiss—were perfect. Well, nearly perfect.

Ian had never known Kelly's husband. He had no idea what kind of husband he'd been to Kelly or what kind of father he might have been to Jade if he were still alive. But he still felt sorry for the man to have missed this.

His cheek brushed against Jade's silky curls. When she looked up at him, Ian opened the book and started reading.

The nightmare was the same one she'd had so many times before. The place was one she'd visited a hundred times in her dreams. As always, Kelly couldn't shake herself out of it.

She was back at the Mission. She was just a girl. Father Mike was waiting for her. She had to go to him. She didn't want to go, but she had to go.

The sun outside was bright white and hot. She felt the push and she was inside. The narrow hallway leading to his quarters was dark and cool. Not nice cool, but stale and dank. She felt queasy, as always.

Kelly tried to remember what she'd done wrong this time. She was always in trouble. Always being punished for being bad. But she couldn't remember what she'd done this time.

She squinted upon entering the dark room. She held her breath, hating the familiar smell. It was like a cellar. She thought she could see things crawling in the dark corners.

"Come in, my child," he called to her in his soft, spiderweb voice. Every time Kelly heard it, a chill went through her, making the hair stand up on her neck.

She didn't want to take a step forward or back. She knew the crawling things had squirmed around behind her, cutting off her escape. She didn't want to go to the voice, either. She looked down. It was so dark, she couldn't see her feet.

"Come closer, child."

A match scratched and flared. The flame touched the wick, and a candle sputtered and lit.

She was not in the Father's quarters. She saw the baptismal font. Liquid the color of blood was bubbling in it. Another candle lit. She saw a cup filled with the blood being held out to her. Kelly shook her head, but her feet were rooted to the ground. She couldn't leave. She stared at the hand as it came closer. Long, thin fingers. White and wrinkled in the candlelight. It was Father's hand.

"What are you frightened of, Kelly?" he asked.

His voice drew her in, held her in its silky strands. "Be a good girl and join me. Join us."

More candles flared to life around her. More and more, until the chapel was filled. The room came to life with undulating waves of tiny white flames.

Kelly looked at the lines of people standing behind the leaders. She knew the faces. The other children she shared rooms with. The people who worked at the Mission's office. The men and women who lived in separate buildings. They were old and young and pregnant. All of them holding their candles, their eyes staring.

She looked back at the Father. The woman was standing right at his shoulder. Sister Jill Frost, so pretty. She was the woman Kelly knew was her mother.

"You're one of us," Jill said in her singsong voice. Her green eyes flashed brilliantly above the glow of the candle.

"Come with us, Kelly." Father's outstretched hand raised the cup toward her. "Take this."

Everyone was holding a cup.

Kelly knew what was going to happen. They were all going to die. Tears rushed into her eyes. She opened her mouth to warn them—to tell them the truth. Her heart, though, was drumming so loud. No, she realized, it was their hearts beating. The sound of it was drowning out her voice.

"Kelly…"

It took all her strength, but she pushed the hand

away. Stunned, she saw it withdraw. She followed the movement with her eyes, distrusting her victory.

The Father's hand moved slowly, deliberately, to someone sitting beside him. Kelly watched him smile as the cup pressed against the person's lips.

She looked down at the face. It was Jade.

Her eyes opened with a start. The skylight. The white ceilings. The pictures on the wall. Kelly blinked a couple of times to make certain she was really awake. Her pillow was damp. She still had tears on her cheeks. Her breaths were short and quick, as if she'd been running.

The old nightmare…but different now. The queasiness she always felt whenever she woke up from it was a hundred times worse today. Never before had Jade been part of the nightmare. Cold dread washed through her when she rolled over and looked at her daughter's bed.

Jade was gone.

Reality and dream collided in the next painful second, ripping through her like a chain saw. Kelly tore the sheets aside and was beside the bed in an instant, her eyes searching the room in panic. No lights were on in the apartment. The bedside clock showed five forty-five. Too early for her to be up. The door of her apartment was open. Jade would not go anywhere unless she'd awakened Kelly.

"Jade," she called as she rushed toward the open door.

The two sets of eyes lifted in tandem off the pages

of the book as she skidded to a stop. The two stared at her, their concern showing in their faces. Kelly backed up a step, holding on to the doorjamb to steady her suddenly rubbery knees. The rush of relief made her almost light-headed, but she fought the urge to snatch her daughter up in her arms.

"Good morning, Mommy," Jade said brightly.

She smiled weakly at them, distrusting her voice. She also had to blink a couple of times to make sure she was awake and that her eyes weren't deceiving her. The two presented such a portrait in contrasts. Jade, a little bundle of yellow blanket, tucked against the man's chest. The look of sheer bliss on her daughter's face was one Kelly rarely saw. And Ian Campbell, unshaven, his hair spiked up in every direction, was holding on to Jade as if she was the most precious package in the world. She fought unsuccessfully against a tremble in her chin and the tears welling up in her eyes.

"You okay?" he asked.

Kelly nodded. "Sorry. Just woke up. I didn't know where she was."

"Uh-oh, time for a Band-Aid," Jade whispered to Ian before pushing away the books and the blanket and getting down from his lap. She ran past Kelly and disappeared inside the apartment.

"I don't have much experience at this stuff," he said, putting the books on the small table by the rocking chair. "But she showed up at my bedroom door, ready to be read to. If I hadn't gotten out of bed and come out here quick, I think she would have climbed in there with me and thought nothing of it. Sitting on the rocking chair was the only compromise she'd settled for.''

He was blushing. Kelly understood his concern about how this might look to someone else.

''I haven't done a background check on you yet, Mr. Campbell.'' She paused and leaned against the doorway. ''But for some reason, my daughter seems to trust you.''

''I think we've moved past trust,'' he said in a lower voice. ''She said she likes me.''

''Yeah…because you're a pushover. What time did she wake you up?''

He didn't get a chance to answer, because Jade rushed back out, carrying a large box of Band-Aids.

''Where does it hurt, Mommy?''

Kelly crouched down before her daughter and looked into her serious face and bright green eyes.

''Nothing hurts anymore, my love,'' she said, giving Jade a bear hug.

The child wriggled free after a moment. ''Then we should put one on, so it won't come back,'' she said with authority, taking one with a flowered pattern out of the box for her.

''See? No cuts or bruises.'' Kelly showed her hands and fingers.

''It won't hurt much.'' With marked single-mindedness, she opened the Band-Aid, peeled the backing strips and put it on her mother's forehead, covering the old scar.

Kelly couldn't help but smile as she touched Jade's handiwork.

"See. I told you it'd feel better." She turned to Ian. "Want one?"

"No, I'm doing great," he said, trying not to show his amusement. He looked up at Kelly. "How many boxes of these things do you go through every week?"

She pushed up to her feet. "I've lost count. I buy them in cases."

When his gaze turned tender, Kelly realized what she'd said and how he'd taken it...and something melted in her.

"I'm hungry." Jade's announcement and the tug on her arm drew Kelly's attention back to her daughter. "I'll make toast."

Without waiting for an answer, the little girl disappeared inside the apartment.

Ian got to his feet and stretched. He seemed to fill the little sitting area. There was something very intimate about seeing him before his shower and shave, dressed in old shorts and a T-shirt. He looked big and warm enough to tempt Kelly to want to cuddle with him herself. She looked down at his bare muscular legs and felt the tingles crawl down her belly.

"So does she get up this early every morning?"

Kelly knew he'd caught her looking at him by the amused expression on his face, and she felt her face burn. Now he was looking at her.

"A little later, usually. Six...six-thirty." Kelly's voice didn't seem to be hers. She'd gone suddenly

hoarse. She crossed her arms over her chest, immediately conscious of how thin the silk pajama pants
and shirt were. She didn't have to look down to know
the tips of her breasts must be poking through. And
her face…and hair. It was too embarrassing to even
think how scary she must look.

"She had a restless night," Kelly finally managed
to finish her thoughts.

"Come and have toast," Jade called out, coming
back to the doorway and motioning to Ian.

He ran a hand over his stubbly chin. "I have to
shower and shave. I'll see you downstairs for breakfast."

"I said toast, not breakfast," she told him, as if he
should know there's a huge difference.

"Wilson doesn't serve breakfast until seven. Jade
and I have a kitchenette," Kelly offered by way of
explanation. "It's good for a bowl of cereal and toast
whenever she wants a late-night or early-morning
snack. You're welcome to join us…unless you want
to get back to bed. I'm sorry, I never even apologized
for Jade waking you up."

His eyes went from Kelly to Jade. Seeing the smile
tugging at his lips, Kelly looked down. Her daughter
was mimicking her stance—everything down to
crossing the arms and rubbing one foot on top of the
other.

"Only a fool would turn down an offer of toast
from two beautiful women," he said, looking back up
to Kelly. "Give me ten minutes, though. I'd still like
to clean up."

It was on the tip of her tongue to offer him the use of their bathroom, but Kelly stopped herself in time. She had to use it herself. And then there were all their personal things cluttering every shelf.

"Come over when you're ready," she said.

The two of them waited until he disappeared inside his bedroom, then turned and rushed into the apartment.

"I like him Mommy. I like him a *lot*," Jade said excitedly, skipping after her mother as Kelly picked up clothing from the chairs and toys off the floor. "Maybe he'll take me out in one of the boats. You can come, too. And I saw these pretty flowers. Maybe…maybe he'll take me for a walk, and we can bring some back for you."

"We can't plan Mr. Campbell's weekend for him, sweetheart," Kelly said, trying not to let her own emotions overwhelm her. She'd always known Jade missed not having a father, but she never realized how quickly she could get attached to someone like Ian. "He's coming back for some toast. Let's take one step at a time."

"What does that mean?"

"It means…" She touched Jade's upturned and wrinkled nose. "That you should get in the bathroom and wash your face and brush your teeth and change out of your pajamas and let me finish making these beds."

"That's not what that means."

The little girl was just too smart. "Okay, it means

that we should only plan on Ian having toast with us this morning. That's it.''

"But he likes me," Jade said with a little tremble of the chin.

"I know he does, my love." Kelly knelt before her daughter and held on to her shoulders, looking into her eyes. "And I *love* you. But sometimes grown-ups have things to do—jobs and places to go and other friends to see. So I think that we shouldn't push Mr. Campbell to give up other things he might have planned for this weekend. Does that make sense?"

"Yes. You're saying Ian is not my playmate," Jade said somewhat dejectedly.

Kelly nodded. "But he still could be our friend. And he's getting all cleaned up and coming over, expecting toast, and you and I still look like this."

The skip was gone from Jade's steps when she finally headed to the bathroom. She hadn't asked for a Band-Aid, though, so Kelly thought the little girl would be able to handle the disappointment.

They were both lacking in company and friends. In some ways, they lived like social outcasts. Kelly knew exactly how Jade felt. Their life in the boondocks of New Hampshire, as much as it had been ideal at the beginning, was not really working out too well anymore. Ian's comment last night, when he'd asked why she hadn't opted for a more suburban existence, made so much sense. Kelly knew it. She'd been thinking about it for a while now. It had started as a germ of an idea this past winter. There was nothing that tied Kelly and Jade to this place or to the inn. And frankly, swimming classes and taking over some accounting books were not enough to excite either daughter or mother. As the summer began to unfold, the thought of moving—of selling the inn for whatever she could get and giving Jade and herself a new start, somewhere where there were people and other children and jobs—was growing more and more appealing.

Standing in the middle of the apartment and watching her daughter trudge into the bathroom, Kelly knew that now was the time. She didn't know how she would break this news to Janice and Bill. Tranquillity Inn was their home, and there would be no guarantee that another owner would want the same live-in staff to stay on.

Well, she decided, that was a problem they'd all face when the time came. Jade was Kelly's first priority, after all, not the Maitlands. And something had to be done.

Nine

Dan was not a hundred yards from the state road when the pickup turned onto the gravel road that eventually wound past the inn. He turned and raised a hand, and Bill downshifted the old truck to slow it before applying the brakes.

"Hey, want a lift?" Janice's husband asked.

Dan snorted and pulled open the creaky door. He dropped the heavy backpack he was carrying on the floor before climbing up onto the cracked and faded vinyl seat of the vintage pickup. He looked over at the driver. Bill was in his late seventies, balding, and wearing the same paint-speckled khaki pants he always wore when he was working. His blue oxford shirt was frayed at the collar but clean. He hadn't shaved in a couple of days, but Dan knew that was a once- or twice-a-week thing for him. Glasses Bill should have been wearing were folded in his shirt pocket. He was a quiet, hardworking old guy, and Dan liked him.

He settled in and looked around for the seat belt. There wasn't one. "So what took you so long?"

"Well, it's a little early for you to be out and about,

I'd say." Bill nodded at him. "Or is it a little late to be getting in?"

Racing the engine, he raised one gray eyebrow.

"You are a nosy old bastard."

"Hey, this nose has gotten this old bastard into a lot of interesting trouble over the years."

Letting the engine settle, Bill engaged the clutch and started along the gravel road. The transmission ground a bit going into second, but slipped easily into third.

"Yeah? And what trouble have you been into this morning?"

"Well, I had to take the last of the stuff over," Bill replied. "We had a few boxes in the carriage house that didn't get picked up last night."

"Did they complain about you being so early?"

"They know I'm an early riser. Also, this way is better. Fewer eyes watching what's coming. Gives them no reason to get too excited."

Dan nodded, looking out his window through the trees. As they came over the top of a hill, he could see the mist rising from a break in the trees that he knew was the lake. He hadn't seen any cars by the road leading in to the camp. But it was still way too early.

"Anything new and unexpected over there?" The pickup hit a pothole in the gravel, and Dan felt his back teeth loosen.

"Sorry about that. Should've gotten out this spring and filled some of these holes." His grizzled face creased into a frown. "Not that it matters now, I guess."

"No, I guess not," Dan murmured.

After a moment, Bill continued. "Anyway, it's quiet over there this morning. They had a lot of folks come in yesterday, and had an inner-circle meeting late last night. They've got more people arriving today, though. Should be a full house before the weekend's out."

"Monday is still the day?"

"As far as I know. But things could change any minute, I suppose."

"Do you have a number?"

"I heard a hundred fifty."

Dan gave the old man a sidelong look. "That's a lot."

"Tell me about it."

The young man pushed himself to focus on the road and the trees and the lake now visible just off to the right. "You wouldn't know there were that many around from this end of the lake."

"That fog is like a curtain across the water, ain't it?"

"Sure is," Dan said, clearing an unexpected tightness he felt in his throat.

Around another bend and the inn came into sight. Bill maneuvered the pickup into the driveway and down to the parking area near the kitchen. Blade's car was already parked by the door. As the truck rolled to a stop, Dan stared at the other cars in the lot. The Desposito truck was the only one already gone.

"So, you going back over there later?" he asked the older man.

"Think so. I'll have to see what Janice has on the to-do list."

"Right." Dan nodded, grabbing his bag and reaching for the door handle.

"You're welcome to come on over, young fella."

He looked over at Bill, who was watching him closely. "Let me know if you think I should," he said, getting out.

The crunching sound of tires on gravel drew Ian to the window. He recognized Maitland's truck. He had not yet been officially introduced to the older man, and this morning—before the other guests came downstairs—was probably the best time for that. Bill Maitland was not the reason why he was here, though. Ian slid his locked suitcase under the bed, hung his wet towel on a hook behind the door and headed for the apartment across the landing.

Jade must have been waiting at the door, because she opened it the moment Ian's knuckles made contact with the wood.

"Mommy is in the shower. Sometimes that takes a while. But she made coffee. And she said I can't touch it cuz it's really hot. But you're a grown-up, so it's okay for you to." Jade held the door wide open. "I'll get you a cup."

As she scampered away, Ian looked down at this little person with the big words, and couldn't help but again be amused. She must have taken a bath or shower, as her hair was wet and combed down her back. She was also changed into a pair of jeans and a white T-shirt. She stopped and ran back to him.

"Oh, you can come in now," she said, taking his hand and leading him in.

He stepped into the apartment and looked around at the open-space combination of bedroom and living room with great interest. The dormers and the skylights were a nice addition, and the white walls and cathedral ceiling made the place look practically spacious. The one thing that caught Ian's immediate interest, though, was the pair of oversize portraits of Jade. They were clearly works of art. They were some of the most stunning natural scenes he'd ever seen captured in a photograph. And they were simply of Jade walking and playing in the woods.

"That's me," she announced to him, still holding his hand.

"I can see that. Did your mom take those pictures?"

"Uh-huh! And this is the bathroom," Jade said, changing the subject as if there was nothing special about those pictures. She pointed at the door to their right. Ian could hear the shower running.

"And here's where we make our toast," she said, pulling him to the high counter that served as a divider and a table between the kitchenette and the rest of the apartment. At one end, a toaster was plugged into the wall.

"Mommy already put out your cup. See?"

The drip percolator had finished filling the coffee-pot, and a couple of cups were sitting near it on the counter.

Ian nodded. "Thanks."

Beside the toaster, Kelly had put out a dish of butter and three jars of jam. Jade climbed up on one of the high counter chairs and reached for the toaster, pressing the button down.

"Shouldn't we wait until your mom gets out?" he asked, anxious that Jade might slip off the chair, or stick her finger in something, or hurt herself in any way.

"She said I could start my toast when you came in."

Ian settled down on the chair next to her, where he could reach her, just in case. He noticed on the wall a tan speaker box with switches for different settings. The device was set to Intercom/Monitor. He reached over and turned the switch to Intercom.

The water stopped running in the shower, and he had a pretty good idea Kelly would be out of there in just a few minutes. Jade told him about the three jams, which were all her favorite. The toast popped up and he quickly took the pieces out before she burned herself. Depositing them on a plate in front of her, he went around the counter and poured out two cups of coffee.

Then he sat back and stared in amazement as Jade went to work. A little bit of butter went on the toast, thick layers of all three kinds of jam, which went not only on the bread, but on her fingers and face and shirt, as well. And it didn't seem that she was done with it yet. So she *was* a kid after all.

Kelly sailed out of the bathroom, bringing with her the clean smell of soap and shampoo. "Oh! You're already here."

For a few seconds, Ian could only stare. Barefoot and dressed, like her daughter, in a pair of old jeans and a white T-shirt, she looked like a million bucks. She wasn't wearing a bra, and she hadn't bothered with any makeup and her wet hair hung loose around her shoulders. To him, she looked fresh and beautiful as a desert dawn. Ian's gaze wandered over her, lingering a little on the shape of that T-shirt. On second thought, he decided, she looked sexy as hell.

"I'm sorry that we're not much at entertaining up here," she said, sitting next to Jade at the counter. "We ask you to come over without ever thinking that you might want milk or sugar for your coffee. I usually take mine black, but I can run down—"

"Black's good for me." He pushed Kelly's cup toward hers and took a sip of his own. "Good coffee."

Ian's eyes fixed on Jade's *pièce de résistance*. The toast was a gooey mass of dripping jam, squeezed between tiny fingers. The little girl held her culinary masterpiece out to him.

"Want a bite?"

"Very tempting, but no thanks. It's all yours, babe." Ian looked at Kelly. "Somebody's got a sweet tooth?"

"These are fruit purees. They don't have a lot of

sugar in them.'' She got up, wet half a dozen paper towels and put them near Jade. ''But my girl is definitely a sugarholic.''

''And you called me a pushover.''

''That's her only flaw,'' she whispered to Ian in a voice that Jade could hear. The little girl, though, was in a world of her own. Diving into the toast, she seemed to savor every bite, even though she got most of it on her face.

''Can I put in a couple of slices for you?'' Kelly asked.

''No way. Not with this jelly monster next to me. Too dangerous!'' Ian made a scared face when Jade showed her teeth and bit into the toast again. ''I was hoping you'd give me a fifty-cent tour of your work, though. You have some amazing things here.'' He motioned with his head toward Jade's photos.

A soft reddish hue crept up into her cheeks. Just as he'd expected, she wasn't used to receiving compliments. Cup in hand, she came around the counter.

''Those two shots were just a spur-of-the-moment thing. It's so much fun watching her do things. She's so interested in everything.''

The pictures were hung side by side. The white matting and silver frames set off the black-and-white photos perfectly. ''When did you take them?''

''Last fall.'' She took a sip of her coffee. ''I was so mad at myself for having only black-and-white film in the camera. The leaves were a thousand different shades of color. And Jade's red sweater made her the centerpiece of a bouquet of flowers. I took the shots, anyway.''

"What makes these so arresting,'' he commented, "is that they're such perfect representations of a child at play. She's a part of nature. She doesn't even know you're there.''

"I have a similar picture of Jade in the woods from two summers ago. She was just a toddler. I'd like to have that one framed like these and hang it next to them. And maybe I could add one each year as she gets older.''

She was planning for the future. Ian liked that.

"And these pictures?'' He walked toward the wall containing dozens of framed photos.

"Family photos.''

"Is that Jade's father?'' He pointed to a picture of Kelly with a good-looking young man who had his arm around her shoulder. The couple looked carefree, happy. No clouds darkened the background sky or the green mountains.

She nodded. "That's Greg.''

"How did you two meet?''

"He was a reporter. I was a newspaper photographer. We had an assignment together, and the sparks just flew. We were married that same year.''

"And how long were you married before **he** was…well, before he…''

"Died?'' she asked quietly, glancing toward Jade. She was busily working on another piece of toast. Kelly sipped the coffee, obviously getting her thoughts together.

"A little over two years," she said finally. "He never got the chance to see Jade. I was about six months pregnant when he died."

Kelly's face disappeared again behind the protective cup of coffee. Without thinking, Ian reached over and briefly brushed the back of his hand against hers.

"You two seemed to travel a lot," he commented, turning his attention back to the pictures. There were at least half a dozen of Greg Stone, in different places around the world.

"We did travel some for fun. But most of these are of Greg on different assignments. Every picture I have of him is framed and out here. I think it's important for Jade to know who her father was."

"Are you in contact at all with his family?"

"He was Australian, born and raised there. We were planning to move permanently to Sydney right after Jade was born. He already had a great job lined up. We'd even started downsizing our belongings. Meeting his family and being close to them was all part of our reason for the move."

"And everyone here knew about it?" Ian asked.

"My parents were old hands at moving. The two of them were retired academics. Neither had ever applied for tenure in their thirty and forty years of teaching. Didn't believe in it. They thought a change of scenery every five or six years was a healthy thing. My father Frank was all for it. He said this would give them a place to visit every year. He knew, despite her initial hesitation, that my mother Rose would eventually warm up to it, too."

Kelly took a sip of coffee, obviously working to keep her emotions in check.

"When my father died a couple of months into the planning process, something changed in my mother. She became a different woman. Even about the move, her attitude changed completely. She became...I don't know, almost adamant for us to move. In fact, she even hinted that she might follow us and live there herself. But then she died, too.

They were silent for a moment, and then Ian spoke up again.

"So you moved a few times growing up?" he asked, glancing at the photograph of an older couple that he knew were Frank and Rose Wilton.

"Only a couple of times, before I went away to college." Both hands wrapped around the coffee mug. "I was adopted."

"Really? How old were you?"

"I was twelve."

"Twelve? That's pretty old for an adoption. You were lucky."

"They were very special people."

"I'm sure they were," he said quietly. "Any communication with your old family?"

She shook her head. "They're all gone." She turned to Jade who seemed to be done eating and was busily drawing patterns with a blueberry-dipped finger on the countertop. "I guess we're ready for the cleanup crew in there."

Ian watched Kelly walk to the kitchen, and then he turned his attention back to the photos. There had been bits and pieces of her life that had been happy. Proof of that was evident in this display. But everybody she'd had was dead. The only family connection remaining for Kelly was her daughter.

He watched the mock wrestling match between mother and daughter as Kelly washed the child's face. Jade's laughter rang out in the apartment. Kelly's smile poured out from her heart. He already knew she would do anything—she would go to the end of the world—to keep her child away from harm. The horrifying thing was that there were others who had to know that, too.

The intercom on the wall buzzed. Kelly, busy working Jade into a clean shirt, was slow to answer it. On the third insistent buzz, she got to it.

"Finally!" The old woman's voice crackled with relief.

"Good morning, Janice," Kelly called, winning the battle and holding the stained shirt in the air as a sign of her victory. Jade continued to jump up, pretending she wanted it back.

"Why did you turn off the room monitor? I was worried about you. Didn't know what was going on."

Kelly looked at the switch on the box, glanced at Ian, and then back at the box again. "Do you need me downstairs?" she asked finally.

"Yes. We need you down here right away. Rita is beside herself with the extra work caused by the extra guests. She has so much more on her plate today. Well, you know the routine."

Ian looked at the clock. It was a couple of minutes past seven.

"I'm on my way down," Kelly told her, switching off the intercom and not answering the next short buzz. She looked up at Ian. "I promise the breakfast downstairs will be a lot more impressive than what we offered you here."

"I liked this one just fine," he said gently, looking from Jade's face back to Kelly's before taking his cup to the kitchen. She took the cup away from him, but he could already tell her mind was running in a hundred different directions.

She took a stretchy band out of one pocket and pulled her hair up in a no-nonsense ponytail. She spent a little more time with Jade's hair, braiding it loosely down her back. Ian used the wet paper towels that were left on the counter and wiped the rest of Jade's handiwork.

"You don't have to do that," Kelly said with a smile and turned to her daughter. "Get your books, love, and some games."

Jade went to a shelf overflowing with her things and started going through them. She took her time and looked at every book she pulled off the shelf before choosing. Kelly was trying to prod her along when there was another buzz from downstairs.

"Why don't you go down," Ian suggested, nodding toward the intercom. "Better than getting another earful. I can walk down with her, if you feel comfortable with that."

"You don't mind?"

"It'd be my pleasure."

Ten

Puzzled, Kelly stood in the door of the porch dining room. Everything appeared to be under control. She could see the balding head of Shawn Hobart at a small table by the window, and Marisa and Dave Meadows were seated a couple of tables away. Freshly made coffee and a pot of hot water were steaming away on the warmers, and the other tables were ready for the guests who would be coming down in the course of the next hour or two.

Rita breezed in from the kitchen, carrying a tray of plates at her shoulder. Kelly opened the serving stand for her and then busied herself folding napkins for lunch as the food was served. Still, as Kelly looked around, she couldn't see what else needed to be done.

"Do you need a hand with breakfast?" Kelly asked after Rita had served the guests.

"Does it look like I need help?" the young woman snapped in her customary combative tone. "There's nothing left to do."

"In that case, you know where to find me if you need a hand with anything," Kelly said pleasantly. She wasn't going to start her day in a bad mood.

Janice was walking back to the reception desk from

the kitchen, a cup of tea in one hand and her cane in the other. Unlike Rita and her sour attitude, the older woman smiled upon seeing Kelly and returned the morning greeting with enthusiasm.

"It's an absolutely glorious day outside. We should ask Dan to open all the windows downstairs. I believe it might even get warm enough today that we could serve lunch on the deck."

"That sounds great." Kelly opened the door and turned on the light in her office. "I just saw Rita. She was offended when I offered to help after everything was already on track for the breakfast."

"Isn't that curious," Janice replied, looking out at the porch dining area.

"Very. Are you sure *she* was the one looking for me this morning?" Kelly asked brightly. Coming downstairs, an alarm went off in her head that was supported by Rita's response. If Kelly's suspicions were right, then she definitely wanted to set things straight. Just because Ian Campbell was staying on the third floor, it didn't mean Janice needed to play the part of chaperon.

"You know her...the moody thing that she is. She didn't have a foot in the door and was already complaining." Janice put her cup of tea down, rested her cane against the wall, and took her time sitting. "I knew you'd be up early, anyway. By the way, where's Jade?"

Kelly was saved from answering as the inn's phone rang.

"I'll get it." She grabbed the phone off her desk

in the office and gave her standard innkeeper's greeting.

"Is this the Tranquillity Inn in Independence, New Hampshire?" The voice on the other end had a few threads of temper, even hysteria, woven into it. "If it is, then you'd better not hang up."

"Yes, I just said it is," Kelly replied, trying to remain pleasant. "And I'm not going to hang up. What can I do for you?"

At the reception desk, Janice was greeting the Stern family on their way in to breakfast. The younger son, Ryan, was standing in the shadow of his older brother. His awestruck stare was the same one Kelly had seen last night. She waved at him, trying to ignore the chill that washed down her spine.

"I called twice last night, but I got nowhere. The woman who answered was not helpful at all." The voice was that of a younger woman, and it was clearly shaking with emotion. "Now listen to me. I've spoken to the bus company. I've called my cousin in New York. The only thing I haven't done yet is to call the police. But that is the next call I'm going to make."

"Let's back up. Are you trying to get hold of someone at this inn?" Kelly grabbed a pen and pad of paper, and pushed the door of the office partially closed, not wanting to disturb the other guests with whatever was going on here.

"Didn't I just say I was?"

"How about if we start from the beginning? I

wasn't the one who spoke to you last night, but I'd like to help you if I can.''

"Who are you?" the voice asked in a distrustful tone.

"I'm Kelly Stone. I'm the owner and innkeeper here."

There was a slight pause. The woman on the phone repeated Kelly's name to someone else in the room with the caller. A muffled conversation followed for a moment before she came back on the line.

"My aunt was coming to Independence to see you," the woman said finally.

"Excuse me?" Kelly asked, becoming more confused by the minute. "Someone was coming to see *me?*"

"Yes. My aunt. Lauren Wells. She's been trying to contact you for over a month now. But you were never available to take her calls. You never returned any of them, either."

Kelly sat down in the nearest chair. "You said Lauren Wells?"

"We don't know the exact connection, but she said she knew you." The woman continued to talk, but Kelly's mind had already rocketed back in time.

Lauren had seemed like some guardian angel who'd been sent to the Mission. She was like the grandmothers you dreamed about...the ones that none of the kids had. She'd come to take her daughter and grandson back, and that made her special, too, because nobody had family that came to take them away.

The adults in the Butler Mission had been plenty upset about Lauren staying there. She was not one of them, and the Father and his ministers couldn't seem to get through to her. It was as if she were deaf to their words.

And Kelly recalled Lauren's daughter, Debbie, too. She remembered her as a pretty young woman who had privileges most of the other women didn't have. Father allowed her to follow him wherever he went, like one of the ministers.

Not long after they'd come out from the city, Debbie moved her little son to the children's center next to the chapel, just as Kelly had been separated from her own mother years earlier. That was while they were still in Albuquerque. All the children were separated from their mothers once they moved out to the desert. Father had said so.

Lauren spent almost all her time at the children's center. Because she had no car, Father's ministers never seemed to worry about her. She never said straight out to Father that she didn't believe in him, but Kelly knew. Lauren became the connection with the outside world that she wanted. She was the fairy godmother she'd read about in the forbidden book one of the other kids kept hidden away. In the end, she was the saving angel for a lucky few.

No, Kelly had never forgotten Lauren Wells.

"Are you still there?" the woman asked from the other end.

"Yes. Yes, I'm here. You were saying Lauren was coming to Tranquillity Inn?"

"She'd even made a reservation there for Friday and Saturday night, last night and tonight. She was leaving Sunday and taking the bus back to New York City, where another of her nieces was supposed to pick her up."

"And how was she getting here?"

"By bus," the woman said, her voice breaking with worry. "I've already called the bus company. They said, as far as they know, she got off at the Independence stop. They can't tell me anything else. The person on the phone last night who works for you just brushed me off."

"I'm sorry about however you were treated."

"Please, just tell me that she's already there, and I'm getting wound up about nothing."

Kelly would have liked nothing better than to do just that. "I'm…I'm afraid she isn't here. But there could be a number of logical explanations for it. We were overbooked for the weekend. Lauren's reservation must have been misplaced. I promise you I'll check with all of our people, though, right after I get off the phone with you. It might be that she showed up and we didn't have a room, so we arranged for her to stay at another local inn. We do that occas—"

"My aunt is seventy-seven years old. Her vision is not too good. She's very particular about calling one of us whenever she's traveling alone. She was not going anywhere else."

Kelly looked at the clock on the wall. It wasn't even seven-thirty. "I don't have any answers for you right now, but please let me check with my people.

In the meantime, maybe she'll call. Once I talk to my staff, I'll be able to give you a more definite answer.''

"Will you call me back this morning?''

"Yes. Absolutely. I promise I'll call you back as quickly as I can. Give me your name and number.'' Kelly wrote the information down carefully. "By the way, do you know why Lauren was so eager to get hold of me?''

There was a very long pause at the other end before the niece finally spoke. "I really can't say.''

The woman was holding back. Something was going on. The niece's hesitation, the calls that Kelly never heard about, Lauren's unexpected trip to New Hampshire, and why another reservation was lost battered at Kelly's brain with a dozen questions. She ended the phone call and her gaze shifted to the corner of her desk, where she'd collected the bits and pieces of the burned letter from the trash can last night.

They were gone. The desk had been wiped clean. She looked down. The trash can was empty, too.

The only things Jade decided to bring downstairs were three one-hundred-piece puzzles, four oversize picture books, and a Candyland game. When Ian told Jade that he'd often heard about the game but never played it, she assured him that she'd be able to teach it to him.

The load was light but bulky, and Ian—glancing at his watch—was relieved when the little girl allowed him to carry everything. Still, their trek downstairs was slow. They had to stop every few steps for Jade to point out the little hole in the stairs that bugs lived in, and the spot on the ceiling where they'd found a bat sleeping last fall, and which step was her favorite for jumping down from, and for an ongoing discussion about which chair in the house was the most comfortable for cuddling and reading.

She even insisted on taking Ian to the specific chair on the second floor in the small alcove at the top of the main stairs.

"And have you tried all the other chairs?"

"Of course," she answered. "Why?"

"I think that one," he said, pointing to a Shaker-style, ladder-back chair, "or this one," he added, rocking a child-size chair, "are more comfortable than that."

"No way!" she said, determined. "Last winter, my mom and I tried every one of them. This was the one we liked best." She climbed up and leaned back, demonstrating how comfortable the upholstered chair was.

He shook his head. "I don't know."

"Yes, it *is*." She raised her little chin stubbornly and then dropped it, looking suddenly thoughtful. "By the way, do you have things to do...or jobs and places to go...or friends to see today?"

He laughed. "Your mom said that, didn't she?"

She gave a quick nod before getting up on her knees on the chair. She turned around in it and looked out the window at the lake. Ian followed the direction of her gaze. The fog was back.

"I was planning to stick around here today," he said. "You know...have a big breakfast, maybe sit on the deck with a good book. Just cool out."

"Can I cool out with you?" she asked in a pleading tone, looking at him over her shoulder.

The vulnerability in the look—as if the whole world depended on the answer he gave her—surprised him.

"Of course you can," he said, gently tugging on her ponytail.

Her immediate smile was about the best reward he could imagine. She turned and started climbing down from the chair. "We have to tell Mommy right away, so she won't ask Cassy to come over."

"What's the problem with you and Cassy?"

"Nothing."

"Where did she take you yesterday?"

"For a walk." The voice turned small again. Jade's hesitation was instantly back.

He looked at her for a second. "Did you see anyone when you were on your walk?"

She nodded slowly. The laces of one of Jade's sneakers had come undone, and Ian crouched down on one knee and began to tie it.

"Who?" he asked.

"I'm not supposed to tell."

Ian's hackles went up, but he stayed calm. He didn't want to scare her in any way. "You can tell me."

She looked down the hallway first before whispering her answer. "Her friends."

"Really," Ian said in the same hushed tone. "How many of them were there?"

"Lots."

"Did they talk to you?"

She nodded.

"Did they hurt you…or touch you…in any way…that made you feel funny?" Ian asked, hoping Kelly had explained this to Jade before.

The child shook her head, but her expression remained extremely somber.

"You didn't like them?"

A quick shake of the head. "I don't want to go back there with her," she whispered, on the edge of tears. "I don't like that camp."

"You were at the camp on the other side of the lake?" Ian asked.

Jade nodded. "I don't like him, either."

"Who?"

"Isn't this a beautiful scene?" The woman's voice was deep and interested. She was standing in the doorway of the room across from the alcove.

Ian fought back his annoyance at the interruption. Holding on to Jade's hand, he stood up. The child immediately hid her face against his leg.

"What an adorable little girl. The father-daughter bond is the most precious. How old is she?"

He was surprised that she'd seen anything but the reflection of herself in the mirror on the wall. This was the same woman who had looked down at everyone last night at dinner as if they were peasants.

"She's almost four, and she's not my daughter, but the child of a friend."

The model came to a stop before them. Sneakers, CD headset, stretchy short shorts and a sports bra that she was wearing as a top. She was wearing lots of makeup for going running, he thought. She looked as if she'd just stepped out of one of the ads that he'd seen of her in a dozen different magazines.

"I'm Ash," she said, looking up from Jade and turning her smoky gaze on Ian.

"Really? Ash who?"

"Just Ash."

"Oh, that's great."

The model was tall. They were almost eye to eye. He was tempted to ask what her real name was, including her last name. He could understand the point of using a fake name on-screen or on the cover of a magazine, but in real life it seemed so bogus for a person to continue to play the celebrity. He decided to be polite, though, and gave her a brief handshake.

"I'm Ian Campbell. This little one is Jade. She's the daughter of the innkeeper, Kelly Stone."

Another wave of shyness had taken possession of Jade, and she refused to acknowledge the woman. This was fine with Ian.

"Are you on your way downstairs?" she asked. She was obviously not about to take a step without them.

Ian considered telling the woman to shove off. He'd hoped to get another couple of minutes in private with Jade to find out more about the trip to the camp the previous day. The little girl's tug on his arm, though, pulling him toward the steps, told him she was ready to go downstairs now.

"I guess we are."

"Mind if I join you for breakfast?"

He looked down at her exercise outfit. "You wouldn't want to run on a full stomach."

She waved a hand dismissively toward the guest-room door she'd left moments earlier and lowered her voice. "I wasn't really planning to go for a run. But Ken is constantly telling me I'm getting too fat. So I have to put these things on and get out at the crack of dawn to make him think I'm exercising. Now, you tell me, do you see an ounce of fat on this body?"

Ian passed on her offer of a perusal.

"This Ken is your boyfriend?" he asked, turning his attention instead to Jade. The child was still tense and uncomfortable. He wondered if his earlier questions or the arrival of Ash were the cause of it. He picked up the books and puzzles and the game.

She gave a bored shrug. "We've been going out together for a while, but he's more like the photographer, manager, pain-in-my-behind type of guy. He's no fun at all." They descended the first set of steps. "So…are you up here alone?"

Ian recognized the "I'm interested" signal. He wasn't, though. He was far from impressed with her.

"Yes and no," he answered as they reached the parlor. "I'm here visiting friends."

"Really? Who?"

"Kelly and Jade." He looked down at the child to

see the twinkle of approval in her green eyes. "And we've got ourselves a heck of a day scheduled. So...enjoy your breakfast."

It was a kiss-off, but she was too dense or too stubborn or too unfamiliar with rejection to realize it. She stood there for a few seconds looking at him with a peculiar smile on her lips. Ash was definitely not accustomed to getting the brush-off from men.

"You're not having any breakfast?" she asked finally.

"Not now. Maybe a little later. Enjoy."

With a polite nod, he let Jade pull him toward the sitting area, where they deposited her puzzles and books on an end table.

"So, is she still standing there?" he asked the little girl, not wanting to turn around and look himself.

"I think she's mad," Jade whispered, a look of mischief coming into her face. "She just stomped out the front door."

Ian looked over his shoulder and saw the door close behind the woman.

"I think Mommy's mad, too," Jade warned in a hushed tone.

Ian's gaze drifted to the office. The door was partially closed. Inside, he could see Janice and Dan parked on chairs behind the desk, while Kelly paced back and forth in the little space on the other side of the desk. She was talking nonstop. There was no mistaking it. She was seething.

Ian had no clue what that was all about. But if the

time had come for putting that old dragon Janice in
her place, then he was all for it.

Shawn Hobart, the disagreeable antique dealer who
was missing the biggest estate auction on the East
Coast—if the boys from Philly were to be believed—
was leaving the dining area. He stood in the doorway
to the porch exchanging a few private words with
Rita. Ian felt Jade edge closer to his side. Her little
fingers came up and disappeared inside his hand. He
looked down to see what was bothering the child now.
She was looking straight at Rita and Hobart.

The alleged antique dealer finished whatever he
was saying and stepped into the parlor. Seeing them,
he returned Ian's nod with a surly one of his own.
The man's gaze, though, moved immediately to Jade.
The child practically crawled inside Ian's skin in her
attempt to hide.

Propriety be damned, Ian decided, lifting Jade in
his arms. She wrapped her hands tightly around his
neck and hid her face against his throat. She was shivering.

This was too much. No child should be so nervous
in her own home. Ian found himself growing angry,
but Hobart quickly crossed the parlor without stopping and went out the same door through which the
model had disappeared a few minutes earlier.

"He's gone," Ian whispered to the child in his
arms.

It took Jade a few seconds to build her courage and
lift her head off his shoulder. She looked pale, and

she was still trembling. Her green eyes searched the dining room, parlor and sitting room.

"What was that about?" Ian asked gently.

She was quiet. Her grip around his neck was still tight.

"Come on, Jade," he persisted, looking into her face. "You don't have to be afraid of anything, honey. I'm a pretty tough Cookie Monster. I can crush all the guys you're scared of with one hand."

Jade looked at Ian carefully. She glanced down at how far above the ground he was holding her. Her expression was very serious when she finally looked up. "There's a lot of them."

He made a fierce face. "I can handle all of them."

After another look around the room, she leaned closer and whispered into his ear. "He was there, too. That man was at the camp."

Eleven

Janice was staring at her as if she were seeing Kelly for the first time—or as if she were looking at some monster that had suddenly sprung out of the ground. Dan's expression was blank and unreadable. Kelly wasn't sure if she'd gotten through to either of them at all.

She wanted one of them to take responsibility, to say they'd goofed. But more importantly, she wanted one of these two people to think back and remember Lauren Wells. Janice went through the reservation book front to back, and there was nothing that indicated the missing woman had even called.

Seeing the two of them together in the office, though, Kelly had another thought. She wouldn't put it past either of them to mess up the registration just to get the other in hot water.

There had been a peeing contest going on between these two from the moment Kelly had hired Dan for the summer. They just couldn't seem to get along. Janice made it clear more than once that she thought it was a waste of money to have the college kid at Tranquillity Inn. Dan claimed the older woman went out of her way to be difficult, finding fault with whatever he did. And working behind the desk had only provided one small incident. She'd found reason to complain about everything he did or didn't do.

Well, Kelly was just about fed up with it, and she let them have it with both barrels, even though she had a feeling Janice was more at fault than Dan. The young man had much thicker skin, though, and he wasn't entirely innocent, anyway. It was just the beginning of their summer season. She wasn't going to go through the next three months like this. Something had to change.

"So what do you want us to do?" Dan said finally, sounding bored. "Kiss and make up?"

Janice pushed her seat away from him to show she was revolted by the very idea of it.

"This is not elementary school. I don't particularly care if you two continue to hate each other's guts," Kelly said hotly. "But this is a place of business. I expect professionalism. I expect courtesy. But most importantly, I expect accuracy and accountability for what we do. This thing…this mess-up with the reservation of Lauren Wells is more serious than either of you know."

"Even if she had a reservation with us—speaking hypothetically—and it was *our* mistake for overbooking…" Janice sent a meaningful glare at Dan. "This woman never showed up at the inn. It's really not our problem, Kelly."

"Janice, a seventy-seven-year-old woman is missing," Kelly said angrily. "This could have been you."

The roll of the eyes was a typical Janice response, and it fired up Kelly's temper more.

"I'm not joking," she snapped. "We're talking about the well-being of a real person. And we compounded the problem at every step."

"I don't see how we—"

"How about these missing messages? This woman's niece told me that Lauren had left a number of messages for me. I never got any of them."

"I'm not the only one who answers the phone around here," Janice said, looking over the rim of her pink frames. "Did they say *when* she called? It could have been off-season. Rita answers the phone all the time when we aren't too busy. Even Wilson picks up in the kitchen when no one is downstairs. Or Bill. He could have taken the call…and you know how he is about writing anything down."

"I was standing right here last night when you brushed off the woman's niece on the phone," Kelly said tensely. "You didn't even try to help her."

"I thought they had the wrong number," she said defensively, her voice quavering. "I made a mistake. After putting in fourteen hours at that desk, anyone could be a little tired and cranky. I'm sorry if I was a little abrupt. I'm sorry that your friend is missing. But she'll show up. So I think you're fussing over nothing."

There were no two ways about it. Kelly no longer trusted Janice—or anything she said or did. She reminded herself this had been coming for a while. But old loyalties had made her ignore it. She took a deep breath now. She wouldn't do anything rash. But she had to make her plans. The inn would go on sale this summer. She had to get out of here before she went crazy.

Dan pulled the brim of his baseball cap around to the side. "I'd like to stay here and listen to you two chat. But the Stern kids warned me yesterday that they'd be out there after breakfast to take out a couple of boats again."

Kelly gave Dan a resigned nod. He wasn't the problem, and they both knew it. She stood back and let the young man leave the office. Janice held on to the handle of her cane and pushed herself to her feet.

"Janice," she said when they were alone. "Do you know if anyone was in here this morning? Cleaning up, maybe?"

The older woman looked at the desk and then back at Kelly.

"Of course. Bill made his rounds and emptied all the trash cans downstairs. Why?"

There was no point in pursuing this, Kelly told herself. There was no way she would get a straight answer to any question that she asked.

"I need a few things changed around here right away," she told Janice before the woman went on her way. "Calls. There's a pink pad on your desk. Any calls for me—or for any of the guests here—I want them to go on one of those slips."

Janice nodded, not seemingly bothered by the request.

"And the mail," Kelly continued. "From now on, no one goes through the mail before me."

"No problem," Janice said in a hurt tone as she headed for the door. "I've only been trying to help."

Ian saw Dan leave the small office first. The college kid gave Jade a wink and nodded to Ian before turning down the back hallway and leaving the inn. Janice and Kelly stood near the open door, and the older woman looked eager to leave.

"I think we should get your mom to take a little break for breakfast," he told Jade, putting her back on the floor. "Why don't you go and get her as soon as Janice is out of the office." He gave the little girl's shoulder a gentle squeeze. "And don't take no for an answer."

She nodded enthusiastically and ran toward the office. The youngest of the Stern boys was leaving the dining room ahead of his family.

"Wait for us at the door, Ryan," his mother called, exchanging a few words with her husband and older son.

The boy was looking into Kelly's office as he went by. Ian saw the collision coming, but there was no time to warn either of them. The two children bumped into each other. Jade, being less than half Ryan's size, landed squarely on her tail. The book Ryan was carrying under one arm fell to the floor, and a couple of papers and what looked to be a black-and-white picture spilled out of the pages.

Ian, going to help Jade up, saw the little girl pounce

on the photograph. The boy immediately wrenched
the picture out of her hand and stuffed it back into
the pages of his book.

"That's *mine!*" Jade cried out, clearly upset.

Ryan stood up and took a step back.

"Mine!" Jade shouted louder, on the verge of
tears.

Ian checked her out. She didn't seem to have any
bumps or bruises. She jumped to her feet, looking
fiercely at Ryan.

"Give it to me," she demanded.

Ian straightened up and turned to see Ryan's parents had joined their son. He was half hidden behind
the father. The older brother was just disappearing up
the back steps.

Jade tugged on Ian's hand. "My mommy's picture," she cried. "I want it back."

Ian looked at Rob and Rachel Stern. She had a hand
wrapped on her son's shoulder in a protective gesture.
The father stepped in front of them in a more combative stance. Ian eyed him carefully, feeling his own
fighting instincts rising to the surface and working to
control them. He knew he could subdue Stern in a
moment, but he didn't want to inflame the situation.

"Would you mind letting her see that picture for a
second?" Ian said in a reasonable tone to the son.
"She thought it was a picture of her mother. If you
could let her see it again, she'd realize she made a
mistake."

Ryan said nothing but shrank farther behind his
father.

"She'd better watch where she's going," Rob Stern said, pointing an accusing finger at Jade. "The little...she just ran into him."

"Relax, pal," Ian said less patiently, straightening to his full height. "This wasn't a traffic accident. And these two appear to have survived just fine. She just wants to take a second peek at whoever's picture that was that your son had tucked in his book."

"Is everything okay here?" Kelly asked softly, stepping between the two men.

"Mommy! He has your picture in that book."

Jade ran to her mother and raised her arms. Kelly picked her up.

"She's my mommy," she announced loudly to Ryan. "Mine!"

"Whoa! Slow down, kids," Rachel Stern said in a motherly tone, turning to Kelly. "We had a little collision here and a mix-up about...I don't know what. But it's all over now."

"Okay," Kelly said, looking up at the two men.

Stern stepped back and turned to his son. "You all right, Ryan?"

"Of course he is," Mrs. Stern replied. "Well, our older boy is dying to go canoeing. We promised to get some in this morning."

With a nod to Kelly, she ushered her family ahead of her toward the door leading to the lake.

Ian said nothing but watched them go, noticing that the book Ryan had been carrying was nowhere to be seen.

* * *

The two gray unmarked cars stopped where the camp driveway made a turn into the small, unpaved parking lot. The state troopers in each car looked down into the tidy camp before getting out of the car. While the two troopers in the second car remained by their vehicle and scanned the center of the camp, Ramathorn and Farva put on their wide-brimmed hats and started down the path toward the lake.

To his left, Ramathorn eyed the array of long cabins that formed a semicircle around the center of the camp. To his right, the largest building, which was undoubtedly the dining hall, sat up on a small hill overlooking the center. Beyond it, completing the arc of buildings that ended at the lake, he saw a cluster of cabins and two buildings clearly marked as the administration cabin and the infirmary. In front of him, as he and his partner walked down the slight incline toward the lake, rows and rows of benches surrounded a newly built, covered stage.

People who looked like normal tourists, separated into groups of children and adults, watched the state troopers from open areas in front of the cabins. Though everyone's eyes were on them now, the younger groups had obviously been working on a variety of craft projects. Older kids and adults were supervising, and other groups of adults were sitting around in circles on camp chairs.

No one was down at the small sandy beach, and no one was out on the water in any boats. A light mist was rising from the lake, but Ramathorn could see the sun shining on the water beyond. It all looked quite normal, and as they passed, each group was gently steered back to their tasks by their leader.

A small assembly of men and women, clipboards in hand, stood between the covered stage and the first rows of benches. They all turned as the uniformed troopers approached.

"Morning," Ramathorn said cheerfully. Farva nodded, standing behind him and saying nothing.

"Morning," a number of them responded.

One of the men—white, about fifty, brown eyes, curly black hair, five-ten and weighing maybe two-fifty—stepped forward and held out his meaty hand. It was a powerful grip. "I'm Joshua Sharpe, Officer. What can we do for the New Hampshire State Police?"

"Well, we're out on a routine drive-through. We like to visit the summer camps in our area when we can, just to make sure everything is going okay, and to let you know we're here if you need us. Are you the camp director?"

"As a matter of fact, I am."

"You look familiar to me. Live around here?"

"All my life," Sharpe said. "My family's been in this area for five generations. I own the property this camp stands on."

"I thought so." Ramathorn looked at the group standing behind him. "So what kind of camp you running here? I seem to remember there were just kids here last summer."

"Well, that's right," Sharpe answered. "But I also happen to be a deacon in a church that decided to take over the camp for the summer. We intend to bring up different groups of our congregation for a week at a time. These are some of the ministers of the church." The director turned and introduced each of the men and women.

"Well, it's always nice to have churchgoing folk in the area. A lot easier on us than the white supremacists and the biker groups we sometimes get."

The ministers laughed, and Ramathorn nodded at the banner hanging at the rear of the Pavilion.

"What's the name of your church, Mr. Sharpe, if you don't mind me asking? That's not a logo I've seen before."

Several members of the group turned and looked at the banner.

"We're a small but growing church called the Ministry of the Divine Blood. We're a kind of charismatic Christian sect, you might say."

"So, you'll be having Bible meetings at night?"

Joshua Sharpe looked at the troopers with concern. "Yes, we will be. There shouldn't be any problem with that. Is there?"

"Not at all," Ramathorn watched the relief register on the faces. "I was just thinking this is a great week to get started. The weather looks good till the end of the week, at least."

One of the younger ministers, a blond-haired, athletic-looking kid who'd been introduced as Caleb

Smith, stepped forward. "We're just hoping the temperature warms up a little. The kids are looking forward to doing some swimming during the day."

"The group would like to make some use of the lake," Sharpe added.

"I noticed you haven't got any boats," the state trooper commented, motioning toward the empty canoe racks.

"They should be arriving in a day or two," the blue-eyed young man chipped in. "The boat outfitters are a little behind in getting the canoes and kayaks out to us."

"Well, that should make everyone happy," Ramathorn said. "Mind if we look around the camp?"

"Not at all." Sharpe gestured with his hand. "I'd be happy to show you around."

Leading the way, the camp director took the troopers through the grounds, showing them all the main buildings, and taking them into a number of the large cabins. Everything was neat and tidy. The dining room was spotless, and they looked in on the kitchen crew, who were busy finishing up the breakfast dishes and preparing for lunch. The infirmary was staffed by a rather gruff RN, who ushered them through without any ceremony.

In all, the camp looked like any other summer camp. As they came out of the director's office, where Joshua Sharpe retrieved a business card for the troopers, Ramathorn watched the young man named Caleb organizing a bunch of kids into a kickball game in a small clearing near the dining hall.

"Thanks, Mr. Sharpe," Ramathorn said, pulling a card out of his shirt pocket. "Here's the number for the barracks in Twin Mountain. If there's anything you need, any problems, don't hesitate to call. We generally have a car up in this area."

"Thank you—" Sharpe looked at the card "—Trooper Ramathorn. We should be fine, but I appreciate you stopping by."

"Just curious, but are you having any special speakers in to address the group? I love a good fire-and-brimstone sermon now and again."

Joshua Sharpe stared at him for a moment, then smiled. "We have a number of fine ministers who will be leading us in prayer, though no one you'd know. Wednesdays will be our lecture nights. So, if you'd like to come by some Wednesday, we'd love to have you."

"Well, maybe I'll just take you up on it. I'm working the next few nights down by North Conway, but this Wednesday could work out perfect. Thanks."

"We'll look forward to it."

As Ramathorn started to turn away, the trooper's gaze fell on a group of cabins they hadn't gone near.

"What are those used for, Mr. Sharpe?"

The camp director turned and looked at the buildings Ramathorn was eyeing. "Those? Those are counselors' cabins. The ministers who are running this particular group are living in them. Not much of interest there, I'd say."

"Well, thanks again for your hospitality and the invite. Have a great day."

As the two troopers walked back to the cars, Ramathorn felt the eyes of the entire camp on them. Waving to a group of kids, he nodded to his backup troopers, and they all hopped into their cars. In a minute they were riding through the woods back to the main road.

"You see anything?" he asked his partner.

"Nothing," Farva said, reaching for the radio. "No sign of him yet."

Twelve

Even though the sun was just getting high enough in the sky to make the day pleasant, Kelly still forced Jade into a sweatshirt. Then, the three of them took their breakfast trays and went outside.

Eating on the deck wouldn't really do. She wanted to go somewhere else, away from prying eyes at the inn. Walking across the grass, Kelly led the way to a picnic table wedged between the edge of the woods and the end of the small sandy beach. The spot was sheltered from the wind, and it was also cut off from the inn by a grove of trees. This was a favorite place for her and Jade to come in the summer months, and Kelly kept a closed wooden bin with all types of sand toys for her daughter beside the picnic table.

Delighted to be out, Jade was far more interested in playing than eating. Still, Kelly managed to win another battle, getting her daughter to eat a small bowl of cereal before she ran off to play in the sand.

Ian sat next to her on the bench, both of them facing the lake. Jade played in the sand not far from them. Neither Ian nor Kelly was very interested in the French toast they'd brought out. There was a deep furrow creasing his forehead. She didn't think he was quite over the little spat with Rob Stern. Frankly, she wasn't over her talk with Janice, either.

"How much do you know about what's going on over there?" he asked, motioning in the direction of the camp on the far side of the lake.

"I haven't heard much about it this year, other than that it's already opened up for the season." She looked at his jaw flex tightly. "You were with me when the van showed up last night, and those people wanted to get their things."

"Have you been over there at all?"

"The first summer Jade and I moved back, I took the wrong turn off the main road once and ended up at that camp," Kelly replied. "There were about a hundred teenage boys staying there. But I don't think the same group leases the camp every year. Why do you ask?"

"Cassy took Jade there yesterday," he said in a lower tone, so the little girl wouldn't hear him.

Worry quickly knotted Kelly's stomach. "How do you know?"

"She told me," he said, looking at the child and motioning toward her. "She also said that there were a lot of people there that she didn't like."

"What…what else did she say?" she asked, forcing herself to stay calm. "What did she and Cassy do there?"

Ian shook his head. "I don't know. I think she was scared more than anything."

"She doesn't like strangers," Kelly said, already knowing a phone call to the baby-sitter would be the first thing she'd be doing when they got back to the house.

"I've seen her shy away from the other guests."

"Cassy should have told me about it," she whispered more to herself than to Ian. "Now I'm not surprised that Jade was so tired last night."

"There's something else, too." He took a swallow of his coffee. "I think some of your guests at the inn this weekend might be part of whatever is going on over there."

"That's happened before," she said, looking at her daughter again. "Janice told me we've regularly had nervous parents stay with us whose kids were campers."

"Did you know your guests that are here now are connected with the camp?"

"No, but I wouldn't ask, anyway. I mean, people could have any number of reasons for staying here." She bumped her cup against his. "Look at you...what would a hotshot cop from San Diego be doing all alone at Tranquillity Inn?"

The threat of a smile softened his intense black eyes. "How do you know I'm a hotshot?"

"I don't know." She studied his face. The high intelligent forehead. The age lines around his dark eyes. The long lashes. The solid square jaw. The hard lips that she'd tasted so briefly last night. "Jade and I can both tell that you're special. So, now you've got me curious. What *are* you doing here?"

Kelly was unprepared when his lips closed the few inches between them and sealed hers with a kiss. Un-

like last night though, her response was quick, her
reaction passionate. It'd been too long since anyone
touched her like this—it felt like forever since she
felt wanted by a man. She poured all her loneliness
into kissing him back.

Ian's strong hand slipped around her, caressing her
back. He drew her tighter against his side. His other
hand cupped her cheek. He tilted her head and deepened the kiss until her mind emptied of everything
but him. Her body molded softly to his.

She was burning inside and out when he finally
ended the kiss. He continued to hold her close, looking into her eyes in a way that made her heart squeeze
with a strange ache. There was something between
them. Something more. She didn't understand it. He
didn't say it. But it was there, just beneath the surface.
They were connected in some way. She knew it.

"Ian?" she whispered.

His hand dropped from her face, and his gaze
turned to Jade. She had both feet—shoes and socks
and all—buried in the sand. Seemingly unaware of
what had taken place behind her, the little girl was
closing her eyes and tossing sand into the air, where
it rained down onto her head.

"You're going to get sand in your eyes, honey."

"No, I won't, Mommy."

A hundred questions were battering at Kelly's
mind. There was so much that she wanted to know
about him. She couldn't bring herself to ask any of
the questions, though. His past was a mystery to
her…as hers was to him. And she understood better

than anyone about keeping certain parts of the past buried.

He toyed with his food. Took a couple of bites. Kelly tried to clear her mind of him. They still sat hip to hip, their legs, their arms and shoulders touching. There was a high-voltage sexual charge running between them, and she could feel its impact from the inside out.

Jade looked over her shoulder and gave Kelly a happy smile. This helped her focus. She slid down the bench a few inches.

No matter what she was feeling now, Ian had arrived yesterday and would be gone out of their lives tomorrow or the day after. But the woman who had given Kelly a second chance at life was missing and perhaps in trouble. Before coming out, Kelly had called back Lauren's niece. She'd shared her own frustration in not being able to find anything yet. She'd encouraged the niece to call the police...and anyone else she could think of. It would be better for all of them to be searching, even if it turned out to be that Lauren had somehow ended up at one of the other inns in the area.

"Can I...can I ask you a police-procedure question?" Kelly asked, pushing the plate away and wrapping her hand around the cold glass of juice she'd brought out with her.

"Go ahead."

She took a sip of the juice, moved a couple more inches away, and turned toward him slightly. "I found myself in the middle of a strange situation this morning when I came downstairs. I had a call from a relative of one of our guests…well, a would-be guest that didn't show up here and that we weren't even expecting.''

''There seems to be a problem with unexpected guests.''

''That was why I was reading the riot act to Janice and Dan in the office this morning.'' Kelly went on to explain to him everything that had been said in the phone call. She also told him of Janice and Dan's refusal to admit they'd had anything to do with the situation.

''And this woman, Lauren Wells, is a friend of yours?''

''Yes…yes, she is definitely a friend to me.'' Kelly nodded, working hard not to allow her emotions to overwhelm her. As far as she knew, Lauren was fine. She needed Ian's help, though—at least, suggestions about what to do next. ''I haven't seen her or heard from her for over twenty years, but I'm sure this has to be the same person. The Lauren I knew would be in her late seventies now, and she's the only person by that name that I've ever known.''

''Was there a reason why anyone at the inn would not pass on any messages from the woman?''

Kelly shook her head. ''None of them would even know who she is…or what connection she had with me.''

''What connection *did* she have with you?'' he asked.

Kelly looked at her daughter on the sandy beach. Her past was not something that she explained to people. It was not part of who she was to feel comfortable talking about herself or her life…ever. She was a cult-suicide survivor. One of four. Other than the social workers who had placed her, and Frank and Rose Wilton who had became her adoptive parents, nobody else knew. Kelly had not even told the truth to Greg, her husband. As far as he knew, she was adopted through the system at a young age. The chapter of her life up to age twelve was closed, and she never intended to open it again.

"Old family friend," Kelly finally answered Ian. "We lost touch over the years."

Ian looked at her steadily before continuing. "And the woman's niece was certain that she didn't know why Lauren was trying to contact you or why she was coming here?"

"If she knew anything, she wasn't saying," Kelly admitted, not entirely comfortable with that conversation, either.

"Do you have a number for Lauren Wells? A way to contact her?"

"Why?"

"Because maybe this whole thing is bogus. Who knows? Maybe this niece is not for real."

"I have a hard time imagining anyone going through all this trouble. And what would they hope to gain by it? She sounded very upset," Kelly argued, shaking her head and planting her elbows on the table. "Assuming there is a problem, what are the steps that should be taken? What should Lauren's family do? What can I do?"

"They should call anyone and everyone who Lauren knows. Friends. Family. Everybody. It's too early yet to file a missing person report. Without some indication of foul play, I doubt the state police will do anything about it. But a phone call wouldn't hurt. At least they'll keep an eye open for her. Also, her niece could make a call to whatever credit card company she uses and find out where and when she made the last charges to the card. The same goes with her ATM card. But again, unless the niece is a cosigner on the account, she might get a runaround."

"Is there anything I could do from this end?"

"If, in fact, Lauren Wells did get off the bus at Independence, then she needed a way to get from point A to point B. Is there a taxi service or any sort of local transportation around here?"

"I don't think so. I mean, who would need it?"

"Is there any snack shop at the bus stop in Independence?"

"There's a little convenience store and a coffee shop kind of place."

"Maybe they saw her get off."

"I'll call them both."

"Also, her family can pressure the bus company to tell them if there were others who got off the bus at Independence. Getting names and addresses is a long shot, but it's possible she befriended somebody on the bus who gave her a ride."

Kelly rubbed an ache on her temple. "I probably wouldn't be as nervous if she were twenty years old.

Then I'd think maybe she just took off with some guy for a crazy weekend.''

"Maybe she's gone off on a spiritual retreat for the weekend," he said in a matter-of-fact tone. He looked at the lake. "Is that camp over there the only one of its kind around here?"

"I don't even know who's there this year. I have no clue if they're adults or kids or teenagers."

Ian looked at Jade again. She was now lying down and drawing patterns in the sand with her fingers.

"What Jade said makes me think there are some adults over there. And if we assume people were arriving yesterday, it could very well be that some of them might have been on the same bus as Lauren." He motioned with his cup toward the fog at the end of the lake. "There might be someone right over there who saw her...or even better, you might find Lauren safe and sound."

Kelly looked across the water. She'd met Joshua Sharpe a few times, but she had never tried to establish any kind of rapport with the owner or the summer camp personnel. Still, she let her neighbor store things at her place for safekeeping every winter. There was no reason why they shouldn't try to help her. "I think I'll take a drive over and see them. It wouldn't hurt to ask a few questions."

"If you want, I can go for you."

She put her hand on top of his. "You'd really do that for me?"

"Absolutely," he replied softly. "And it wouldn't be only for you."

* * *

"Last time we were here, I kicked myself for not getting a few shots of Ash with the lake and fog as a backdrop."

"No big loss," Ian muttered to himself. He wasn't happy that the four of them had ended up riding over to the camp together, and he didn't mind if the photographer knew it, either.

Kelly had suggested having Bill Maitland take Ian over, since the older man had already been to the camp a couple of times this weekend and had met some of the new people there. This was fine with Ian. He'd been looking for a chance to meet and talk to Bill, anyway.

As they were getting into Kelly's four-wheel drive, though, Ash and Ken Burke had come striding across the parking area. Two camera bags swung from the photographer's shoulder. Bill apparently knew about the extra people they were taking over, which turned out to be the reason they were taking Kelly's car.

After quick introductions, Ash took the seat behind Bill, and Ian sat in front. He could tell that she was back into her ice-princess mode. But her outfit and the way she'd touched his palm when they shook hands were clearly intended to send a different message. She was wearing a sleeveless, black lace bodysuit with a V-neck that plunged nearly to her waist, and a sheer black wraparound skirt that mostly trailed behind rather than covered her miles of legs. Ian worried about Bill having a heart attack before they got there.

OFFICIAL OPINION POLL

Dear Reader,

Since you are a book enthusiast, we would like to know what you think.

Inside you will find a short Opinion Poll. Please participate in our poll by sharing your opinion on 3 subjects that are very important to all of us.

To thank you for your participation, we would like to send you your choice of **2 FREE BOOKS** and a **FREE GIFT!**

Please enjoy them with our compliments,

Sincerely,

Pam Powers

Editor

P.S. Don't forget to indicate which books you prefer so we can send your FREE gifts today!

What's your pleasure...

Romance?

Enjoy 2 FREE BOOKS that will fuel your imagination with intensely moving stories about life, love and relationships.

OR

Suspense?

Enjoy 2 FREE BOOKS that will thrill you with a spine-tingling blend of suspense and mystery.

✔ Whichever category you select, your **2 FREE BOOKS** have a combined cover price of $11.98 or more in the U.S. and $13.98 or more in Canada.

Simply place the sticker next to your preferred choice of books, complete the poll on the right page and you'll automatically receive **2 FREE BOOKS** and a **FREE GIFT** with no obligation to purchase anything!

We'll send you a wonderful surprise gift, ABSOLUTELY FREE, just for trying our books! Don't miss out — MAIL THE REPLY CARD TODAY!

Visit us online at
www.FreeBooksandGift.com

YOUR OPINION POLL
THANK-YOU FREE GIFTS INCLUDE

▶ **2 ROMANCE OR 2 SUSPENSE BOOKS**

▶ **A LOVELY SURPRISE GIFT**

DETACH AND MAIL CARD TODAY!

OFFICIAL OPINION POLL

YOUR OPINION COUNTS!

Please check TRUE or FALSE below to express your opinion about the following statements:

Q1 Do you believe in "true love"?

"TRUE LOVE HAPPENS ONLY ONCE IN A LIFETIME."
○ TRUE
○ FALSE

Q2 Do you think marriage has any value in today's world?

"YOU CAN BE TOTALLY COMMITTED TO SOMEONE WITHOUT BEING MARRIED."
○ TRUE
○ FALSE

Q3 What kind of books do you enjoy?

"A GREAT NOVEL MUST HAVE A HAPPY ENDING."
○ TRUE
○ FALSE

Place the sticker next to one of the selections below to receive your **2 FREE BOOKS** and **FREE GIFT**. I understand that I am under no obligation to purchase anything as explained on the back of this card.

Romance

193 MDL DVFS
393 MDL DVFU

Suspense

192 MDL DVFR
392 MDL DVFT

0074823 ‖‖‖▌‖‖▌‖‖ ‖‖▌‖‖‖ ‖‖▌‖‖ FREE GIFT CLAIM # **3622**

FIRST NAME	LAST NAME

ADDRESS

APT.#	CITY

STATE/PROV.	ZIP/POSTAL CODE

(BB3-04)

The Reader Service — Here's How It Works:

Accepting your 2 free books and gift places you under no obligation to buy anything. You may keep the books and gift and return the shipping statement marked "cancel." If you do not cancel, about a month later we'll send you 3 additional books and bill you just $4.74 each in the U.S., or $5.24 each in Canada, plus 25¢ shipping & handling per book and applicable taxes if any.* That's the complete price, and — compared to cover prices of $5.99 or more each in the U.S. and $6.99 or more each in Canada — it's quite a bargain! You may cancel at any time, but if you choose to continue, every month we'll send you 3 more books, which you may either purchase at the discount price...or return to us and cancel your subscription.

*Terms and prices subject to change without notice. Sales tax applicable in N.Y.
Canadian residents will be charged applicable provincial taxes and GST.

If offer card is missing write to: The Reader Service, 3010 Walden Ave., P.O. Box 1867, Buffalo NY 14240-1867

BUSINESS REPLY MAIL
FIRST-CLASS MAIL   PERMIT NO. 717-003   BUFFALO, NY

POSTAGE WILL BE PAID BY ADDRESSEE

THE READER SERVICE
3010 WALDEN AVE
PO BOX 1867
BUFFALO NY 14240-9952

NO POSTAGE
NECESSARY
IF MAILED
IN THE
UNITED STATES

"I love the look of this fog," Ken Burke continued, apparently unperturbed by Ian's attitude. "Twenty years looking through a lens and I've never seen anything like it. This is certainly a chance I'm not going to pass up again."

"So you've been doing this for a long time?" Ian asked. He figured the short, muscular guy's age to be early forties—making him twenty-odd years older than Ash.

"Sure have. Always had an eye for beauty."

"Or is it for the close-up?" Ian asked, turning in his seat and looking at Burke.

"So you've seen my work."

"Not really. But seeing all those lenses, I'm guessing."

"Well, for me that's where the real beauty is. The closer you look, the more a subject's beauty emerges," Burke replied, meeting Ash's gaze as she looked over at him. "As a man, you must appreciate that."

"As a cop, I have a little difficulty with that," Ian commented. "In my business, the closer you look, the more a subject's guilt emerges. But I will concede that one or two good close-ups of a crime scene are more effective in court than almost any testimony."

"So I heard correctly. You're a cop," Ken said.

Ian pinned him with a direct look. "Heard correctly from who?"

The man's face went blank. He clearly wasn't certain if he'd admitted something he shouldn't have.

"Shawn Hobart told me," Ash said, leaning forward and putting her arm up on the back of Bill's seat. From his vantage point, Ian could have seen everything of interest all the way to her navel. "You ate dinner with him last night."

"And you and Shawn are old friends?" he asked, raising an eyebrow but not looking down the path she wanted him to travel.

"We met for the first time this morning…when I went running," she said, looking out the front window and moving her arm in a way that pulled the lacy fabric back. The dark edge of her nipple emerged.

Bill—trying to get a good look in the rearview mirror—missed driving around a pothole, and the car jerked, bouncing everyone in their seats. Ash, who was not wearing a seat belt, almost landed on the floor.

"Sorry," the old man grumbled, turning his attention back to the gravel road.

"Shawn Hobart didn't strike me as an athletic sort of guy," Ian pressed. "I can't imagine how you got him to put in a mile or two in gray flannels and boat shoes."

A deep blush darkened her cheeks. "No wonder you're stressed out at your job. You can't carry on a simple conversation without becoming offensive."

With a huff, she sat back in her seat as Bill turned onto a dirt road.

Ian was on a roll, though, and he wasn't going to give up now. He looked over at Bill Maitland. "So who are the people who've taken the camp this year?''

The old man went around another pothole. "It's the owner of the camp himself, Josh Sharpe."

"You know anything about him?"

"He's a young fella," Bill said, glancing at Ian. "Well, maybe a few years older than you. Family was from around here. From what I hear, he don't work. Just lives on whatever was left to him by his parents."

"A lot of money?"

"Don't know, exactly." Bill darted a glance in the mirror at the two in the back seat. "Old money, anyway. In fact, at one time the lake and everything around it was theirs, including the—"

"Look, Ken," Ash interrupted, pointing at a section of the lake coming into view through a large gap in the trees. "Maybe we should stop here and take some pictures."

"Not on my time," Ian said shortly. He turned his attention back to Bill, who suddenly appeared amused at the way they were getting along. "So the Sharpe family owned the inn before Kelly's parents bought it?"

"Josh Sharpe converted it, renovated it, and got it going."

"That right?"

Bill nodded. "I used to work for him. Janice and me both. We ran the inn for him."

Ian wasn't sure if Kelly knew this or not. "Why did he sell?"

The old man shrugged. "I think it was too much of a headache for him. He had no interest in running it. So he put the place up for sale, and it sold. Just like that."

Ian saw Ken pull his camera from one of the bags, and start taking pictures of Ash's profile as the car rolled down the road.

"What's with all the astrology stuff?" Ian asked. The camera stopped clicking for a moment. "How come all the rooms have plaques and zodiac names?"

"We're staying in the Sagittarius Room. That's the zodiac sign for my birthday," Ash put in, leaning forward again. Obviously, she'd forgotten that he'd hurt her feelings before.

"Half human, half beast...but watch out for the arrows," Ian replied.

"I'd definitely watch out for the arrows, if I were you," she said, sitting back and crossing her arms.

Ian turned to Bill again. "So what about the astrology stuff?"

The old man let out a long breath. "Well, it all started with Mrs. Sharpe, Joshua's mother. She was into those things big-time, and years ago—when the inn was only being used as a summer home—she even had a planetarium and a calculation room here." He kept both hands on the wheel, going around a bend. "My Janice picked up where the old woman left off. She can really get into it deep, if you talk to her...well, if she likes you."

"She knows her stuff," Burke asserted. "You tell

her your birthday, exactly when and where you were born, and she can lay out your whole life story.''

This was the last thing Ian needed right now... someone laying out his life story.

Bill turned onto another gravel road, which brought them almost immediately to an unpaved parking lot. There were only a couple of cars there.

Ian's gaze lifted from the lot to the rows of cabins. A white-haired woman was stepping out of the cabin nearest them, and Ian tried to recollect everything he knew about Lauren Wells. He'd asked Kelly if she had a picture. She'd thought she might have an old one, but she couldn't put her hand on it this morning.

''So, Bill, you're going to get someone to give us a fifty-cent tour of this place?'' Ken asked, getting his equipment out of the car.

Ian didn't hear the older man's answer. His attention was solely focused on the rows and rows of benches around the front of a newly built covered stage by the edge of the lake. From the rafters above the stage, a rolled-up banner of some kind had been hung.

His blood ran cold, though, when he saw a large baptismal font on the stage.

''I told Rita to let everyone know at breakfast, I'm only serving dinner until eight o'clock tonight,'' Wilson told Kelly. They were standing in the back hallway, and he was blocking her path to the stairs. ''The kitchen is shutting down completely at nine.''

"That's perfectly all right," Kelly told the cook, trying to keep a wiggly Jade under one arm and keep her laptop tucked under the other.

"You need a hand?"

"No thanks, I'm fine. I've got to get her upstairs, though, or this sand is going to be everywhere," she told Wilson, going past him and starting the long climb up the steep staircase.

Jade had sand in her ears, in her nose, and in her hair. Kelly stripped the little girl's clothes off and put her right in the shower the moment she got to her apartment.

As she sat in the bathroom and kept an eye on her daughter, Kelly booted up her laptop. She wanted to dig out Lauren's address and a picture. She knew she had them in a file she'd saved. But Ian's question about how the two of them were connected had thrown her for a loop.

Kelly's memories of her childhood—of her first twelve years of life—were dreamlike and surreal. What she recalled most was the frequent moving from place to place with a group of people who never seemed to have private houses or backyards or swing sets for their children. There were no fathers who went to work or mothers who walked you to a school bus stop. When she was very young, school consisted of tutoring in small groups with kids who were constantly coming and going. There were no real brothers or sisters.

When she got older and had to go to the public schools, she was so different. For her, there were no soccer games or swimming lessons. No vacations. No having your own clothes or shoes. No having anything to say about what you wore. Nothing that made her feel like the other ten-, eleven- and twelve-year-old girls that she watched enviously in the halls at school. Or read about in books. Or heard the new kids at the camp talk about.

If Kelly ever had a life outside of the Butler Mission, she had no recollection of it. Her earliest memory was a time when she must have been around three years old and sick with a sore throat and fever. At the time, the group was living in a cluster of gray ranch buildings in a desolate place near a big city. They moved her from her bunk room with the other kids to a special room where a couple of the other sick children were kept. She still remembered waking up in the middle of the night and hearing someone sitting next to her on the bed. The woman was young and pretty and had big green eyes the same shade as her own.

Jill Frost was her mother, and she stayed by her daughter's bed all that night. For the couple of days following that, Kelly had been allowed to follow her mother around. As soon as the sore throat and fever were gone, though, the two were separated again. Kelly went back to the children's cabin, and Jill to the part of the ranch where the women lived and worked.

Kelly had tried everything to be closer to her mother. Tears and temper tantrums had no effect, and even a recurring illness did not bring the mother back

to the child's side. She could see Jill in the distance
sometimes, and even talked to her briefly in passing.
But that was the extent of their mother-and-daughter
relationship.

As the years passed, Kelly and the other children
were taught the reasons why they lived as they did,
so different from the rest of the world.

They were told over and over again that they were
the Chosen Ones. It was their mission to serve and
help others. They were traveling the same path as the
Lord. They were not separate families, but all one
family. That was why there had to be sacrifices, self-
lessness, poverty, frequent moves. They had to work
hard, study hard, pray hard. It was their duty to spread
the wisdom of their leader, Father Mike, to the other
children who joined their group. It was the responsibility of those like Kelly to mentor the young, to teach
the newly arrived and to report any disobedience.
They were His flock, and it was their calling to live
and do as Father Mike instructed them.

Even at a young age, Kelly realized it had not been
her choice to live here, so she rebelled. More often
than not, she dreamed of someone arriving at the Mission, looking for her, wanting to take her out. Her
real father, perhaps, or her grandparents. From the
time she could read, she became fascinated with
phone books. They were a carefully protected item,
though—a precious commodity that was kept under
lock and key at the office of the Mission. She knew
they had people's names and addresses and phone
numbers in there. People with the same name as hers.

Perhaps they were related to her. If she called them, perhaps they'd come for her.

She stole the phone book a couple of times over the years, but she was always caught. She never called anyone. No one ever came for her.

Sometimes, very rarely, someone would leave the Mission. But when that happened, there were always tears and hard feelings. After they were gone, Father Mike would gather everyone together and pray and weep and storm about in fury, in the end calling down His wrath upon their vicious enemies. Those who left were damned forever, and anyone who tried to communicate with the deserters would suffer the pain of eternity in an everlasting lake of fire.

Kelly obeyed what he said because when he said those words, he was always looking into her eyes... into her terrified soul.

Michael Butler was not a violent man. He never raised his hand to her or to any of the other children, as far as she knew. But there was something about the way he looked at her—as if he was seeing someone else inside of her. It was freaky. When it was just the two of them, he talked to this other person and Kelly would stand frozen to the ground. She could still think, argue against what she was being told, but it would all be futile once she was called before him. By the time he was done with her, she felt nothing but the Father's will.

This had been the way when they'd all gone through the rehearsals in the weeks leading up to that last night. To those at the Mission, the Khumba Luxor would be the great moment. The alignment of the planets would open the way to heaven. The saints were holding open the door for them to ascend through. It was a celebration of the highest moment on earth for the Chosen Ones. It was the Rapture.

To Kelly, however, it was the end. Still, she had no will—no strength—to fight the Father, nor any means to run away from it.

Kelly looked at Jade. The little girl was contentedly lining up a half dozen of her toy people against the shower wall. She was talking softly to them, perfectly happy with the warm water washing down on her.

And then Lauren Wells had saved her. In taking her out of the camp that final night, Lauren had given Kelly back her life.

Five of them had left the Mission that night. Only four had survived the escape. Kelly didn't think Lauren had really known with certainty the tragedy that was going to take place that night at the Mission. She herself had wondered so many times over the years how many really knew.

In the aftermath, the police and the media had been brutal. The social workers had succeeded fairly well, though, in keeping the identities and the faces of the surviving children off the television screens and the front pages of the newspapers. This had been another place where Lauren Wells had played the part of their champion. In spite of her grief in losing her daughter and grandchild, Lauren had taken on all comers. She had faced the wolves while the other three were quietly being moved to safe shelters within the system.

This was when Kelly had last been in touch with any of them.

Jade waved at her from behind the glass, and Kelly waved back. "Ready to come out?"

"Five more minutes." The child pressed ten fingers against the glass.

Kelly nodded to her daughter before looking down at the screen of her laptop.

Technology was a true blessing. Her computer was her private domain. Nobody accessed this laptop but her. As a result, she had no need for boxes of old newspaper clippings. No faded pictures lying around. Kelly kept everything she had about the Butler Mission and the other survivors locked securely in her computer files.

While working at the *Times,* she'd had access to so much material, and she'd made use of the resources. Every article, obituary, photo and academic study that touched on the Butler Mission was now copied into her computer. Every government and law enforcement file that had been made public was here. And that wasn't all. The results of her own research were here, too. She'd gone as far as finding out the new last names of the other survivors. As of six years ago or so, she knew what part of the country they lived in, what they did, how they were.

But that's where she'd stopped. Greg had moved into her life, and she'd taken a different road.

Kelly opened up the old files. She scrolled down the listing of the hundred-plus articles that had been written about the Butler Mission suicide over the

years. Some of them were scanned copies. Others
were in a text format. She searched for the first articles on the car accident and the Mission suicide.
Years ago, she remembered seeing a picture of Lauren
in one of them.

As she looked at the partial titles of the early articles, one jumped out at her. Then another. She ex-
panded the screen, looking at the entire titles.

> *Trooper Finds Wife Among Victims…*
> *State Trooper Campbell Testifies at Mission Cult*
> *Hearing…*
> *Campbell Quits Force…*

She opened the first of the article files. It was one
of the personal interest articles that ran as a sidebar
along with the straight news about the suicide.

> *State Trooper Ian Campbell, one of the two of-*
> *ficers first to arrive at the scene of the Butler*
> *Mission mass suicide, found his wife of less than*
> *a month among the dead. Anne Campbell, a so-*
> *cial worker with the New Mexico Department of*
> *Child and Family Services, was visiting the…*

Kelly's heart was beating hard enough that she
could feel it pounding in her ears. She felt sick to her
stomach. She looked at the picture of the man,
dressed in his uniform, walking up the steps. Tapping
the touch pad, she zoomed in on the face of the grim
young man.

Ian.

Thirteen

Joshua Sharpe, clearly in a hurry to go to Errol, had only been able to give Ian a few minutes of his time. Speaking quickly, he explained the camp was running like a retreat this summer, mainly for his own church in Boston. He intended to run it himself, allowing only a few different religious organizations to use it for the same purpose, each taking a week here or there later in the summer.

Before leaving, Sharpe called over one of the camp counselors, Caleb Smith, to help Ian with whatever else he might need. Ian remembered him as being the young man who'd come to the inn with his friend to empty the cottage last night.

After Sharpe had driven off, Caleb began to show Ian around, but his cheerful demeanor slipped a little when Ian started asking questions.

"When did you arrive?"

"I just came in yesterday."

"Drive in?" he asked, looking around at the few cars in the small parking lot. A line of portable toilets stood near the end of the lot.

"No, my buddies and I came by bus. Why?"

"To Independence?" Ian turned to him in surprise.

"That's right."

"You didn't happen to see an old lady get off the bus with you?"

Caleb thought for a minute, shaking his head. "No, I don't think so."

"Can you think hard about it? It's pretty important to her family."

"No," Caleb said more definitely. "I don't recall anyone getting off with us at Independence. But then again, there were five of us, and we weren't paying much attention."

"Think any of the others might remember seeing her?"

"Listen, I'm sure nobody got off with us."

"Okay," Ian said, hearing the change in tone. "How many people have you got coming this week?"

"About a hundred fifty or so, I hear."

"That the whole congregation?" Ian asked.

"I don't really know."

Ian glanced again at the nearly empty parking lot. "Where are all their cars?"

"We transported everyone in from a commuter lot out on the state road."

"Oh, good idea. Is that how you got here from town?"

"Yeah. The van picked us up." Caleb said, tucking his clipboard under one arm.

"Do you have a registration list? Something with the names of the people you're expecting this week?"

Ian's question threw Caleb for a second. After fumbling around and scratching his face with the edge of his clipboard, he turned to an older man who was walking past and repeated the question.

"Yeah, there's a complete list, but Josh would have it." The man walked on.

Anyone who might have been some help seemed to be on the go. The one person put in charge of helping him was absolutely useless.

"Do people stay at the inn and spend the days here?" he asked, turning his attention back to Caleb.

"I'd imagine they do. Some folks aren't real campers, if you know what I mean."

"Do you know if anyone's doing that this week?"

"I don't really know. Josh's list would have that," Caleb said apologetically. "We're still trying to get all our ducks in a row for the summer."

"I'd like to talk to your friends who were on the bus coming in," Ian said, focusing again on Lauren's disappearance. "Would that be a problem?"

Caleb looked briefly at the tables with children's activities going on. "That'd be no problem, but they're all in the middle of stuff. You have to keep kids busy, you know. If you have a picture or something of your friend, I can show it to them when they're on their lunch break."

"I don't have one on me now, but I'll get one."

A woman poked her head out of the door of the infirmary and called to Caleb. He waved at her.

"I can ask my friends. If any of them remember anything, they could swing by the inn at the end of the day and look at the picture…you know, and see if it's the same person." He looked at his watch.

"No. I'll come back," Ian replied. "And I don't want to hold you up. You go do what you've got to do. I'll just poke my head around the camp before I leave."

"That's okay. She'll…uh, she'll wait." Caleb motioned toward the first row of cabins. "I have time to show you around."

Ian glanced at the edge of the lake. Ash was stretched out on top of a picnic bench, and her boyfriend was clicking away with his camera. They'd already drawn a small crowd. Up by Kelly's car, Bill was leaning against the vehicle with his arms crossed over his chest and talking to the same counselor Caleb had asked about the registration list.

Ian tried to think why Cassy had brought Jade here yesterday. "Is this your first year working at the camp?"

"No," Caleb answered. "I was here last year, too, but for only a month of the summer."

"And the rest of your crew?"

"Some of them are back from last year. This is too good a job to pass up for the summer."

Maybe there was an explanation for the babysitter's action after all. As he followed Caleb toward the first cabin, Ian looked down at the stage. "What's on the banner?"

"A welcome greeting for the families," Caleb answered, holding the door open for him.

"And the baptismal font?"

"Just that." The young man smiled. "We have new people who've never been baptized."

Ian knew things were not always that simple, but he let it go and walked past Caleb into the cabin.

The bright red pickup truck sped into the lot, coming a little too close to the phone booth for comfort, and Special Agent Ed Dershiwitz of the FBI's Boston Field Office switched the phone to his other ear. Turning, he glared as the vehicle skidded to a stop in one of the convenience store's parking spaces. His SAC was presently in Concord, coordinating the last stages of the operation.

"Listen, Ed. I talked to O'Hara in the attorney general's office an hour ago. We can't get the warrant to go in there until we know for sure he's there."

"They're armed, damn it," Ed said thinly into the phone. "Automatic weapons, assault rifles, bullet-proof vests, explosives, the whole nine yards. I saw them. They were keeping everything in the two cottages at the inn. He may or may not simply be sending the faithful on to their reward. There could be more here, and those weapons are reason enough for us to go in."

"Ed, you're not hearing me. O'Hara will not produce the warrant until we know Tyler Somers is there."

"We might be dealing with kidnapping, too. The old woman, Lauren Wells, was heading this way. Now she's missing."

"We already know that. Had a couple of calls on it. The locals are keeping their eyes open for her."

"She might still be alive. If we go in now, we can get her out."

"No one has seen her. We don't know if she's there, any more than we know if Somers is there."

"Jesus Christ!"

"You listen to me. You're not the Special Agent in Charge here, I am. We have an objective that we will accomplish."

"But we can get her out alive if—"

"We can get over a hundred fifty people out alive if we wait until Monday morning," the SAC snapped. "Our sources say that's when he's going to show up…"

Ed held the phone down by his leg, trying to regain his temper. When he raised it to his ear, his commander was still talking.

"…chasing this slimy bastard for over twenty years. If we don't get our hands on Tyler Somers this time, every wacko in America will figure he can pull this shit anytime there's a full moon. This is the first time that we know for sure he's showing his face."

Ed shook his head and looked in the back of Bill's truck. The groceries he'd picked up for Wilson sat lined up in a dozen brown bags. "Did you get anything else on Campbell?"

"Yeah." Ed heard the papers rustling through the wire. "He's on his own. Completely. He was offered a promotion with the San Diego force last month, but he said no. Just threw it in their faces and walked out, taking a personal leave. If you think he's a loose cannon, we can take him out of there.''

"Not yet. It's okay having him around, so long as he doesn't get in the way." Ed reached over the side of the truck and touched the five-gallon tub of ice cream in the first bag. It was getting soft. "I've got to get back. I've got to put my Dan hat on and get back to work.''

"We're planning to move at first light on Monday. We'll rendezvous at the mile marker on the state road.''

"Right.''

"And Ed…Dan, let us know if you see him sooner. I can have that warrant in an hour.''

Ken and Ash were not done with their photo shoot, so Bill offered to take Ian back to the inn and then come back for the other two.

On the ride back, Ian found the old man to be very pleasant, willing to answer any questions and to offer advice…solicited or unsolicited. Ian was surprised that the two of them got along so well. When they got back to the inn, Ian went looking for Kelly.

"Is there anything I can help you with?'' Janice said, appearing out of nowhere behind him as soon as he poked his head inside the empty office.

"No, I need to talk to Kelly.''

"She's very busy this morning,'' Janice said tartly. "If you have any questions about the menu today, we'll be starting to serve lunch in another fifteen minutes. The menu is already on the board. Also, dinner will be early tonight. The entrées—"

"I'm looking for Kelly," he repeated, looking beyond the pink glasses and white hair toward the deck. The Meadows couple was there, sitting in a pair of Adirondack chairs. By the lake, he could see the Stern boys pushing a canoe into the water.

"If there is a problem with the room—"

"No problem. Thanks for your help," he said as pleasantly as he could muster before heading for the stairs. She wasn't in the office, she didn't look to be on the deck or by the lake, and Bill had her car, so she had to be here. He hoped that she was up in her apartment with Jade.

Ian wished he had better news for her about Lauren. Still, he needed to talk to her about a few things he'd noticed at the camp. There was no one on the second floor. He took the back staircase two at a time and was surprised to find Kelly sitting in the rocking chair on the landing at the top, waiting for him.

Her face was somewhat flushed. Her eyes were red-rimmed, and he decided she'd been crying. The brisk rocking of chair blades on the wooden floor spoke volumes about her nerves.

"What's wrong?" Ian asked quickly, immediately looking for Jade. He glanced in through the open door of the apartment and saw the little girl sitting on the floor between the two beds, deeply into a giant floor puzzle. His gaze moved back to Kelly, and he felt a twist in his gut as a tear rolled down her cheek. "What's going on?"

"Do you have something to tell me?" she asked quietly.

Ian looked into her pained face as the chair continued to rock. She rubbed her hands up and down her arms as if she couldn't get warm. He looked around her and saw the laptop sitting open on the floor by her feet.

"The Internet's a wonderful thing," he said finally.

"It's not the Internet. I've kept files," she said. He could hear the note of temper edging into her voice. "And I've been looking up a few things."

"Like me."

"Like you."

He ran a hand through his hair in frustration. "Kelly, I—"

"What are you doing here? What do you want from us, Detective Campbell?" she asked bitterly.

"I don't want anything from *you*," he returned, matching her tone. "I'm here to protect you."

"Protect me? Who are you protecting me from…you, yourself?"

"What's that supposed to mean?"

She pushed herself to her feet so fast that the chair continued to rock madly on its own. "I had nothing to do with what happened at the Mission. I was twelve years old. I didn't know all of them would actually kill themselves."

"I don't blame you."

"I don't know why your wife stayed that night. I'm sorry that she did. I'm sorry that you suffered…that you had to be the one who walked in there and found her…found the rest of them. The whole thing was so unfair. Life is unfair. But I was a kid. I… It wasn't my fault. I couldn't stop them even if I'd stayed. I…I just had to go, and that was my chance. I couldn't take it anymore. I…I begged Lauren to take me. I was scared. I was so…scared.''

Ian closed the distance between them and drew her into his arms. She was crying softly, shaking uncontrollably. He pressed Kelly's face against his chest and held her tight. He caressed her back, pressed a kiss into her hair. He understood what guilt felt like. The guilt of surviving loved ones. He'd lived with it for the past twenty-two years. That Mission was in his territory. He'd let his own wife walk in there. He'd let her die. He hadn't even seen it coming.

"Is Mommy okay?"

His own vision was blurred. He saw Jade standing in the doorway of the apartment, one bare foot rubbing on top of the other. Green eyes gazed up with great concern at the two of them. Ian nodded, unwilling to trust his voice at the moment. Kelly pulled herself out of his arms. She turned to her daughter and crouched before her.

"I'm okay, honey." Her voice still quavered. "Why don't you go and finish your puzzle. I'll be right here if you need me."

"Do you need a Band-Aid?" the little girl asked, touching the tears that continued to fall down Kelly's cheeks.

She shook her head. "Not now. But why don't you save one for me for later."

"Will you tell me when it's later?" Jade asked, caressing her mother's hair.

Kelly pulled her into a tight embrace before letting go. "I sure will."

Jade looked up at Ian as she backed toward the door. "I have boy Band-Aids, too, if you want one."

"Thanks." He cleared his voice, smiling at the little girl. "I'll take one later, too."

The intercom in the apartment buzzed. Following Jade in, Kelly answered it. It was Janice.

"We could use your help serving lunch, Kelly."

Thoughts of strangling the old woman ran through Ian's head.

"You'll have to do without me," Kelly said shortly. "And Janice, I don't care what happens, please just handle it." She turned off the unit completely and turned to Ian. "We need to talk."

He couldn't agree more.

"Wait here." She went down the stairs. He heard her close the door at the bottom. She came back up a few seconds later. "I don't want any more interruptions."

"We can talk in my room," he said, motioning toward the closed door. "There are a few things there that I need to show you."

She wiped her face with the back of one hand and nodded, following him across the sitting area. She stopped as she reached the doorway.

Ian pulled his suitcase from under the bed. She was looking back toward her own apartment and Jade. Sitting on the bed, he unlocked and opened the case. He

could feel her eyes on him. He knew she would see
the gun when he opened the suitcase to get the thick
manila folder. It was inevitable. When he looked up
at her, she was staring at the pistol, her concern showing in her face.

"I'm an officer of the law. I carry a gun. When
I'm not carrying it, I keep the pistol unloaded and
under lock and key."

Her arms crossed. She leaned against the doorjamb.

Ian locked the case, put it away and sat down again
on the bed. He opened the folder on his lap. "Why
don't you come and sit down."

"Why didn't you tell me who you were when you
came?" she asked.

"I did tell you," he said. "I used my own name,
my own address. I even made sure you knew what I
·did for a living. If any of that struck a familiar chord
with you, it was okay with me." He patted the bed
next to him. "As far as why I'm here…"

She didn't move from the doorway. "I've never
been driven to search for answers. I didn't dig into
what happened. Other than collecting a bunch of information and letting it sit in my computer, I decided
somewhere that I'd just as soon forget. Is this something that I should know?"

"Yes, it is," he said seriously.

Her steps were hesitant, but she came and sat on
the edge of the bed, a foot away from him. She tucked
her hands between her thighs, watching everything he
did. Ian opened the file folder, pulled out a print of
an obituary from the San Diego paper, and handed it

to her. She stared at it for a couple of seconds, and he knew the moment she made the connection.

"William Bridger...William. That's him. He left the camp with me. He's dead?" she asked, going pale and looking up at Ian before turning her attention back to the newspaper obit.

Ian gave her a summary. "Thirty-six years old. Ran a small center that offered day-care service for mentally retarded children. Well liked and respected. Popular with the kids and their families. No wife and kids of his own."

"This doesn't say how he died."

He handed her a second sheet containing a copy of an article about a fatal fire in a day-care center.

"They claim it was an accidental fire at the center," he said. "A cigarette butt dropped into a trash can. Happened on a late night this past April. He was the only one there, but he couldn't get out in time for some reason."

"Was it an accident?"

"You want the police report or my opinion?"

She looked down at the paper again. "San Diego...shouldn't it be the same?"

"Not in this case," he said, digging out a write-up of the accident from another paper. "He was a smoker. But he'd supposedly quit last Christmas. Nobody else in that building was a smoker. Not even the custodian. Also, there was something wrong with the lock in the little office he was in. He seems to have been stuck in there."

"Isn't what you just told me enough to call for a homicide investigation?"

"They investigated, but there was no hard evidence to suspect foul play. Everybody liked him. He was a very down-to-earth guy, apparently. He was not romantically involved with anyone at the time. There were no suspects. No one to point a finger at." Ian dug into his file again.

"You have something else?" Kelly asked, shivering slightly.

He handed her another obituary. This one was from the *Chicago Tribune*. She looked at it, already knowing what it would be.

"Sydney Gerhart. Oh my God, this…this is the baby Lauren took out with us. Sydney." Kelly looked at the black-and-white picture of the young woman that ran with the obituary.

"Twenty-three years old. Graduate student at Northwestern. Shared an apartment on the eighth floor of a high-rise with two other girls." He took out a copy of something that looked like the summary page of a police report of the accident. "She fell off the balcony of her apartment in the middle of the afternoon."

"An accident?"

"The whole thing is still under investigation. But there are no eyewitnesses, no suspects, no evidence of forced entry into the apartment. Her boyfriend was questioned a couple of times, but he was in class at the time and there's nothing that ties him to her death."

"None of her roommates were at home?"

Ian shook his head. "The investigation is still open only because of the possibility of suicide. But that's a long shot because there was no note, and she seemed like a well-adjusted young woman."

Kelly's chin trembled. Her eyes were filled with tears when she looked up at him. "We went our separate ways. None of us knew each other. But in a way, they were like family to me. And now they're both dead. What's going on? Are these two deaths related?"

Ian hoped she was ready for what he was going to unload on her. He moved over on the bed, took paperclipped bundles of paper out of the folder, and stacked them in piles between them.

"I couldn't just walk in here and tell you or show you these things. You would have thrown me out, not believing any of it." He took her hand when she tried to pick up the first stack of paper. Kelly's green eyes looked up into his. "I believe William's and Sydney's deaths are directly related to what happened at the Butler Mission twenty-two years ago."

Her hand drew back immediately, as if she'd been burned. Out of reflex, she looked through the open doors for Jade.

"Everyone died," she whispered, finally looking back at him. "Father Mi...Reverend Butler died."

"Only those who were at the Mission that night died," Ian said, forcing himself not to see in his mind again what he'd witnessed so many years ago. He picked up the first stack of papers off the bed and flipped through the pages until he found what he was looking for. "Tyler Somers. This picture is from the last time that he had his picture taken at a DMV office in New Mexico. It dates back to before he left the Mission. Do you remember him?"

Kelly didn't reach for it, but leaned close enough to look. "Brother Ty. He was really close to Father Mike. He worked in the office a lot. He was the front person. In a way, he was our contact with the outside world. He answered all the questions from the families of people who were at the Mission. He left the same month that…everything happened. I don't know where he went."

"Michael Butler was too wrapped up in his end-of-the-world routine to bother filing any charges. But what showed up after the cult suicide was that Somers had practically emptied the bank accounts on his way out."

"I don't think there was much to take, anyway. We were pretty poor."

He shook his head. "The families living there *thought* they were poor. Michael Butler had a mailing list of over two hundred thousand people that he sent a letter and contribution envelope to twice a year. He appealed to people's generosity to help him care for the runaway and abused young mothers and children who showed up every day at his door with nowhere else to go. He had a pretty convincing package, and he was able to hook in even a few major contributors."

"How much did Ty Somers take?"

He shook his head. "I don't know, but I'm sure the FBI agents who've been chasing him for all these years can tell you."

"So…you're not working for someone else. You're not acting on behalf of some government agency? You've done all this investigating on your own?"

Tell her only the truth, Ian reminded himself. He'd traveled all the way across the country to find her, and it looked as though he'd gotten here in time. He didn't want to lose this second chance to find out what happened. To find out why.

"I couldn't let go," he started. "I lost my wife twenty-two years ago. In the wake of that, I lost my faith in my own judgment. Worst of all, I missed out on the chance to ask the questions that were driving me crazy. Questions about the cult, about Butler. About Anne. I needed to know if Anne's death was a suicide or a murder. But I couldn't find any answers."

He took a deep breath and continued. "Moving away—going from New Mexico to California—should have helped. I was no longer living in the middle of all the memories. But I found I still couldn't let go. So I started keeping track of things. Like a hobby. I started collecting anything and everything new and old about the Butler Divinity Mission."

"I did the same thing, but it was only for a short time," Kelly told him. "That was how I had copies of articles about you in my laptop. I stopped collecting them when I got married, and then, after Jade was born, I couldn't move far enough away from it.''

"She's a great kid. You've done a great job raising her.''

Kelly's expression softened. ''She's very special. What she's done to me here—'' she touched her heart ''—is to make me feel more than I have ever felt for another human being. The love I feel for her is more than I ever felt for my husband…or for my adoptive parents, either.'' She looked down at the papers on the bed. ''I've been so scared, though, lately. I've lain awake at night, worrying that something might happen, and I wouldn't be able to protect her. And now, you're showing me all this.''

"I'm sorry it had to be this way.''

She nodded. ''So, is Tyler Somers somehow involved with Sydney's and William's deaths?''

Ian thumbed through the package until he found what he was looking for. ''After the Mission suicide, Somers went underground for a while, changing his identity a number of times. He started a couple of other Missions of his own in Colorado and later in Texas under different names. Both of them were failures. He just didn't have the charisma that Butler did. Not enough people joined his cults. He couldn't develop the funding network that Butler had, either. The bottom line, apparently, was that he never could establish a core group of people who believed he had a direct line with God…like his teacher claimed to have possessed.''

He showed Kelly flyers that had gone out on one

of Somers's fund-raising campaigns. "Meanwhile, as these other sects came and went, he added a whole list of criminal charges to his dossier."

"What charges?"

"Possession and transportation of illegal firearms, interstate flight, racketeering, mail fraud, reckless endangerment to minors, extortion, tax evasion...and he's wanted for questioning in connection with the disappearance of a dozen women and children. He's been on the FBI's Most Wanted list for over ten years."

She took the packet from him and looked through it page by page, including the FBI's sketches and pictures and the list of identities Somers had used over the years.

"About five years ago or so, I heard a rumor of him being sick with some kind of cancer," Ian said, picking up another packet of papers off the bed. "I think it also might have been about then that Somers realized he had a goose that was laying golden eggs, and he wasn't cashing in on it. Michael Butler died twenty-two years ago, but a number of his generous supporters lived on. There were people working in the office in Albuquerque, and there was a smattering of people whose families had pulled them out of the Mission before the end. Anyway, it appears that a lot of these people elevated their belief in Butler, changing him from a clergyman into the 'Prophet Michael.' Apparently, they quietly stayed in touch with each other, forming a kind of silent network to keep the faith alive and to continue to support what they thought were Butler's causes.''

Ian showed Kelly printouts of a Web page. At the top of the page, there were the letters *''BDMMDB.''* Beneath the letters, there was a logo depicting a golden crescent moon with three red drops falling into a cup from one tip of the crescent.

''Butler Divinity Mission. Ministry of the Divine Blood,'' she whispered.

Ian nodded. ''The Web site was established a decade after the suicide. No search engines point you to it. They had a low-level security screen before you could access it. But it was easy to get past that. Basically, word of mouth is how a person finds the site.''

''And here I was, thinking that it was all gone.''

Kelly shivered as she looked through the pages. Nothing specifically identified any connection with the original sect or Reverend Butler, but if you were a part of it, you recognized it. And the ''Truths'' page contained the philosophy that she'd had drilled into her as a child. There were even sermons that alluded to ''The Prophet,'' undoubtedly a reference to Butler.

''How did you find it?'' she asked.

''My wife, Anne, must have been on an original mailing list. I received a notice of it in the mail when the Web site went up on the Internet.''

She gave the pages back to him. ''So Somers rejoined the group?''

''He didn't only join it, he took it over and spearheaded the effort to revive it,'' Ian explained, showing Kelly the piles of propaganda that had gone out since Ty had taken charge. "He was, after all, a member of Butler's original inner circle. So far as these people knew, he was the trusted arm of the Prophet, and he'd been wandering in the desert, preparing to lead them in Reverend Butler's name."

"But what about stealing from these same people? Some of them must have know about it."

"Somers claimed that his departure from the Mission was planned by the Prophet himself. To provide for those who had been spirited away from their just reward, Butler personally sent him away to carry on. To be his voice. To gather the surviving believers for the Second Coming. I have to assume that over the years, Somers had learned how to put together enough astrological and scriptural evidence to make a pretty convincing case."

Kelly ran her hands up and down her arms. She looked at him, anger mixing with frustration. "How could these people believe him? He's a crook. Everything he says is a lie. Wasn't it enough for them to see what happened to those who followed Butler? The two of them are one and the same."

"Not if you believe in what they say they can do."

Kelly said nothing. She knew how the minds of people could be controlled.

"Butler was crazy," Ian continued. "But Somers is *armed* and crazy. That makes him more dangerous. But there's something else. In all the propaganda he's been putting out this year, he keeps referring to a new messiah. A Chosen One that Butler also sent away."

"He's talking about himself," she said tensely.

"No, Somers is the right hand of the Prophet. The one who would lead all of them though to eternity is someone of Butler's own divine blood. He's been referring to a child that was taken away on the day of the suicide. The Prophet's child that they call Luna-K.''

Fourteen

Denial.

Kelly felt the impulse shut down her thinking even as Ian said the words.

The Prophet's child.

She stood up abruptly and walked toward the door. Before she could step through it, though, guilt and grief unlike any she'd ever felt descended on her in one violent sweep. Her feet froze to the ground. Her hands pressed against either side of the door, stopping her body's forward motion.

"No," she told him brokenly over her shoulder. "No, it's not me."

"I thought it could have been William or Sydney. But before I could get to either of them, they were dead." He was standing behind her. "You're the only one left."

"It can't be." She shook her head, unable to hold back the tears. "I'm not like him. I didn't believe in him. I hated him. He didn't send me away. I ran away. It was my own doing. I…"

Putting a hand around her waist, Ian gently pulled her away from the open doorway and pressed her back against the wall of his room. Even in the middle of her panic, she realized Ian was thinking of Jade. He didn't want her to see her mother like this. Kelly closed her eyes. She let the tears fall. All those dreams. Jill, her mother, was always near the Father. She could see him now—reaching out for Kelly, offering her the cup. They were not dreams. She was seeing what he expected her to do.

"No," she told Ian, shaking her head. "I won't let him do this to me. I won't let him use me to kill innocent people. If I'm that demon's offspring, then I'll kill myself first before allowing anyone to follow me to the same ending that he took all those innocent people to. It's not going to happen. I won't let it."

"You're *not* any demon's offspring," Ian said gently, lifting her face until she was seeing him through a teary blur. He wiped her tears with his thumb. "Butler was just a man, and none of us are responsible for our father's sins. You're a loving and caring mother to a wonderful daughter. Whatever Somers claims, none of that changes the kind of person you've become. You spent twelve years in that Mission, but you've lived twenty-two years away from it."

Kelly clutched at his wrist, desperate to remember something that would clear her of being Butler's daughter. Like a noose around her neck, the thought that she was his offspring was choking her. But there was nothing she could recall that indicated anything else. The more she forced herself to think back, the more incriminating the moments were that she remembered. The woman she knew as her mother was always close to Father Mike. Kelly had to go and see the sect leader more than any of the other children. He was much more interested in what she did, in where she went, in what she was studying than any of the others.

"You're here. You found me. Does this mean that they can do the same thing?" Kelly asked.

"I suspect they've known for a long time. I think they know where you are, what you do, and who's around you."

Leaning against the wall, Kelly hugged herself tightly. She couldn't panic. She had to think. "Lauren...Lauren Wells. Is this why she was trying to get in touch with me?"

"It makes sense, doesn't it?" Ian answered. "I spoke to her a couple of times on the phone during the early days...when I was beginning to look for answers about Anne—about if she was part of the cult or not. Lauren was friendly, open and helpful. She was very much aware of all the aftershocks that were still going on after the Mission suicide. I think she had a much harder time than any of the three of you in forgetting how close she'd come to saving more people. So I wouldn't put it past her to keep track of all three of you. If she was, then she might have known something happened to William and Sydney."

"And, since then, has been trying to tell me." Kelly shook her head. "Did you talk to anyone at the camp? Was anyone on the bus? Did they see her?"

"I talked to one of the kids who came over last night to pick up the stuff that was in the cottage. He and a few of his friends were on that bus, but he said he didn't see her. He was lying.'' Ian reached into his pocket. "I found this in—"

The shouts could be heard through the open window of the sitting area. Hearing the cries for help, Kelly and Ian rushed to look outside. Four people were standing on the shore of the lake. Some fifty yards out in the water, a canoe was capsized, and there were two people in the water. From the cries, it looked to be the Stern boys.

"How deep is the water?" Ian asked right away.

"Very. It drops off very fast. It doesn't look like they're wearing life jackets. Where's Dan?" Kelly asked, recognizing the people on the beach as Bill and Janice and the parents of the boys. The father was moving into the water, but one of the boys went under.

"I'll go," Ian said, starting down the stairs. "Don't leave Jade alone. Don't trust anyone to watch her, either."

Her daughter was already beside her. Kelly picked up the child in her arms and followed Ian down.

As Dan pulled the old truck into the parking area, he saw Ian Campbell sprinting toward the water. He only had a partial view of the lake from where he was, so he jumped out of the truck and took a couple of steps toward the beach. He saw the capsized boat and the flailing arms.

"You sure took your fucking time picking up this stuff." Blade stepped out the back door. He paid no attention to what was going on at the lake. "What are you waiting for? Bring the bags in."

"Later," Dan called over his shoulder, running toward the water.

Rachel Stern was only good for making lots of noise and had not put even a toe in the water. Her husband was not much better. He was wading out at a snail's pace toward his sons.

Ian Campbell, though, was already near the boat. Dan saw him dive under as the younger son's head disappeared below the surface. Dan raced into the water, closing the distance rapidly with strong strokes. Ian and the kid broke to the surface ahead of him.

"There we go," Ian said, holding the kid up by the back of the shirt. Ryan Stern was coughing out some water he'd swallowed, but not thrashing or trying to get a grip on his rescuer. "We're all right."

The older Stern boy seemed to be treading water with ease. As Dan reached the boat, Ian was pulling Ryan toward the shore. The boy's face was red from coughing, but Dan thought he'd live, no problem.

"Get the other one," Ian said, swimming past.

"I'm on it."

A couple of strokes and Dan was beside the boat, where Craig Stern was now holding on to the bow of the canoe.

"Can you swim in?"

"Yes," the older Stern boy replied. He was shivering, and Dan guessed it wasn't because of the temperature of the water, which was quite bearable. He looked scared.

"Then start swimming." Taking hold of the bow-line of the boat, Dan started toward the shore, pulling the canoe behind him. "And where the hell is your life jacket? Didn't I tell you two that you don't take a boat out without having them on?"

Craig nodded and started swimming toward the shore. Ian was already wading toward the beach. The boys' father was standing with Ryan in the shallow water, putting a towel that the mother had handed him around the younger son's shoulders.

An audience was waiting for them at the shoreline. Marisa and Dave Meadows were standing and watching by some chairs. The photographer and the model were also on the lawn. Dan realized, though, that everyone's attention was focused in one place.

Kelly was knee deep in the water. She took Ian's hand as he approached and whispered something to him. He said something back and wrapped his arm around her as they made their way out of the lake.

No one appeared to be too concerned with the two boys who could have drowned. Everyone was watching Ian and Kelly.

Ian was no lifeguard, but he was smart enough to recognize when someone was trying to pull the wool over his eyes. Especially when that someone was a twelve-year-old.

As he came out of the water, Kelly thanked him for going after the kids, and Ian told her the truth. The boy was faking it. The whole thing was staged. Ryan could swim just fine. He felt her muscles grow tense even as he told her what he thought. Then he just held on to her, because he didn't want her exploding at anyone on that beach, and he told her that.

Luckily, Jade was the first person who ran toward them.

"I want to go swimming, too. I want to go swimming with Ian," she protested, jumping up and down in her bare feet at the very edge of the water.

"Not now," Kelly said, marching off toward the Sterns, who were coming out of the water and being handed towels by Janice.

"It's too cold." Ian faked a shudder and took the little girl by the hand. "Plus, your mommy is ready to rip into a couple of kids and their parents for not following the rules about going out in boats."

Janice dropped some towels on a bench for Ian and went back up to the inn. He and Jade walked over and stood by the bench as Kelly had a few words with the Stern family. They watched her as she pointed to the signs. Snippets of the one-way conversation reached Ian as Kelly reminded the family why it was the inn's policy to give everyone a crash course in water safety before taking any boat out. She reminded them that it was only yesterday that Dan had instructed them about the rules, and that it was their responsibility as adults to make sure their sons followed those rules.

"Good work out there," Dan said, joining him by the bench.

Ian tossed him one of the towels. "Where were you?"

"In town. Picking up food for the kitchen. Don't want any boating survivors going hungry tonight." He ran the towel over his head and neck. "But this thing wasn't my fault. Kelly told me we won't be having any lifeguard duty for another week or so, when it's actually warm enough for people to go swimming. Of course, who knew about those two?"

The two boys were wrapped in their towels. Showing miraculous resilience, Ryan seemed to be completely over his near-death experience. He was standing next to his brother and staring devotedly at Kelly.

"Actually," Ian said, "I think they would have done just fine by themselves if you and I hadn't jumped in."

"You think so, too?" Dan answered, sending him a knowing glance. "I say, next time we let them take in a gallon or two before we decide to go in after them. Check out the way they're looking at Kelly. You'd think they were *trying* to get her attention."

"Not a good way," Ian replied, frowning.

"Not a good way at all," Jade added in her little voice, mimicking his frown.

He looked down and found the child standing between him and Dan, her feet apart and a giant towel draped around her shoulders, just like the two of them. Ian was still smiling when he looked up. Dan seemed amused with Jade, too.

"So, how good a friendship do your mother and Kelly have?" Ian asked the younger man.

"Good enough that she hired me here for the summer."

Kelly was still talking to Rob and Rachel Stern. Janice had disappeared inside the house. The Meadows couple was starting up toward the inn. Ash was pretending to ignore her boyfriend as he took some shots of her with the boathouse—along with Kelly and the Stern family—in the background.

Ian looked down at the little girl standing at his feet. "Do you think they're good enough friends that Kelly and Jade could just pop in and visit with her for a few days?"

Dan looked up at him. "I didn't know Kelly was planning on going anywhere. Why would she want to?"

"Answer the question," Ian told him pointedly.

"I guess there wouldn't be a problem. No, I'm sure she wouldn't mind. But she does like twenty-four-hour notice. Even I have to give her that." He tugged on one ear. "I keep thinking maybe she has a live-in boyfriend these days and has to push the guy out before I get home."

The Sterns were starting back to the inn, and Rachel Stern was all apologies as the family moved away from Kelly.

"Keep that topic to yourself for now, will you?" he asked Dan.

The other man nodded, and Ian and Jade headed over to where Kelly was standing, her hands still on her hips. She was looking with some perplexity at the departing family.

"Why, Ian? Why did they stage this?" she asked.

"Maybe you and I were spending too much time

alone,'' Ian told her. ''In fact, right about now, I won-der who's upstairs in my room, going through the stuff that I left all over my bed.''

''You need to change,'' she said, abruptly swinging Jade up on her hip and leading the way.

''I want to play in the sand,'' Jade complained, pointing back toward the water.

''Later, sweetheart. We can play later.''

Ian's clothes were still dripping wet. He left his soggy shoes and socks behind on the bench and fol-lowed Kelly as she bypassed the door going in from the deck and headed for the lobby door.

A lunch buffet had been set up, and the newlyweds were fixing their plates. Kelly went by the reception desk and was heading down the hall that took them to the back stairwell when Janice came breathlessly after them.

''That was a close call. Wait...'' the old woman called. She was leaning heavily on her cane with each step and with her other hand was motioning to them to stop.

Kelly slowed down and shot a frustrated look over her shoulder. ''Whatever it is has to wait, Janice.''

''I need to tell you something.''

''Later. I'm wet. Mr. Campbell is soaked. We need to change first.'' She started up the steps.

''I remembered the reservation,'' Janice called after her. ''Lauren Wells. I know where she is.''

This brought both of them to a dead stop. Kelly backtracked and turned to look at the older woman. ''Where is she?''

"I guess my memory is not what it used to be," Janice said. "She tried to make a reservation quite a while ago. But we were already booked, so I put her name on a waiting list. She called later, though, and had her name taken off the list. That's why I don't have it written down anywhere."

"Her niece said she was still coming to Independence. She got off the bus at the village. If she wasn't coming here, then where was she going?"

"To Josh Sharpe's camp," Janice said. "When she called to cancel her reservation, that's where she told me she was going. She was staying across the lake."

"I was there this morning," Ian interrupted. "Caleb Smith, who seems to be running much of the show there and who was also on the same bus as Lauren Wells, denied seeing any older woman."

"Well, I can't help that," Janice said sweetly. "Mrs. Wells was on that bus yesterday. A van from the camp picked her up."

"How do you know all this?" Kelly asked, moving Jade from one hip to the other.

"Mrs. Wells called a couple of minutes ago from the camp office herself. You were talking to the Sterns outside, so I didn't want to interrupt. She did say, though, that the cabins were a little too rustic for her, so she was wondering if we had any rooms where we could put her up."

"I hope you said yes," Kelly said excitedly. "Jade and I will double up in the carriage house with you and Bill and give her our apartment."

"That wasn't necessary," Janice replied quickly.

"I explained to her about the room Mr. Desposito and his friend are staying in, and how it's only half-painted. They're planning to check out by ten o'clock tomorrow, so I offered to have it ready for her by noon. She was thrilled with the arrangement."

Lauren Wells's disappearance was far too neatly packaged and explained. Ian tried to see the eyes behind the pink frames. He waited for Janice to show some sign—no matter how small—that she was fabricating this entire story. But there was nothing to indicate she was lying. Still, he knew she had to be…right through her teeth.

"Maybe I could take Kelly over there to see her," he suggested, knowing full well that he wasn't going to take Kelly and Jade a foot nearer that camp than where they were standing right now.

"I can't see why not, Mr. Campbell. She did say she saw you and the other couple at the camp this morning. But she didn't know you were looking for her."

"Did you tell her that her niece is going crazy looking for her," Kelly asked. "That she's probably already called the state police?"

"Yes, I did. And she said she'll call her this afternoon." Janice waved a comforting hand. "I'm sure that will all work out just fine."

Kelly visibly relaxed. She asked Janice a couple more questions before going ahead of Ian up the stairs.

"So she's okay. My God, I'm so relieved."

Ian didn't think Kelly was prepared to hear what exactly was going through his mind. At least, not at the moment. And he wasn't about to tell her when he knew for a fact that these walls had ears.

Fifteen

Stopping her by the door leading to the third floor, Ian went ahead of them up the stairs. Kelly saw the tension in his shadowed expression. She closed and latched the old door at the bottom of the steps and followed him up to the landing.

"Was someone here?" she asked.

"I don't think so," he said as he pointed to her laptop. The top was closed. Kelly specifically remembered leaving the computer open on the floor beside the rocking chair. As she opened her mouth to say something, he pressed a finger against his lips and motioned to her to follow him. She did.

Inside her apartment, he pointed to the intercom system on the wall. She came closer and looked. The room monitor had been turned on.

Kelly recalled turning the thing off when she and Ian had been talking before. She felt the anger rising within her. She reached over to shut it off, but Ian's hand closed around hers. He shook his head, motioned for her to wait where she was, and went quietly out to the sitting area in the hall.

"Kelly, can I use your shower?" he called in a

normal tone. "Or are you going to make me go down-stairs?"

"You can use this one," she answered.

"You can play with my toys in the shower if you want to," Jade chirped, diving out of Kelly's arms and running toward her toy chest to dig out her favorites.

"Barbie dolls?" he asked, lightening his tone.

"They're all headless…in keeping with a grand tradition," Kelly answered. "The male action figures are in much better shape. Jade only maims them by taking off their arms or legs."

He closed the apartment door and tested the lock. Kelly had changed this one last year, so she knew it was in much better shape than the one to his room. She watched him tuck one of the chairs from the kitchen against it. He also fastened the latch high on the door. She almost never used that.

"Okay, you can have five of them." Jade ran back to him excitedly, carrying two handfuls of dolls. "This one doesn't like soap in his eyes, so be careful. And this one gets scared when you first turn on the water, so give him a hug. These other three are all fine. But be careful, she's a bully."

"What happened to her head?" he asked, holding the naked doll at arm's length.

"She sent it away to get a haircut," Jade said with a smile, not missing a beat.

Kelly was glad those two could laugh. The tension from not knowing what was going on was shooting pains from the back of her head to her temples.

She tried to ignore it and turned to her daughter. "How about if we build with blocks and watch one of the Sing-Along tapes?"

"Okay. And Ian can watch it with me when he's done with his shower," she announced before running off to get her favorite tape.

Kelly rarely let Jade watch TV, and on those few instances that she did, she limited her mostly to one of half a dozen children's Sing-Along videos they had.

"I want you in there with me," he whispered into her ear, motioning toward the shower before she could go and help Jade.

It was totally unexpected, but Kelly felt a shiver run through her in a way that had nothing to do with fear and everything to do with his lips touching her ear and his breath tickling the skin of her neck. She managed a nod and first went to help Jade with her toy blocks and tape. By the time she returned to the bathroom door, she could hear the shower running. She paused, not sure if she should go in or not. At the same time, she didn't want to knock, for fear of someone listening downstairs knowing she was in there with him.

Kelly realized how ridiculous propriety was in the light of everything else that was going on right now. She gave one light tap on the door and stepped in.

He'd taken off his shirt. Kelly's eyes involuntarily moved down from the broad, muscled chest to his flat stomach and to where Ian had already undone his belt and the button of his wet khakis.

"If you'd taken any longer, I would have jumped in."

Kelly shook her head and forced herself to concentrate on his face. Her bathroom was too small for the two of them. Other than a small window, high on the wall, there was no other ventilation. She was thankful that he was only running the cold water. Even at that, though, a cold mist hung in the air and glistened on his naked skin.

"Kelly..." He took her by the shoulders and pushed her back against the vanity. She sat up on the counter. "I think you should pack a bag, put Jade in your car and drive as far as you can away from here."

His statement had an immediately sobering effect. Kelly looked into his face. "What is it that you haven't told me?"

"Ty Somers is planning his Rapture...or moment of truth...or whatever it is, for this Monday."

Kelly was glad she was sitting, as she didn't think her legs could have supported her. "The day after tomorrow?"

He nodded.

"Why? What makes you think that? How could he do that? Does he already have these people together? Where is he?"

"It's all explained in the Web site...sort of," Ian replied. "It has to do with the time it takes for Jupiter to travel around the sun. But it's more astrological than scientific. It's been a little more than twenty-two years since the last similar alignment between the moon and sun and Jupiter. The Hindus have a big celebration of the event that they call Khumba Mela or something, and it culminates this Monday. Anyway, the idea is that when the three celestial bodies line up, the portal to immortality opens for the faithful. Somers calls it Khumba Luxor and connects it to both scripture and some mythic Egyptian priest. It's supposedly the same secret that Reverend Butler passed on to him before sending him away. The suicide happened on the night of the last alignment.''

''That's a lie. Butler wasn't into any astrology stuff. He was into his own interpretations of scripture, it's true, but what happened was because he went nuts.''

''You were too young to see it, but he was apparently a big believer in all of that,'' Ian told her. ''I read his journals and his sermons. It was there, but he always conveyed astrology as being part of Scripture. He wasn't about to lose his fundamentalist followers.''

Kelly stood up, but there was no room to go anywhere—nowhere for her to pace. Ian opened the bathroom door a crack and looked out at Jade. Kelly could hear her singing with the video.

''Where are they gathering?'' she asked, feeling sick to her stomach. She already knew the answer.

He closed the door again. ''My guess is, at the camp across the lake.''

Like a March wind, cold dread pierced her body, chilling her to her very core. She sat down again on the edge of the vanity and hugged her arms around her queasy stomach.

Kelly looked up at him. He was standing by the door, his powerful arms crossed over his chest. "You've found out all this on your own."

"Pretty much."

"Do the authorities know this, too?" she asked hopefully. "You told me Somers is on the FBI's Most Wanted list. Why can't we just call them and tell them what's going on…let them nail him now."

"They know what's going on, too. I think they're handling it in their own way, whatever that might be."

"How do they know?"

"I called them last night, after I found this." He reached into his pocket and took out a soggy credit slip. "It was in the van that came over to pick up the stuff that was stored in your cottage."

Kelly leaned over as he opened the piece of paper. The water had dissolved most of the writing, but she could still make out the name Wells.

"This had the name Lauren Wells on it. Knowing about Sydney's and William's deaths, I was afraid she might be the third victim. So I called a friend I have at the Bureau—someone who I know was working on the Butler Mission suicide way back when. I gave him the info. He didn't commit himself one way or the other, but he led me to believe they're on top of it."

"Lauren went over there of her own volition. Maybe she's been won over somehow."

"After what she went through, do you think that's possible?"

Kelly frowned and shook her head.

"You were *told* that Lauren was over there," Ian reminded her. "The truth remains to be seen about that."

"Janice?" She rubbed the pain on her temples. "And Bill?"

Kelly recalled the older woman's fascination with astrology. Even the names of the rooms. She'd always insisted on placing people in the "appropriate" rooms if she could. All of it had been right under her nose, but Kelly hadn't seen it. And this thing with the intercom being turned back on—and all the interruptions to get them downstairs.

"Are they part of the new Mission cult, too?" she asked. "They've been part of my life for…"

"Almost ten years." He placed a hand gently on her shoulder. "I wish I had all the answers but I don't. Not yet. But my inclination is to say that you should suspect everyone around you to be a possible cult member. That's why I think it's important for you to take Jade and get out."

"How far could I go? Where could I hide?" she asked. "If they've worked so hard even to get people that I thought were like family to me involved, don't you think they'll come after me—or try to stop me?"

"I still think you have a much better chance of running than trying to stay and face them." He cupped her chin, raised her face and looked grimly into her eyes. "Jade makes you more vulnerable than you think."

Kelly knew he was right. Everybody that worked at the inn, any person who'd ever met or talked to her, knew how she felt about her daughter. "Would you come with us?"

His jaw clenched, and she saw the decades' old pain in his eyes. "I'll help you. I'll find you a place to stay. I'll even get you a police escort when the time comes for you to go. But I can't go myself."

Kelly knew what it was. She knew he was still trying to bury his dead.

"Anne died twenty-two years ago," she said quietly.

"I know that." He turned away and shut off the shower. He ran a frustrated hand across his neck. "But I have to do this, Kelly. I have to understand why she did it."

"I think once she gets over her complaining about where she's going to put all this stuff, Ellie's going to be very happy with the pieces we got," Victor said, looking up from the auction catalog covered with his boss's notes as well as his own. "Wow, look at that baby move."

Brian slowed down a little as a sports car cut in front of them in a no-passing zone. "Nice car," he commented.

The road from Guildhall, where the auction had been held, had taken them into the mountains along the northern edge of the White Mountain National Forest. Climbing quickly from the Connecticut River valley that formed the border of New Hampshire and Vermont, they'd traveled along a mountain road that provided spectacular views, rendering both speechless at the sight of the sun reflecting off the highest peaks, which still had patches of snow on them, even now. With the bright blue sky as a backdrop, the mountains looked like a picture postcard. From there, the road they took led north, winding along the Androscoggin River. At Errol, they turned toward Independence.

"Do you realize we successfully bid on twelve of the fifteen pieces Ellie was very interested in, as well as…" Victor paused to count off the items in the catalog. "Six, seven, eight…nine of the maybe-if-the-price-is-right pieces she wanted?"

"I like the pair of Francis Trumble Windsors."

"Tomorrow morning, we just have to go to Rumford to pick up that Goddard-Townsend bureau and the Peter Stretch tall clock," Victor said. "I hope we have enough room back there."

"We've got room."

"Do you have the map of Maine?"

"You put it in the glove compartment," Brian replied. "It's an easy drive from here."

"If you say so. You know I hate leaving the city."

"It's nice up here," Brian said. "I wouldn't mind coming back this way."

"I'll take Philly or New York anytime. You know me. I like having people around."

Victor looked out the window as they rode along in silence for a few minutes. His mind drifted back to the auction. "That Benjamin Randolph highboy will make her happy. She might even keep it."

"It shows some beautiful workmanship," Brian said.

Victor nodded. "It's always amazing to me that pieces of furniture—like that highboy and the tall clock—can be built by a Philadelphia craftsman over two hundred years ago and then end up somewhere like northern New England."

"And still be in such great shape."

"Well, I like the idea of us bringing them back to Philadelphia," Victor said, looking down at the catalog notes. "Ellie wrote down here that she's getting the tall clock for that nice lady at 1500 Locust."

"Here's our turn," Brian said, nodding to the inn's sign up ahead.

As they turned off the state highway onto the gravel side road, Victor put the catalog into the briefcase on the floor. He looked up as Brian steered around a pothole.

"What's *this* all about?" Victor said, peering down the gravel road.

The sun was behind them, reflecting golden rays off a new Cadillac that was sitting on the edge of the road. They were still a mile from the inn, and Shawn Hobart stepped out of the car as the truck came into sight.

"Looks like your good friend, Shawn Hobart."

"Don't stop, Brian," Victor said. "He's such a creep."

"That's okay with me. I'll just go around—"

"No, you've got to stop. What if he needs help?"

"Looks like we don't have much choice," Brian said. Hobart was stepping out in front of them and waving them down.

"Well, that's pretty nervy!"

"I wonder what he really does for a living," Brian mused as they slowed down.

"Whatever it is, at least we know he's no antique dealer around here," Victor replied. "No one at that auction ever heard of him"

As the truck stopped, Hobart moved to the driver's side. Brian rolled down his window.

"Thanks for stopping."

"No problem," Brian said. "Need help?"

"As a matter of fact, I do."

Victor frowned at the alleged dealer. "Well, we'd like to help, Mr. Hobart, but Brian's a carpenter, not a mechanic. And we've had a full day at the auction. So why don't you hop in and we'll take you to the inn and you can call for help there."

Hobart stared at Victor for a moment, then turned back to Brian. "I just need help positioning the jack."

"You have a flat?" Brian asked, looking out at the car.

"The tires look fine to me," Victor put in.

"The front tire on the other side. The thing is totally flat," Hobart replied. "These new cars have specific places to put the jack, and…"

Victor yanked on the door handle and got out, muttering to himself, "I can tell you exactly where you can put the jack."

As he hopped down, Brian and Hobart came around from the other side of the truck.

"Did you look in the manual, Mr. Hobart?" Victor asked.

"As a matter of fact, I was just doing that when you two came up the road."

Hobart followed Victor and Brian around the front of the car. The two of them looked down at the tire in surprise. It was not flat.

"What's the big idea?" Victor said, turning around.

The silver-plated pistol in Shawn Hobart's hand was an even bigger surprise than the tire. Behind him, two younger men holding assault rifles emerged from the woods, and Victor felt a sense of dread wash through him. Hobart stepped forward, raising the muzzle of the gun until Victor was looking down the barrel.

"I told you not to stop," he said to Brian.

Ian would be turning forty-six at the end of the summer. "Grandpa" was what he was called by the kindergartners the department was hiring these days and putting out on the street as cops. He was five years older than the captain of his detective unit. He didn't care. This is what he had to do.

If you believed the bullshit put out by the department brass, he was too valuable to work the streets anymore. They wanted him behind a desk, running special operations, serving as a liaison between the narcotics, vice and homicide units, so they'd offered him a promotion again. They were moving him into management. But Ian didn't want the extra money. He wasn't interested in a better retirement pension or more vacations. He didn't care about any paper-pusher job. His only interest was to be put on the front line, on the street, where his blood would be pumping and his mind would be clear of everything except the suspect that he was about to apprehend.

That had been his way of thinking, anyway, before being introduced to the joys of finger painting with Jade. Now, though, he thought maybe he was really meant for a career in art.

"You have to do the green next," the little girl instructed, pointing to the paints Kelly had poured into saucer-shaped plastic dishes. Ian now understood Kelly's wisdom in bringing everything out on a battered old kitchen tray and setting them up at one of the picnic benches. The bench she'd picked was an older one that had been moved to the edge of the parking area. It was in a spot that was sheltered from the wind but still caught the last rays of sun. She had also dragged the end of the hose out, leaving it next to them.

She's done this before, Ian thought, eyeing the green paint.

The three of them had eaten an early dinner. The guests who were back at the inn were being served now. Kelly had left the dining-room duty tonight to Rita and had locked herself in her office to make a couple of calls. Ian thought he'd succeeded in convincing her that she had to leave the inn, at least for a few days. She just needed to stay out of harm's way until Monday was behind them.

Kelly had told him that she would contact some friends she'd stayed in touch with in New York. One of them was Dan's mother. The college kid was the only one in this entire place that she trusted. He was the only one that she'd hired herself.

She'd promised to be ready to leave tomorrow morning. And Ian *would* make sure that she got out of here safely...before the madness started.

"Green, Ian," Jade said, prompting him.

The large poster board they were working on was a masterpiece of color already. Ian looked down at his hands. One was yellow. The other one was dripping with blue.

"I'm going to make my own green." He rubbed his hands together and showed her the results.

"That's no good. Use this one," Jade directed as she dipped her finger into the paint and held it up in front of his nose. "See? *This* green."

She was holding the finger too close to his face for him to focus on, and Ian didn't miss the puckish look that crept into her face. She had paint in her hair and on her face and all over her clothing. Other than his hands, so far, he'd managed to stay clean.

He caught her hand just before she had a chance to smear it on his face.

"Arm wrestling with a three-year-old," Kelly scolded, coming across the parking area.

"She's almost four," Ian argued.

"Well, that's okay, then."

"Look at her. The little imp is a royal mess." He backed away when Jade tried to put her other hand on his shirt. "How many times a day do you have to change her clothes?"

"This will be her third change today. That's actually a pretty good day."

"Green!" Jade shouted, not giving up wrestling with him as she complained to her mother. "Show it to him, Mommy."

Kelly dipped the tip of her finger in the paint and held it up. "This one?"

"Yeah," Jade said excitedly.

Ian let go of the child but couldn't get his hands on Kelly before she dabbed the paint on his chin.

"That does it." He grabbed her by the waist, but like her daughter she seemed to have six extra hands. The paint was flying at him from every direction.

He got up from the bench, carrying Kelly away from her source of ammunition. Jade, however, was an excellent markswoman and didn't think twice about picking up the tray of paints and winging it at the two adults.

Using Kelly as a human shield worked. The blue and yellow and red hit her on the back of the pants and T-shirt, and as Ian turned her around in his arms, the green saucer connected as well, leaving a bull's-eye on her chest.

"I can't believe this." Her arms stretched out to the side, she looked down at the colorful mess she'd become.

Ian carefully let go of her and stepped back. Jade, standing only three steps away, started giggling. "We painted Mommy."

"You little paint pixie," Kelly growled, chasing after her daughter for a couple of steps. Jade screeched in delight and went around the table. She swung around toward Ian. "How could you let her do this to me? Look at me."

She was more relaxed than Ian had seen her since arriving at the inn. She also looked damn cute covered with all that paint.

"Hey, we were having a quiet, civilized time together. You were the one who started the trouble."

"*I* started the trouble?" She took a threatening step toward him.

Ian didn't back away. He stared at the green paint on the front of her T-shirt. For a few mad seconds he imagined how interesting it would be to take off those clothes and smear the rest of that paint over her naked body.

"I think it's only fair that you should get some of this, too," Kelly said, coming closer. "How about it, Ian? Just a little hug?"

She didn't have to ask twice. Reaching out, he took a fistful of her shirt and pulled her toward him hard enough that she fell into his arms. He kissed her lips before she could voice a complaint. His hands were on her back and bottom and on her neck and into her hair, and he could feel the paint on his fingers. A soft moan escaped her throat, and she rose up on her toes and wrapped her arms around him, answering the kiss with so much passion that he lost all interest in where they were and who was their audience.

"Me, too."

Jade's voice knocked them apart abruptly. Kelly's

face reddened with embarrassment. Ian scooped Jade up into his arms.

"None of this 'me, too' stuff," he told the little girl. "You started all of this, you little monkey."

"So? I want a hug, too." Not waiting for him, she wrapped her arms around his neck and hugged him tight.

For a couple of seconds, Ian's throat knotted up, but it was not from the pressure she was exerting. He pressed the child's head against his shoulder. His gaze and Kelly's locked. She reached up and touched his cheek before hugging him, too, with Jade sandwiched between them.

"Did you make the call?" he asked her softly.

She nodded. "We're all set." She placed a quick kiss on his lips.

A car coming down the gravel driveway made Kelly pull away and look back. Ian recognized the driver. He was annoyed when Shawn Hobart saw them and immediately pulled in close to their picnic table, kicking up dust as he skidded to a stop.

When Jade saw who was driving, she tried to crawl higher on Ian's chest. He handed the child to Kelly and stepped in front of them.

"You're asking for trouble, coming this close," Ian told Hobart as he got out of the car. Hobart hung a small leather bag over one shoulder.

"Yeah, well, I'll be watching that there's no paint spatter on this finish."

"We're not making any promises."

Hobart nodded to Kelly. "I hope I'm not late for

dinner. Your front desk warned me this morning of the change of the hours for dinner."

"You're cutting it close, but we won't let you starve, Mr. Hobart," Kelly said politely. "I'm sure Wilson can scrape together something for you in the kitchen."

Turning her back on the man, she began to clean up the mess they'd made on the bench and in the grass. Sundown was approaching fast. The shadows were getting longer and the air was getting cooler.

"So how are things across the way?" Ian asked, openly inspecting the mud on the tires and the fenders of Hobart's car.

"Across the way?"

"At the camp." Ian motioned with his head at that direction. "I stopped over there this morning. A very impressive setup. I had a chance to chat with Joshua Sharpe, and then Caleb showed me around. A lot of people seem to be showing up. And it's good that they have a list. It makes sense to know who's supposed to be there, and who's not. So what's your function? Are you one of the ministers or just a member of the congregation?"

Color was rising on the skin on the man's neck. He moved his bag from one shoulder to the other.

"I'm just here as part of our church retreat," he finally said in a gruff voice.

"A member of the congregation, then?"

"You could say that."

"They invited me over for some of the sermons,"

Ian lied. "I forgot to ask the name of some of the guest speakers, though."

"I don't know anything about that." Hobart made a big production of pointing the key chain toward the car door and pressing the autolock. "Got to get some dinner."

"When are you going back over?"

The older man's expression darkened with annoyance. He glanced at Kelly. "I didn't know I had to report in to other guests."

"I was only going to ask you to pick me up a schedule of the activities and the speakers," Ian said calmly. "But I wouldn't want to put you out."

"I'll see if I can get you a schedule tomorrow," Hobart grumbled as he walked past them and proceeded toward the inn.

Sixteen

Kelly couldn't take a suitcase or any kind of carrying bag that would bring attention to what she and Jade were planning to do. She looked around at a room full of memories, knowing she had to leave it all behind—for now, at least. The very few photographs she dared put in her handbag would have to be selected after her daughter was asleep.

Ian's suggestion was for the mother and daughter to walk out of the inn tomorrow morning and get in their car, pretending to go and do some routine chore—going to church or visiting one of Jade's friends or something like that. They didn't want to raise any suspicions at all. Kelly didn't want to tell him how bitter and fearful she'd become about religion, after her early upbringing. She definitely didn't have the heart to tell him that Jade had no friends. And she couldn't bring herself to admit to him what a huge effect his presence was having on both of their lives.

"Is Ian going to tuck me in tonight, too?" Jade asked from her bed.

"He had some things to do, but I saw him give you a hug before he went downstairs." She gently rolled up the old yellow blanket and put it next to Jade on the bed.

"I know." The little girl sighed dramatically, cuddling with her favorite blanket.

Kelly pushed a strand of damp hair out of Jade's face. It had taken some hard work to wash Jade's hair and scrub every bit of paint off her face and hands. Both of them were finally squeaky clean, though. And both of them were dealing with unexpected feelings for the same man.

"Will you stay up here, Mommy?" Jade asked in a little voice when Kelly turned off the bedside light.

"Yes, honey. I'll be right outside the door, doing some grown-up reading."

"Love you," she whispered, closing her eyes.

"Love you, too," Kelly whispered back, brushing a kiss over her daughter's forehead.

She had to get up from the edge of the bed, had to tiptoe away…before the tears came. She was an emotional tumbleweed right now, and there was no telling what direction the breeze would roll her tonight.

Downstairs earlier, she'd struggled but had been barely successful at remaining civil with Janice. As the guests were finishing dinner in the dining room, she'd told the older woman that she was going up early and the rest of them could take care of locking up for the night. Kelly hadn't said so, but the thought ran through her head that they were in control, anyway.

Kelly wasn't sure when this mess had started. She wasn't sure how many years her life had been a lie.

She'd always thought she had escaped the Mission, but she now wondered how completely the strands of Michael Butler's vile web ran through her life. Could it be that everyone, every chapter of her life, had somehow been a part of it?

She wasn't going to stay here to find out. Not with Jade at risk. She knew what these people were capable of. She'd move her clear across the country, if need be. Out of the country, even.

Kelly turned off two other lights in the apartment and walked to the sitting area.

She'd been able to connect with Sally Davies, Dan's mother today. After saying that she and her daughter were going to be in New York City for three or four days, Kelly had needed no other reason for coming. Sally had insisted that they stay with her.

If they didn't know she was running away, then they wouldn't come after her, Kelly reasoned, walking into Ian's room and taking the file with all the information off his dresser. Her worry was not about how to get from here to there safely, but how to deal with Ian staying behind.

Kelly went back to the sitting area on the landing and sat down, opening the files on her lap. The obituaries were on top. Brother Ty's...or rather, Father Ty's new army of believers could obviously commit murder, and she was terrified at the thought that Ian could be hurt, even killed. At least she had the peace of mind of knowing that Ian was a policeman. He was trained and capable, and he knew better than anyone what he was facing.

Old attachments were difficult to break, Kelly thought, thumbing through the rest of the information in the thick file. Toward the bottom of the pile, she came across a copy of an article that she hadn't seen before. The piece was dated one year after the Butler Mission suicide. She looked at the picture of the woman on the first page. Anne Campbell. Kelly remembered her because she was an outsider. She was young, beautiful, full of life. She tore her gaze away from the picture and read the headline.

Social Worker Was a Cult Member.

Kelly quickly scanned the article. The investigation following the mass suicide had concluded that Anne Campbell's presence at the Mission compound that night was voluntary, and that the twenty-two-year-old social worker was a member of the religious sect and a willing participant in the suicide.

Kelly let out a frustrated breath. She understood why Ian had to stay. She knew why he had to find the truth.

Ian's socks were damp and his shoes soggy. Dropping a pillowcase containing other clothes on the picnic bench, he slowly gathered up the wet items and stuffed them into the makeshift laundry bag as he surreptitiously studied the cottage closest to him.

This was where Dan was staying, and it was the first time he'd seen the door left ajar. He looked back toward the house. Daylight was quickly fading, and the shadows of the trees covered the area around him. A few minutes ago, when he'd been coming down the back stairs, he'd heard Dan and Wilson arguing in the kitchen. The cook had been ripping into the kid about not washing the floor under one of the food-prep tables, and Dan had returned a few choice words in response to being called back to the kitchen to repeat a perfectly satisfactory job.

Ian walked to the cottage door and slipped inside. A bedside light had been left on, and he had a clear view of the entire place. The first impression that struck him was how clean the place was. No clothes tossed on any chair or on the floor. No leftover food composting on the small table. No beer cans decoratively stacked on the windowsills. No piles of magazines sporting covers of athletes or musicians or buxom models. The guy was certainly not fitting the profile of what Ian thought most college kids were like these days. Dan's living quarters definitely did not match the image Ian had in his head.

He could see an oversize bag and a black suitcase stuffed under the bed. He eyed a backpack that had been left on the bed. On a dresser next to him, the kid's wallet and watch and some change caught his eye.

Ian flipped open the front of the wallet. Dan's New York license—picture and address—matched what and who he claimed to be. Ian picked up the watch and glanced at the back.

Congratulations, Ed.
Love, Mom & Dad
June 2001

Ian heard the footsteps outside and turned the watch over in his hand.

"What are you doing in here?" Dan asked, clearly annoyed as he marched into the cottage.

"Admiring your watch," Ian said, tossing it to the younger man. Dan quickly strapped it on. "High-school graduation present?"

"Yeah, something like that. What do you want?" He pocketed his wallet and looked around the room before grabbing a windbreaker that was hanging from a peg on the wall.

"I'm looking for a laundry machine," Ian replied, motioning to the pillowcase filled with clothes at his feet. "I definitely underestimated how much clothing I needed when I packed."

"There's a washer and dryer in the basement of the inn," Dan said, grabbing his backpack and ushering Ian toward the door. "Take the door across the hall from the kitchen. You can't miss it."

Outside, Ian stood around as Dan made a point of locking the door of his cottage. "Hot date?"

"How did you guess?" The young man gave him a long look before running off into the darkness in the direction of the parking lot.

Ian stayed where he was for a minute or two. No cars left the parking area. He knew that Dan didn't have his own wheels up here, and he wondered if the kid was traveling on foot...and where.

The dining-room lights were out. Going back to the inn, Ian noticed that Victor Desposito's rental truck was not back yet. Wilson Blade's car was already gone.

Nobody had locked the door. Stepping inside, Ian could see lights on in the sitting area beyond the reception desk. He could hear the muffled voices of people sitting in the chairs there. Ian poked his head into the kitchen, where the lights were turned off. The door across the way, which he assumed led to the basement, was ajar. Ian opened it farther and saw a light burning in the basement. Listening carefully, he heard the sound of someone moving boxes around. Ian was wearing his pistol holster behind his back, clipped to his belt. Reaching around under the Hawaiian shirt he had on, he unsnapped the leather holster strap.

"Hello," he called. "Someone down here?"

The noise stopped. He moved quietly down a couple of steps and crouched low when he had a good view of the space at the foot of the steps. The dank smell of basement and the distinct odor of mice filtered into his nostrils as he surveyed the area. Washer. Dryer. A couple of shelves above them filled with detergents and things. A slate laundry sink on one end. In the center of an adjoining alcove, a giant furnace and a pair of huge water heaters sat at the ready. A large table, probably used for folding laundry, sat in the middle of the space, and a fluorescent light overhead buzzed and flickered every couple of seconds. Five laundry lines with clothespins on them had been strung from the beams at the far end of the basement, where Ian could see an abandoned washing machine that had to date back to the 1940s.

The true age of this section of the house showed in the thick, rough-hewn beams. They were dark and ancient and covered with cobwebs. Ian moved silently around the cellar. When he looked into the alcove behind the furnace, spider webs trailed onto his face. As he brushed them away and backed out, a brown mouse scurried out from under one of the water heaters and ran along the wall, disappearing into a crack at the base of the stone foundation.

There was no one in sight, but there was a door at one end of the cellar that seemed to lead to another section. It was open slightly, and Ian could see a light on in a room beyond.

Dropping the bag he was carrying onto the table, Ian headed toward the door. A new padlock hung open on an old latch. The light in the room went out as soon he reached the doorway. Instinctively, Ian stepped out of the way. He was not about to become a clear target.

A second later, Rita emerged carrying a large black plastic garbage bag. Through a tear in the bag, Ian spied crimson-red fabric.

"I thought I heard somebody down here," Ian said good-naturedly. "Do you need a hand with that?"

She swung the bag behind her and closed the door with her foot.

"What are you doing down here?" she said brusquely, closing the latch and fastening the padlock.

"Dan told me this is where the laundry is."

"Just leave it. Somebody will do it for you later."

"No, I don't have anything better to do right now." He looked over his shoulder at the machines. "They look pretty standard to me. I think I can handle it."

"Suit yourself," she said, dragging the bag toward the stairs.

"Are you sure you don't need a hand bringing that up?"

"No," she said curtly, lifting the load and starting up the stairs.

"Going over to the camp?"

His question caused her to miss a step. She stumbled but caught herself. She lost her grip on the bag, though, and she had to trap it against the stairs with her legs. As she did, the tie at the top gave, exposing the clothing packed inside. Red. Everything was solid red.

Rita cursed under her breath and twisted the top closed again.

Ian realized that she had no intention of acknowledging or answering his question. "I saw Wilson's car is gone. Do you have a ride tonight?"

"I'm fine," she said emphatically. Without another word, she ran up the stairs with her load.

Ian followed the sound of Rita's footsteps across the floor above. She didn't leave through the rear door, but walked down the back hall to the vicinity of the reception desk. A couple of minutes later, a number of people moved toward the main entrance. He heard footsteps going down the front steps and then the sound of car doors opening and closing. Ian guessed the engine that came to life in the parking area was the Sterns' minivan. He waited until the car drove off.

There was nothing in this room that interested him. With its gray stone walls and painted concrete floor, the space had been organized to fit the lie that had been fed to Kelly all her life.

Ian took out his flashlight. The padlock on the door was a good one, so he took a penknife from his pocket and pried out the two nails that attached the latch to the door. Swinging them out of the way, he opened the door and flashed the beam of his light into the separate section of the cellar. There was a low hum emanating from a far corner. The room appeared to be a storage space of some kind. He stepped in and flipped the light switch beside the door.

The room, located under the reception area and the parlor, was larger than the laundry area, but it was mostly filled with carefully organized boxes. Chairs and desks and beds were neatly stacked against the walls, near more metal shelves filled with boxes. Everything seemed to be labeled. Ian closed the door behind him and looked at a stack of boxes to his left.

He stared at the labels for a long moment. They were all marked New Mexico. He felt the hairs on his neck stand up. He looked again at the things stored there.

Everything was clean. No coating of dust could be seen on anything. Even the smell of the room was different, and he looked into the far corner. The hum was coming from a dehumidifier.

Ian picked up a chair sitting next to a table. There was a label on both the chair and the table: New Mexico. Study. Butler. He looked at the label on a reading lamp. The same information.

A chill ran down his spine. It was all from the Butler Mission in New Mexico. Everything belonging to the self-proclaimed prophet—from the bare-bones furnishings in the buildings to the books from Butler's own apartment—had been put on auction to pay the burial expenses of those victims whose families had not come to claim their bodies. Ian remembered the auction taking place. He hadn't been able to bring himself to go, but he knew that there was a good-size crowd who did come to bid on the property. He'd thought it was ghoulish then, but he hadn't had any idea.

It was all right here.

Ian tore open the top of a box by his feet. It was packed with books. A loose inventory sheet lay on top. He scanned the titles. They all had to do with religion in some way—books on the apocalyptic scriptures, Hindu mysticism, the writings of St. Germaine, Atlantis and ancient Egypt, the Dead Sea scrolls. The list went on. Part of Butler's personal library. He dropped the sheet back in the box and moved toward the wall. Metal shelving housed smaller boxes. The dates on these were more specific, and everything was filed in chronological order.

Ian opened the box dated February.

In it, he found a series of curled black-and-white photographs. He stared at the images, feeling his gut twist at the sight of the smiling faces. Groups of people were working together, moving beds and furniture into a building. Sitting together at meals. Standing at a church service. Butler speaking to a rapt crowd.

He opened another box. And then another. All similar pictures. It was a photographic record of the Butler Divinity Mission. These photos had not been at the Mission the day of the suicide.

Ian moved along the shelves and pulled off one of the earliest dated boxes. Butler looked so young in these pictures. They had to be photos of the first days of the Mission, while they were still in Albuquerque. He shoved the box back onto the shelf and pulled down another, thumbing quickly through the pictures. He was about to put the top back on when one of the photos caught his attention. Ian pulled out the picture and looked carefully at the face of the woman who was seated beside Butler in the shot. A coffee table separated them. She looked like she was conducting an interview.

Rose Wilton, Kelly's adoptive mother.

Ian searched inside the box again, digging deeper. He found more pictures of her, all of them with Butler. Different days, different outfits.

He looked at the date on the box. These were taken before Kelly was even born. She would have never known of the old connection.

Kelly had never escaped the Mission. She'd never been safe.

Ian felt the walls of the cellar begin to close in on

him, but he fought off the sensation. He had to see it all. No, he thought, he had to see the last days.

Moving down the rows of boxes, he looked at the date on each until he found the one he was looking for. It was a different kind of box. He took it down off the shelf and tore open the sealing tape. There were no curling prints in this one, but only a single photo album. Ian carefully lifted it out.

His hands were shaking as he opened to the first page. He turned the page. Each one contained a lone photograph mounted beneath a plastic sheet. His chest was tight and he could barely breathe, but he looked at each picture. They were all gathered in the chapel. All of them were listening to Butler, their faces lit with excitement. Several pictures of the font. The cups. The passing out of candles.

Ian closed the album and carried it to the chair that once had belonged to a monster. He sat down and opened the album again.

Halfway through, he came to a picture of Butler holding up a cup. He stared at the face of the man, trying to discern something there that would explain what was about to happen. Nothing. He turned the page.

Each page after that was a record of those coming up to receive their cup from their spiritual leader. The photographer had taken the pictures to capture the believers three at a time. One was taking the cup while the other two waited patiently.

Ian felt the tears burn his eyes. He tried not to focus on the lost children, on the trust that was evident in so many of the faces. He flipped the pages faster and faster. He was searching for one thing, one person.

And then he found it. He found Anne—smiling, confident, beautiful—taking the cup of poison from Michael Butler's own hand.

Seventeen

Dan lay motionless in the grove of trees by the unpaved parking lot, trying to ignore the damp cold seeping up into his body. He'd been lying here for well over an hour, and his joints were stiff. He could smell the earthy scent of pine and soil, and he listened to the voices of the group members as they left the dining hall en masse and returned to the cabins. The sun was long gone when they began filtering down toward the benches and the stage, and he could see from their silhouetted forms that many were wearing robes or carrying them over their arms.

Time dragged by in endless ticks of his watch, but when he felt it was dark enough, Dan moved toward the back of the dining hall. The sound of the people gathering at the benches in front of the covered stage reached him as he crossed to the building. Pressing his back against the wall, Dan strained his ears, but he couldn't tell if anyone was still in the dining hall or the kitchen.

He was not in the shadows for even a minute when a light went on in a window above him, throwing a long rectangle of yellow onto the dirt lane behind the dining hall. Hearing a voice coming toward the back of the building, he quickly moved to the Dumpster and squeezed himself behind it just as the door above him opened.

''It'll take two of you to carry the large vat down, you know.'' The voice sounded as if it came from a young man standing at the door, and the response from within was muffled. ''Just hurry up. The font has to be filled before the service starts.''

The door banged shut and a pair of sneakered shoes came down the wooden steps. Dan's muscles tensed as the young man approached the Dumpster. The top creaked open and a number of empty plastic containers were tossed in, the hollow sound echoing. The top banged down but the man didn't immediately move away.

Dan wondered if he'd been discovered. He held his breath as seconds ticked by. His mind considered the possible situations and his own responses. Pretty limited, all in all. Against his back, he felt the vibration of a door closing somewhere in the dining hall.

Then, as the sound of a keyboard came across the speakers, he heard the young man move away, turning the corner and going toward the camp center. Dan let out a deep breath and edged out of his hiding place. Peeking around the corner of the building, he could see brilliant footlights lit the stage, two of them focused on the banner hanging at the back. His field of vision of the stage itself was obstructed from here, though.

Over the lake, the moon was just beginning to rise,

but it was enshrouded in a strange, unnatural-looking fog that clung to the near edge of the lake.

Someone spoke into a microphone, asking everyone to be seated as they'd been instructed. The keyboard player fired up, and the chords of a gospel song filled the air. People in the congregation immediately began to sing.

Staying low, Dan ran in the shadows until he reached a small cabin behind the administrator's office. Ministers in red robes and white sashes were standing by the door of the camp office, which overlooked the center and the stage. As he watched them, a solitary figure robed in white emerged from the office. The entourage quickly formed around their leader, but Dan recognized "Father" Ty Somers immediately.

"Bingo," he breathed.

As the escort moved toward the stage, Dan edged forward. From here, he had a clear view of the front of the stage and much of the swaying, singing congregation, as well. Dan judged everyone expected was already here. They were all dressed in identical blood-red robes.

The stage itself was lit up like a photography studio, with lights and screens arranged carefully and unobtrusively. Directly in front of the stage, a half-dozen members of the cult's inner circle took their places, facing the assembly, ready to lead the congregation in prayer and song. Joshua Sharpe was standing at the far end. On the stage, a baptismal font stood near the front edge, and a microphone had been set up near it. In the very center, on a large chair draped in a shimmering white cloth, Tyler Somers sat down, withdrawing into an attitude of deep meditation, his body motionless and his eyes shut.

Dan saw Ken Burke move down the center aisle toward the stage, his camera clicking as he recorded the scene. From the edge of the stage, the photographer focused on Somers, then turned and photographed the congregation. Moving to one end of the Pavilion, he turned and took shots of the ministers.

Dan looked at the font by the front edge of the stage. Right beside it, an empty easel stood with red and white sashes draped over it. There were cups on a small table on the other side of the font. A flash of concern shot through him. He looked at his watch as the singing stopped.

Somers stood up and moved to the microphone, and silence fell over the assembly. He smiled and held up his hands. A woman cried out a blessing on him from somewhere toward the back, and he nodded.

"May the great Lord and his prophet and saint Michael smile down upon us, children."

A great "Amen" sounded out in response.

"Sit, brothers and sisters, for we have much to discuss."

The congregation settled onto the benches.

"THIS is the time of our Rapture!" Somers began thunderously. "THIS is our time…our turn…OUR PATH!"

As he was speaking, the fog behind him began to

dissipate. Without looking, he gestured with his hand at the lake.

"The planets and the stars have aligned themselves once again, children, opening the way for us across the universe. Do you see it, brothers and sisters?"

The moon, huge and white, suddenly became visible in a cloudless night sky, and the moonlight reflected brilliantly in the lake, its beams broken up into a million shards on the surface of the water. It looked like a path of gold across the lake.

Cries of "Yes!" and "I see it" rang out.

"It is our path," he continued. Somers moved back and forth across the stage, looking into the eyes of his congregation. "We are the Chosen Ones. It is our destiny!

"Think, brothers and sisters, of how our lives follow the divine plan. In this, we conform to His will. There is no struggle in this. We join Him willingly, in happy and joyous exaltation of Him and His saints who have gone before us. Our path is His design, His divine plan."

Somers raised his hands to the heavens.

"Use me, Michael, as the instrument, as you are eternally the instrument of the Ideal One. Guide me from the shores of the fiery lake, you saints who have ascended through the ages, guide me at this time of Tribulation. Teach me, holy ones, how to walk the eternal path at our moment of Rapture."

A shout came from the believers, "Bless him, Michael."

"Brothers and sisters, let us join our hearts and our

souls to recognize the light-bearer, the one who holds open the door to eternity. In our unification, in our sharing of the Divine Blood, we shall no longer walk on the dark path of our limited human reason. Unified with Him, we share in the divine energy that dispels human ignorance. Out of this energy comes the garment of eternity, the great seamless garment of the living Divinity.

"Look to the skies." Somers pointed toward the rising moon. "Born of the divine sun which created all energy, that planet is a sign of our redemption. Just as the moon is a magnet in this existential plane, controlling the ebb and flow of the tides of the great oceans, the Divine Magnet that created the universe controls the ebb and flow of the very shadows and the light. Now is the time when the Divine Magnet draws us, with a transformed consciousness, into the ascendant plane. As we break off the ties of our frail human existence, we renew the ancient covenants in which we are called back home into the very bosom of Him.

"Now is our time, my family. When Khumba Luxor last occurred, aligning the celestial bodies and opening our spiritual path, our Prophet Michael led our brothers and sisters through the eternal door. Now the stars and planets are again in place, and the Prophet left us His own divine offspring, our own Luna-K, to lead us past the tenacious ties of this earthly existence. Born of the House of Cancer, she is the moonchild to take us home. Nurtured and guided to this place and time, Luna-K shall become herself the pathway of the holy flame. For us, for this moment, for this Khumba Luxor, the Father has left us his own child, the conduit of the divine energy force. She is the holy flame, the Divine Magnet, the day and the night, the conscious and the unconscious, the Creator and Destroyer. She is here, brothers and sisters, to lead us home…''

Somers continued to work his spell upon the congregation, telling them the meaning of the event that they were about to participate in. Alternately praising them for their faithfulness and then chastising them for their sinfulness, he gradually raised the pitch of his message as he went, enveloping them in his power. The emotions of the believers spilled out as he spoke. Then, when he had them firmly in his grip, he returned to his earlier exhortation.

''The time when we shall ascend into the heavens has come,'' he cried out. ''Can you see them, sisters and brothers? Can you see the Prophet, sainted and clothed in white? Can you see him there waiting for us? Can you see him with our brethren who have gone before, standing before the White Throne, their arms open to us? Welcoming us?

''Prepare yourselves, children. The glory of our ascension awaits. The current of energy that will carry us is again open to us, His Chosen Ones. As the Christ showed us on that Easter morning, we have been given our passage. There is no life's end for us. We have the chariot of fire. We have with us the eternal Thread of Contact. We have the Angel of His Blood.

Luna-K—the Moonchild, the Divine Magnet, the holy flame—is with us.''

Somers raised his hands over the multitude. A picture of Kelly was carried up and placed on the easel beside the baptismal font and draped with the crimson and white cloths. People cheered and there were shouts of joy from the congregation. Ken Burke's camera continued to click away.

''Luna-K will lead us, my children, out of the limited colors of human existence into the infinite spectrum of eternal light. Into the heavenly world of ascended saints and divine beings. They await us…and our time is near! Prepare!''

As the keyboard began a low somber chant, assistants hurried down the aisles, quickly distributing candles. Somers went to the white throne and sat down, clearly overcome with exhaustion at being the vehicle of the message. His hands were draped over the armrests and his chin was on his chest. A minister came with a cup of something to drink, from which he managed a sip before wearily rising to his feet. Burke focused his lens on Somers's face.

Within minutes, the congregation was standing with their candles lit, swaying in unison to the slow rise and fall of the music. Somers stepped up to the microphone again.

''Brothers and sisters…my soul will rise.''

''My soul will rise!'' emanated from the mouths of the entire multitude.

''See the shadows melt away,'' he chanted.

''My soul will rise!''

"See the veils melt away."

"My soul will rise!"

"Foolishness is human thought."

"My soul will rise!"

"It melts and vanishes into the air."

"My soul will rise!" The pitch of the assembly was rising.

"All that I AM is everywhere."

"My soul will rise!"

"Everywhere, everywhere I AM!"

"MY SOUL WILL RISE!"

"The realm of angels awaits you."

"MY SOUL…"

On and on, the chanting continued. Dan looked at the members of the congregation that he could see. Their faces had clearly taken on a trancelike appearance. No one looked anywhere but at the stage. The candles were burning down, but no one was paying the least attention to them.

"…SOUL WILL RISE!"

"The cleansing flame awaits you."

"MY SOUL WILL RISE!"

"Come and drink the divine blood."

"MY SOUL WILL RISE!"

Somers stopped abruptly, raising his hands to the group. "Come, children. Drink the waters. We are nearing the Rapture."

Silently, the entire assembly—even the children— filed forward. At the front of the line, each member blew out the candle in their hand and received from Somers himself a full cup of liquid from the font, which the ministers handed to him. Ken Burke photographed each one as they received the cup. Then, just as silently, they all returned to their seats and stood with their cups raised toward their leader.

Dan stood up, unsure what to do. When the members of the congregation were all standing at their seats, Somers took a cup himself.

"Drink to the memory of those who preceded us, children. Drink to the path that lies ahead of us. The door to eternity is open."

As everyone drank from their cups, Dan looked on in horror.

But his shock was momentary, for he heard the footstep behind him and twisted his head only in time to see the flash of the knife in Wilson Blade's hand.

Eighteen

By ten o'clock, Kelly was curious about what had happened to Ian. By eleven, she was worried enough to go looking for him.

She checked on her sleeping daughter first. Peering out the window, Kelly could see the shapes of her own car and Ian's in the moonlight. The space where the Desposito party had parked their rental truck the night before was still empty. She couldn't see the rest of the lot from this angle. She looked down at the lakefront from a window on the opposite side of the apartment. All was quiet there. A light in Dan's cottage was on. Far off across the water, she could see lights burning brightly from the camp.

Kelly came down the stairs. The second-floor hallway was quiet, lit only by two night-lights at either end. There were no lights coming from under any of the doorways. Either the guests were not back yet or they had already settled for the night. For a moment, Kelly thought of the complication her leaving tomorrow would cause Janice. She quickly shook the thought off, reminding herself that most, if not all, of these people were tied in some way to the new Mission across the lake. Probably only Victor Desposito and his friend were not part of it; they were the only ones scheduled to check out.

She was halfway down the back stairwell when Ian came around the corner.

"I got worried," she started. "I—"

"We shouldn't leave Jade alone," he said, quietly coming up. "I locked all the doors."

"I don't think everyone is back," she said, backing up to give him room. The hallway was dark, but she noticed the flashlight in his hand. "Everyone has a key to the front door, though."

"Do you have a phone in your apartment?"

Kelly nodded. "I only use it for outgoing calls, though. The ringer is turned off. If nobody picks it up downstairs, then the answering machine kicks in."

Ian ushered Kelly ahead of him up the stairs. She noticed the close attention he gave to latching the door and testing it.

It wasn't until they were upstairs that Kelly turned around and saw the change in him. Though his expression was unreadable, she could see the tight control he was keeping on his feelings. His jaw clenched and unclenched. She could feel the tension in him.

"Did something happen?"

He shook his head and walked by her into the apartment. She followed and watched Ian lean over Jade's bed and gaze at the child for a few moments. The little girl was sleeping peacefully, and he gently touched a strand of Jade's hair before straightening up.

His face hardened again as his eyes scanned the

apartment. Wordlessly, he opened the doors of her two closets, looking inside at the entire space, even turning his flashlight on to inspect the closet ceilings. She watched him look under the beds and inside the large blanket chest she kept against one wall. He checked the kitchen cabinets and her bathroom, as well.

Kelly felt a chill wash through her, realizing the cult members might go so far as to hide someone or something in her apartment. She knew they'd been listening to her. It was all so different than the way she remembered it.

As much as she'd hated it—as much as she'd known she didn't belong—Kelly remembered very little overt coercion at the Mission in New Mexico. The nights leading to the final suicide at the Butler Mission were filled with rituals everyone was required to participate in, but no one had held a gun to anyone's head. It had been peer pressure, not the threat of violence, that had made Kelly herself stand in the line. And even that last afternoon, when Lauren was taking four children away from the Mission, Kelly had seen members of the cult watching their departure. True, no one assigned to security that night had seen them, but no one else had tried to stop them.

Ian conducted a quick search of his own room. Kelly waited in the sitting area until he turned off the light and came back out.

"Will you please tell me what happened?"

"I don't think you want to know," he said, turning

off the two lamps in the sitting area. He opened the shutters and the light of the rising moon poured in.

Kelly saw him study the parking area below. "Ian, I've listened to you and gone along with everything you've told me so far, believing that what you've been telling me is the absolute truth. What I *don't* want is you holding back now."

"Okay." He turned his back to the window. "But first, I think you should know, the earlier you leave, the better."

"Sure, whatever. But—"

"Also, I'll need to make a call before you go."

"That's no problem."

"Kelly, when you were working with this Sally Davies, do you remember her ever talking about a son?"

She stared at him a moment. "Sally was divorced, living alone. When she called me this spring, she mentioned that Dan used to live with his father. Why?"

"We'll know tomorrow, after I make a call and find out who's buttering Dan's bread."

Kelly sat down on the edge of a chair. "He's not who he says he is?"

"I don't know. But if I don't get a straight answer tomorrow morning, then I'm taking you and Jade out of here myself. I'll find you a place to stay temporarily until this thing is done with."

"And you'll stay with us," Kelly repeated, feeling her spirits lift for the first time since all the revelations about the lies began to pile up on her.

"I have to come back for Monday."

Kelly swallowed the painful knot of protest rising into her throat. She pushed herself to her feet, paced the length of the sitting area, and looked at Ian across the darkness of the room. He was leaning against one side of the window, pretending to be looking outside. But there was something more. She walked to the other side of the window, mirroring him.

"Suspecting Dan of being someone else is not the only thing that's bothering you, is it?" she asked, reaching over and gently touching his hand. "Something happened."

His answer was slow in coming. It took him a few long seconds before he turned and looked at her, before he actually saw her.

"I want it to be over," he said in a low voice. "Once and for all. Over and done with. I never want to look back at that again."

"The Mission," she said softly.

She heard the grief in his tone. When their gazes locked, she knew his eyes held a thousand unshed tears.

"Ian," she said gently. She closed the distance between them and wrapped her arms around him. She pressed her head against his heart. "I've had a break from it, at least. Despite all the lies around me, I thought I was leading a normal life. That it was behind me. But you haven't had that. You've been torturing yourself with this for so long."

She looked up and touched his cheek with the tips of her fingers.

"Pull the plug on this," she said firmly. "Call in all the law enforcement agencies you can. Let the others handle it. There's no guarantee that you'll get any answers to Anne's death by going to that camp yourself. It's more likely that you'll *never* have an answer to what happened."

The silence was complete as they stood by the window, the soft, pale light of the moon enveloping them. Kelly could see the moonlight reflected in his eyes.

"But I do know the answer," he said quietly. "I just don't know how to put it all behind me."

"You know? But how could—"

Ian was kissing her before she could finish her question. He kissed her with such longing that she couldn't do anything but answer his need, allowing her own need—held so deeply within her—to burst to the surface.

He pulled her away from the window and pressed her back against the wall. She burned with excitement as his hands roamed over her body. His mouth was hard and demanding, and he deepened the kiss.

She leaned into his touch when his hand found her bare breast beneath her shirt. His hands were everywhere. She moaned with pleasure when he pressed his hand in the most intimate of places through the thick denim of her jeans. She found herself arching against him, wrapping her arms around his neck, kissing him with mindless passion as the sweet pressure within her swelled. Suddenly she realized she was at the fringe of coming apart. Kelly tore her mouth free, calling on her last shred of common sense.

"Not here," she whispered hoarsely.

His mouth tasted the skin of her neck. He was slow to take his hands off her body.

"Let's go to your room," she whispered against his ear.

His eyes were black when they met hers. She could see he was thinking now, too. "We shouldn't. I'm complicating your life more than you need it to be, right now."

Kelly shook her head. "If you are a complication, then I *want* my life complicated." She entwined her fingers with his and pulled him toward his room.

Ian followed her, his gaze burning her with its intensity. Once inside the small guest room, she closed the door most of the way and turned to him.

"First, I have something to tell you," he said raggedly. "The reason I...I'm hurting right now. Tonight, I found out that my wife was at that Mission willingly. She bought the stuff Butler was selling. She went to her death...with all those others...smiling." He paused, fighting to keep his composure. "All these years, I've been chasing a ghost I never really knew. There was no crime to be solved. Her honor didn't need to be restored. She did what she wanted, when she wanted, and I was a fool for not seeing it then...and for not realizing it for another twenty-two years."

"You're *not* a fool," she scolded gently, coming close to him and grabbing a fistful of his faded Hawaiian shirt. "I can see who you are. You're a man capable of loving deeply. You're a man of honor. I'm sorry that your marriage worked out that way." She tugged at his shirt, making sure she had his attention. "But, Ian, I'm glad that you showed up here when you did. You're giving my daughter and me another chance at life."

Ian looked at her as if he was seeing a side of her that he didn't know. Kelly didn't let go of his shirt and returned his stare.

"Where did you learn to act like a tough guy?" he said finally, the trace of a smile breaking across his lips.

"I used to live next to a little theater on East Ninety-third," she said, letting her fingers trail down the front of his shirt. "It only showed movies from the 1940s. Bogie, Cagney, Ladd..."

He caught and flattened her hand against his hard stomach. "Kelly, I'm...ancient. You have to know I already have a deep crush on you and your daughter. What I'm trying to say is that things might get a little sentimental on my end. So are you sure you want to mess with me?"

Kelly smiled and brushed her lips against his, teasing him until he was ready to deepen the kiss, but she pulled back. "Yeah. I really want to mess with you."

"In that case..." He let the words trail off as he unclipped his holstered pistol from the back of his belt.

Kelly saw him eject the cartridge before he put the weapon on the bedside table. She stood there watching as Ian unbuttoned his shirt, took it off and laid it next to a couple of other shirts lying on the chair.

"Your turn," he said to her, his eyes skimming her body, causing her skin to tingle.

Her husband was the last man she'd made love to. And that life felt as if it had taken place aeons ago. Still, Kelly was surprised at Ian hinting that she might be too young for him. She felt almost crazed with desire for him right now, and she wanted him to feel that way about her, too.

"My turn?" she said softly.

Ever so slowly, she pulled her T-shirt up and over her head. She dropped it on the floor.

"How am I doing?" she asked, seeing his gaze focus on her breasts.

"Just perfect," he said hoarsely.

"Still my turn?" she asked, opening the top button of her jeans, then the next one and the next one after that.

That was as far as she got before Ian took her in his arms. In an instant, she was flat on her back on the bed and he was there with her, kissing her deeply as they struggled out of the rest of their clothes.

Kelly gave a soft cry when Ian entered her. He immediately tried to withdraw, but she held him, stretching up and kissing his lips as she lifted herself toward him. It had been so long.

"Tell me if I'm hurting you."

"This is so right," she whispered back. He slid back and then thrust again. Her body stretched and took him in deeper. Kelly arched her back and let the waves of pleasure build in her body.

She kissed his lips and looked into his eyes as he

made love to her. She could see into his heart and his
soul. There was grief there for so many faces, so
many people. And there was anger there, for a
woman. Kelly was seeing a dark passageway of un-
certainty. She tried to see more, looking deeper.

It was there, as she knew it would be—love, pure
and true, glowing within the protective sphere surrounding his heart.

As their bodies molded to one another, so did their
souls, and Kelly saw it the moment they became one.

Ian came closer, sealing her mouth with his, and
the love dance became frenzied. Higher and higher
they rose until Kelly heard him cry out just as she did
herself, and they soared off together through a pul-
sating cloud.

The night before, he'd cursed the old bed for being
too narrow and too short. Tonight, Ian decided the
creaky old thing was the perfect size. The only way
the two of them could stay on it comfortably was for
Kelly to lie with her body draped over his.

He liked looking up at her with her face on his
chest, her chin propped on the back of her hands. Her
hair was a mess, and the curls lay in disarray on her
beautiful skin. It would be so easy for Ian to lose
himself in the new beginning that they could each
give the other. Another chance at life, she'd called it.

Walk away from this disaster across the lake, he
told himself. Take her and never look back. Kelly had
said it. Let someone else handle the catastrophe that
was about to unfold.

Unconsciously, Ian reached up and traced the scar on Kelly's forehead with his finger. They were both scarred in their own way. He wondered how far they could run…or if they could ever forget.

"You know about my other scar, too. The one on my ankle."

His hand stilled.

"I remember you, you know," she said quietly. "The night of the accident in New Mexico. You were there…talking to me."

Ian gently caressed her hair. "I didn't know if you remembered or made the connection."

"I didn't at first. But now I do."

"I was afraid to say something about it before. I was an adult then and you were a kid. It seems a little strange, feeling the way I do about you now."

A smile pulled at the corner of her lip. "We're *only* eleven years apart, not fifty."

"Twelve years."

"I'll compromise. Eleven and half." She placed a kiss on his chest. "And I know for a fact that you had other interests back then."

"That's true," he whispered, his mind drifting to Anne and what he'd seen in the basement. There was so much there. He'd only had time to scratch the surface. An ugly but important surface.

"How did you find out about Anne?"

"What do you know of your own basement?" Ian answered Kelly's question with one of his own.

"My basement? We have our laundry machines there. Why?"

"Why didn't you go past that room? Weren't you curious to see the rest of the cellar?"

"You mean the back section of the basement? Janice and Bill use it to store their personal belongings. I've been in this house for two years, and I've never gone past the front room where we do the laundry."

"They needed more room than you gave them in the carriage house?"

Kelly gave a small shrug. "I had no reason to distrust them. And it wasn't like I needed the space myself. I sold almost everything from my apartment in New York before moving. The little I brought along all fit up here."

Ian guessed that Janice was involved with the Butler Mission, but he hadn't decided on Bill's involvement yet. The tough old bird didn't quite fit the profile, as far as Ian could tell. But then again, finding Rose Wilton in those photos had been a surprise.

"What was in that back room?" Kelly asked.

"It's a kind of repository for everything. The history of the Mission. Butler's sermons, books… everything needed to educate the next generation of martyrs."

Ian felt her body stiffen.

"The next generation?" She pushed up and stared at him. "And it was all right in my own house for all these years."

He told her about the books and the furniture and the photographs—most importantly about the photos.

"Your mother, Rose Wilton, was in some of those pictures."

Kelly stared at him in disbelief.

"Not in the later photos. These were snapshots of some of the early days. She looked like she was conducting an interview."

Kelly was silent for a long time, and he let her think it through.

"She taught cultural anthropology," she said finally. "That included religion, so it figures. She never told me about it, though, never acted or hinted in any way that she'd had any connection with the Mission."

"She wouldn't, just as Anne didn't. If my assumption is correct, Rose had a job to do—keeping you safe and delivering you here."

"And Frank?"

Ian shook his head. "I just don't know. I only glanced through a few of the boxes and records. I could be wrong, and Rose's connection could be entirely innocent. But what I can't understand," he said with a frown, "is how they could think a potential recruit would ever buy into their beliefs after seeing those pictures."

"Not everyone would see them," she replied. "I remember, even at my age back then, realizing that there was an 'insider' doctrine and an 'outsider' doctrine. The sect had levels of membership, based on trust. The more important you were, the more you knew of the secrets. Plus, we were constantly told we had to protect our beliefs from our enemies. So what was put out for public consumption—for potential donors and for new members—was different."

"New members like Anne?"

She nodded. ''I know now how it was done. It was just standard psychology. Father Mike's way with people like her was to appeal to her compassion and gain her trust, then practice basic mind-control techniques.''

''You mean brainwashing?''

She gave a small shrug and slid to his side. ''Elements of brainwashing and hypnosis are part of it. Peer pressure is part of it, too, but so is the constant negativity members are barraged with. Chanting is used as a part of the praying, to create subconscious associations. A few years ago, when I started researching some of this stuff, I was amazed to see how many bright, educated people from stable backgrounds have been drawn into different cults.''

''Most of Butler's victims were underage kids or young women who'd gone there, thinking it was safe.''

''I know. They thought they were getting into one nice, big, happy family. Once there, though, they quickly lost their freedom to make choices. They gave them up freely, thinking Father Mike knew what was best for them. It all spirals downward after that. They bought into his doctrines because there couldn't be anything better for them elsewhere. They were gradually implanted with phobias, too, about what would happen to them physically or spiritually if they ever turned their backs on the cult.''

''They were programmed.''

Kelly nodded. ''I was a kid, but I felt it, myself. The weird thing was that I knew it then. That doesn't usually happen, from what I've read. Still, he used his power of mind control on me, too. I became a different person when I was in Father Mike's presence. He had some power, some charisma that he knew how to use on people. When I was standing in front of him, he controlled my behavior, my thoughts, my emotions. My will.''

She entwined her fingers with his and looked up into his eyes before she continued. ''Don't make a judgment about who your wife was, or how much she loved you, or whether she cared about your marriage, based on a couple of pictures. She was programmed, Ian, just like Rose. They were victims. As a social worker, Anne was important to them before the suicide. Her education, her job, the potential media coverage, they were all factors. Don't judge her as a rational person.''

There was so much to think about.

''And look at how much we don't know about the cult,'' she added. ''You investigated it, and I was a member since childhood, but you and I both thought what happened twenty-two years ago was a onetime deal. That it was over. But obviously, it isn't.''

He looked at her, feeling his jaws tighten. What Kelly said was true, and what it all meant was that he *had* to put a stop to it. Not just for Monday, but forever.

On nights like this, stars did not seem real. They did not project the appearance of celestial bodies of gas and matter. To the human eye, they looked more like a million tiny tears in a black velvet universe. They only seemed to hint at a greater light, a greater illumination, which lay beyond the cosmic fabric of the night.

Here, beneath the flawed and covering sphere, the New Hampshire sky was crystalline and the moon, following its ordered path, was beginning its descent into the western sky. White and cold, the lunar orb bathed the lakeside with its tall pines and maples in a pale blue light. From beneath the trees, black, shape-changing shadows crept and grew along the uneven ground until they touched the walls of the inn.

Outside the apartment on the third floor, the slate plaque depicting a crescent moon rocked slightly in the breeze coming through the landing's open window. Inside, all was quiet and still. The room was dark, except for two shafts of light coming through the skylights. The two beams moved slowly, relentlessly across the floor. A child's bed lay in the path of one, and the light climbed the side of the bed inch by inch.

The little girl grew restless in her sleep, then turned and rolled onto her back. The yellow blanket clutched in her arms dropped to the floor. The beam of light continued to rise, curling upward over the edge of the bed and caressing her small shoulders. She lay motionless, her arms at her sides, her innocent face quiet and calm.

Like some ethereal presence, the moonlight moved across the pillow. It molded itself to her, filling the folds at the neck of the little girl's T-shirt, the slight rise of her collarbone, the curve of her ear, the soft lines of her cheek. Like some otherworldly wraith, the pale light took possession of all it touched.

When the moonlight touched her eyelid, Jade's eyes suddenly opened.

She didn't move. She made no sound. The moonlight continued its inexorable progress across her unblinking eyes. Jade stared upward at the ceiling until the moonlight bathed her entire face, and then she sat up.

The little girl did not look either right or left. Pulling back her blankets, she swung her legs over the side of the bed and placed her feet on the floor. Her face was in shadow now, but it made no difference. As if still asleep, she stood up beside the bed and did not move for a long moment. Then she moved silently to the chair where her clothes were laid out for the morning. She pulled on her jeans and carefully buttoned them. Picking up her sweatshirt, she slipped it over her head and worked her arms in. Sitting on the chair, she tugged on her sneakers.

Dressed, she sat where she was for several minutes, staring vacantly across the apartment. She did not see the moonbeams as they crossed her mother's empty bed.

As if she had received some invisible, inaudible signal, Jade stood up and walked slowly across the room. Without looking where she was going, she went around furniture and past the counter that separated the living area from the kitchenette. When she reached the open door leading from the apartment, she went out without hesitation.

The muffled sound of voices coming from the room beyond the sitting area did not disturb her, and she passed the partly open door noiselessly.

The stairwell was steep and pitch black, but it was no obstacle. Three steps up from the bottom, Jade leaned out and easily unlatched the door. Descending the rest of the way, she opened the door and went into the hall, leaving the door open behind her.

Softly and slowly, she walked down the long hall, touching each room's zodiac sign as she passed, but never once looking at them. The house was silent, and no one came out of any room. At the end, she turned and stood at the top of the stairs leading to the parlor. The last of the setting moon was shining in through the window, bathing her in its pale light. She stopped and went to the window. For a long time, she did nothing but stare with unseeing eyes out at the lake and the woods. Then, slowly, she lifted her hand and waved into the darkness.

Turning, she went down the stairs, her arms dangling loosely at her sides. The parlor was lit only by the lamp on the reception desk. The dull black eyes of the moose above the fireplace stared vacantly as Jade's green eyes. The little girl stood at the bottom of the staircase. The inn was deathly quiet. Then she turned and padded across the lobby to the front entrance. Turning the latch on the door, she went out.

The air was cold and crisp, but she felt nothing. As she went down the front steps, the air from her mouth and nose formed little wisps but quickly dissipated into nothingness. The gravel crunched beneath her feet. A moment later, she left the parking area and started across the dew-covered grass. Down the hill she walked until she reached the lake. Ahead of her, the water was flat as glass.

Jade turned then and walked along the water's edge—past the cottages and the boathouse and the beach—following the lakeshore until she drew near to the woods. About ten yards from the black line of trees, she stopped.

The moon had set beyond them, and the sky in the east had not yet begun to lighten. There was no sound coming from the forest. No owls, no hunting coyotes, no bullfrogs, even, calling out from the lake. Nothing but silence and darkness in this hour before dawn.

Out of the trees stepped a solitary figure.

Cassy held out her hand, and Jade walked without hesitation to her, placing small fingers in her sitter's hand. The teenager looked up at the darkened windows of the third floor for a moment and smiled.

Then, wordlessly, she turned Jade toward the trees, and they were gone.

Nineteen

The sky outside was just beginning to lighten, and the loud chirping of birds promised the coming dawn. Kelly leaned over Ian to look at the clock. It was 5:01.

"Time for me to go back." She placed a kiss on his lips and tried to get off the bed. His arm wrapped around her. Kelly looked up into his face.

"Everything will be okay," he whispered.

She nodded, wanting to believe him, telling herself that she was not alone in this. While they were making love or talking, she was happy. The magnitude of what they were facing seemed somehow manageable. But now, the nervousness had set in.

"I'll bring the phone back here," she said, sitting up on the edge of the bed. She reached for her shirt and jeans and hurriedly pulled them on. The air was cold. "I want Jade to sleep as long as she can."

Ian pushed the covers back too and sat up next to her. "What time does Janice start in the morning?"

"No earlier than six-thirty or so. Wilson gets in around six, though."

"I want to make the call before there's a chance of one of them eavesdropping downstairs. I don't want to jeopardize Dan's cover, if he was planted here for a purpose.''

Kelly stood up. ''I'll get it for you right now.''

Quietly, she opened the door wide and stepped out into the dark sitting room. A breeze coming in through the window chilled the air. She ran her hands up and down her bare arms and walked to the window to close it. The Desposito rental truck had not returned last night. She closed the window, telling herself there was too much other stuff on her plate right now to be worrying about a pair of guests who'd probably spent the night carousing. It wasn't the first time.

Walking into her apartment, she immediately reached over the kitchen counter for the telephone handset. Rays of dawn had started streaking through the windows onto the spacious room. She heard Ian's steps behind her and turned around, handing him the phone.

He'd pulled on his pants but was still shirtless. For a few seconds she just had to stand and stare. How handsome a man he was and how quickly he'd come to mean so much to her. It was like she'd found an old flame. Last night hadn't been simply about passion. It had been about the different ways they were connected to each other.

He rubbed his thumb gently across her lower lip and motioned that he was taking the phone out.

Kelly nodded and tiptoed across the room toward Jade's bed. A couple of steps was all it took before she noticed the blankets had been pushed back. The bed was empty. Her daughter's old yellow blanket was lying on the floor next to the bed. Her shoes and the clothes on the chair were gone.

The taste of bile climbed into the back of her throat. Suddenly, she couldn't breathe. She whirled around, her eyes searching every corner of the room. She rushed toward the bathroom, turning on the light. She wasn't there. Kelly ran out.

"There's no dial tone," Ian whispered from the open door of the apartment. His gaze immediately focused on Kelly. "What's wrong?"

"Jade." The name came out in a painful sob. "Jade's gone."

He immediately turned on the overhead light and looked around the room.

"Check the closets, under the bed," he said grimly, pointing as he backed out of the apartment.

She wasn't there. Kelly knew her daughter. Her little girl had never liked hiding in closets or crawling under beds. She followed Ian as he turned on the lights and went quickly down the stairs.

"God...no!" she cried, peering past Ian's shoulder. The door at the bottom of the staircase was wide open.

"You go down this hallway. I'll take the back steps," he told her. His voice rang through the upper floors. "JADE!"

Kelly switched on the lights in the hall. She didn't give a damn about waking anyone up. She yelled her daughter's name as she ran. She turned the corner, hoping Jade would be in her favorite alcove at the top of the stairs leading to the lobby. Nothing. She rushed down the stairs and saw Ian coming out of the hallway behind the reception desk.

"The back door is still locked," he told her, motioning to Kelly to check the dining-room door that led to the deck. He headed for the front door.

The sun was coming up outside. The door to the deck was locked, too. Still, Kelly felt no relief as she looked at the thick fog rising off the lake beyond the beach.

"Please…please…Jade!" she called out, hurrying through the rooms downstairs. She spied Ian outside on the walkway, and felt her hopes die. Tears rushed into her eyes and a sob choked her. She ran to the open front door and caught up to Ian in the parking lot.

"The door was unlocked and the screen door partially open," he told her. "I closed it myself last night. That's the way she got out…or how they took her out."

"How could they take her just like that?" Kelly asked desperately. "How could we not have heard them?"

"The door at the bottom of the stairs wasn't forced," he said, frowning. "She let herself out."

"*JADE!*" she screamed at the top of her lungs. A couple of birds taking flight and the sound of the breeze in the leaves in the trees near the lake were her only answer. Nothing more. No Jade. No answer from anyone.

The oddity of it hit Kelly the same time as it must

have hit Ian. The two of them had made enough noise to wake the dead. She stared up toward the house, looming ominously over them in the light of dawn. Not a single person had come out of their room. No one had looked out the windows or appeared to ask what was wrong. The inn was full of people, but there wasn't a breath of life in it.

Ian's attention was on the parking lot. The only vehicles left were Ian's car, and Kelly's four-wheel drive and Bill's old truck.

"Janice," she whispered, running off barefoot in the direction of the carriage house. Jade went there sometimes. She liked having Bill read books to her on the chairs beneath the maple tree by the front door. The grass was cold and wet on her feet, but Kelly was barely aware of it. Only the pain that was ripping at her insides distracted her at all.

"Please…please!" she cried, going to their front door. "Let her be here…please. JADE! Janice…Bill!"

She pounded on the door. There was no answer from inside. She turned the knob and the door opened. Kelly shoved the door and almost fell into the dark living room. The smell of old furniture and mustiness greeted her. The curtains were all drawn shut. She fumbled her way toward one of the tables and turned on a light.

Charts, zodiac signs and old maps were everywhere, pinned to the walls, spread on the tables and chairs and on the sofa. There were boxes and old books scattered on the floor.

Kelly stared, unable to comprehend the mess. This was so unlike the Janice she knew. The Janice she *thought* she knew. She saw the label on the closest box. *New Mexico. Butler.* Just as Ian said he'd found stored in the basement.

"No...please God, no!" Kelly cried, walking through the house. She went to the bedroom. The curtains were closed there, too. She turned on the light. Two empty beds sat on either side of the window. In her mind's eye, she saw her adoptive parents, Frank and Rose Wilton, sleeping in this very same room.

It was no coincidence that they bought this particular inn when they'd retired from teaching. It was part of a master plan that at least one of them had been party to. From the little Kelly had heard from them about the move here, there had been no shopping around for other inns in other states. Frank once told her that Rose had simply fallen in love with Tranquillity Inn, and that was what triggered the move. At the time, that was good enough for him.

Years of living here brought disenchantment, though. Kelly remembered Frank telling her privately that buying the place had been a mistake. Rose had said the same thing, with a note of bitterness in her voice, after Frank's death. But by then, it was too late.

It all became clear to Kelly now. The script was written. They'd played their part, consciously, and when they disrupted the play, they had to die. First one and then the other. For whatever reason, Rose must have broken free of the cult after Frank's death, so she had to pay the price. They had both been crushed by the machinery that had brought Kelly to this moment.

A lie. Her entire life had been nothing more than an elaborate lie. She had no choices. No control. Even in leaving the Mission. They'd let Kelly go. It was all planned.

Kelly tore aside the curtains and pulled open the sliding glass door. She stumbled toward the lake. She couldn't think, she couldn't see. Everything was a gray fog. She tripped over a boulder protruding from the grass and sank to her knees. The feel of the wet grass on her hands shocked her.

"LET HER GO!" she screamed. "I'll do anything. Please let my daughter go!"

The phone in the office and the one on the reception desk were both dead. Through the window, Ian saw Kelly come out of the carriage house, moving like a robot. At first, he thought she'd found Jade. Then he saw her on her knees, screaming and crying, and his blood ran cold.

He went up the stairs two and three at a time to the third floor. He grabbed his gun and snapped in the cartridge. He took the keys to his car, his wallet, and pulled a shirt over his head. He stuffed his feet into his sneakers. Running into Kelly's apartment, he grabbed her keys off the counter and picked up her shoes off the floor. He looked out the window. Kelly was walking slowly toward Dan's cottage.

He ran down the stairs as fast as his legs could take him. They wouldn't hurt Jade, Ian kept reminding himself. They had to keep her safe to force Kelly's cooperation. They would keep both mother and daughter alive, at least until tomorrow.

Monday. This entire thing was supposed to start on Monday. As he ran outside, Ian cursed himself for not acting sooner, for not driving them out of here during the night.

Kelly was knocking on Dan's cottage and calling Jade's name. He saw her shove the door open and walk in.

When he reached the cottage, she was standing just inside the door. The back of her hand was pressed against her mouth, and her face was ashen. She was staring at something across the small one-room cottage, and Ian stepped in front of her, blocking her line of vision.

He could smell the blood before his eyes even adjusted to the dim light.

Dan lay on the small bed on the far side of the room. Duct tape bound his arms tightly to his body and his legs were taped together, as well. His sightless eyes were open and staring at the door. His shirt and jeans were covered with a deep reddish brown that Ian identified immediately, and it was not difficult to see where the blood had come from.

The throat had been cut through from one ear to the other, severing the jugular and the carotid artery, the windpipe and most of the cartilage and ligaments. Whoever had murdered the young man had slashed the throat with such savagery that he'd nearly taken off Dan's head.

Ian turned and pushed Kelly out of the cottage. She was shivering violently. She looked up at him, but Ian didn't think she was still seeing anything but the gruesome image inside.

"Kelly," he whispered, pulling her close into his arms. "I need you to keep it together."

He felt her nod and try to take a breath.

"They're probably all around us. They're watching us, honey. Don't fall apart on me."

She pressed her face against his chest. She continued to shake. Ian looked around them. A thick mist was rising off the grass. The lake had a cloud hanging on the surface of the water. He glanced up at the parking area.

"We're going to walk to the car. I'm going to drive you out of here."

"No," she answered, pulling away. "I have to find Jade. I'm not going without her."

"There's nothing we can do against all of them. It's two of us and probably close to two hundred of them," he told her, pushing her gently toward the car. His eyes scanned the line of trees, the dark windows of the house. They were so exposed. "We'll drive out of here and get help. They won't hurt Jade. She's their trump card to get at you."

Kelly didn't look convinced. She continued to shake her head as he moved her steadily toward the car. They were nearly at the gravel driveway before she spoke again. She was still crying. "I won't go without her. I have to go to her. She's got to be scared."

"We'll come back for her together. I promise, Kelly. Let me get to a phone and make a call, and I'll bring you back."

When they reached his rental car, Ian yanked open the passenger door and pushed her in. Hurrying to the driver's side, he stayed low to avoid being a target. Dan had been in their way, so they murdered him. Ian knew he would be next.

He turned the key. The engine would not turn over. He tried again and again. Nothing. He cursed inwardly. Of course! What made him think they'd make it easy for the two of them to drive out?

He didn't bother to get out and open the hood. There probably wasn't a spark-plug wire left on that engine. Plus, he'd be a clear target in front of the car.

Kelly had stopped crying. She was looking at the key in the ignition, obviously realizing what was happening.

"You stay here. I'm going to try your car," he told her, squeezing her hand. He waited until she looked up and their gazes locked. "She's okay, Kelly. Keep telling yourself that. They won't hurt Jade. You're the one they want."

She didn't say anything, but Ian knew she understood. He took his gun out, grabbed her car keys. Slipping out of one car, he was inside the four-wheel drive in a couple of seconds. He didn't waste time. Putting the key in the ignition, he turned over the engine. He expected it to be dead and it was.

Ian glanced at Bill's truck across the way. He weighed the risk of running to it. He had no key and decided against it. These people wouldn't go through the trouble of disabling two cars and leave the third for them to use. Walking out of here was not much of a choice, either. There were five miles of woods and back roads between here and the state highway. Plenty of opportunity to lie in wait.

Kelly was getting out of the other car. Ian climbed out and went quickly to her.

"The boats," she said, wiping her face with her hand. "We can take one of the canoes across."

He pulled her against the car and made her crouch down.

"We can do that, but first we have to think of a way to warn whoever was backing Dan up. I wasn't expecting anything to happen until Monday. I don't think they were, either. By the time they show up tomorrow, it might be too late."

Her breath was still catching in her chest as she tried to take a lungful of air and let it out.

"Not across to the camp. To an inlet over there," she said, indicating with her eyes but not pointing. "One of the county roads comes pretty close to the lake, about three-quarters of the way across in that direction. We can take a canoe, pull ashore, and it's only a few minutes' walk. There might be some morning traffic."

"You're a genius." Taking her hand, they moved quickly toward the lake. Once they were on the water, he thought hopefully, the fog would hide them and there would be no way to guess which direction they were going.

He dragged the canoe closest to the lake to the water's edge. Grabbing two paddles, he motioned Kelly to get in. She scrambled to the bow. Ian threw the paddles into the boat and shoved them off.

"Remember where you've come to, Kelly," Ian said as he climbed in. Picking up one of the paddles, he drove it into the water, propelling the canoe forward. "Michael Butler and Tyler Somers and the rest of them have been controlling the people and the circumstances around you, but they can't control you. You're a free individual. You think and act the way *you* want. You're in charge of your own mind. You're not like the rest of them in that camp. You are *not* afraid. You're strong, Kelly. You can fight th—"

Ian felt the bullet rip through him, knocking him over even before he heard the gunshot. It was only as he was tumbling over the side of the boat that the searing pain started, bright lights flashing in his head.

"NO!"
Kelly dropped to her knees, staring for an eternity at the blood-spattered side of the boat, at Ian's body disappearing beneath the surface of the lake. Her stunned mind just could not fathom what she was seeing.

"NO!" she screamed, looking all around her. Fog. Trees. Water. It was a nightmare. Nothing but a horrible nightmare. She tried to wake up. All of this had to be a lie. This couldn't be happening.

But then reality broke through her stupor. It was happening.

The boat wobbled as she looked frantically over the edge. She could see clouds of Ian's blood, already spreading and disappearing. Some bubbles were rising to the surface, but that was all she could see in the dark lake water.

She was over the side in an instant.

The water was colder than she expected, shocking her momentarily and causing her to gulp a mouthful. Coughing and sputtering, she kicked her feet, treading water for a moment. They were not far from shore, but she knew the lake was already fairly deep here. When she could fill her lungs, she dived straight down where the bubbles had been. With the morning fog blocking out the sun, the lake was black even a few feet beneath the surface. Kelly could see nothing of him.

She swam to the surface and took another deep breath. Diving deeper this time, she reached the lake bottom. The water was very cold. Her ears were pounding with the pressure, but she felt around frenziedly for him. Once, she thought she'd found him when her hand touched something. Reaching out again, she realized it was only the anchor rope from the swim float. Letting go of it, she continued to search in a widening circle until her chest was burning.

Kelly's lungs were about to burst when she broke the surface again. Gasping for air, she looked around her.

"Ian!" she cried. The canoe was floating not twenty

feet from her, one end of it bumping against the float, but there was no sign of him anywhere.

Filling her lungs again, she dived a third time. Even as she went to the bottom, she realized that he'd been in the water a long time now. She was tiring quickly, and she couldn't stay under for very long. She came up again, pushing her hair back from her face and feeling a horrible sense of hopelessness settle into her.

"Mommy!"

Kelly spun around, her eyes searching the shoreline for her baby. "Jade!"

"Mommy!"

Blinking away water, she saw her. Jade was there on the beach behind the inn, with Janice and Cassy standing on either side of her.

Twenty

Jade was crying.

At the sight of her daughter trying to free her arms from the two women, everything Kelly was feeling—relief, grief, fear, exhaustion, the cold water—all of it was pushed aside by one emotion. Anger.

Kelly knifed through the water toward the shore. The blue van from the camp had pulled onto the grassy area near the lake. Two men armed with rifles were standing on either side of the open front doors of the car. Kelly wondered which one of them was responsible for killing Ian.

Tears burned her eyes again, but she pushed her head under, washing off any sign of weakness. The water became shallow, but Kelly took two more quick strokes before starting to walk out.

"Mommy!" Jade's cries got louder. She was trying to get to Kelly.

Kelly looked at Cassy first. The teenager's complete attention was on Jade. She was whispering something to the little girl, who became suddenly calmer. Janice's focus, though, was on Kelly. A strange smile was painted on the old woman's face. She appeared to have a death grip on Jade's wrist.

"Welcome back, holy sister," Janice said, her eyes widening behind the pink frames. "We're here to take you to the Mission. It's our time, Luna-K, and you must guide us."

Every inch of Kelly's body tensed, and then her blood boiled over. She tore her gaze away from her daughter and delivered a solid punch to the side of Janice's face. "I'm not Luna-K."

The old woman shrieked as she let go of Jade and fell backward on the beach. Her glasses were lying in the sand, and her hand was at her bloody mouth. When she turned, Kelly saw Cassy running with Jade under her arm past the gunmen to the van. She took a step and the two men raised their weapons, pointing them at her.

She couldn't fight all of them, not all at once. She wouldn't be able to get past the guns to her daughter, either. But that didn't cool her burning emotions.

"But you're Luna-K," cried the older woman.

Kelly looked down at Janice. "You're an evil woman. I trusted you. My parents trusted you. And what did you do to them? Their deaths were not accidents, were they? You killed them." She gave a solid kick to Janice's foot. "And believe me, you don't want to die, Janice. There will be no saints or angels waiting for you with open arms when you get there. You're a lying, cheating, murdering bitch."

Janice inched backward, pulling her feet in. "You have only one family, Luna-K. We've been your protector for your entire life."

"Don't you dare call me that!"

"You're the holiest of all. You carry in your veins the blood of the Prophet Michael…"

"Stop it!" Kelly went after her, but two sets of strong hands grabbed her from behind. She struggled like a wildcat against them, but one of the men twisted her arm painfully behind her. The other one grabbed her wet hair and turned her roughly toward the van.

Jade was standing beside the door. But she wasn't crying. She wasn't trying to come to her, although no one was holding her.

"Jade."

The child only stared and didn't move.

A man's voice whispered something from the van, and the little girl looked over her shoulder at the open door. Kelly realized they'd taped paper inside the back and side windows, and she couldn't see who was inside. Her blood froze when she saw the white-robed man climb out of the van.

Many years had passed. Kelly had tried so hard to eradicate the faces and the horrors of the Butler Mission–cult days. She had not succeeded. Despite the years, she recognized Tyler Somers immediately.

"Hello, Kelly." He said the words and then paused. His eyes searched Kelly's and then he held her stare.

She felt the pull. The lulling feeling of helplessness washing through her. She couldn't fight them. They were everything and she was nothing. She felt the men let go of her arms. No one was holding her, but she wasn't going anywhere. This was the same trick that Father Mike had used. This was part of their old hold on her.

"No!" she protested vehemently, tearing her eyes away from Somers and taking a step toward him. She stumbled but managed to keep herself on her feet. "I'm not doing this. You're not playing with my mind. I was there once. I got out. I'm not going back."

"We just want you to take your rightful place among us," he said in a soft voice. "We've waited a long time for Luna-K to lead us in our greatest moment."

"You can't make me tell a bunch of clueless zombies to kill themselves for…for what?"

"For our eternal reward." When she wouldn't look into his eyes, he turned with a resigned sigh and whispered to someone—perhaps Cassy—in the waiting van. "There are so many more important matters that require my attention right now. I shouldn't have had to come here to convince you."

Janice limped toward the van. The back of the woman's jogging suit was covered with sand. Kelly focused all her attention on Jade. She knew what was happening to the child. Jade had no control over her actions. She was at their beck and call.

"I was hoping you'd come to your senses on your own, but I want you to know that we're leaving this world with or without you, my child. You were born of Michael. And I warn that you will be cursed for ten thousand eternities if you continue to break your father's heart…if you continue to disobey his wishes.''

''I don't believe that crap. I never did. My father—if he *was* my father—was as sick as you. And neither of you have the power to…''

Kelly's words trailed off as Somers reached into the van. Someone placed a clear plastic cup filled with a dark liquid into his hand.

''If there has to be a surrogate for you, Luna-K,'' he said, ''Michael will understand…and so will our congregation.''

Somers handed the cup to Jade, and Kelly screamed.

''No! *NO!*'' Her arms were once again held by the two gunmen on either side of her. ''Don't take it, Jade. It's me…Mommy. Don't drink it!''

''Drink it, Jade,'' Somers said in a low voice to the child.

''Don't do it!'' Kelly kicked and screamed, trying to break free, but to no avail.

The little girl held the cup with both hands, brought it to her lips and drank the contents. When she was done, she handed the cup back to Somers.

Kelly looked at her in a daze. It was as if time had stood still. She stared, waiting, not knowing how long it would be before the poison took effect. In her mind, she found herself imagining some rescue about to take place. Armies of soldiers pouring onto the beach. Ian coming out of the water. Ambulances rushing down from the inn and saving her baby.

But nothing happened. No one would help her. She

looked around her at the woods and the lake and the inn…and then stared at Jade as feelings of guilt washed through her.

Kelly had brought this child into the world. The images of different moments in their life paraded before her weary eyes. The infant she'd held in her arms. The nights when just the two of them had looked out the window at the stars. The smile that Jade gave only her. The look on her face just before going to sleep. She could see Jade now, walking through the woods. Picking the flowers they both loved. Reading her books. Her mischievous laugh. Jade was like some perfect little human being inside of this child's body. Kelly blinked back the tears and looked at her. She looked so small, so vulnerable.

"Please," Kelly begged. "There might still be time. We can still take her to a hospital. They might do something for her. I'm the one you wanted, anyway. Please!"

"Yes, you were the one we wanted," Somers said profoundly.

"Then you can have me," she said desperately. "Get her to a hospital. Let her live, and I'll do anything you want."

He seemed to contemplate her offer. Kelly's nervous glance went from Somers back to Jade. She tried to see any sign of the poison affecting her child.

"Full cooperation," Somers demanded.

"In exchange for the guarantee that no harm will come to Jade. That she'll be taken to a hospital and given the best care…now!"

He crushed the cup in his hand and tossed it to the ground. "No hospital is needed. This is just a red fruit drink...this time."

Kelly couldn't stop the quivering of her chin. She wanted to believe him but she couldn't. What if he was lying? What if this poison took time to work? She shook her arms free of the two men. They let her go.

"I need to hold her," she said brokenly.

She took hesitant steps toward Jade, and Somers waved off the gunmen. No one tried to stop her.

Kelly crouched in front of her daughter. She touched the child's cold face. The silky hair. The thin shoulders. The large green eyes were open, looking directly at her.

Kelly took Jade in her arms.

"There are a few of our disciples who will not be joining us in our ascension tonight," Somers told her. "You've met Ken Burke. As a young man, he did an outstanding job of documenting Michael's final earthly moments and his ascension to the divine plane."

She remembered Burke now. That was why he'd looked familiar.

"He's doing the same thing for us, making sure our next generation will have a complete understanding of our last moments in this earthly wasteland. You don't have to fear. He'll watch over the two children...as we watched over you."

"Two children?" Not letting go of her daughter,

Kelly looked up at Somers. "What do you mean... two children?"

"Jade's soul mate. I received the vision and I have ordained him. He will be a part of *her* life until her time comes. You already know the child."

"Ryan?" she asked, her entire body breaking out in a cold sweat.

Somers nodded.

She was giving life to her daughter for a short time. Jade would be a victim of this group, as Kelly was being forced to play her part now. There would be no end to the vicious cycle. No one would be left to stop them.

"Our final devotions started last night. Your people are eager for you to arrive for tonight's ascension," Somers told her, motioning Kelly to get to her feet.

"But wait! The alignment happens on Monday," Kelly said, hoping she was using the right terminology. "You said *tonight*."

"The moment of alignment takes place in the Eastern World tomorrow at sunset, but here in New Hampshire, the Khumba Luxor is tonight. We intend to meet the Prophet at the moment when the eternal door is open. With you leading us, we'll do just that. You will guide us along the divine path...and no one will interfere."

Crazy, Kelly thought. He must have known the authorities were on his tail. But he was going to do it. In spite of all the pain he had caused, all the murders he'd committed, he would die making a name for himself instead of rotting away in some prison.

"If at any moment you rebel against us, if there is any sign of disobedience on your part, you will be eliminated, and Jade—or rather, the innocent Luna-J—will have the honor of being our guide tonight," Somers warned. "Those of us who know both you and your daughter find her far purer of heart, anyway."

Kelly had no doubt he was talking about her relationship with Ian. She caressed her daughter's hair and thought about how quickly Jade and Ian had bonded, as well. He was the only person she'd ever met that she knew Jade would have been safe with.

She pulled her daughter into a tight embrace. The tears coursing down her cheeks were for both of them, and for the man they'd both lost too soon.

"It's time to go," Somers said impatiently.

Kelly saw the two gunmen approach. She lifted Jade into her arms and walked to the open door of the van. Cassy was sitting in the back seat by herself. Janice was in front of her. Another woman that Kelly didn't recognize was sitting behind the driver's seat.

Kelly moved all the way to the back and sat next to Cassy. The young girl tensed immediately and looked away, but Kelly didn't care. Of all the people in the van, she had the best chance of getting help from the teenager.

"Are you asleep?"

"How could I be asleep?" Brian answered gruffly. "You haven't stopped moving once all night."

"I really have to take a leak. And no way am I going to go in my pants," Victor said tensely.

"I don't think it really matters. Do you?" Brian said calmly.

His arms and hands were bound with tape behind him, as were his feet. They'd taped his arms to a metal loop on the side wall of the truck. It was a fixture used for lashing in furniture, so Brian knew it was strong. On the other side of the truck, Victor continued to squirm in the semidarkness.

"Just go," he told Victor. "I promise never to tell anyone about it or give you a hard time."

"Yeah, right! If we get out of here, you'll tell everybody in Center City."

"And South Philly, too," Brian replied.

"See, I told you."

"Of course, that's if we ever get out of here."

Brian looked around the confined space in the back of the truck. Pieces of furniture were jammed all around them. Thin streaks of light were coming through a couple of rusted seams where the walls of the truck met the roof. The rental truck Victor had gotten for free from one of his many cousins in South Philadelphia was not in the greatest shape. There were even a couple of pieces of plywood covering a number of rusted areas on the floor.

Brian flexed his legs, pushing at the edge of one of the plywood boards. He'd been doing it repeatedly during the night to keep the blood flowing to his bound feet. He wasn't so lucky with his upper body. It'd been hours since he'd felt anything in his shoulders and arms. They didn't feel like part of him anymore.

"What time do you think it is?" Victor asked.

"After eight."

"How the hell can you be so sure?"

"I'm hungry," Brian replied. "You have to take a leak. I have to eat. My stomach says it's after eight."

"Your stomach is hardly what I'd consider a finely tuned clock, Brian. Besides, we had a hot dog each for lunch and no dinner. Your stomach might be telling you it's eight o'clock at night."

"Well, it's morning." Brian pressed his head back against the wood panel covering the sheet-metal wall. "And I'm so hungry that I feel sick to my stomach."

"Well, just go ahead and throw up. I'll never tell anyone," Victor said wryly before growing serious. "What do you think they're going to do with us?"

"For the hundredth time, I don't know."

Shawn Hobart and his Rambo gang had been men of few words. They sure did seem to have been waiting for them on the road. Still, there were no explanations. No questions answered. They weren't robbing them. Nor did they seem to be interested in hanging a couple of gays from the nearest tree for old time's sake. They did seem to be well armed with plenty of guns and lots of duct tape, though, and before they were done, the two of them were trussed up like prize pigs ready for the barbecue spit.

What Brian couldn't figure was why Hobart or one of his thugs had driven the truck for a few miles on a gravel road before just stopping and leaving them.

Brian had no clue where they were. He had no idea if anyone was coming back for them. Sometime during the night, they'd given up calling for help. They didn't seem to be within earshot of anywhere.

Brian closed his eyes and pushed at the plywood again. Strange. The entire thing was too damn weird.

"I don't have the heart to watch you waste away like this. Do you want a piece of gum?" Victor asked.

"Sure. What the…?" Brian looked over in shock as his friend rubbed his wrists, one at a time, and peeled off more of the tape from his shirtsleeve. "How did you manage to cut through the tape?"

"Hobart's a moron. He underestimated my preparedness." Vic flashed him the nail clipper he always carried in his back pocket. He looked at the tiny file critically. "I didn't realize how dull the silly thing was, though."

Feeling hopeful for the first time in hours, Brian watched Vic go to work on the tape around his ankle, peeling and unwinding it, layer after layer.

"I have to take a leak first," Victor told him as soon as he had his feet free.

"Don't even think about it," Brian warned. "You've held it this long. You can hold it until you get me out of here."

"That could be days. You know the door is latched on the outside."

"Get my hands undone, and I'll have us out in under an hour."

"An hour?" Vic complained. "Forget it."

"Vic, get my hands," Brian ordered in his sharpest tone.

"Fine. Fine. Fine." Vic moved across and pushed Brian forward so he could reach his bound hands. "So what's this genius plan for getting us out of here?"

"My toolbox." As soon as his hands were undone, Brian moved them gingerly, trying to ignore the pain shooting through his arms as the numbness went away.

"You left that in the front, right by my feet."

"No, I used it back here. It's behind the Randolph highboy," Brian told him. "That's the first piece we loaded."

"You left it in front."

"No," Brian insisted as Victor started helping him get the tape off his ankles. "I needed my power screwdriver to fix the hardware on the band that we used to hold the highboy."

"I'll bet you—"

"No betting. Just help me move some of these pieces around." Brian pushed himself to his feet and stopped, putting out a hand on the wall until the woozy feeling passed.

"My bladder can't take too much pressure." Despite his complaints, Victor started helping Brian with moving the pieces in different directions to make a little space so one of them could look in back.

"You're thinner than I am. Why don't you crawl through here and see if you can reach the toolbox?"

The look he got told Brian that Victor still didn't

believe the thing was there. "I'm taking a leak inside it if it's back there."

"Be my guest," Brian replied. "Just take the tools out first."

Victor started working his way between the pieces toward the back. Brian waited until he guessed Vic was getting close.

"Is it there?"

"Do you hear me peeing?" the other man called out.

"Vic," he said sharply.

The sound of a power screwdriver revving reached Brian's ears.

"No toolbox. Only this," Victor said as he worked his way back.

"It'll do."

Brian took the tool and looked around on the floor of the truck. Lifting up one of the plywood boards on the floor, he spotted a number of small areas that had actually rusted through.

He looked up at Victor. "It's a good thing your cousin Vinny gave us the crummiest truck on his lot."

"Yeah, he showed a lot of foresight giving us this one, wouldn't you say?"

Without answering, Brian crouched down on one knee and went to work. Drilling a line of holes through the rusted floor, he sat back as Victor pounded out the thin metal with the corner of the plywood.

"Your hour is up," Victor announced after his third go at the floor.

"It hasn't been ten minutes."

About an hour and a half later, Brian was covered with dust and sweat and his hand and arms were cut in a dozen different places, but they had a hole big enough to try to crawl through.

"I'll go first," Victor said bravely, leaning the plywood against the wall.

Brian poked his head down through. There were no cars around them. No one he could see. Only lots and lots of trees. And they were parked in the middle of a gravel road.

"Be careful," he said, pulling his head back in.

"You can leave in a more civilized manner," Vic told him. "I'll open up the back door."

"Good, because it's going to be a squeeze for me."

Brian gave his friend a hand and helped him lower himself through the hole. The sharp edges tore at the shoulder of Vic's shirt, cutting him. Brian was surprised Vic didn't voice one word of complaint. The two of them had been through hell since yesterday afternoon, and Brian was pretty proud of how they had come through so far, but this was extraordinary for Victor. His friend's handsome face reappeared seconds after he'd cleared the opening.

"What's wrong?"

"No valet service," Victor replied. "You'll have to come out this way, and be quick about it, too."

"Why?"

"Take a look." Vic backed out, and Brian poked his head out again. Victor pointed to a small device taped between the muffler and the gas tank and some wires leading toward the back of the truck.

"They've set us up to be a fireworks display. I touch that back door, and we'll be flame-broiled…just in time for lunch."

Brian put his feet in the hole and started working his way out.

Twenty-One

It was a miracle that Ian even realized what his good arm had hooked on as he sank deeper in the water. Grabbing the rope and trying not to panic, he immediately started pulling himself slowly upward along the anchor line toward the floating swim platform. The water was black and cold, and his left arm was numb and useless. Still he pulled himself along, running out of breath with each passing second.

Ian knew he'd be dead if he surfaced anywhere near the canoe, but the rope was rising on an angle, and the vague thought emerged that he might be able to hide on the far side of the float.

He heard Kelly go into the water, and he knew she was looking for him. He couldn't let her find him. He was sure they wouldn't hurt her. They'd taken Jade only as a way of forcing Kelly to go along with whatever they had planned. No, they wouldn't hurt her—not yet, anyway.

His lungs were burning, and the pain in his left shoulder was fierce. Suddenly, he couldn't stay under any longer, and he let go of the rope, kicking for the surface. Before he broke through to the air, though, his head glanced off something hard, stunning him momentarily even as he surfaced.

Gasping, Ian had no idea what was going on. His face was above water, but he was in an enclosed space. He reached out with one hand and realized instantly where he was. A foot or so above him, he saw light coming through the slatted wood of the swim platform. The metal bracket for the anchor rope was attached to the underside of it. The enclosed space was only about three feet square, and his head had grazed one of the hard foam blocks that the structure had been built on.

Gradually, his breathing slowed. He was starting to get some feeling back in his arm, and that wasn't a good thing. The pain in his shoulder was getting worse, but he tried to ignore it.

He heard Kelly call his name. She was still in the water. When he heard the note of desperation in her voice, Ian found it almost impossible not to call out to her. Turning around, he tried to peer through the narrow spaces between the foam blocks. On one side, the canoe bumped against the float and then drifted past. He couldn't see her anywhere.

Far off, he heard Jade's voice. She was calling Kelly. Grimacing from the pain as he moved to another side, he found he had a partial view of the shore. Jade was standing on the beach with her abductors. The camp van was on the grass behind them, and two young men with automatic rifles stood by the open door.

"Bastards," he whispered.

Suddenly, Kelly appeared in his line of vision, wading out of the water. The float shifted a little, and again he couldn't see them.

The words were muffled, but he heard Kelly's voice rise a couple of times. Ian considered swimming out from under the float, but he didn't know if there were others along the edge of the water, perhaps looking for his body to surface. Even if he got out, though, he knew he wouldn't be able to support himself in the water and still get a decent shot off at the two armed men. That was, if his gun would fire.

Time had no meaning and he lost track of it. He knew he had to be losing blood. He tried to stay afloat, holding on to the anchor rope. When he heard the doors of the van slam shut and the engine roar to life, he couldn't wait any longer. Taking a deep breath, he dived under the water and kicked his way beneath the foam blocks. When he surfaced beside the float, he could see the van disappearing around the inn. There was no one left on the beach, and no one he could see hiding in the trees, either.

Kicking hard and pulling with his good arm, he managed to get to shallow water and wade ashore. His entire body was aching now, and he pulled his shirt away to inspect his shoulder. The wound was bleeding but not as heavily as he would have thought. The bullet had gone in the back, near the left shoulder joint, and had come out beneath the collarbone, grazing his chin, which was bleeding more than his shoulder. He tried to move his left arm and found he could use it, though he had little strength in it. When he moved it, the bleeding in the shoulder increased.

"It could've been worse," he muttered. "You could be dead."

Ian pulled his pistol from its holster and looked at it. He needed more firepower than this, he thought. Looking at Dan's cottage, he started for it but then changed his mind. First, he had to stop the bleeding somehow and patch himself up.

Going into the boathouse, he found a cabinet containing towels and a first-aid kit. Ian dumped the contents onto the wood floor and dug out two gauze pads. Tearing one of the packets open, he slipped it under his shirt and pressed it into the wound behind his shoulder. He sat down hard as the pain shot through him. Opening the other packet, he applied the gauze to the exit wound and replaced the shirt over the dressing.

As he stood up, he saw a roll of duct tape on a workbench. He went over to it, thinking of the young man lying in the cottage nearby. He shook off the image. He had work to do if he was going to be of any help to Kelly. Using one hand, he carefully wrapped his wound, going over his shoulder, under his aching arm and around his chest before repeating the cycle.

When he was done, he steeled himself for the inevitable. He had to go into Dan's cottage.

Ian's eyes scanned the inn property as he moved quickly to the cottage. There was no sign of life at all up by the main building. Slipping through the

door, he glanced for an instant at the body. His heart
went out to Dan…or Ed…or whatever his name was.
He wondered if there was a wife involved, or kids.
He wouldn't want to be the one to take the news to
them or to the young man's parents.

Taking another look at the dead body, Ian knew
exactly what kind of people he was dealing with. As
crazy as Butler had been, this was much different than
what the New Mexico Mission was all about. Somers
and his thugs were cold-blooded killers. He hoped
Kelly remembered his warning.

He looked around the room for a likely hiding
place. Whether the kid was working for the state police or the FBI, he wouldn't come out here without
weapons to protect himself in an emergency.

Two storage lockers contained only rain gear and
a jacket. The drawers yielded nothing, either. He
wouldn't leave anything in the open where anyone
could find it.

Ian looked up toward the rafters and knew he'd
found the storage area. Rough old planks had been
laid across the rafters. Fishing gear and boxes, backpacks, sleeping bags and what looked like rolled-up
tents had all been stored up there. Actually, Dan had
done just that…hidden his things in the open.

Ian dragged a chair to the middle of the room,
climbed onto it and reached up with his good arm.

"But it doesn't make any sense to go that way,"
Victor said, standing his ground.

"We're heading for the state road," Brian said again, continuing to push him away from the truck.

When they were a good distance from the vehicle, Victor dug in. "We're far enough away, Brian. We're not going to get blown to pieces if those explosives decide to do their thing."

Brian said nothing but looked down the road.

"Now look," Victor started. "Let's consider our options."

"We're going to get out of here."

"I agree, but walking God knows how far through God knows what may not be the best way to do it."

"We can't be far from the state road."

"But we are! They drove for a while before leaving us here." He looked around him. "In fact, I know exactly where we are."

"You do, huh?"

"See that boulder sticking out of the ground by the road there? The one that looks like Benjamin Franklin's head?"

"Come on, Vic."

"Seriously. I saw that each time we drove in and out of the inn. There's a side road right up…there." He pointed up the road to a spot that was just visible. "That dirt road is near the inn. I'm telling you. The inn is right there. It'll take us five minutes to walk to it."

"Vic, if we *are* close to the inn, why did they drive us here, booby-trap the door and leave us where, if the truck blew up, anyone within a hundred yards would be obliterated?" Brian paused, staring at him.

''Don't you think there's something nasty going on? I think we should get the hell away from here.''

Victor shook his head impatiently. ''Do you even remember how far away the closest gas station or convenience store was? Or anywhere we could find a phone?'' He didn't wait for Brian to answer. ''Five miles, at least. Be logical. Hobart is not so stupid that he'd leave us in our truck in the middle of the road here and then go back to that inn and pretend nothing happened. We'll walk toward the inn—just for a little ways—and take a look.''

Brian nodded grudgingly. ''Okay, but just to take a look…and I don't like it, Vic.''

To Victor's relief, they were exactly where he thought they were, within a half mile of the inn. After walking for just a few minutes, they spotted the building through the trees.

''Look at it.'' He pointed toward the parking area. ''Hobart's car is not even there.''

''There's something weird going on here,'' Brian warned. He was still holding on to the power screwdriver, and he tucked the tool under one arm. ''This might be more dangerous than what Nate and Ellie went through with that Betsy Ross flag last year.''

''Hey, we helped with that, didn't we?''

''We followed directions,'' Brian said reasonably. ''We had the FBI, the Philly police and Nate watching out for us. Everyone was looking over our shoulder, and they gave us one little job to do and we did it. This is different.''

''We're not going to do anything stupid, Brian.''

"Hobart and his goons were *armed*, Vic." Brian shook his head. "Do you remember all that shooting in Ellie's apartment? People get killed when there are guns involved. You and I were lucky enough to save our own asses this time. The next time Hobart runs into us, I wouldn't count on that happening again. I'd just as soon have the police handle this."

"I agree. We're saying the same thing." Victor took a couple of steps toward the inn and then stopped. Brian wasn't following. "Come on."

Brian shot a look of frustration at him. "Where are you going?"

"Ian Campbell is a cop." Vic paused and pointed at the sedan parked in the gravel driveway. "That's his car. We go very quietly to the inn. If you want, one of us can go in and the second one can watch the other one's back."

"With what?"

"You're getting too technical on me."

"Vic, this isn't a TV movie."

Vic waved him off. "Look, we know there's a phone in there. We sneak in, use the phone, or talk to Ian, whichever comes first. Then we let the professionals take charge."

Brian hesitated. "I still don't feel good about it."

Vic pointed to the inn. "We walk two hundred yards." He pointed the other way. "Or we walk two hours, or three, or four. And still there's no telling that we won't run into some of those armed creeps in the woods. Come on, Brian. Besides, think of the food in that kitchen."

His friend thought about it for a moment, then acquiesced, albeit reluctantly.

"Since you put it that way," he grumbled. Together, they moved quietly toward the inn.

Now that they'd stopped talking, everything was too quiet. There was no activity around the inn. There were only three cars in the parking lot, and that was strange, too, considering they knew every room in the place was booked. Vic didn't point any of this out, though, for fear of Brian changing his mind and taking them back in the opposite direction.

Hanging around the shop with Nate Murtaugh, Ellie's gorgeous husband, this past year had given Victor a whole new taste for police procedures and FBI stuff. Nate never talked about specific cases, of course. He'd left the Bureau to get back to what he'd gone to school for—practicing law. But Nate still oozed toughness and cleverness and self-assuredness. It was the kind of strength and confidence that Ian had. He was sure the other man had lied about being a cop. He had to be in the FBI.

"So, do you want to wait here while I go in and use the phone?" Brian asked when they reached the line of trees beyond the parking area.

Vic looked at the inn again. "I'll be no good to you here. But let's not go in the front door," he said, summoning his courage and starting quickly across the gravel driveway.

"If they start shooting, don't stand there and argue," Brian warned in a low voice, catching up to him. "Just duck."

"Argue? Of course I wouldn't argue." Ten steps across and nobody had shot them yet. Vic felt his confidence building and started around the inn in the direction of the door near the kitchen. "I don't know why you'd say something like that."

"I don't know, either...except that yesterday you made sure to let Hobart have it with both barrels for the way he was treating us."

"He's a creep. I have a few cousins in South Philly I'd like to introduce him to."

"He was armed, Vic. I'm going to have Nate give you a lecture about respecting guns."

As they drew near the kitchen door, Victor started to respond, then stopped. Looking down by the beach, he could see a canoe floating near the shore. There was no one in it. He looked around him. There was no smell of food coming from the kitchen.

Suddenly, Victor felt very uncomfortable about everything. Maybe Brian was right. Maybe they should have gone in the other direction...away from the inn. Then he saw Ian come out of the cottage by the edge of the lake.

He was wet. He was heavily armed. And he was wounded.

Arriving at the camp, Kelly told herself she would do nothing to look as if she were betraying Somers's trust. Jade was with her, and Kelly intended to keep her daughter right by her side.

As the van stopped, she fought down her panic and got out smiling, just as she was instructed. She shook

the hands of dozens of people who greeted her
warmly, many kissing her hand. She waved to others
who were walking back to the benches for the continuing devotions.

Not allowing herself to appear either surprised or
distressed by the throng of red-robed children in the
camp with their parents, she even forced herself not
to turn away as Ken Burke showed up with his camera and began to snap pictures continuously of Kelly
and Jade.

Some of the people looked very familiar to her.
There were faces that, if she focused closely enough,
she would have sworn she'd known at another time
in her life. People like Ken Burke were out of the
past she'd been trying to forget. But forgetting wasn't
her priority right now.

She was still wet. They'd draped a blanket around
her before she left the van, and they now offered her
dry clothes and a robe to change into. Kelly noticed
they'd given her a white robe very like the one Somers was wearing. Hers, however, had a hand-stitched
crescent moon logo on the breast.

Rita appeared at her side. She'd been assigned to
escort Kelly to one of the cottages to change. Kelly's
inclination was to give the young woman the same
treatment she'd given Janice, but she held her temper.
As always, Rita was sharp-toned and curt in telling
her where they were going and what they were doing.
As they walked through the camp, Kelly noticed that
the pair of armed guards—whom she'd learned in the
van would serve as her ''protective'' escort—had left

their rifles behind, carrying only handguns concealed beneath their robes.

Kelly's main concern was Jade. She had been in her daughter's place twenty-two years ago. In her research about what had happened at the Butler Divinity Mission, the first thing Kelly had done was to try to understand how mind control worked...and how to break a person free of it.

When they reached the cottage where she was supposed to change, Kelly put her hand up to stop Rita from coming in, too. "I need privacy."

"Then she stays with me." Rita reached to take Jade from Kelly's arms.

"No," Kelly said with enough authority and lack of emotion to make herself sound convincing. "Father Ty said she stays with me...now and for the rest of the hours of devotion that are left."

The younger woman's eyes widened, as if she was seeing Kelly in a new way, and nodded.

Kelly knew now that Butler and his inner circle—including Ty Somers—had been consciously using established mind-control techniques on those at lower levels in the sect hierarchy. Their goal was to take control of the thinking and the actions of the cult members. Creating and using triggers aimed at all five senses, they were able to manipulate how a person received and processed information. Nothing they did was new. The techniques they used had been studied and documented thoroughly over the past fifty years.

Kelly was certain they'd used the same methods with Rita as they had with Jade. She doubted if the young woman realized that she was a puppet in all this. She wondered if, deep down, Rita even understood the significance of how empty her life had been up to now…the significance of how completely she had given up her will to make choices. That was what made the actions of Somers and the sect leaders a crime and not simply a tragedy.

"I'll wait right here," Rita said tersely, opening the door for her. Quickly, she laid Kelly's robe and a change of clothes on a chair by the door before backing out.

Kelly saw the two men take up positions not far from the cottage. The smell of burning incense reached her before they even stepped through the door. It was a basic trigger meant to prompt programmed memories and behaviors. She recalled the same incense burning in all the dormitories at the Mission in New Mexico. They'd had it always burning in the chapel, too. It was no accident.

As the door closed, Kelly grabbed a pitcher of water left with a couple of glasses on the table and dumped it on the smoldering stick. The sharp hiss of it going out gave Kelly a deep feeling of satisfaction.

She looked up and was immediately faced with a huge, white tapestry hanging on one wall. Numerous photographic images had been transferred onto the cloth and carefully hand stitched onto the tapestry. Michael Butler. Kelly herself. There was even a picture of her as a child, standing by the Father's knee. Images of the crescent moon and zodiac signs had been artfully arranged around them.

Jade tensed in Kelly's arms. She immediately turned her daughter's eyes away from the tapestry. Michael Butler's face and crescent moons had always been triggers for Kelly, too. She remembered how, for years after leaving the Mission, she continued to be afraid of being outside at night during specific phases of the moon. Even now, she forced herself to think of the faces of her husband on their wedding day. Of Jade on the day she was born. Of Ian in the half light of dawn.

There were no locks on the door. The two windows were covered with pieces of plywood nailed to the wall. Kelly went to the tapestry and ripped it down. Turning it facedown on the floor, she pushed it into the corner.

She held Jade tighter in her arms and tried to think what other tricks they might have used on her child. Somers's voice was definitely a trigger for Jade, just as Butler's voice had been for Kelly. But she didn't know if there was anything else. She knew that the sense of taste or even the sense of touch were used, but perhaps they hadn't had enough time for all that with Jade. She prayed that was true.

Kelly's clothes were very damp, but Jade didn't seem to mind. She had her head on Kelly's shoulder. Her little body was limp. Still, though, Kelly knew her child could hear her. She thought hard, trying to remember the articles she'd read years ago about mind control and deprogramming. They all stressed the importance of bringing out of the subconscious memories of good times, of warm feelings and posi-

tive occurrences and safe situations the victim knew
prior to being subjected to the abuses of mind control.

"We're going to find our way out of here, my
love," she whispered to Jade. "And we're going to
get in a car and drive far away."

Jade's arms remained looped around her mother's
shoulders. She didn't say anything in response.

Kelly walked around the sparsely furnished room.
A cot, the table, and the chair by the door were the
only furniture. Water was still dripping onto the floor
from the table. The only exit was the way they'd
come in. Her focus wasn't dwelling on the unlikeli-
hood of escaping at the moment, though, but on re-
claiming Jade's freedom of mind. Kelly wanted her
daughter with her. Her real daughter.

"What do you say we stop for breakfast along the
way? Somewhere we can order toast and lots of
jelly."

Again, there was no answer. Kelly thought about
sitting Jade in the chair and braiding her hair. She
wanted to do something that was part of their daily
ritual. The child's arm tightened around Kelly's
shoulders, though, as soon as she tried to put her
down.

"I like this," Kelly whispered, rubbing her daughter's back, pressing a kiss against her forehead. She
started pacing the room and continued to talk about
all the things they liked to do together. About the
good books they'd read and the walks they'd taken.
She could feel Jade starting to relax a little, but she
didn't dare hope.

"What do you say we forget about toast and go for a serious waffle with ice cream for breakfast instead. We can even make it sugarcoated."

"And M&M's?"

Her voice was so small that at first Kelly wasn't sure if it was her imagination. "What did you say, honey?"

"And a billion M&M's on top?" Jade slowly lifted her head off Kelly's shoulder and looked into her face. "Can Ian come, too?"

Kelly pressed Jade's head back on her shoulder so she wouldn't see the tears springing into her eyes. "Yes, my love. We'll take Ian, too."

She was responding, Kelly told herself. Her own Jade was with her again. But tears wouldn't help solve the trouble that lay before them.

"I want a Band-Aid, Mommy," Jade whispered tearfully.

Kelly searched the back pocket of her pants. Deep down, she found a soggy Band-Aid and pulled it out. She dumped the robe and clothes off the chair and dragged it to the table. Sitting Jade in front of her on a dry portion of the table, she handed her daughter the Band-Aid. "Where should we put it?"

The little girl looked around on her fingers and arms in search of the right spot.

"How about here?" she said, pointing to her ankle.

Kelly recognized the spot as the same place where her own scar was located. She helped Jade put on the bandage.

The door of the cottage opened without a warning.

Rita stepped in. "You're taking too long. Everyone is waiting for you," she said brusquely.

Furious, Kelly leaped off the chair and charged the woman. "Don't you *dare* interrupt us again."

Rita quickly backed out of the cottage and stood just outside the door.

"We will come out when we're ready," Kelly told her imperiously. "Do you understand?"

Rita nodded her head a couple of times, and Kelly slammed the door in her face.

"I'm scared, Mommy."

Jade's voice brought Kelly's attention back to her daughter. She walked across to Jade and took her in her arms again. "Don't be, my love. I'm right here."

"They're mean here."

"Only if we let them," she said soothingly.

"They say things I...I don't understand."

"I know."

Kelly considered that for a moment. She'd witnessed more than a few of Michael Butler's lengthy sermons. She wondered if she could muster up the courage to stand before the crowd outside and come up with some rendition of her own. They had given her a white robe. She was supposedly their spiritual guide into the divine world. She wondered, though, what she could say that might steer these people away from the abyss they had been programmed to desire.

Still, it was worth a try. At the very least, she could attempt to put things off until tomorrow. That was when Ian had told her the authorities thought the final ritual was to take place. She had to buy everyone some time. Of course, that was if Somers would allow her to break into his realm of power.

She looked down into Jade's face. It was definitely worth a try.

Twenty-Two

Ian didn't pull any punches. Time was at a premium, so he explained the situation to Victor and Brian as clearly and succinctly as he could, telling them who was dead and who was missing and what was happening at the camp. He thought the two men dealt with it pretty well, listening to everything without saying a word.

They'd moved inside the house and were talking in the sitting area. Ian didn't want them to be spotted by anyone from the camp that might be coming around to keep an eye on things at this end of the lake.

He told them exactly what he wanted them to do. Their response—or rather, their lack of response—was what made him nervous now. Neither had asked any questions or had shown any objection to his plans. They were reacting like a pair of veteran law enforcement officers, rather than a Philadelphia antique dealer and a carpenter.

Ian nodded to Brian. "Okay, let's just go over it one more time."

"No problem," he replied, glancing at Victor. "We raid the kitchen for a half an hour or so to give you a chance to get near the camp. Then we play the part of demolitions experts and blow up a couple of cars and buildings.''

''You can be the demolitions expert,'' Victor interjected. ''I'll be Rambo. I'm getting that gun down from over the fireplace.''

''You're going to shoot yourself for sure if you take down that gun,'' Brian responded. ''I'll put you in charge of matches.''

''Brian!'' Vic snapped. ''You can be such a chauvinist sometimes. Nobody said you were in charge.''

''I'm only looking after your—''

''Guys! Guys!'' Ian interrupted. ''Let's focus on what we have to do here. I don't want you to think you're going to engage in hand-to-hand combat, or get into a firefight with a bunch of gangsters. All I'm asking you to do is blow up one of the cars, or maybe the boathouse, or even the rental truck you just—''

''Not the rental truck,'' Vic jumped in immediately, shaking his head. ''There are too many valuable antiques in there. Ellie would never forgive me. And then there's my cousin Vinny.''

''You've got the gist of what I'm saying.'' Ian put his hand up to stop Victor from continuing. ''There's a large metal gasoline can with the lawn equipment in the boathouse. All I want is a little fireworks on this side of the lake. Bill's truck might be the best choice because if you can detonate that gas can under the truck's gas tank without blowing yourselves up in the process, we should have a pretty good explosion.

Plus, it's far enough from the house that you should be able to avoid burning down the entire East Coast.''

"An explosion, not just a fire," Brian repeated.

"Right, no bonfires. I want to make sure there's at least one solid bang. It has to accomplish two things. First, the distraction gives me a chance to get inside the camp. Second, the state police or the agencies Dan was working with should figure out that something must be wrong when the report goes in, and they'll come to find out what's cooking.''

"But you told me and Brian to go and hide in the woods after we start the fire—I mean, blow up the truck. How are we going to know when the good guys get here? And what happens if we come out, thinking the right people have arrived, and it ends up being the wrong guys? And—''

"Victor," Ian said wearily. "Just use your judgment.''

"Bad advice," Brian chirped up.

Vic turned on his friend. "Look, I'm tired. You're tired. Ian is more tired than both of us. And he's been shot in the shoulder, to boot. But do you see either of us acting like a jerk?''

Ian walked away from the two men, shutting out their argument just as he'd forced himself to ignore the throbbing pain in his shoulder and arm. The bleeding had stopped, at least. He'd have to wait to get the wound sewn up.

It was the same thing with Brian and Victor. They'd handle it. He had to have confidence, he told himself, and hope they didn't hurt themselves. In the meantime, he had to get to the camp and fast. Somers was obviously moving the schedule up, but Ian didn't know by how much. The thought of Kelly and Jade being there made him increasingly queasy. He definitely couldn't wait around here, counting on the FBI or the state police to arrive in time.

"I'm going," Ian announced.

Both men stopped their argument immediately and turned to him. Victor looked at Ian's shoulder with great concern. "Are you sure you can manage with that wound?"

"I'll be okay. One hour."

"Fireworks." Brian sent him a salute. "One hour."

It went against every impulse in her, but Kelly forced herself to put on the white robe over the dry clothes.

Rita's patience didn't last too long. This time, though, she knocked instead of barging in. From the voices outside, Kelly guessed there were others who had collected by the door, as well.

"No, Mommy," Jade whispered, tears gathering in her eyes again. "I don't want to go with them."

"You'll stay with me." She lifted Jade in her arms and opened the door. The greeting committee outside made her want to cringe.

Ken Burke and Ryan were standing on one side of the door. On the other side, Ash and Cassy had joined Rita. The two gunmen were not far off. There were

also a number of children watching from the area between the cabins and the benches.

The photographer lifted the camera and snapped a
couple of close-up shots of Jade and Kelly. The child
immediately hid her face on her mother's shoulder.

"We'll take her now," Ken announced, letting his
camera dangle from his neck as he reached for Jade.

"No way in hell," Kelly said quietly but emphatically to the man, bringing him up short. She extended
her hand toward Ryan, speaking much more gently.
"Why don't *you* come with me."

The expression of awe in the boy's expression increased ten times over what Kelly had seen before.
Cold, clammy fingers slid into Kelly's hand. She
turned next to Cassy. For the first time, the teenager
looked hesitantly at her. "You walk with me, too."

The girl looked frightened, but she nodded.

The model was a tough one to figure. Still, she was
a new recruit, which gave Kelly hope.

"And you, too," she ordered Ash.

The tall woman looked as impressed with the pro-
ceedings as Ryan. She stepped forward, joining Kelly.

This is how it had to be, Kelly told herself. She
had choices. She had the possibility of power. This
was all about assuming a position of authority. This
was the last thing that Somers would expect her to
do, as long as he could control Jade.

Moving toward the open-air chapel, Kelly saw the
older man on the stage. He seemed to be in the midst
of a fiery sermon. Most of the benches were full. The

red-robed congregation was responding to his calls of devotion.

Kelly started walking, circling around behind the back row of the benches. Ryan stayed with her. Only a step behind them, Ash and Cassy followed. The rest of the group only watched in obvious confusion.

Meditation. This was the way Michael Butler used to start his services. Before he'd go to the pulpit, he'd walk endlessly in the back of the congregation, meditating and praying, sometimes aloud and sometimes in silence. He made sure everyone could see him, though, as the "spirit" took possession of him.

Plus, he let the anticipation build.

Kelly waited until they'd gone the entire length of the benches before starting to talk to Ryan. She kept her voice at a level that Cassy and Ash could hear, as well.

"I was twelve, too." She smiled down at the boy.

"I know," Ryan answered. "I've been studying your life. I know everything about you…and your daughter."

It was a creepy reminder that she'd been watched for all of these years. Kelly forced herself not to get distracted by this.

"Are the Sterns your real family?" she asked. "Is Craig your brother?"

"I…I think so."

Jade tried to climb higher into her arms. Kelly had to let go of Ryan's hand momentarily before adjusting her daughter. She immediately went back to taking the boy's hand, though.

"Do you know why you were picked?"

"My mother's sister was Jill Frost. The Prophet Michael chose her, so that makes our family special."

Rachel Stern was her aunt. The realization was not a pleasant one, and at this very moment it only meant that insanity definitely ran deep in her family. Kelly didn't remember Rachel from the Mission. She guessed that Ryan's mother had to be a younger sister, but none of this mattered now.

"So, do you play any sports, Ryan?"

The question seemed to throw the boy for a loop. He looked up, confused. "I...I like to...to play basketball."

"Do you play on a team?"

"No."

"Why not?"

"I...I have chores and studies that I have to do," Ryan said in a quiet voice.

Suspicion, Kelly told herself. She had to plant seeds of suspicion. "Where do you go to school, Ryan?"

"I'm homeschooled by my mother."

"So do you and a group of other homeschooled children get together every now and then and do fun stuff? Play basketball?"

"No."

"That's strange."

"Craig and I have time to play together."

Kelly let go of Ryan's hand and gently touched his hair. "Do you have any neighbors? Any other children that you play with?"

"No, just Craig."

"Ryan, do you have *any* other friends?"

The boy shook his head slowly.

"That's wrong, honey," Kelly said calmly. "I was the Prophet's daughter, but I went to school with other kids."

"You did?"

She nodded. "And I went to college later, too. I had friends and jobs, and I celebrated Christmas and traveled, and lots of other fun stuff."

"That's not what I learned about you."

Kelly frowned. "I don't know what they told you, but don't you think I'd know about my own life?"

Ryan stared up at her, clearly perplexed. She could see his mind racing. Kelly looked over her shoulder at Cassy.

"You went to school with other kids, didn't you?"

Cassy blushed but nodded.

"How did you hear about the Prophet?"

The teenager continued to follow, but Kelly saw her looking down at her hands. "From Caleb."

Kelly looked around the camp in search of the young man that she'd met for the first time two nights ago. He was on the stage with Somers.

"Do your parents know about it?"

Cassy gave a quick shake of her head.

"Where do they think you are now? This weekend?" Kelly asked, slowing down so the four of them were walking together.

"They think I'm baby-sitting at the inn."

Kelly forced back her inclination to scold the

young woman. Positive, she told herself. "Do you remember Christmas when you were Ryan's age, Cassy? Or Thanksgiving? Or playing with other kids?"

"Sure," she replied. "Thanksgiving was always my favorite holiday."

"I can smell that turkey right now," Kelly said softly, leaving the thought hanging. She turned to Ash. "You're not much older than Cassy, are you?"

"I'm twenty-two."

"Why are you here?" Kelly asked gently, already guessing the answer. Ash would be the big headline for the Divinity Mission. A couple hundred people committing mass suicide would get plenty of media coverage, but the public could obsess on it for decades if there was a beautiful celebrity mixed in with them.

"Ken asked me to come."

"Do you know what's going to take place to-night?"

She nodded. "We're all going to meet the Prophet."

"We're all going to die," Kelly said plainly.

"But death is only a curtain to a dimension that we can't see. You will be the guide past the curtain. You'll lead us to a far more beautiful world waiting for us on the other side. There, it won't matter what we look like."

"Who told you this?"

"Ken did," Ash said, smiling at her boyfriend. Ken was continuing to take pictures of them as they made a turn at the end of the benches and started back again. She turned her attention back to Kelly. "I've gone through the Prophet Michael's writings, the ones that I have been given the blessing to read. These were his beliefs.''

Kelly took Ryan's hand again and squeezed it gently, making sure the boy was paying attention to what was being said. ''The Prophet Michael was my father. He spoke the absolute truth to me…before his death *and* after.''

''He's talked to you?'' Ash asked in awe.

''He visits me often in my dreams. He also appears to me at every full moon.'' Kelly looked at each individual face, making sure she had their undivided attention. She did.

''He must be proud that a new Mission of followers is going to join him,'' Ash said excitely.

''Does he really talk to you?'' Cassy asked.

Kelly nodded to both women. ''He talks to me all the time. But what he shares with me is far different from what that man up there has been babbling about. I'll tell you this…the Prophet Michael does not recognize Tyler Somers or any of these so-called ministers.''

''What do you mean?'' Ash asked, stunned.

''The Prophet Michael's message, when he was alive, was about kindness and charity. About leading a good life of service. He lived his life as an example for all of us. That was why we all lived in a Mission in New Mexico. We didn't have cars or houses or even clothes that we called our own. We worked hard all the time, giving to the community, to people who needed help. We lived through years of suffering before the right time came.'' She paused and let her gaze sweep over the crowd. ''This group is very different. The leaders who have assumed power by using my father's name are very different.''

Kelly noticed that quite a few of those sitting in the benches were being distracted by her continuous movement behind them.

"The only thing these people know is comfort,'' she continued softly. "This gibberish that Tyler Somers has been preaching about the stars and 'our' time is false. My father, the Prophet Michael, has told me that these believers have not yet paid their dues. They have not served others. And they're being duped.''

Everyone around her was looking at her wide-eyed.

"What does the Prophet say is going to happen to us…to them?'' Ash asked, a quiver of nervousness in her voice.

"He says, let them kill themselves. But that's the extent of it. This is not the time of Rapture, and taking one's life prematurely is a sin. Those who die today will all descend into the fiery lake. The bodies of those who die today will be eaten by worms. Dust to dust. But no curtain shall lift, Ash. No doors will open. No divine world will be revealed to those who die today.'' Kelly spoke as passionately as she could. "The Prophet says that there is no one in this group, not even me, worthy to cross the same threshold that he and his disciples passed over, twenty-two years ago.''

Ash stopped, looking at her in a daze, as if she'd just been awakened from a deep sleep. "You know this, but you're here.''

Kelly stopped, too, as did the others with them. "Cassy can explain it to you better than I can. But I will tell you this...I wasn't given any choice about being here.''

The teenager's face was crimson now. She didn't look anywhere but at the tips of her sneakers. Even Ryan had lost some of that starstruck look. He was glancing over the robed congregation at the stage with a healthy look of fear on his face.

Kelly saw Ken lower his camera and look with concern at their group. He knew something wasn't right. The others staring back at them from the benches saw the same thing.

''Ken is not drinking from the font tonight, but I'm supposed to.'' Ash's voice was very tense. ''I'm going to get out of here.''

''They won't let you,'' Cassy said under her breath. ''They have guns. The security guys have orders to kill anyone who changes his or her mind during these last hours of devotions. I heard Caleb tell the others.''

Ryan moved close to Kelly's side. She put a hand on the boy's shoulder. Ash twisted her fingers together.

''What can we do?'' the model asked, looking wary as her boyfriend approached.

''Stay with me. Do what I say,'' Kelly told them, turning away from the photographer. She started moving along the backs of the benches again.

She'd succeeded in partially clearing three people's heads. Only a couple hundred more to go.

Twenty-Three

At the last minute, Ian decided to take a quick walk through the cellar before leaving the inn. It hadn't taken long to find what he was looking for. The red robe was about six inches too short, but he didn't think it would matter.

Ian moved as quickly as he could through the woods, staying away from any roads and some fifteen or twenty yards away from the walking paths, as well. The dense undergrowth in the woods offered the best cover. He had to get to the camp unseen. His plan was to circle around to where a number of portable toilets had been lined up by the parking lot on the outskirts of the camp. He made it without any problem and crouched in a grove of trees, waiting for his chance. He donned his robe.

The traffic of red-robed believers going in and out of the blue and brown stalls was light. Two younger men, standing at one end of the row of toilets and listening to the sermon coming from the stage, appeared to be the watchdogs.

No guns were evident, though they could have easily been armed beneath their red robes. Ian crawled as close as he could and waited until the opening and closing of the doors gave him his best chance. Pushing to his feet, he casually walked around the far end of the line and inside one of the toilets.

Looking out through the slatted air vents high on the wall, he waited to make his next move. He certainly couldn't see much of the camp from here.

The doors of one of the adjacent toilets banged closed as a man walked out, and Ian opened the door and followed him toward the camp's center. He could hear a preacher now, haranguing the congregation through the public address system. No one was coming from the direction of the open-air chapel.

As Ian came within sight of the stage, he saw a white-robed man at the microphone. The pale, older speaker was the source of the fire-and-brimstone sermon. Perhaps it was illness that had aged him, but he looked far older than the pictures Ian had seen of him. Still, Ian had no doubt he was looking at Tyler Somers.

Ian continued to walk slowly behind the other man. As he moved toward the right side of the concentric rows of benches, his gaze swept across everyone else onstage. There was no sign of Kelly. When he reached the end of the back benches, the man continued toward the cluster of cabins. It appeared that he was heading to the infirmary.

Then Ian saw her. She was dressed in a white robe, like Somers. Jade was in her arms. He looked at the people who were walking with her on the far side of the crowd on the benches. There were others watching her, too, from the area between the benches and the long cabins beyond, and from the congregation itself. She was certainly a fine distraction, he thought.

Glancing up at the stage, Ian could see that some of the ministers were looking at her with annoyance in their faces. Somers himself was engrossed in the theatrics of his delivery—he was obviously winding up for a big finish—and didn't seem to be aware of her. The young man named Caleb was on the stage, as well. Ian started moving casually toward the cluster of cabins near where Kelly was. There were small groups of people, some of them families, who were sitting at picnic benches with untouched food in front of them. Obviously, eating lunch while Somers was talking was frowned upon.

Just as Ian looked back toward the stage, someone took hold of his arm and began to steer him in the direction of the first cabin. Ian looked into the wrinkled face of the old man at his elbow.

"Hello, Bill."

"You don't want to be running into him right now."

Ian glanced in the direction that Bill was looking and saw Wilson Blade. The cook stood up from the last row of benches and turned toward them.

"I don't think he's seen you yet. Let's just keep walking, Mr. Campbell," Bill said, using his body to shield Ian as much as possible. He nodded to a cabin farthest away from the center. "That's an empty one, right there."

"Whatever you say." Ian moved along, hunching his shoulders and keeping his head down.

Behind them, Somers wound up his sermon to some "Amens" and murmuring in the crowd. A keyboard started in on some country folk-type tune, but Ian wasn't interested. They moved together, like two old friends, past the front cabins, and went directly to the empty cabin.

Bill opened the door, poked his head in first before motioning Ian to go in.

"Did he see me?"

"He's looking this way. But I don't think he recognized you." Bill walked in behind Ian.

The room was small and appeared to be used only for storage, as there were piles of boxes stacked in one corner.

"Not a good day to be hanging around the camp." Bill said casually, peering out the single window of the cottage in the direction they'd come.

"We don't have much time. Can you get me close to Kelly?"

"Do you work with Dan?" Bill asked.

Ian considered the question. Bill could have blown the whistle on him as soon as he spotted Ian in the camp, but he hadn't. Now that he thought about it, it only made sense for Dan to have a mole in Somers's organization.

"Dan's dead. They cut his throat and left him on his cot back at the inn. I found him there this morning."

Bill looked down, visibly shaken. He turned away from the window and took a step toward Ian.

"I...he was supposed to meet me here last night.

He never showed up." The old man shook his head. "He was little more than a kid. I can't believe they killed him."

"He's not the first, though I'm glad to hear you say that." Ian looked into the man's wrinkled face. "How long have you two been working together?"

"Only since Dan came up this spring. But I've been passing information to his people since before Kelly moved here."

"So you were never a member of Butler's Mission?"

"I wish I could say that." He turned toward the window again. "All that religious mumbo-jumbo has never meant much to me, but for more years than I care to admit, I just did whatever Janice wanted me to. She believes in that stuff—hook, line and sinker—so I just went along, for better or for worse. But all that changed when this Somers fella decided to get rid of Frank…and then Rose. Frank and I had become pretty good friends. He never knew that Rose was one of them. She was the reason they got Kelly to begin with and also the reason they bought the inn from Josh Sharpe. It was all part of the plan, but there's not a shred of loyalty among these people."

"So they were both murdered?" Ian asked.

Bill nodded. "Like I said, Somers and his people wanted Kelly up here. So whatever had to be done was done. When Frank wanted Kelly to move with her new husband off to the other side of the world, he had to die and so did the husband." Bill thought about that for a moment. "Rose wasn't herself once she realized what they did to Frank."

He checked his watch. Reaching into the robe for his gun, Ian moved to the window. Everything looked to be the same outside. He saw no sign of Blade.

"They're running everything ahead of schedule," Bill said. "This is a last-minute change."

"Unfortunately, Dan's people don't know that."

The old man sat down on one of the boxes, still too rattled by the news. "I asked Dan to come and check things out. None of us coming over from the inn last night knew that this was the final call. That we weren't going back. Or at least, I wasn't told," he corrected himself. He looked over at Ian. "The security guys are big on guns here. If Dan wasn't shot, then I can only think of one person who would've done it that way…with a knife, I mean."

"Wilson Blade?" Ian asked.

Bill nodded. "He was the watchdog at Tranquillity Inn. He was Kelly's own personal pit bull, though she never knew it."

The door opened without a knock, and Bill leaped to his feet. Ian slid behind the door before the intruder spotted him.

"What do you want?" Bill asked without a trace of friendliness.

"Watch your fucking tone, you old goat," Wilson Blade said, stepping in. "And just what do you think you're doing in here? Who was the other g—"

As the cook cleared the door, Ian drove his good shoulder into Blade's chest, slamming him into the corner and knocking him to his knees. Even as the pain in his shoulder exploded across his chest and into his head, Ian realized that Bill was shutting the door behind him. Trying to remain steady on his feet, he pulled out Dan's .45.

Blade shot to his feet, red-faced, and pulling out a wicked-looking hunting knife. "What the fuck...?"

His eyes widened as he realized it was Ian. Brandishing the knife, Blade lunged at Ian. As he came, Ian sidestepped him and smashed the barrel of the pistol across Blade's temple, staggering him momentarily. Stepping in, Ian put his knee into the man's face, lifting him up. He was not about to lose his advantage. Ian swung the pistol again, hammering the butt of the handle square on the center of the cook's forehead.

Blade dropped the knife and crumpled to the dirty wood floor.

Ian staggered back, clutching his shoulder. He could feel the blood coming through the robe.

"What the hell?" Bill said, looking at Ian's shoulder. He glanced down at the unconscious man at their feet and again at Ian. "When did that happen?"

"This morning. Like Dan, I was in the way. They had to take care of me when they came to take Kelly."

He looked around the small room, trying to decide what they could do with Blade. There wasn't much. And he didn't think at this point that it really mattered. The man was out cold.

"You're bleeding pretty bad."

"I'll live." He glanced at his watch again. "Is there any way you can access a phone to call out?"

Bill shook his head. "Only one line out, as far as I know. In the administration office. There's an extension in the infirmary, but they're both guarded more closely than Ty Somers's bank balance. There's no way."

"Then we'll have to rely on my distraction." Ian quickly explained what he hoped would take place across the lake. "I don't know if it'll work, or if the authorities can get here in time. I was hoping we could stop a standoff *and* a mass suicide."

"Somers wants to go and take this group along with him. I think he'll make Waco look like school recess if he has to," Bill warned. "I heard two of the security fellows telling Caleb about that truck being rigged to blow up on the road. Sounded to me like if the thing blows, then Father Ty was planning to use the noise to get everyone to come up for their final drink."

Ian felt suddenly ill.

"He doesn't give a damn about the moon and stars and all that shit," Bill continued. "He wants to die and take a lot of folks with him. Unfortunately, what you've got planned is gonna play right into his hands."

"Get me to Kelly," Ian said urgently.

The number of people walking with her was increasing by the minute. Speaking all the time she walked, Kelly lengthened the path they were going, coming farther down the sides of the benches before going back. The distraction was working.

Somers's hold on the audience began to waver the moment Kelly extended a hand toward Craig, Ryan's brother, motioning for the boy to come to her. Without a moment's hesitation, the teenager left the bench and deserted his parents, joining Kelly and the others in their walk. She had then motioned to a child, to another teenager, to a young woman, and so on. Some had come even without an invitation.

Kelly could hear whispers behind her and from the back benches as she passed. From the bits and pieces of conversation, she knew her objection to Somers's plan was being discussed.

Let the word spread, she told herself.

Somers had moved to his seat on the stage, taking a break from his sermon. Kelly watched as several of his inner circle were whispering to the older man. His gaze shifted, fixing finally on what Kelly was doing in the back.

It was only a matter of minutes before she saw Caleb leave the stage and start toward her. Kelly had to hold on to whatever shred of authority she could wield. She did not waver in her path as he approached, nor did she stop inviting others to join her.

When she turned around at the far end of one row, she realized that Caleb had placed himself directly in her path. She wasn't going to step around him. She wasn't going to give any hint to this congregation that she was anything but a person of vast superiority to any of the ministers in attendance. She continued toward the young man.

"You wish to speak to me, Caleb," she called out loud to him, "then you will walk with me."

Caleb's face did not hide his annoyance as the group approached. At the last moment, though, he moved to the side and fell in beside her. It was a good thing he did, for she had every intention of barreling right into him, if necessary.

"Father Ty requests your presence on the stage," the young man said.

The time had come. Kelly glanced over her shoulder at the group she'd collected. Roughly thirty people. She wasn't alone.

"Follow me," she told them, going around the last row of seats and heading directly for the stage.

"These people have to take their seats," Caleb told her as they walked. "No one is allowed to stand with Father Ty and you on the platform."

Kelly stopped and faced him. "*You* are allowed to stand on the platform, aren't you? What gives you that right, other than the fact that you carry guns under your robe? What do you have that they don't?"

Her comment was loud enough that a hush fell over those walking with her and those in the seats nearest them. Kelly looked back at Cassy and noticed a look of disgust on her face as the young woman stared at Caleb.

She continued toward the stage. The other ministers near the stage seemed obviously concerned. Kelly saw Somers motion to Joshua Sharpe, and the heavyset man rose immediately to his feet. So did Shawn Hobart, who was sitting beside Sharpe. The two moved to block her before she reached the five steps leading to the platform.

"Welcome, Luna-K, daughter of the Prophet," Joshua Sharpe said in greeting.

Kelly forced herself to remain in character and only nodded dismissively.

"May I?" he asked, reaching for Jade.

"No!" she barked. "She stays with me. And all of these good people—and whoever else who might care to join me—I invite to come forward and sit on the steps and on the edge of the platform. I want all of them to be close to my heart and body and soul. It was the same way that the Prophet Michael kept his disciples close to him."

Despite the continuing keyboard music, her voice carried above it. There was an unusually loud "Amen" from her group and from a few people near the front row.

She reached out and motioned for Sharpe and Hobart to step aside and open a path for her. Both men looked back at their leader for his approval. The music stopped and there was suddenly dead silence in the open-air chapel.

Too many people were watching the little power struggle. Somers nodded, and the two men stepped aside to make way for her.

Kelly refused to accept either of their proffered hands and climbed the stairs on her own. She turned around and supervised as her group was blocked by the steps. Going along the front of the stage, she encouraged some of her followers to sit on the edge of the platform. She was happy to see a few more had joined them at the last moment.

From the corner of her eye, she saw Somers rise to his feet. Looking somewhat impatient, he motioned for her to take the chair that had been set up near the font. Kelly noticed two very large bottles of red liquid that were partially hidden behind a banner at the far end of the stage. She ignored her picture sitting on an easel by the font. Instead of following the older man's direction, she headed for the microphone. He realized her intention and reached it first.

"My brothers and sisters, Luna-K has returned," he announced. "Let us welcome her."

He started to clap, and the congregation joined him, cheering loudly. He took his hand off the microphone, gesturing for her to speak, but then extended both of his arms to take Jade.

Kelly's blood ran cold in her veins. All the courage and confidence she'd built up came dangerously close to dissipating.

"Come to me, Jade," he said in a calm voice.

Kelly felt her child go limp in her arms.

"No," she said sharply. Her voice rang into the microphone and the crowds quieted. All eyes were on the two of them.

"I am the Prophet's daughter. And Jade is his granddaughter. It is vital that the Chosen Ones see us together at this important time. It is essential that Michael look down and see his offspring together."

Anger brought color into the old man's pale face. He nodded grimly.

"Luna-K, you have my permission to hold on to your child…for now," he said menacingly. "But it's time for you and your daughter to take your seat, as I am ready to lead our people in the next phase of our devotions."

"Devotions," she said, pulling the microphone from the stand. "That's one of the things I'd like to address with all of you here. I will speak for a moment, *Brother* Ty."

She stared at Somers, who glared at her for a second or two before backing away a step. She turned to the congregation.

"Some of you may be wondering about the reason for my pacing back and forth along those walkways at the back of our fine chapel here in the woods."

A few smiled knowingly. Others nodded their heads, curious. Kelly switched the microphone to the other hand, shifting Jade away from Somers.

"The Prophet Michael," she said powerfully into the microphone as Somers took a step toward her. "How many of you were fortunate enough to meet that holy man in person?"

She walked away from Somers. More hands went up than she would have expected.

"How many of you remember how he used to march and pace the Mission chapel, smiling and acknowledging everyone before any of his sermons?"

The same hands went up. The faces were bright

with remembrance. Kelly saw Somers coming toward her.

"That is exactly what I was doing," she announced into the microphone. "I was following my father's instructions."

There was a murmur as she moved to the front of the stage.

"And he had instructions for you, as well, when he appeared to me last night during my moments of private devotion," she said, shooting a threatening look at Somers. "My saintly father was concerned about the lack of love, the lack of compassion, the lack of the unity that he sees among his people. He's concerned that his words have been forgotten. That his divinely ordained purpose is no longer observed here."

The small group sitting on the steps and at the edge of the stage responded with words of concern. She walked past them to stay away from Somers. She saw the older man motion to his assistants to close in on her.

"The Prophet told me that the Chosen Ones…you, my friends…want the rewards of the work you have not labored at. My father rejects the idea that you could join him without an invitation, without being worthy."

Cries of "No…no!" rang out from the benches.

"He told me that you have been deceived by the words of a self-appointed leader who is not recognized by the Prophet Michael or by the heavenly hosts above. This man is that deceiver."

She pointed the microphone at Somers, only to have it torn from her hand by Shawn Hobart. She ignored him, continuing to address the shocked congregation in a loud voice.

"This man was cast out of the Mission before the final day. Tyler Somers is a coward and a thief. He is a dying man who wants a flock to lead to hell, as that is the only place where he'll be spending etern—"

The explosion across the lake turned everyone's head at that direction.

The silence in the camp lasted for only a moment, though, as Somers snatched the microphone from Hobart's hand.

"This is our moment," he shouted into the public address system. "Our enemies are upon us."

He reached for her with one hand, but she ducked away.

"Do you hear them? It is just as I foretold," Somers continued. "The gates have burst in, and the unbelievers are among us. Now is our time. We must leave this wasteland behind us. We must rise through the Eternal Door."

The ministers on the stage had leaped into action the moment Somers began to speak. Caleb and Sharpe were pouring a bottle of the red liquid into the font, and Hobart was carrying the other bottle to them from the side of the stage.

Kelly moved to the front edge of the stage and called out to the people gathered beneath her. "What this impostor is telling you is not true. This is not the time and he is not the guide!''

"Do not listen to her," Somers shouted into the mike. "*She* is the impostor! Someone silence her blasphemies!''

"My father told me—"

Kelly stopped dead as she felt a man's hand wrap tightly around her ankle. She looked down and her heart almost stopped at the sight of his face.

"Ian," Kelly whispered, staring at him in shock. She crouched down. "You're—"

"Come on. Come down," he told her urgently as Tyler Somers continued to exhort the confused congregation.

"Stop him!" Somers yelled into the microphone, pointing at him. "I told you, our enemies are against us. This is the agent of Satan himself. This man is the antichrist. Stop him before he taints us all."

Kelly took his hand and jumped off the stage and onto the ground. Jade lifted her head off her mother's shoulder as Ian started to pull Kelly toward the end of the benches.

"Ian!" the little girl called out happily.

Somers was still yelling into the microphone and the entire scene was one of chaos. Caleb and Hobart were rushing across the stage toward them, and two young thugs appeared, cutting off any chance of escape, moving in to the end of the row, blocking their path.

The pistol appeared in Ian's hand in an instant and screams and shouts came from the congregation.

Somers was still shrieking, but Caleb and the others stopped at the sight of the gun. Kelly felt herself and Jade suddenly yanked against Ian's body and the gun pressed to her forehead.

"You come one step closer," Ian shouted, "and she dies!"

Kelly knew what he was doing. He was trying to buy them time.

"He's lying. Stop him," Somers yelled into the microphone to those in pursuit. He turned back to the rest of the congregation. "Join me, my brothers and sisters, come and take the cups."

"I've been waiting twenty-two years for this," Ian said loudly. "My wife died at the Butler Mission. She was killed the night of the suicide. I've been waiting a lifetime to avenge her death."

"The cups. They're here. Come and take them." Somers motioned toward the row of drink-filled cups lining the very edge of the stage. He acted as if Ian and his taking of Kelly and Jade were nothing but a nuisance. Kelly saw Janice move quietly to the front of the stage.

Caleb jumped off the stage and grabbed a woman off the first bench, shoving her toward the drinks.

"Hurry! Now!" He grabbed the next person and pushed her in the same direction, too.

"Not without Luna-K." The woman shook her head and looked in confusion and fear toward Ian, still holding a gun to Kelly's head. Other people backed up from the stage.

"My father, the Prophet Michael, does not support

this act," Kelly shouted to them. "This is all wrong. The time of Tribulation has not passed. All of this talk of the Rapture is Ty Somers's deceit. It comes not from my father, but from a sick mind."

The crowd shrank back more. Some of the people started to cry. Others huddled with each other in fear.

"Get them. Bring them to me," Somers screamed.

Guns appeared from under the robes, revealing the true colors of those closest to Somers. Caleb continued to line people up by force, as Hobart pushed the cups into their hands.

"Luna-K," a woman screamed. "Luna-K, save us."

"Luna-K will take the first drink. She will guide you," Ty announced.

Kelly hadn't realized until that moment that another gun was directed at them from the stage. This one was held by Joshua Sharpe, and it was pointing at Jade. She pressed her child's head on her shoulder and shrank back against Ian. They were surrounded by armed men. They had nowhere to go.

Ty raised a hand. "I'll let your daughter go with this man. They can leave the camp so long as you join us on our journey." He paused, motioning toward Sharpe. "Or he will shoot and she'll die, and then you'll die, too, along with your lover. We'll have you traveling the road with us one way or the other, Luna-K."

Kelly shielded Jade from Sharpe's gun.

"Take her," she said to Ian in panic as she saw

Joshua Sharpe glance back at Somers. "Take her away, Ian!"

"Not without you," he said, shoving both of them under the stage.

"Ian," she screamed as a shot rang out.

There were screams all around them as shots continued to fire. People were running. She pulled Jade close to her. She saw Cassy dive in beside her, and then the Stern boys were there, as well.

"Please, God! Ian," she called out.

They'd kill him. There were too many of them. More shots.

"Ian." She tried to look out, but all she could see were feet stampeding by.

And then she heard the sound of helicopters and loudspeakers blaring overhead and dozens of cars and vans roaring down through the camp.

She pulled the others close to her and curled her body around Jade.

Twenty-Four

The hospital waiting room had no windows. Kelly liked it this way. She didn't want to see the full moon outside. She needed no reminders of what might have been. She had seen and heard enough to keep her running for the rest of her life.

She'd left the chaos at Lake Tranquillity as quickly as she could. An army of state troopers and federal agents had poured into the camp as she'd huddled beneath the stage. She'd been told Bill had fired the first shot, wounding Joshua Sharpe. Ian had kept the rest running for cover as the agents poured in. The cult members had quickly laid down their arms in the face of such overwhelming force.

Victor and Brian had been responsible for the perfect timing of the assault. While the two men had been scrounging in the boathouse for materials to make a decent explosion, Victor had found some old telephone line. They'd located the cut phone line, and Brian had quickly fixed it. The call to the state police had been made before the actual explosion, which they went ahead with, hoping that the distraction might help Ian.

There had been numerous arrests in the camp, the

most important being that of Tyler Somers. Buses were brought in to transport the rest of the sect. Most of the kids were being turned over to state agencies. These people, the majority of whom were innocent of any conscious wrongdoing, would need long periods of therapy to unlock their phobias and release them from the bonds that held them to Michael Butler and his successor.

And then there were those whom she held personally responsible for so many crimes—people like Janice, Rita and Wilson. She was relieved to see them taken away in handcuffs. Bill was going to be an important witness for the prosecution when the time for the trials arrived. To her great surprise, she learned that Bill had been involved with the FBI for several years now. Kelly already had been told that her husband's death and both of her parents' deaths were being investigated as probable homicides. The murder of Lauren Wells wasn't discovered until this afternoon, when they found the old woman's body in one of the cottages. Kelly felt horrible, knowing she'd been the reason that the woman had come to Lake Tranquillity. Lauren had come to warn her, and she had become a victim herself. The third victim.

Kelly would have been the fourth in a long line of them.

There would be no end to any of this anytime soon. Feeling extremely vulnerable, Kelly gathered Jade closer to her chest and cuddled the yellow blanket around them both. The child was sound asleep. They had taken Ian away from the camp in an ambulance.

She would not have survived any of this if it weren't for him coming into her life again and saving them from a horrible death.

Now she prayed for him to pull through. She asked a gentle and loving God to give them one more chance. She realized now that everyone needed some kind of belief. Including her. The difference was that she'd recently learned she could maintain the freedom of her mind and still believe in something more. Something greater.

She heard his voice before she saw him. Kelly glanced up and saw Ian being rolled in a wheelchair toward her. She looked with concern at his legs. He was dressed in his own clothes. His shoulder was bandaged, and his arm was in a sling. She gazed into his face. He smiled at her.

"Don't move," he told her quietly when she started to wake Jade and get to her feet.

He asked the nurse to leave them.

"How do you feel? Shouldn't you be in bed?" She took his hand, her eyes welling up.

He brought her hand to his lips and pressed a kiss against her palm. "I'm okay. All sewn up and good as new." He shrugged at the chair. "This is just hospital procedure. They wheel you in, they have to wheel you out. Did you have a chance to go back to the inn and pack?"

She nodded. "I gathered your stuff and a suitcase for Jade and me. That's all we need." They'd talked about it before Ian had been taken away in the ambulance. She didn't want to stay at the inn. They were moving to a hotel near Conway until the authorities were done with them.

He brushed a tear off her cheek. "It's over, love."

"They told me there would be a lengthy investigation. I'll need to provide statements and give testimony. I can't walk away yet," she said sadly, feeling everything closing in on her again. "And there's no saying that this thing won't follow me. Who's to say that some other nutcase won't pick up where Somers ended, five or ten years from now."

"Kelly, it's over," he said gently. "And whatever you have to go through, I'll be there with you. And when all the legal stuff is done with, we'll be on the road."

"To where?" she asked, choking on the words.

"Anywhere you want. The three of us. We'll pick any corner of the world you fancy and start fresh— with everything. New identities. Everything. I've already had an okay from the Justice Department on that."

She shook her head in disbelief.

"But do you really want to do that, Ian?" she asked nervously. "Are we worth it?"

"My God!" he breathed, leaning toward her in the chair.

His black eyes were misty as he drew her face close to his.

"You are all that I want now. You're worth more to me than my next breath…more than my life," he whispered, kissing her lips. "I love you, Kelly."

Tears fell onto her cheeks. She kissed him with all

the love she felt in her heart for him...with all the hope he himself had given her.

Jade was squeezed between them. She managed to work herself free and look sleepily into both of their faces.

"Does anyone need a Band-Aid?"

Authors' Note

We all seem to know or hear of someone who has suffered a radical personality change. We cringe when we hear about the destructive cults that suddenly appear too close to our comfortable world. Too often, unfortunately, they go unnoticed until it's too late for something to be done. Jonestown. Heaven's Gate. Waco. When they occur, these tragedies make us wonder how such a thing could have happened. And, in case of the creative minds of two fiction writers, the tragedies of the past make us say, what happens if somebody had the chance to stop it? Well, we hope you enjoyed *Fourth Victim*.

Following our customary fashion, we could not leave behind some of the characters of our past books. So we hope you enjoyed visiting with Victor and Brian, who initially showed up in *Triple Threat*. And for those of you who asked for a cameo of Nate and Ellie, we tried but couldn't find them a room at this inn. Maybe the next book.

For the many people who visit New Hampshire every year, we wanted you to know that Lake Tranquillity, the campground and the inn were purely products of our imagination. So, don't get lost in the woods in search of any warm water lake anywhere near Errol!

Again, we cannot finish a book without thanking our sons for their endless love, patience, and sense of humor. You are two amazing young men, and we couldn't be prouder of you.

As always, we are so grateful to those of you who continue to read our Jan Coffey and May McGoldrick books. We love you for your kindness and support.

We also love to hear from you:
Jan Coffey
c/o Nikoo & Jim McGoldrick
P.O. Box 665
Watertown, CT 06795
or
McGoldMay@aol.com
www.JanCoffey.com

It's time for Susie to decide on her order.
Does she want canapés in Cannes or
a bagel and lox right here in New York?

MIRA®

JUDITH ARNOLD

Blooming ALL OVER

Bagels with a shmear of love...only at Bloom's.

There may be a bigger deli than Bloom's somewhere in the
world, but there's certainly none better! That doesn't mean
it's the only place Susie Bloom ever wants to dine, though.

Writing "The Bloom's Bulletin" is a fun sideline, but Susie is
keeping her options open...not just with the store, but also
with Casey, the ever-so-sexy Bloom's bagel master. Casey is
pushing for marriage, but Susie has her qualms. Can a girl
from Manhattan settle down with a guy from Queens?

**"Oddball characters and humorous hijinks abound in Arnold's
touching, romantic tale of an Upper West Side delicatessen."
—*Publishers Weekly* on *Love in Bloom's***

Available in July 2004 wherever paperbacks are sold.

www.MIRABooks.com   MJA2059

MIRABooks.com

We've got the lowdown on your favorite author!

☆ Read an excerpt of your favorite author's newest book

☆ Check out her bio

☆ Talk to her in our Discussion Forums

☆ Read interviews, diaries, and more

☆ Find her current bestseller, and even her backlist titles

All this and more available at
www.MiraBooks.com

Jan Coffey

66919	TWICE BURNED	___ $6.50 U.S.	___ $7.99 CAN.
66859	TRUST ME ONCE	___ $5.99 U.S.	___ $6.99 CAN.
66703	TRIPLE THREAT	___ $6.50 U.S.	___ $7.99 CAN.

(limited quantities available)

TOTAL AMOUNT $_____

POSTAGE & HANDLING $_____

($1.00 for one book; 50¢ for each additional)

APPLICABLE TAXES* $_____

<u>TOTAL PAYABLE</u> $_____

(check or money order—please do not send cash)

To order, complete this form and send it, along with a check or money order for the total above, payable to MIRA Books, to: **In the U.S.:** 3010 Walden Avenue, P.O. Box 9077, Buffalo, NY 14269-9077; **In Canada:** P.O. Box 636, Fort Erie, Ontario L2A 5X3.

Name:_____

Address:_____ City:_____

State/Prov.:_____ Zip/Postal Code:_____

Account Number (if applicable):_____

075 CSAS

   *New York residents remit applicable sales taxes.

    Canadian residents remit applicable GST and provincial taxes.

MIRA®